BITTERSWEET TAPESTRY

BITTERSWEET TAPESTRY

A NOVEL OF EIGHTEENTH CENTURY EUROPE

The Derrynane Saga

Kevin O'Connell

The Gortcullinane Press

ISBN-13: 978-0-9974076-2-4
ISBN-10: 099740762X

Library of Congress Control Number: 2019904887

Gortcullinane Press, The – P.O. Box 157, Severna Park, MD 21146 USA

Published by The Gortcullinane Press

'The Lament for Art O'Leary by Eileen O'Connell' as translated by Frank O'Connor and as appeared in A Frank O'Connor Reader reprinted by permission of Peters Fraser & Dunlop (www.petersfraserdunlop.com) on behalf of the Estate of Frank O'Connor

Cover design by Jennifer Quinlan, Historical Editorial

For Marion,

my mother, my friend, my first riding companion

with love, gratitude and many happy memories

Her earliest advice – oft-repeated – was simple:
"Take the jump . . . if ye fall, ye fall"

Following it – if only occasionally – has made for an interesting life!

ACKNOWLEDGEMENTS

The One Person Without Whose Vision, encouragement and support the *Derrynane Saga* would have never been conceived much yet written is my beloved wife, Laurette Hankins. My gratitude to her is boundless . . . as throughout the process she has been patient, steadfast and loving . . . listening to even the most random of ideas, reading and editing the roughest of thoughts and sharing the kind of creative insights as only an accomplished, talented musical performer in her own right would be able to.

I remain indescribably grateful to (and for!) my extraordinary editor, Randy Ladenheim-Gil, for her continuing understanding and invariable good cheer. Her editorial and critical skills, including her vast knowledge of obscure facts and word origins, her brilliant and precise fact-checking as well as her insights and subtle nudges have gone a long way to making the writing of now-three novels a memorable and enjoyable experience. I so look forward to continuing our collaboration as the *Derrynane Saga* progresses.

As I have previous characterised her, Laura Oliver remains the consummate mentor – from the very beginning, she has been a gentle, steadying presence, wise and thoughtful.

Vanessa Fox O'Laughlin continues to cast a long, supportive shadow across the Atlantic from Dublin. As with my earlier books, so too with *Bittersweet Tapestry* she has been a wise advisor and an enthusiastic spirit-lifter, though it is with regards to this book that she has also been something of a rescuer.

In the Spring of 2018, when I was, to put it mildly, "becalmed" – and indeed rather frightened (as the thoughts, the words were simply not coming) – by my first bout of "writer's block" it was Vanessa who patiently listened to my cares and concerns. In the process, she identified a number of possible causes, which she was able to reduce to a pair of probable ones. As she wisely counselled me through them – the result was a near-immediate break in the intellectual and creative log-jam.

Eileen O'Leary stood quietly on the long, open porch that ran along much of the rear of Rathleigh House. It was, she had noticed as she'd passed the tall, mahogany-cased hallway clock shortly after ten o'clock, on what was a near-perfect mid-July morning. Beyond the low, stone-walled close of the house, the estate's vividly green fields undulated as far as she could see, broken in places by occasional outcroppings of granite and dotted with a sparse variety of both soft and hardwood trees, until the panorama was ultimately interrupted by a low range of gentle, still-misty hills.

After a moment, leaning her six-foot and perhaps an inch or even more frame back against a pillar, her arms crossed, she smiled broadly as she watched Bull, her striking, near-singularly chestnut Frisian stallion, now twelve years old, whom she'd raised from *a wee little pony*, gambolling about the green meadows of West Cork, tossing his classic long black wavy mane, his dramatic black tail streaming, as joyfully as he ever had over the manicured pastures of the Habsburg imperial palaces at Schönbrunn and Laxenburg, or in the magnificently ornate rink of the Spanish Riding School in Vienna.

"He has a friend!" she heard Anna Pfeffer correctly observe as the young Austrian trundled a basket of wet washing out onto the porch.

Eileen turned. "He does indeed, *two* of them; see." She pointed, gesturing at a frisky yearling colt racing towards Bull and a bay gelding almost Bull's age. "I am happy for him . . . I feared he might have developed a 'sense of entitlement,'" she laughed, "after the lofty places in which he was stabled in Austria."

Anna smiled knowingly. "*Ja*, it is indeed a long way from his fancy Lipizzan friends at the Winter Riding School!"

Eileen reached for one edge of the basket and, after trundling it across the yard, she and Anna dropped it on the grass near the clotheslines, where together they hung some of the family's washing, draping some pieces on nearby hedges whilst spreading out bed sheets on the grass near the kitchen house, which Ann, Rathleigh's housekeeper, and several of the serving girls referred to as the house's "drying ground."

As they were finishing, holding her arm across her sunburnt forehead, Anna covered her eyes against the bright sun; flashing a dazzling smile, she observed, "Life is different for all of us, *ja*, Lady Eileen?"

Eileen nodded in response. "Is very different, Lady Anna, *ja*, indeed!"

Laughing, the women strolled back to the house for tea. As comfortable as both had become to effortlessly alternating amongst German, English and French many times in a single day, since departing France, they found themselves speaking mostly English.

The most obviously tangible evidence of their transition from the life they had shared in the imperial palaces of Austria to the one they had only recently begun in Ireland were the simple, comfortably light wool dresses each wore—the older woman's a soft grey, the younger's a light blue—both long-sleeved, though Anna's were at the moment rolled up, and full-skirted, each covered by a crisp, long white apron. Eileen stood some five or perhaps even six inches taller than Anna, but the women shared long, thick manes of hair, both gleaming in the midmorning sunshine, Anna's being rivulets of gold, Eileen's a singular blue-black.

Rathleigh was unusually quiet this particular morning. Little Conor O'Leary, several weeks short of his second birthday, was napping. Eileen's husband, Arthur—he remained, though presently on-leave, a commissioned officer in the Hungarian Hussars of the armies of the Empress Maria Theresa—and his father, whose name Conor bore, were in the closest town, Macroom, for the day. The women, who barely three months prior had, at least formally, been mistress and servant—though having in the not-quite-nine-year process become close, and were now the dearest of friends—working and living together at the apogee of Austrian society, had adjusted quickly and happily to their new status and, indeed, Arthur O'Leary had observed just this week that "Life is become quite . . . *normal* . . . yes, that is the word, *normal*" and he had smiled, as the two attractive women to whom he was speaking enthusiastically agreed.

For those not quite nine years, the young woman born Eileen O'Connell at remote Derrynane in County Kerry, her family's home and the base of operations for their far-flung and highly profitable smuggling business, had served as governess, as well as teacher, riding mistress, companion and confident, to the two youngest daughters of the Empress Maria Theresa, Archduchesses of Austria and Lorraine, Maria Carolina and Maria Antonia, and Anna Pfeffer had been her maid—or at least that was her official designation.

During that time, Eileen's relationship with the younger archduchess, whom she called Antoine, had become more maternal than anything else. Indeed, the young girl had confessed frequently to the tall, attractive young Irishwoman that "more a mother to me than the empress you are," even ultimately coming to address Eileen, when they were alone, as Mama. After Eileen and O'Leary had wed at Christmastime 1767 and were expecting their first child, as the long, hot summer of 1768 had lumbered somnolently into August, once O'Leary had joined his wife and the young girl she still affectionately spoke of as "my wee little archduchess" at Laxenburg Palace in the rolling countryside beyond Vienna, the three immediately began to be referred to there, quite warmly, as *La Petite Famille,* a characterisation of which, when she was made aware, the empress smilingly approved. Indeed, so close had become the relationship that, moments after Conor O'Leary had been laid in his mother's arms, Eileen had smilingly informed the newborn that "Even an 'older sister' of sorts it would appear you have. . . ."

When Antoine—now become Marie Antoinette, dauphine of France— departed Vienna for Versailles in April 1770, so, too, had Eileen and Arthur, striking out for Ireland and a new life for both of them. Eileen's older sister, Abigail, now O'Sullivan, who had accompanied her to Vienna, had remained in Austria, serving now as principal lady-in-waiting to the empress.

When the O'Learys, along with little Conor and Anna, also bound for a life she'd never even been able to dream of, arrived at Rathleigh, they were immediately embraced by Squire Conor O'Leary, Art's distinguished, widowed father, who was instantly proud beyond belief of little Conor, his first grandchild and namesake. The elder O'Leary, a devout Catholic, had—

no one ever discussed openly how—publicly retained both his cherished faith and his position in society, serving as lands agent for the prominent Protestant Minhear family of Carrigaphooka. What was quietly referred to as being the "permanent lease" of Rathleigh House and its own not insignificant lands, the rents received from its tenantry being only part of what was said to be his substantial remuneration, along with certain significant "protections" afforded him and his family by his patrons.

The squire quickly assumed charge of their homecoming and of the newly expanded household in residence, in the process quietly putting his still but now only occasionally dour housekeeper Ann's anxious worries about Anna's role to rest, assuring her, "The girl is the Lady Eileen's dearest friend. The captain indicates their plan is to find her a good Irish husband." Thus relieved, Ann had taken careful notice of the very pretty, not-quite-twenty-year-old Austrian, with her trim shape, blue eyes and long golden hair, quickly coming to find her buoyant personality as well as her German-accented English surprisingly pleasant, concluding that an early marriage to a young local squire was indeed quite probable, the names of several men even coming to mind, which she immediately shared with Eileen.

Some weeks following their arrival, it was during the course of what had been expected to be yet another uneventful Wednesday straddling the cusp of spring and summer, the morning having become a very hot, nearly windless afternoon and the women having removed the quickly dried washing, when the usual, highly animated commotion of the Rathleigh dogs, now eight of them of varying sizes, shapes and, save for the three huge Irish wolfhounds, largely unascertainable breeds, heralded the arrival of something never before there seen; indeed, a sight rarely if ever seen in Cork, perhaps in all of Ireland.

With the squire and Captain O'Leary in the vanguard, a slow-moving procession of four—"No!" Eileen called out from the striking, whitewashed house's middle upstairs window, "'tis five, there are *five* of them!"—massive, lumbering drays, pulled by twice that number of determined-looking, sad-faced oxen, whose rough, thick leather reins rested in the skilled, callused hands of an equal number of weathered teamsters; they were O'Connell men, part of a covey of ships' captains, mates, sailors and drovers, all employed in the far-flung, and largely illegal commercial maritime activities of Eileen's family, the O'Connells of Derrynane. As they drew closer, Eileen recognised several long-time, familiar faces.

As Eileen and Anna, with little Conor racing ahead, opened and immediately stepped out of the gleaming, black-painted front door and onto the broken stones in front of the house, a still-mounted Art dramatically stretched his arms wide and called out into the still, hot air, "Some parcels from Vienna, my ladies!" Dismounting, he scooped up his little boy and laughingly joined the wide-eyed women, Squire O'Leary handing the reins of his horse to an awed young groom and walking slowly towards the family, shaking his head.

"Never, mind you, *never* have I ever seen the likes of *this*." As had his son, the squire now opened his arms as the cavalcade that had halted in a semicircle; dominating the space, more bemused than anything else, he stepped close to his son and permitted Conor to wriggle from his father's arms into his own.

Each wagon carried not less than four massive wooden crates; three of the five were also laden with trunks and satchels, lashed together by thick ship's ropes.

Eileen finally managed a hesitant, almost breathless, "Our belongings? This is what *all* of this is, what these contain?" and O'Leary nodded and stood aside as an enormous, red-haired man, whom Eileen had instantly recognised as Donál Cahill, stepped towards her.

"My Lady Eileen," he said warmly, "you *do* remember me?"

His smile broadened as it was immediately apparent she did, to the extent that, also smiling broadly, she opened her arms to the man, who was huge, like her late father, Donál Mór, and like her dear brother, Morgan, who blushed as she embraced him as best she could, exclaiming, "Most certainly I do, good sir, my dear, dear Cahill!"

It was Squire O'Leary who indicated to the teamsters that they should climb down. "Food and drink await you, good men, and lodgings for the night—or longer, should you wish!" He gestured them to follow a wide-eyed Ann, who kept gazing back at the huge wagons and massive crates.

As his men followed Ann to the kitchens, Donál Cahill advised the O'Learys and Anna that the cargo had travelled overland from Vienna, carried by commercial haulers, engaged, he had been told, by "*the Lord High Chamberlain,*" his eyes widening in awe as he repeated the exotic-sounding, unfamiliar title, adding "*. . . himself!*" to Le Havre, where one of the O'Connells' vessels awaited its arrival, thence carrying it on to Cork, where it was placed in his hands. There, he and his men had loaded them on their convoy, which had thence lumbered across County Cork in the direction of Macroom.

"Indeed, 'twas parts of now three days we had been in transit when first we came upon you, gentlemen," he gestured to the O'Leary men, "on the road from Macroom." Art related to the women how, as they neared the crossroads, the right cross leading to Rathleigh, he and his father had inquired as to the destination of the rather incredible-looking caravan, only to learn from Cahill, "It is to a place called Rathleigh House we are bound, sir, indeed had you not inquired, it was my intent to ask of you whether we were correctly proceeding thence."

It was then that Cahill had advised of the origin of the shipment and O'Leary concluded of what its contents consisted.

Breathless and wide-eyed, both Eileen and Anna were anxious to see everything, though they agreed to wait until morning to begin what would prove to be a challenging logistical undertaking: Whilst primitive crane devices—basically, blocks and tackle—had been used to hoist the large crates onto the drays, neither they nor anything remotely similar existed in West Cork.

After a hearty breakfast had been spread on and consumed from plank tables erected in the yard, the crates were each in turn slowly, largely disassembled, such of the wood as could be salvaged, as well as the mounds of packing material, set aside.

This having been accomplished, it was on to the broken rocks of the drive and the thick, summertime-green grass beyond that were gently placed all the elegant furnishings, including magnificent Indian and Chinese carpets, from the three apartments Eileen, first alone and later with Art and their son, had occupied at the Imperial palaces of the Hofburg, Schönbrunn and Laxenburg, including a dizzying array of books and paintings, as well as the O'Learys' and Anna's clothing, much of it packed in the trunks and valises, along with a myriad of other personal belongings.

As the day progressed, Eileen was bemused to discover that, wholly separate from the other clothing, all of her very formal court dresses, as well as her only slightly less-so afternoon dresses and the outfits' related accoutrements had been carefully packed, along with her riding habits and few items of casual wear. "We shall have to host grand balls each month for the good people of Cork so as to permit me to yet again don these," she said, gesturing at the elegant ball gowns, now bursting out of their open trunks, sitting haphazardly on the lawn.

"I shall not have forgotten how to . . ." Anna smilingly gestured, wiggling her fingers in a tying motion, "Mistress," as she recalled how frequently, sometimes three or even four times in a single day she had dressed and undressed Eileen. They all laughed as O'Leary swung first his wife, then Anna and finally the three of them together, in an exuberant reel about the yard.

"I no longer have to be tied into my clothing. . . . I am actually able to dress myself!" Eileen laughed.

By the end of the still hot but benignly sunny day, all the various pieces of furniture had been trundled inside and placed in practically every room of the commodious, though still not terribly large house that was Rathleigh. "Remember, the Hofburg alone has hundreds of rooms," Anna reminded the group as she was thrilled to have been given the beautifully carved, roomy bed from the O'Learys' quarters at Schönbrunn.

"There is so much here that once you are to be wed you may select virtually any and as many pieces as you wish for your new home, my darling," Eileen told her quietly.

Paintings were lined up against the walls in various rooms and corridors, most of the carpets rolled up wherever they might fit. So, too, were all the clothing and accessories hung, placed, folded, laid—and, towards the end of the day, stuffed—into any available, suitable space.

The process of unloading, moving, carrying, placing and distributing proved to be so extensive and time-consuming that it was not until late in the evening, after all had eaten and Cahill and his men had retired in anticipation of an early morning start, that the mysterious, heavy, outsized wooden crate that had been packed so carefully, with so much wadding, that its contents rattled not at all, had been placed in the parlour, seemingly in accordance with the carefully lettered card that was affixed to it:

TO BE OPENED ONLY WITHIN YOUR RESIDENCE AND ONLY AFTER ALL OTHER CONTAINERS HAVE BEEN EMPTIED

It was Anna who noticed that the handwriting might well have been Abigail's; at least it could have been a very careful version of her familiar hand. "How lovely, Mistress . . . er, *Eileen*," she laughed, correcting herself as she found she still occasionally reverted to her years' long way of addressing her friend, "a gift from the Lady Abigail and the major, *ja?*" she wondered aloud. The husband of Eileen's older sister was also an officer, albeit in a different regiment: in the Hungarian Hussars.

That Eileen was uncertain was evident as she nodded and thoughtfully bit her lower lip, a look of puzzlement on her somewhat weary face. "'Tis so large, so heavy, so tightly packed . . . I cannot imagine . . ."

Art, coatless, his sleeves rolled up in the still-warm, semi daylight of a Cork midsummer night, playfully brandished a crude iron crowbar as if it were a sword, observing, "I should suggest that by the use of this instrument we shall be able to solve the mystery, *ja?*" Everyone was smiling as he began to very gently pry off the nailed slats on one side.

The nails creaking, O'Leary removed the side wall that the slats had held to the box, his father taking it from him and peering into mounds of batting. Kneeling on the floor, Eileen and Anna began to tentatively tug at the strips and balls of heavy cotton and flannel packaging, until Eileen scratched her finger on something rough and strangely cold. She then tried to move the contents. "'Tis heavy; I cannot budge it, whatever this is," she exclaimed, nor could either of the O'Leary men, who agreed to completely disassemble the container, which they proceeded to do, though even then not fully revealing the mysterious item, which appeared to be roughly three, perhaps almost four feet in height, and, as Eileen had indicated, quite heavy.

Using a small knife, O'Leary quickly cut the heavy twine that had, when tied, secured the still-significant remaining padding carefully wrapped about the object.

As they knelt on the floor, sitting back on their heels, all of the strings cut, Anna finally removed a heavy draping from what seemed to be the top of *it*, revealing the sculpted head of a horse.

Eileen quickly pushed away the remaining coverings. Her eyes wide now, she ventured, "Oh my, I believe I know this . . . this I have seen, yes, yes, I recognise it. . . . 'Tis from the Hofburg, from the palace."

Standing now, his tanned face sheened with sweat, the crowbar at his side, O'Leary nodded emphatically. "Yes, 'tis from the palace; indeed, it is, yes!"

In the midst of the broken-apart crate, the yards and mounds of packing material littering the parlour's elegant Indian carpet, now stood a striking piece of statuary, some forty-odd inches in height, a depiction of a proud Lipizzan stallion, which, it would shortly be confirmed, was one of several similar pieces of sculpture that had, for a number of years, graced a series of quiet niches of that wing of the Hofburg to which was appended the Spanish Riding School.

A thick, cream-coloured envelope had been carefully placed, partially under the objet d'art, where it rested on the still-intact flooring of the crate. Bending, O'Leary carefully raised one side of the sculpture while Anna tugged at the envelope, handing it up to the captain, who, looking down, read, "Capt. Arthur O'Leary/the Lady Eileen O'Leary, Rathleigh House, Co. Cork, Ireland," this clearly having been written by Abby O'Sullivan. By now genuinely weary, O'Leary handed the envelope to Eileen, gesturing for her to open and read it. He finally sat heavily in a brown-leather winged chair, crossing his legs, resting his head against the chair's high, gently worn back, momentarily closing his eyes.

Still sitting back on her heels on the ornate Chinese rug, Eileen unfolded the heavy, fine pages. Easily recognising a familiar, uniquely elegant script, she was immediately able to tell by whom the letter had been written. "'Twas written by the empress herself!" she exclaimed breathlessly, her eyes wide, and without pause began to read, her normally husky voice even more so, as, translating almost effortlessly from Maria Theresa's flawlessly written French, she spoke the words softly, precisely:

My dear children:

Since first we learnt of your decision to depart from us, we began to consider what might be an appropriate remembrance of the time, happy we trust it has been, which both of you have spent with us and have decided on the object now before you, something we trust you will find to have some special meaning, something which we hope will become a part of your home in Ireland, as it has been of ours, of your home here with us.

The empress then proceeded to describe in some detail the history of the statues, their precise location—"Yes, now I recall precisely where I had seen this!" Art exclaimed—and related her understanding of how both of them had become fascinated with the Lipizzaners, slyly indicating that she had long been aware that Eileen had, on more than a few occasions, been given the virtually unheard-of opportunity to actually ride one of the horses, then continuing:

Your obvious love of and appreciation for horses, especially those of this magnificent breed, in ways that only extraordinarily skilled and accomplished equestrians such as you both are, could possess, led us to believe that this token would prove the appropriate remembrance of your years in Austria.

The empress went on to request that they display the statue in a *"place appropriate at your own home, a place where you may each see it daily, and, as Conor and I am certain your future children reach an age at which they, too, can understand and appreciate this, that you will tell them of our splendid Lipizzaners and speak fondly of your days with us here in Vienna."*

Only after pausing for a moment, a soft smile and quiet tears on her face, Eileen read the empress's concluding thoughts, closing, *"with our gratitude for your many years of service to us, and of the singular affection and care you have both shown to she who is now the dauphine of France, assuring you that we daily ask God's blessings on you and your family."*

It was signed, with her customary flourish, simply *MARIA THERESA.*

Versailles—Summer 1770

The dauphine of France was restive in her magnificently carved and gilded bed; her husband had just paid one of what had, in the very few months of their marriage, been his occasional nocturnal visits to the same bed, which resulted, as had all the prior ones, in a brief, uncomfortable conversation, one or perhaps two awkward kisses, some fumbling touching, followed by a brief, inartful parody of the act which was the intended purpose of such visits. As a still-erect Louis Auguste moved abruptly away from his wife and then from the bed, seemingly, incongruously unaware of that fact until, as he smoothed his simple cotton nightshirt, it became quite obvious, his face red, his large, rough hands fluttering before his tented shirt, he grabbed his silk dressing gown from the foot of the bed, wished his wife a "Good evening, Madame, and a restful sleep" and hastily departed.

Even a quarter of an hour later, Marie Antoinette seethed quietly, her small, delicate hands clenched in tight fists as she rolled from her back to her right side, then onto the left, where she now lay, facing the open windows of her ornate bedroom. The hems of the heavy, full-length brocade draperies rested just above the floor, whilst those of the lighter, sill-length drapes danced gently as a steady, warm wind brushed against the bulk of Versailles. She could see the milky, otherworldly twilight of a reluctantly setting sun being challenged by what would become a nearly full Île de France July moon. The delicately ticking, small Sèvres clock on her mantel indicated it was just ten o'clock. *Perhaps if it were the dark of night when he comes . . . perhaps then, it might be . . .* she reflected. Realising that true nighttime darkness actually lay several months ahead, she closed her eyes tightly, then opened them with a sigh, or perhaps it was a low groan.

She closed her eyes briefly again. Though she was not precisely sure how *it* was supposed to be done, she was quite certain what was occurring between herself and Louis was nothing close to the manner in which the act was properly performed. *I so wish I had asked Eileen. . . . Perhaps she believed someone else would "educate" me; if so, she unknowingly permitted me to remain ignorant. Oh, why did she not simply tell me everything?*

My dearest sister Charlotte . . . I know not from whom she learned about it; only that it was not Eileen. . . . Charlotte knew if not everything, so very much about this! Yet I did not understand what she was trying to explain to me. I should have asked questions of her about . . . "coupling," as she called it, likening it to a sword and its sheath, she said . . . the man, the husband . . . he–he . . . he does what Louis has done, but . . . there must be more to it than this . . . than what he does. She shook her head. She recalled the one time when she had reflexively arched against him when he was just inside her, and Louis had gasped and immediately withdrawn, departing without a word. How she missed Eileen; she missed her terribly! *To whom can I turn? Am I to inquire of Madame Etiquette about this?*

She sighed yet again deeply and closed her eyes. *I think not!*

As the breeze, now freshened and growing slightly stronger, reached her face and her bare arms, her fists slowly unclenched. Lifting her nightdress, first her fine, elegant fingers, then her smooth, open palms played gently over her still-small, firm breasts and stomach. Drifting in and out of a light, restless sleep, she clenched the muscles where her husband had but briefly been, closed her eyes and tightened them again, then—first gently, then more than a few times not so gently—finally touched herself *there*, rubbing, slowly, sensually, sighing softly; perhaps she may even have sensed herself quietly moaning. It was only as she'd spoken aloud, certainly much more softly, the words, she became quickly aware that she'd moaned to herself, "Ohhh . . . Hugh . . ." that she sat bolt upright, her breathing rapid, her face flushed.

Calming herself, the very young—she would mark her fifteenth birthday in November—future queen of France slid off her bed and, smoothing her delicate, summer-light silk gown, padded slowly across the thick Chinese carpet to the open window, grateful for the cooling breeze on the smooth— "flawless" they said it was—skin of her flushed, sweat-sheened face. Assuring herself that she would most likely not be seen, Antoinette rested her arms on the sill and sighed, immediately thinking, *I am grown so very weary of sighing; I sigh far too much, all too frequently.* Her eyes on the massive moon. its shape not clearly discernible against the creamy colour of the mid-summer night sky, fleeting images flickered in her mind's eye:

The afternoon in early June at Schönbrunn, little more than a year ago, mere days after becoming formally betrothed to the dauphin of France, when she first met Hugh O'Connell, *in the most laughable manner,* she smiled as she recalled, *I was chasing Mops along the high terrace of the palace, only to burst upon a small gathering that included my mother and Hugh O'Connell, the brother of my dearest governess, Eileen, as well as the head of the empress's household, Abigail O'Connell O'Sullivan, he being newly arrived from Ireland, minutes from having been introduced to the empress.*

We did not particularly like each other at first . . . She smiled wistfully into the hushed semidarkness of the velvety night as there came to her mind snippets of what she had come to remember as those magic months of the summer and autumn of 1769, *spent largely at my best-loved, enchanting Laxenburg,* the palace she treasured most, for a palace it almost was not: broad rather than soaring, with the appearance of being instead a very large country house, comfortably welcoming rather than majestic. *During which time Hugh and I were virtually inseparable as, always of course chaperoned in one way or another, even if it was with a covey of mounted outriders, we roamed, on foot and most frequently on horseback across the green, open space beyond Laxenburg. When Eileen had inquired, "What is it that you find to do with all the time you two spend together?" I merely smiled and said, "Why, Mama," for that was how I had come to address her, as, both then and now, it most accurately reflects the true nature of our relationship and the level of our mutual affection, "we* talk—*about so many things, about everything!"*

As indeed they had and, in the process, they had guilelessly become what each called the other's dearest friend. So dear, in fact, had Hugh become to her that when he had departed Vienna in the company of his, Abigail and Eileen's uncle, General, the Count Moritz O'Connell, en route to Paris to join the armies of Louis XV as a cadet, to be trained for service in Dillon's Regiment, of the famed Irish Brigade on a snowy day early in the winter of the current year, she felt her heart was broken. That grim morning, as she stood—by choice, alone—in a high window of the Hofburg, watching those she knew the empress had come to refer to as "our special Irish," she finally had admitted to herself that so much more than being merely "special," it was they who actually were her family! That she had promised to summon him to Versailles as soon as she arrived as dauphine had sustained her from that time forward.

Sadly, when she actually succeeded, against all odds, in procuring his company at Versailles, for her, Hugh's visit had not been anything close to the joyful reunion Antoinette had hoped and planned it would be. Almost immediately upon her arrival at Versailles, several of her women, especially the countess de Noailles, to whom she had come to openly refer, quite caustically, as *Madame Etiquette*, as well as the strikingly beautiful young woman who was first her companion and then, very shortly thereafter, became the unofficial head of her household, the Princess de Lamballe, Marie Thérèse Louise de Savoie-Carignan, the widow of the grandson of the Sun King's bastard son, later acknowledged and legitimised, had begun reminding her—not at all gently, Antoinette would quickly come to feel, and repeatedly—that she must reconcile herself to the fact that the life she had known in Vienna was no more. Save for Mops, her beloved, albeit annoying little pug dog, who, at the very last moment, had been permitted to come to France, that being due solely to the skilful diplomacy of Count Mercy, her mother's ambassador to the court of Versailles, aided by her beloved governess, she was repeatedly told, everything and *everyone* she had cherished in Vienna were no longer part of her life.

It seemed to her that once she had spoken to Lamballe, *in utmost confidence,* of Hugh being her "dearest friend," the princess—said by many at court to be an eccentric pedant, sheltered and ridiculously naïve in the ways of the world, and prudish in the extreme—had almost daily taken to reminding her that "the dauphine of France you are, wed to the dauphin; thus wed, you and he shall become king and queen of France. This you must never forget!" *How could I possibly forget? You remind me every day!* She recalled that even on the very morning of the day, just last month, of Hugh's visit, the princess had spoken to her of this yet again.

It was on account of this and even more of what had occurred during the afternoon and particularly the evening of that day, that the young dauphine had finally forced herself to take critical notice of what she conceded to be the striking appearance and attributes, physical and otherwise, of the twenty-one-year-old Savoyard. Marie Thérèse Louise stood perhaps three inches shy of being six feet tall—several inches taller than the dauphine herself—her luxuriant blonde hair, more the colour of softly, deeply rich rather than shimmering gold, her flawlessly though frequently simple dress; her complexion presented a natural healthy glow, and as a result, she largely eschewed rouge and powders. Her choice of couture— from the simplest afternoon dress or riding habit to the most magnificent formal evening robe—was always impeccable and invariably flattering to her near-perfect figure. As were her clothes, her manner itself was quietly elegant, though to Antoinette she frequently seemed tentative and even timid. Compounding all of this, only recently, and to her discomfited surprise, had the dauphine come to realise the young woman spoke English fluently. As her mother's emissary to the court, Count Mercy himself informed her of this fact, adding ". . . and in the most *delightful* manner," observing that Lamballe's spoken English was charmingly threaded with a singular Franco-Italian accent. Her voice was soft, almost sensually seductive, its tone gentle and elegant, her words seemingly almost always carefully chosen.

Though Antoinette had not witnessed it, the princess was also said to be fragile, delicate and overly sensitive, it being court gossip that she'd actually fainted upon seeing a still-life painting of a lobster cooked red and resting on a platter with other food.

All of this aside, she recalled that once Hugh had arrived and they were yet again together, she had almost immediately come to feel that the supposed chasm between them was in the minds of others. It was not until after she'd successfully introduced Hugh to Louis XV, the French sovereign and the Irish cadet immediately having taken a liking to each other, and was excitedly displaying a giddiness that virtually no one at Versailles had witnessed in her before, leading him away by the hand from the palace and towards the fountains and gardens which she'd wished him to see, that Lamballe had—*and mere feet from where Hugh stood!*—turned her aside and said, *yet again,* "I fear, indeed, I regret that I must remind you again of that subject about which we have spoken already several times today. . . . You must remember that you are now the Dauphine of France, the future Queen of France . . . and that you are wed! . . . and . . . and . . . and . . ." As Lamballe continued, the all-too-familiar litany quickly became a monotonically numbing cascade of words that she no longer heard.

Antoinette's eyes rolled even now as she recalled the ill-timed, wholly out of place lecture. And they brimmed with tears anytime she called to mind that, at the actual moment, later on in the afternoon, when she'd formally introduced Hugh and Lamballe to each other, even as they stood, the three of them chatting in the Versailles gardens, how—*and how totally out of character it was*—Lamballe had not only taken Hugh's hand but had held it tightly between both of hers, only obviously, reluctantly, releasing it—*and in a giddy, playful manner at that!*—when the dauphine had dismissed her.

. . . And . . . and following his dinner with Louis and myself, when her specific instructions were, her sole purpose was to conduct Hugh to where an officer from the Irish Brigade awaited him to return to Paris, I learned the following day she took it upon herself to provide him with an extensive "tour" of the palace, her arm rarely being separate from his own! And to promise to visit him "at school," which she, I am told, though I am uncertain whether it is true, has already done, supposedly laden with breads and foods from her home in Paris, as well as possibly even from Versailles!

All of this said, despite that she had accepted what she came to refer to as the realities of her life, what perhaps especially saddened Antoinette was that, by all accounts—and she had heard virtually all of them—Hugh had been and apparently was as taken by Lamballe as she obviously was with him. *And so they remain,* she sighed. *Of this I am frequently informed. This I know for certain.*

She nevertheless regretted that neither she nor Hugh had attempted to speak directly to the significantly permanent alteration of their relationship, and, even more profoundly, she was deeply saddened to think that he had so immediately become enamoured of the beautiful Savoyard. *It appears now that he differs not at all from most of his gender—a fine figure, a beguiling expression, pleasant words—especially, it would seem, ones spoken in "fluent English" in a "most delightful manner" and with a "charming Franco-Italian accent,"* she sneered, mimicking Count Mercy bitterly, even in her thoughts, *and his head spins. It must be that it is thus for most men . . . would that the dauphin of France were* thus!

So lost in her memories, her thoughts. her dreams, Antoinette had not heard fingernails delicately scratching on the slightly ajar door to her bedroom. Only when she finally sensed the faint sound on the door did she turn, just as it silently opened.

"Madame, my dearest dauphine," began the Princess de Lamballe as she half-curtseyed, her hands delicately crossed over her ample breasts, lest the bosom of her elegant, flowing, light blue satin dressing gown inadvertently fall open. The gesture by her invariably prim companion, who was widely spoken of at court—notwithstanding her lofty position, being the only Princess of the Blood—as being stuffily priggish in the extreme, caused Marie Antoinette to smile. "I sensed you might yet be awake . . . I only wished to . . ."

The dauphine gestured for the striking young blonde to fully enter the room, then, by patting the mattress, to join her on her massive bed, as she had done on several recent occasions.

Moments later, the former archduchess of Austria leaned back against a puffy mound of down-filled pillows at the headboard, as her companion perched comfortably against the sturdy right-side bottom bedpost, several of the same pillows behind her own back.

"Now, my darling princess, let us visit," smiled Antoinette playfully, although she was painfully aware that the only reason Lamballe knew she was most likely awake was that one or more of the servants had almost certainly advised her that, yet again, Louis had come to and very soon thereafter departed her apartments. *Every aspect—howsoever minute, howsoever private—of my life is known to all in this place!* She was irritated at them all, including Lamballe, though she generally had grown fond of the young noblewoman, and—despite this and other annoyances, one continuing to be especially hurtful—she had, for the most part, come to enjoy her company.

The pair chatted quietly, discussing a random, meaningless sequence of topics, some gossip, some news, the only mention of any real interest to Antoinette being that Lamballe had confirmed that Madame Rose Bertin, one of several prominent Parisian dressmakers vying to serve the new dauphine, would be coming on Tuesday morning, ". . . though well before Your Highness's attendance at Mass." The dauphine smiled noncommittally; truth be told, she felt the Bourbons' attendance at daily Mass *en famille* was, as she'd informed the princess on several prior occasions and yet again this evening, "silly," as always, shocking the devout princess, although she confessed that she was enjoying immensely all of the attention she continued to receive from Paris's leading dressmakers and milliners.

Finally, Marie Antoinette rested her head back against her pillows; closing her eyes, momentarily reflecting and quickly concluding *If not at this moment, when shall I ever . . .?* she opened them and, sitting up straighter, looked pointedly at her companion.

"If I may, my dearest princess," she began—Lamballe smiling softly in response—"I have been meaning to mention . . . to ask you, indeed . . . to . . ." She paused and cleared her throat, after a moment resuming, "Regarding Monsieur Cadet O'Connell and his recent visit, I was, if I may say, most *intrigued* by your effusive kindness, your *generous, welcoming* of my friend . . ."

Noticing that Lamballe's mouth was open in a small "o" and that her cheeks had become a bright red, the dauphine paused, but only briefly. "What I am attempting to say is that I have not . . . indeed never have I seen you . . . conduct yourself, indeed, *behave* in such a manner, if I may say that . . . in my brief time here. Your demonstrative spirit and gestures, your apparent sheer joy! It was really quite . . . remarkable, and most surprisingly so!"

Her blush not at all receding, the princess spoke softly, seemingly not quite believing she was saying the words she spoke: "Highness, the truth is that never have I felt so profoundly, so immediately attracted to any man, to any boy . . . never, in my life." She lowered her eyes, whispering, ". . . and I am not a precipitate person. . . ."

"I do not believe, nor am I saying, you are," Antoinette interrupted gently, "Merely that by your continuing to hold Monsieur O'Connell's hand in both of yours even as we spoke in the gardens following my introductions . . . In truth, I was rather shocked." She laughed lightly, airily, despite that she felt darkly serious. "Indeed, even as Monsieur O'Connell was to depart our company following his dinner with the dauphin and myself that evening, the fact that you immediately took his arm, conducting him away from us . . . proceeding thence to lead him on an extensive—and lengthy—tour of the palace . . . as I am told . . . the details of which I continue to learn."

Lamballe's lips were quivering, her complexion now gone ghostly pale, and she began stammering. "It was only as I have said, Your Highness . . . Madame, I was . . ." Colour gradually returning to her face, she swallowed, and then continued, her voice suddenly, almost eerily, resolute, "I *am* most taken with the young man. . . . I have never experienced such deeply profound feelings; I . . ."

"But, my darling princess . . . you were . . . your husband, he . . ."

Abruptly sitting straight up and away from the bedpost, her back rigid, no longer resting against the pillows, one of which had fallen off the bed as she moved, her palms resting on, then suddenly gripping her thighs just about her knees, Lamballe's cheeks flamed, displaying a naked rage, an emotion the dauphine could not believe the woman could summon, and her words erupted.

"My husband? My *husband,* the grand-sounding *Monsieur Louis Alexandre de Bourbon-Penthièvre, le prince de Lamballe!*" she said mockingly, practically spitting out his name and title. "You will know that he was little more . . . indeed, he was *nothing more* than a *pox-ridden libertine!* " Both of her hands now clenched in tight fists, she shrieked, the high pitch of her voice seemingly resonating off all four walls, off the ornate gilded ceiling itself. "*This* despite his high birth and magnificent title, notwithstanding his heritage . . . descended from Louis XIV himself! Your Highness must be aware that never was this 'marriage' anything but one in appearances only! The only kindness done to me by this wretched, this repulsive, *this utterly disgusting man,* was that he never forced himself upon me, leaving me chaste and unsullied—and most assuredly free of the loathsome diseases that cost him his worthless, miserable life!" Her face sweat-sheened, she paused abruptly, breathing heavily, her full bosom rising and falling, then shockingly displaying for the first time before her mistress, indeed perhaps before anyone, a sneering haughtiness, she added in an icy tone, "As by wedding me, he rendered me a Princess of the Blood . . . by dying he made me a very, *very* wealthy widow . . . Madame."

The dauphine remained wordless in stunned amazement both at the revelation as well as the passion displayed by someone so genteelly fragile as she'd deemed Lamballe to be.

At that, in the powerful stillness, releasing her fists, Lamballe suddenly collapsed backwards, first grazing the bedpost—that she did so prevented her from falling heavily onto the floor; instead she toppled over gently, like a doll. Antoinette was quickly at the foot of the bed, holding her moist, shaking palms, slowly easing the princess into a sitting position. Gently turning her, she placed the pillow that had fallen off the bed behind her head and leant her back against the footboard. The dauphine then quickly fetched and held a cup of tepid, sugared water to her companion's dry lips. Finally, the princess opened her eyes and drank shallowly.

"Your Highness, please forgive me . . . I have never spoken . . . please forgive . . . me," Lamballe whispered, and fainted again.

It was perhaps ten days later when Marie Antoinette yet again raised the topic of Hugh O'Connell, though having grown genuinely weary of the subject, her own feelings about him by then being, at the very best, ambivalent, she was slowly coming to accept the realities of this aspect of her life. Her now not-always-mild animus towards her lady-in-waiting nevertheless remained. She resented Lamballe's tiresome, no longer subtle cautions about her having to accept that she had left everything and *everyone* behind her. She even more deeply resented the princess's behaviour on meeting Hugh O'Connell, not to mention her conduct since that time, her ire heightened by which Lamballe appeared blissfully unaware—or, even more troubling, perhaps callously uncaring as to her mistress's obvious albeit patently unexpressed feelings.

The dauphine and her lady were strolling slowly along the Grand Canal on a still, humid afternoon. As she glanced over at the princess, Antoinette reflected, *this dear, fragile and in some ways perhaps even damaged woman . . . she who seems so otherworldly . . . is it that she is just now grown conscious of her beauty and grace . . . such that a siren of sorts she suddenly appears to have become? Is it that I fear she will lure my once dearest friend to some disaster? Or is it rather that she does, or even that she might genuinely care for him that troubles or even more profoundly saddens me?* Staring blankly into the afternoon haze, she paused. . . . *Yes, it saddens me deeply . . .*

At one point, after they had strolled in silence for several minutes absent any prodding from Antoinette, indeed absent any reason at all for her to have done so, Lamballe airily, almost matter-of-factly began to relate that she had several days earlier visited Hugh at the École Militaire *once again!* ". . . bringing with me . . . as I had promised him I would on any such visit," she laughed gaily—Antoinette instantly sensing an almost- cruel haughtiness as well—"more of the bounties of the kitchens and bakery of my home." She laughed again. "As he was on prior occasions, Monsieur O'Connell, he was once again so very delighted . . . both at my coming as well as by my 'gifts,' though it appears the officers remain less so," she observed, this time her manner clearly being purposely haughty.

Antoinette stopped abruptly, her face red. "Do you mean to tell me that you have been journeying into Paris absent my consent, *princesse?*"

Having taken several steps beyond where her mistress had halted, Lamballe turned and retraced the distance; she smiled almost guilelessly, or was it, the dauphine immediately considered, *arrogantly?* "You will recall, Your Highness, that given my own station in life, given that I, as the Princess de Lamballe, continue to maintain my own residence, indeed my home, at the Hôtel de Toulouse, that you yourself had said I would continue to have full and free access to Paris, apart from my service to Your Royal Highness." She lowered her eyes.

Her cheeks hot, Marie Antoinette was unable to mask her shock, realising that, indeed, and for the reasons the princess had stated, she had indeed decreed just what the princess had said. *I of course knew this!*

The dauphine took a few steps forward, this time Lamballe standing still, and turned back towards her companion, her voice shaking, her right forefinger stabbing the heavy air. "I shall say just one thing, *my dearest princess*—" she hissed softly between clenched teeth, "and then the matter, it shall be spoken of by us no more, never again: that you continue to lecture me about caring for someone from 'my past' and then *pursue* him like a siren, this . . . this is cruel, this I resent!" She paused for a long moment. "Yet you are henceforth free to see . . . indeed to consort, in public or in private, as you wish with Master O'Connell."

Sensing herself triumphant, Lamballe stood still, *regally* . . . and *proudly, perhaps even smugly*, Antoinette immediately noticed and would recall, otherwise displaying no emotion at all as the young, presumptive queen completed her thought, her voice slightly elevated. "You are correct in that I am *of course* dauphine of France, and that I shall indeed become queen one day. Given that, I have come to believe that I have far, *far* more important matters with which I must cope than what may be but a pleasant memory of a young Irish boy in Vienna."

The women silently faced each other until Antoinette added, pointing her right forefinger at Lamballe's bosom, "And *you* shall no longer lecture me like a child. *Do you understand?*"

The princess nodded only once, and very slowly, lowering her eyes only momentarily before immediately looking directly, quite sharply, down into the dauphine's eyes, both, seemingly perhaps for the first time, conscious of how much taller than her mistress she was.

Antoinette extended her hand to Lamballe and the two walked, again largely in silence albeit they continued hand in hand, for almost an hour more.

That night as she lay—alone, to her relief Louis not having appeared— in her bed, Marie Antoinette would, reflecting upon when she had first introduced Hugh to Marie Thérèse Louise, recall that at that very moment she had felt a slight yet actual physical twinge, acknowledging, for the first time, the reality that it was only with Marie Thérèse Louise de Savoie-Carignan or someone like her, that Hugh O'Connell would spend his life *. . . and not with me, nor I with him . . . as that could never have been, and at that very moment my heart experienced a gentle prick of sadness.* It proved to be a deep, quiet and hauntingly profound sorrow that, though she would never speak of it to anyone—not even to Eileen—would remain with her forever.

County Cork, Ireland—September 1770

More quickly than many had thought they would, certainly more so than most people in West Cork had hoped, July had become August, and a gentle autumn began in earnest late that month.

The summer had passed largely uneventfully. Art and Eileen had worked closely, buying and selling several horses, including a yearling who looked remarkably like Bull. Leaving his father free to devote more of his time to his multifaceted position as land agent for the Minhear family at Carrigaphooka, a continuing source of the O'Learys' secure status and wealth, Art oversaw the farming aspects of the Rathleigh business as the summer crops moved towards harvest and plans were made for a winter wheat crop. At a large outdoor gathering at Rathleigh, and by means of a number of in-home visits, the O'Learys had, true to their word, seen to it that Anna Pfeffer was successfully introduced to their neighbours, especially the local Catholic gentry, to the extent that by September she had begun to receive calls from several younger squires, seeming to be especially taken by a young gentleman whose hair was almost as blond as her own, one Master John Collins of Derryleigh.

Of the young men whom Anna had met, Collins was, in both O'Leary's and Eileen's estimation, clearly the most outstanding: Perhaps six foot three and solid, he carried himself with an effortless elegance, whether walking, riding or dancing. He spoke in an almost softly genteel voice, his several years of study at Salamanca having further polished a seemingly innate aristocratic manner. The youngest of five children—and the only son—he had been doted on by, in addition to his indulgent parents, a bevy of, in some cases, considerably—he was five years younger than his closest sibling—older sisters, who adored "wee John" and whom he, in turn, loved dearly and to whom he would always remain devoted. Each of them had now been wed well to a mix of Protestant and Catholic gentlemen in the area.

Young John had returned from Spain only weeks before Squire James Collins's death in mid-1767; having stoically concealed what he had known for months was a fatal illness, the elder Collins had fiercely clung to life so as to, he hoped, enable him the time to discuss one last time with his heir all that he must know as he became squire of Derryleigh. Despite the squire's significant age—he was approaching sixty at the time of John's birth—he and his son had been close, and it was during the years of the younger

Collins's growing that, quite early on actually, he had begun to subtly impart to his son the wisdom and wiles which had served him well.

The Collins clan—like the O'Learys and the O'Connells, for that matter—were devout, relatively wealthy Catholics. Unlike many of the other families, however, Squire Collins's grandfather had quietly embraced the Church of Ireland, and the male heirs, including young John, were nominally Protestant. It was "Squire James," as he was affectionately referred to by the Derryleigh tenantry and indeed by a number of people of all stations in the neighbourhood, who had, equally quietly, as he said, "Finally and at long last cast off, indeed tossed away the bloody heretical yoke of Protestantism once and for all!" He proceeded to formally install a small chapel, which could, if need be, effortlessly and quickly resume its outward purpose of being a kitchen house, where Mass had henceforth been regularly celebrated by a man generally known to the neighbourhood only as the estate's chief steward, Tomás, a sturdy, sunburnt, one-time sailor, with a mane of slate-grey hair and piercing black eyes, who was, unbeknownst to anyone other than the Collins family, Father Tomás Ó Sé, a priest of the Society of Jesus, a veteran of what would prove to be virtually the final stages of the Jesuits' "English mission," for whom Derryleigh seemed a respite after his years of ministering to the still largely hidden Catholic gentry of England.

All this considered, what Anna had found most endearing was the sweet, gentle shyness of this big, handsome Irishman. As O'Leary had predicted—and as Eileen had brought herself to hope—Anna and Collins had fallen wonderfully, blissfully in love.

Adding to the O'Learys' domestic contentment, Conor O'Leary had turned two in August and remained a happy, seemingly self-assured little boy. "Does he fear nothing?" Anna had cried out to no one in particular as, by catching his feet just as he was propelling himself through the rails, she had interrupted the little boy's attempt to squeeze through a paddock fence where a young, not terribly friendly stallion was confined, pending being broken to the saddle.

At least twice weekly, O'Leary had resumed his customary practice of riding into Macroom later on in the day, occasionally taking care of items of business, seeing friends and spending part of the evening in the company of a variety of men, occasionally included his brother-in-law, the husband of Eileen's twin sister, Dr. James Baldwin, whom O'Leary had actually come, at least to some extent, to like. Over copious amounts of stout and porter and a large meal, the men, mostly in their twenties and thirties, discussed neighbourhood affairs, the weather, crops, horses and, inevitably, politics.

"There will come in Ireland the time when the *Sassenach* shall find themselves compelled to leave, whether it be by force of arms, and then whether domestically or by invasion . . . or by some grand scheme of peaceful, diplomatic resolution, the precise source of which I cannot now imagine," O'Leary had observed one strangely chill night in early September.

"*Never* will they depart voluntarily," interjected Charles MacCarthy, a stout, young red-haired farmer and horse breeder, from whom it was that O'Leary had acquired the chestnut yearling that resembled Bull. "Driven from these shores they shall have to be, and, indeed, I believe strongly *they shall indeed be* . . . though not in our time, not in the time of our grandsons, I fear," he opined, in a voice much softer than O'Leary's.

Draining his tankard, O'Leary thudded it gently on the rough table, where it was quickly refilled with thick, creamy, dark porter by the comely auburn-haired barmaid.

"'Tis from Catholic Europe that assistance will come, 'tis *to* Catholic Europe that Catholic Ireland must, and eventually, I strongly believe, shall, look for succour and aid," O'Leary emphasised, his strong voice now filling the public house as Dr. Baldwin winced, even as a number of men, seemingly a majority of those in the house at other tables and standing at the bar banged their tankards in agreement.

Significantly not so was a small, serious-looking group composed of some of the king's men and their own friends, gathered about a large corner table, exchanging tight looks and whispered comments, softly murmured so as to be heard only amongst themselves: *Ah, yes, we hear again O'Leary; perhaps he believes it shall be he who leads the goddamned bloody Papist army of which he speaks, of which I am sure he and even more so that pompous old bastard O'Connell the general incites to action. . . . Is he to now remain here, with the O'Connell girl he is said to have seduced from her home? . . . No, return to Austria he shall— to resume chasing glory . . . and blond German girls, of both I am certain. . . . At least tonight he dresses in acceptable clothing, setting aside his gaudy, traitorous uniform. . . . Ah, fear not, we shall see him strutting again. . . . They must strut, these arrogant traitors, these "Austrians" and their "French" friends. . . . As you mention the bastard, I saw old General O'Connell, I did, cavorting about Macroom like a popinjay in his bloody finery, whilst last here he was, he is "ennobled," I learnt, can you imagine? . . . That pretentious old bitch parading about with him, his wife! One of the girls at my house says a "countess" or some such she is. . . . In the event, we shall have to maintain careful watch over O'Leary . . . and I should think the O'Connell girl, as well—the arrogance of the bloody, goddammed O'Connells of bloody, goddammed Derrynane I am certain must exceed even that of O'Leary. . . .*

The muttering continued, heads were shaken, glances cast furtively across the room towards the table, where the talk had turned to the weather.

Later, as their group was departing, gently touching his shoulder, Dr. Baldwin halted O'Leary, and the others stopped as well, gathering tightly about in the still, wintry darkness of the market square. "Brother," the physician addressed his brother-in-law, though Eileen and Mary were still far from becoming close, "most careful you must be, sir, of voicing such opinions, even in this close company." He gestured back towards the public house. "You have brought a wife and child to live here, even though 'tis to Catholic Europe that you yourself shall regularly return; you must consider them, their safety and security."

O'Leary nodded. "Thank you, *brother*, that is truth indeed, yes, but *Eibhlín Dubh*, a stalwart subject of Her Imperial Majesty, the Empress Maria Theresa, she remains, that strength she herself can and shall draw upon in any adversity."

Squire Collins, the quiet young man who had captured Anna's attention, leaned forward and quietly lifted a finger for recognition. "But, Captain O'Leary, sir, is it not reality that the king's men, the king's laws *here* do indeed present a threat to your family's security and safety and well-being, a threat that the imperial armies in which you serve are unable to thwart, no matter how strong remain your loyalties, and those of Mistress O'Leary, to the empress."

Silence hung over the men, the night air chill, almost cold now, and damp; in former days, O'Leary might have challenged a man who had stated even that obvious truth, but tonight he nodded thoughtfully, stood quietly, looking into the near total darkness, and nodded again, this time very slowly, directly at John Collins. "What you say, Squire Collins, is truth, verily it is. I shall attempt to be, shall we say, perhaps more *circumspect.*"

County Cork, Ireland—Winter 1770–1771

A curiously chilly autumn gave way to a heavy, cold and it would prove to be abnormally snowy winter in Cork; though it would not long accumulate in drifts the way it had in Vienna, the ground would nevertheless be periodically snow-covered from Christmas until after St. Brigid's Day. As the days grew shorter and the outdoor labour and activities fewer, the Rathleigh household turned inward to one another's company. Books and music, stories and singing, grateful for warm fires and ample food, contentment not universally enjoyed that and many another winter in West Cork.

Through the autumn, following a call paid by him to Art alone, and the requisite permission to do so as a result granted, Squire John Collins, tall, just thirty, blond, quietly gentle, almost pensive at times—and wealthy—began to pay regular visits to "the Lady Anna," as he now referred to her. Under the propriety required, albeit the bemused and surely benign gaze of the O'Learys, the couple would sit, visiting quietly by the fire, or stroll chastely about the Rathleigh grounds, Anna wrapped snugly in her long, black Vienna cloak, her hair goldenly stark against the heavy, soft, wool fabric.

In addition to loving Anna dearly as a friend, Eileen now confided to her husband that she felt a strong maternal affection and, with it, maternal worries and cares as well. As she carefully observed the now obviously courting couple, her affection increased, and her worries and cares were abated. She smiled benevolently when she heard, and less frequently watched, Anna laughing her wonderfully warm laugh or, several times, as she overheard the couple sharing a joke about Anna's still not always flawless use of the English language, even once hearing John Collins responding to a question from the pretty Austrian girl with a smiling *"Ja!"*

A week prior to Christmas, the couple had come quietly, and quite formally, to "Captain O'Leary and the Lady Eileen," as John Collins addressed them, and indicated that they had arrived at *an understanding.* "The Lady Anna having accepted my . . . my pro . . . my proposal," the normally well albeit extremely soft-spoken Collins hesitatingly began, "in the absence of her father, her mother, I thought it not inappropriate . . . and indeed—" he took Anna's hand in his own— "the Lady Anna has agreed for us to speak with your good selves. We should be most grateful if . . ." and O'Leary, nodding towards Eileen, smilingly raised both of his rough palms in a gesture Eileen remembered seeing for the first time as she and Art had sat similarly across from Squire O'Leary approximately three years earlier in the very same room.

"I believe that we *both*—" Eileen smilingly nodded her head in effusive agreement—"could not be any happier to fully assent to your proceeding to conclude your *understanding.*"

Indeed, they could not have been more pleased with the arrangement, and later that evening, as they visited in Anna's room, Eileen lauded the young Austrian's choice: "Not only is he a good man, a good, pious Catholic—indeed a devout one I understand him to be—but a wealthy and superbly educated one as well, and . . ." she smiled impishly, ". . . and, oh my goodness, is he not a soft one on the eyes." She laughed as Anna blushed and giggled. A bit taller than O'Leary, Collins was a hefty, solid man, broad-shouldered and large-handed. He wore his golden-blond hair long, with a neat, tightly beribboned plait. His voice was melodically deep, his eyes a singular blue. "Easy on the eyes indeed, my darling," Eileen whispered as she kissed her dearest friend good night.

With the betrothal and the fact that Captain O'Leary's orders did not require him to return to Vienna until late February, Christmas 1770 was an especially festive time; the wide-eyed joy of little Conor, just four months beyond his second birthday, and still unsure why he felt as he did and why it was so wonderful, reflected the collective joy of the household.

Eileen had begun to tell him stories of the birth of the Christ Child and of the angels and the shepherds, of how Mary rode a donkey to Bethlehem whilst Joseph walked, and where the Baby Jesus had been born, so that more than once as Christmas drew near, whilst they were in the barn, the precocious little boy, who was only beginning to talk, simply pointed at a hay-filled feeding box and smiled.

As if it were an unexpected gift, even the long-dreaded Christmas visit of Catherine O'Leary proved to be a surprisingly pleasant one, virtually devoid of any significant contention. As she strolled slowly, curiously, from room to room, Catherine took awed note of the furnishings that had come from the imperial palaces. "You had three apartments, in three different palaces . . . and all the furnishings and rugs, books and paintings I have seen, these were *yours* . . . there?" she had breathlessly inquired of Eileen, who quietly—and, to herself, quite smugly—nodded in the affirmative, adding softly, " . . .by the grace and favour of the empress." Additionally, Catherine was rendered virtually speechless by the Lipizzaner statuary, ensconced for the winter in a corner of the large entry hall, especially when her father told her of its history and how it came to be there, later quietly sharing the empress's letter with his by-then wide-eyed daughter.

"I believe your iconoclastic sister is become an unwitting monarchist," Eileen advised Art as they walked in a quickly gathering dusk a few days before Christmas.

"If 'tis our history in Vienna and the type, quality and volume of the goods and wares the empress has lavished on you, on ourselves, that serve to keep her in this thrall, I say 'hurrah and thanks be to God Himself, and to Her Imperial Majesty'!" He chuckled, patting his wife's arm.

So enjoyable was Catherine's visit that the O'Learys were actually pleased to have her extend it through the celebration of Twelfth Night; she departed midmorning on the following day. "May 1771 prove to be a happy and prosperous year for us all!" Catherine called out as her carriage lurched away, the horses' hoofs and its wheels crunching exceptionally loudly on some of the broken and crushed rocks, the night's heavy frost having delicately cemented some of them to one another by morning.

That evening, in bed, Conor now ensconced in his own adjoining small room, the couple quietly agreed that given the quality of Catherine's visit and that of what Eileen had, somewhat grandiloquently, referred to as the Christmas ball they had attended in Macroom was, by and large, both a joyous and successful occasion.

"I must confess, my darling, though I never expected to, I truly enjoyed wearing court dress yet again." Eileen laughed softly, both of them agreeing how lovely Anna had appeared in a drastically altered dress of Eileen's. Eileen had worn a robe of heavy red velvet, with full train, whilst Anna's was of green brocade, delicately laced with gold thread, both of the women's hair having been done by each other in a fairly successful mimicking of the French style, based on engravings of women "said to be mostly of ill-repute," Eileen had noted as she advised that she'd first seen the pictures in *Town & Country* magazine, founded in London just the year before, as well as their memories of how Madame la Dauphine's hair had been fashioned upon departing Vienna and during the journey to France.

The grand event had been held on the Friday evening of the week of Christmas, culminating a merry progression from Monday's Christmas Eve festivities, the Great Day itself on Tuesday and St. Stephen's Day on the twenty-sixth, in the hulking, some said cavernous, generally nondescript, rough grey-stone building located on the far side of the market square in Macroom, away from both the market house itself, near where O'Leary and Eileen had met, as well as from what remained of the battlements on the front wall of Macroom Castle. The unnamed building—informally referred to by some as the Space—was more typically used for markets and livestock auctions in bad weather, but this night had been utterly transformed, scrubbed clean of any suggestion of its customary uses, glittering with a blaze of well-placed torches and candles, swags of Scots pine subtly perfuming the air, its draughty, invariably chilly interior comfortably warmed by a roaring fire in the pair of massive—so large that a man could stand upright in both—hearths. The blazes had been set early in the day and kept spectacularly roaring so that by evening the empty space would be as warm as possible, as so it was. Virtually anyone in the vicinity who enjoyed performing in public, their instruments ranging from the dramatically complex violin and viola, along with the Irish harp and uilleann pipes, to the simpler, yet perhaps even more joyful bodhrán, flutes and whistles, had gathered to provide the evening's music. Almost all those invited had contributed significant quantities of food, along with vast amounts of liquid refreshment, all delivered by a day-long procession of well-ladened wagons and carts on Thursday and Friday morning. It proved to be a rare gathering of much, if not most, of the local aristocracy, Gaelic Catholic and Protestant alike. In the spirit of the season, guests included some of the king's men and their wives, despite that most members of both orders considered them their social inferiors.

The night was cracklingly cold, the silent countryside illuminated by a full yellow moon and a myriad of stars that seemed to have been haphazardly scattered across the chill black heavens. Blazing torches greeted the revellers as they approached the hall. Both O'Learys were wrapped in their thick wool Vienna cloaks: O'Leary's worn tonight over his coat like, fur-trimmed pelisse, a part of his uniform, being of black wool, severe, with elegant gold clasps at the neck and the chest, whilst Eileen's was her still-stunning red wool, grey fox-trimmed and lined one. The occasion was the first time since their accelerated public courtship in the fall of 1767 that O'Leary had appeared publicly in Ireland wearing his full-dress uniform, including his sword, and the first time ever that Eileen, joined by Anna, would be seen in the magnificent court dress as worn in Vienna. It did not go unnoticed.

"*Popinjay*, see, Morris, I told you, as I have told you many times, to fear not that the traitor O'Leary would strut yet again . . . and yonder so he does, in full plumage . . . as does the O'Connell girl. From her outlandish costume, she fancies herself noble, indeed *royalty*, it appears!" scoffingly gestured Deputy Under High Sheriff Nathanial Dilby quietly to Abraham Morris, high sheriff of Cork as, in marked contrast to the elegance of Anna, Eileen and a number of the women, especially those of the Catholic gentry, a number of them having direct access to Parisian fashion, with their primly, plainly, almost severely attired, clearly uncomfortable wives, they stood stolidly, unsmilingly to one side as, along with their Protestant neighbours, many of the *bloody goddamned Papists* and their merrily laughing wives already swept about the floor in a series of round dances.

At one point, after O'Leary spoke with the musicians, pounding on his thighs to indicate the appropriate cadence, upon hearing them strike up an Irish tune that had never before been played as it would be, he and Eileen took the floor alone to dance the graceful, elegantly complex Ländler, which they had both mastered in Vienna. As they danced close to their small group, with John Collins's smiling acquiescence, O'Leary gracefully handed his wife to him and led a blushingly reluctant Anna out onto the floor. Between Anna and Eileen's comments, the others now knew it was an Austrian folk dance, a favourite of long standing.

Turning his back to his wife, Morris faced his deputy. "God's blood, sir, how I detest, indeed how I *loathe* that man!" he hissed as O'Leary and Eileen later again floated past, their eyes gleaming only for each other, their feet seeming to barely touch the polished floor as they elegantly twirled and processed lightly away.

"He shall ultimately be brought to justice, Your Honour," growled Dilby, "of that I have no doubt. . . . He shall be incautious to the point of recklessness, in word or deed or both . . . and such shall cost him his life or, at the very minimum, his freedom, sir!"

The sheriff's weary eyes flashed dimly. "Indeed, yes, I agree . . . so he shall, and when he does, we shall be prepared to act in the king's name, enforcing the king's writ   . . . yes!" His dour mood markedly lifted by the prospect of an eventually hanged, no! much more simply, an eventually shot, in either case, an eventually most certainly dead Arthur O'Leary, after seating their now wholly miserable wives, who did not even care for each other's company, on rickety side chairs, he and his companion proceeded to treat themselves to copious amounts of the abundantly available spirits, in a strikingly brief period of time, repeatedly toasting each other, as well as to Christmas, the coming year, the king, the king's justice and his—and their—continuing dominance over Ireland, specifically the hegemony they maintained over ninety percent of whose population they sneeringly referred to as the "mere Irish."

Within the hour, as O'Leary and Eileen were quietly making their way slowly about the hall, in a continuing effort to have visited with as many of their friends and acquaintances as they were able, they found themselves unexpectedly facing a red-faced, glistening High Sheriff Abraham Morris, his eyes watery, his stance unsteady, as he suddenly set himself directly in their path.

"Why . . . if iz not Ghen-eril O'Learlee himself!" the short man began, his voice combatively loud, "and, and . . . his luverley wife . . . You *are* Missus O'Lear-lee, mmmmh . . . *Lear-ree,* are you not, girl?" he slurred, looking up and gesturing towards a clearly shocked, unpleasantly surprised Eileen.

She quickly turned to her husband, hissing, "Who *is* this foul little man?"

Barely having heard Arthur inform her of Morris's name and position, her carriage customarily regal, her expression as she looked down again on the squat, stout, sadly unattractive man one of disdain bordering on contempt, Eileen *sniffed* audibly and turned sharply to walk away. Feeling

O'Leary's white-gloved hand delicately placed on her arm, she then turned back, her voice icy. "*I* am the Lady Eileen O'Leary   . . . *Mistress* O'Leary to you, *sir*," she purred condescendingly, almost viciously.

O'Leary instantly regretted detaining her.

"Hmmfh," Morris managed, visibly swaying in place, despite that his feet were flatly planted, his legs spread wide. "One would have uh mpressshum . . . from your wurvs and by your cos-soom—" smirking, he gestured wildly at Eileen with an unsteady right hand— "that you see yerself as being wurvfy of res-speck . . . of *my* russ-sphecht," he again slurred, now wagging his left forefinger up at Eileen as he pounded his chest with his right. "I know nah wun reason why, nah wun bloody damme reason . . . you arr-gunt gurl, you . . . why, you slul . . . you *schlutt* . . . you *SLUT* yeh . . . fuh'ing Romish *SLUT* . . . *you,* you run 'way wiff'"—snorting, he waved both hands at O'Leary, who stood uncustomarily mute—"*him* . . .who d'ya tink . . . you *think*, you . . . you . . . are, hmmm?"

By then having separated herself from O'Leary with a single step, gesturing for her husband, whose hand was on his sword hilt, to remain back, her cheeks now bright and, having permitted her train to cascade back onto the floor, some of it puddling in front of the broad skirts of her gown, as if to sharply separate her elegant self from this "foul little man," her arms at her sides, Eileen turned to look down yet again at the momentarily silent man, his eyes now focused quite noticeably on the ample décolletage her robe provided. "You will look at *me*, sir . . . at my *face*!" she commanded and, unthinkingly, he did so instantly, his rheumy eyes shooting up, his mouth still slack.

As he did, Morris having spread his feet as wide as possible, with a force sufficient to make a statement but not nearly enough to injure, she unhesitatingly slapped the drunken man across his face with the palm of her by-then ungloved right hand. The *smack* was quite audible in the hushed hall.

His body first lurched precariously forwards and back, swaying then sideways, finally managing only a shocked "You Pape-piss bisch!" and a laughably comical, wholly impotent parody of taking a swing at her, which evoked hilarity and mocking remarks amongst those closest to the pair, Morris swayed even more visibly as Eileen continued in a calm, firm voice:

"I would remind you"—from this point, in her disgust, she pointedly refrained from addressing him as *sir*—"that I am the daughter of Donál Mór Ó Conaill and Maire ní Dhuibh of Derrynane, County Kerry. I am the wife of Captain Arthur O'Leary, an officer of the Hungarian Hussars in the Imperial Armies of Austria and Hungary, of Rathleigh House, in this county. I am the proud mother of his first son, his first child; I am just returned from most of a decade spent in service at the highest levels of the court of Her Imperial Majesty, the Empress Maria Theresa in Vienna. I am well-read and travelled; I am fluent in four languages, competent in two others, I am well-spoken, whilst *you* . . . you are *none* of . . ."

Shaking her head, she caught herself, but then continued. "I *am* most assuredly worthy of respect in this, my country, the very same respect accorded me at what is perhaps the highest court of Europe. *You* shall behave accordingly," she again commanded haughtily, "you repulsive little man."

Pausing momentarily, her gently heaving bosom the only indication of the passion she felt, she then spoke, loudly enough to be heard by most of the people in the hall, ". . . *and* . . . should I *ever* learn that you have used *that* or any similarly foul word in reference to me *ever again*, be assured," she paused dramatically, pointing her long, elegant right forefinger directly at him, "be *fully* assured, little man, that *I . . . shall . . . kill . . . you.*"

People gasped. Morris's mouth fell open. In the deadly silence, he finally managed, "Zat's uh fret! You dare fretten me?"

Laughing cruelly, Eileen condescendingly shook her head. "Indeed not, small, foul, nauseating man, that I shall kill you I assure you 'tis a *promise* . . . and I rarely break my promises," she sneered, quite loudly.

At which point, gathering her train, she slowly, disdainfully turned and swept elegantly away, leaving O'Leary silently looking down at a sullen, enraged Morris, his cheeks blazing, his rheumy eyes wide.

Directing his gaze upwards towards the uniformed officer, "You, *you, you* . . ." attempted the sheriff, unsteadily stabbing his stubby left forefinger now at O'Leary, who, stepping nearer, immediately, though noiselessly, grabbed the shorter man's left wrist, drawing him instantly closer to himself.

Not releasing his strong grip on Morris's wrist, leaning over, close to him, O'Leary seethed calmly, speaking quite softly. "You will *never* again arrogate to yourself the authority, indeed any right whatsoever, to speak as you have to either my wife or to myself. . . . Do you understand *that . . . you little turd?*"

Sweating profusely now, his jaw drooping, his eyes unfocused, Morris looked up at O'Leary; waving his right hand shakily, he suddenly called out, quite loudly, "Wachting you, I am . . . I . . . we, uh king's loy-yul . . . we all sall be wachting, you, you trayrus arr-gunt Papis' bas-ard, you. . . fuh-ing, yoo sonofuh . . ."

At that moment, Morris gasped and *mffffff'd* audibly as O'Leary tightened his grasp on the man's left wrist and hand, the sheriff impotently attempting to shake himself free, the grip instead becoming ever stronger, the veins in O'Leary's right hand bulging unseen within his white glove. His eyes blazing, O'Leary then twisted his hold, bringing Morris to his knees with a dull thump, heads turning in the crowd, scattered gasps and whispers from those standing close by now being heard.

After a long moment, O'Leary abruptly released him.

Morris immediately fell forward—hard!—a solid, audible thud heard well beyond the spot where his forehead struck the frigid stone flooring. The gasps were replaced by an audibly buzzing cacophony of murmurs, expressing, depending, in some though certainly not all cases on the individual's religious persuasion, anger, disgust, embarrassment, scorn, derision, ridicule and eventually a great deal more than slightly cruel and wholly ecumenical laughter. Loud, caustic laughter.

Having stepped back, his arms now crossed, O'Leary watched with loathing as a momentarily stunned, dazed Morris attempted to struggle to his feet toppling forward several times in the process; sweating, shaking, his glazed eyes still wide, the little man finally achieved a semi kneeling position, supporting himself by resting his palms flat on the floor in front of him. Just as he did, his at least somewhat less intoxicated undersheriff shuffled up and took his arms, steadying him, lifting him, balancing him as Morris finally stood somewhat upright, nevertheless swaying again.

The unpopular sheriff's condition visible to all, from amidst the crowd, an Ulster-burred voice called, "Dilby! Dilby! Dinna let 'his honour' go, he'll n'er rise er agin!" and most of the assembled roared and then howled even louder as Morris's rubbery legs appeared to fail him, Dilby's firm grasp under his arms being the only reason he did not fall flat. A polished, clipped voice rang out from the other side of the assembled: "Let him go, sir; just let the disgusting, sloppy little sod go!" and to many it appeared that the undersheriff was perhaps considering the patrician-sounding advice.

Stepping slightly farther back, in marked contrast, his hands gracefully, disdainfully folded on his hips, O'Leary spoke crisply, in a commanding though neither a strident nor a combative tone. "Very well then, sir, *you* will thus be advised, *Sheriff,* that it is *I* who shall be taking careful note of *your* own conduct, official and otherwise."

Squinting, his deputy whispering something in his ear, Morris listened in seething, drooling silence as O'Leary continued, this time purposely raising his voice. "Should you, under cloak of office or no, *ever* attempt to do, or cause to be done, any harm to *anyone* in my family, I shall . . ."

"*Shay it! Shay it, you diz-loyal Papis' bass . . . bass-ard . . . you foul trayrus Popish . . . you, you . . . fuh-hing . . .*" Morris incoherently screeched, his dry, shrill voice now echoing to the rafters, his hands formed into weakly clenched, impotent fists at his sides. "*Frettin* me and *'rest* you I *sall here, now, innuh . . . name of . . . of uh king! Shay* it *now!*" he shrieked, "*you . . . you chile of uh hoor uh Rome, you . . . you . . . !*"

His forehead glistening, O'Leary paused, breathing deeply, Eileen by now returned to his side, Dr. Baldwin and—though she clearly, hesitantly— Mary O'Connell Baldwin, as well as Anna and Squire Collins, joined quickly by Squire O'Leary and Catherine, all standing in a protective semicircle behind them both, he stood, in dramatic silence, finally, theatrically continuing, slowly, deliberately and at full volume. "As I was *attempting* to say before you interrupted me: Should you do so . . . *I shall*—" he paused histrionically, looking about— "see to it that you suffer the most dire of consequences . . . *at law . . . the law of His Majesty, our great and good King George the Third! . . . God bless and save him!*" the young officer exclaimed, his expression as he looked down at Morris one of condescending contempt and absolute victory.

Seemingly finished and starting to turn, O'Leary, fully aware that all eyes in the silent hall remained on him, abruptly halted, dramatically taking a step back. Smiling broadly at the sheriff, he extended his hand, for which a befuddled Morris did not possess the acuity to reach, much less grasp. Chancing that he would not, with a flourish, O'Leary theatrically withdrew it, paused, then said, again loudly, "Ah, no matter, 'tis still Christmastide! So now a very happy Christmas, a prosperous new year to *you*, Sheriff, notwithstanding . . . and to your good undersheriff . . . and to your ladies." He gestured grandly to the dark corner where the men's wives cowered alone.

Then, taking Eileen's hand, he extended his free arm to the room, calling out, ". . . and to all of you, to all of *us . . . a happy new year!*" Hand in hand, the O'Learys rejoined the crowd to thunderous applause and cheers from all the Catholics and, it appeared, virtually all the Protestants as well.

As the music and the festivities resumed inside, Morris was last seen bent over, loudly retching against the wall of the building, the torches wildly flaming in what had become a steady night wind illuminating the moment.

Paris—Winter 1771

It was mid-afternoon, a sunny, breezy but chill February Sunday. The wind off the Seine was sharp, causing a chop on the swift-flowing river, whilst suggesting the scents of the mountains, the forests of central Europe, as wispy clouds swept westward towards the distant Atlantic.

The pair of young regular French army other-ranks, standing at parade-rest on either side of the principal entrance to the sprawling grounds of the École Militaire, the academy for the training of officers for the armies of the king of France, established by Louis XV in 1750, took more than casual notice of the approach of what was a subtly elegant closed coach, well before the conveyance drew near. Indeed, one would have been hard-pressed not to: Meticulously crafted of the finest, darkest walnut, its natural colour and grain preserved beneath, enhanced by many coats of gleaming clear shellac, the coach's exterior was artistically gilded—indeed it appeared to have been delicately filigreed in strategic places, much like a fine firearm. Its fittings were of premium brass, its wheels—save for the unavoidable road dust and mud spatters—a lustrous black, with matching iron hubs.

The youthful guards had every reason to be surprised by the carriage's abrupt arrival at their gate; it being Sunday, there had been virtually no other traffic in this still somewhat remote area of Paris. The quartet of colourfully liveried, in the distinctive soft blue and gold hues of the eminent Bourbon-Penthièvre family, young outriders reined in their gleaming white Arabian mounts tightly, their tack jingling merrily as they did.

The bulky, middle-aged coachman—similarly clad, though presenting a far less elegant appearance—drew in his team as well. Taking note of the absence of any officers, whose presence would have indicated that their arrival had been expected, he silently bemoaned his impatience with the situation: *C'est toujours pareil . . . Always the dammed same . . . each time she comes here, Her Highness refuses to advise these people in advance of her plans, of the precise time of her arrival. It seems she somehow considers it beneath herself to do so, so she makes the officers feel as if they should be able to somehow magically anticipate an event which they cannot, and so I must wait.* . . . The man was correct in both his suppositions, the officers at the military school had not been made aware by his passenger or anyone on her behalf of the time of today's visit, and some of them were indeed at least mildly resentful of the imperious attitude of this particular visitor. "At least she now comes every Sunday . . . every dammed Sunday!" he muttered to himself.

Despite that all this was once again today the case, within the majestic coach's brown-leathered, brass-studded confines, its solitary occupant, the striking blonde Princess Marie Thérèse Louise of Savoy, gave it virtually no thought. She was, as always, magnificently attired, this day in a deep emerald-green velvet afternoon dress, her lengthy train sprawled behind her back, draping the right side of her seat and collected about where her feet rested, on a small, densely thick Chinese carpet. Her trim, nearly bare shoulders, as well as her ample décolletage, were masked rather incongruously as she sat comfortably enveloped by the thick folds of a rough, tightly woven Scottish arasaid, its dense, heavy, blue-brown plaid wool gathered at her bosom by a large, strikingly crafted pewter brooch, the centre of which featured an O'Connell stag encircled by an intricately fashioned ring of heather and shamrocks, the garment and the clasp both having been obtained in Scotland and sent from Derrynane at Hugh O'Connell's request.

Feeling altogether satisfied, the princess was not at all perturbed by the situation; rather, far from being so, she joked playfully with her mounted guard, forcing them to smile, and finally to even laugh, as she jested about what she called the "lack of breeding" of so much of the "supposedly aristocratic" French officer corps as they awaited the junior officers whom she knew would be coming to assist her in the conduct of what she had come to refer to as her "business" today.

Leafing through a small stack of London newspapers as well as the current number of *Town & Country,* the young princess smiled contentedly as she reflected that her visit to the school today was only the latest in a series of such weekly calls she had begun making not long after she had first, quite unexpectedly, made the acquaintance of young Monsieur Cadet Hugh O'Connell in June 1770. With him now having completed the first of the approximately two or three years of study required in order to be commissioned a sub-lieutenant, in Hugh's case, attached to Dillon's Regiment of the historic Irish Brigade of France, the couple had come to acknowledge what each felt was a profound love, they had only just recently begun to openly discuss marriage, slowly exploring building a life together. Reflecting on this realisation, she smiled and sighed serenely.

Even as she glanced at an illustration of what *Town &Country* maintained were the latest ladies' hairstyles in London—albeit she playfully sniffed, *London,* in faux hauteur, she nevertheless seriously doubted the English capital could boast any hairstylists possessing the talents of those in Paris, *certainement pas mon cher* Leonard!— she recalled, as she still did almost daily, how she had, to her own shocked surprise, not to mention that of the entire court, been immediately taken with the tall subaltern-to-be, disregarding— surely insensitively, certainly selfishly, perhaps even cruelly—the possibility that her mistress, the dauphine of France, might have continued to maintain some residual feelings for the young man with whom she had grown close prior to both their coming to France the previous year. Indeed, the young royal had within weeks of meeting O'Connell, and true to the promise she'd made to him on that occasion, visited the École Militaire laden with pastries and breads, which she'd purchased from the bakery of Versailles. Since then, the bounties had increased in magnitude, diversity and frequency, such that, as today, she was ofttimes accompanied by one or more wagons.

Lamballe's reverie was interrupted as she was, as she had been on prior occasions and as she had fully expected to eventually be again, advised that a pair of junior officers, in the distinctive red-coat, padded, white waistcoats and breeches – raiment of *Le Regiment de Dillon* were approaching the coach.

As they drew nearer, to the horror of her footmen, she casually reached out and opened the carriage door herself. Gathering her train over her right arm, she alighted gently, her low-heeled shoes crunching lightly on the white gravel. She was gently bemused by the Irish officers' shocked reaction— *C'est toujours pareil,* she laughed aloud—to the contents of a pair of rough farm wagons waiting behind her coach. The first held a dizzying array of specially prepared breads, pastries, as well as fresh meat, fish, fowl and vegetables, from which entire meals could be crafted, which had emerged from the kitchens and bakeries of her majestic Paris home, the Hôtel de Toulouse, the massive mansion she shared with her father-in-law, Louis Jean Marie de Bourbon, the Duke of Penthièvre. The second wagon contained cases of wine and casks of brandy.

As had become her practise, she'd saved her most dazzling smile, the warmest of greetings for those young officers assigned to accompany her, as she once again charmed them, accepting their special gratitude for the as-always conspicuously displayed cases of the finest of French wines as well as several casks of the extraordinary brandy that Richard Hennessey, a one-time Irish Brigade officer, had begun producing the liqueur near Cognac in 1765, which she hoped, as they invariably did, mollified them when they were assigned to facilitate her now-regular visits to the school.

Standing between the handsome pair, she beamed up at them. "So, monsieurs, you will join me as we progress now to the kitchens, *oui?*" She gestured the young men into the coach. "Once there, you shall assist me in completing my business which is but one reason for my return, *oui?*" Though she weekly brought breads, pastries and similar baked delights, only once monthly did she arrive with the volume of food and drink which she'd again delivered today.   On each occasion, however, it had become increasingly clear that the gifts were being made solely because of her relationship with young O'Connell – as that her "business" deliveries permitted a weekly visit with the cadet.

Her relationship with Hugh had, as Daniel Charles had recently written to both Abigail and Eileen, quickly progressed from being "the worst-kept secret in Paris," becoming instead the talk of Versailles and amongst the hordes of royal, noble and aristocratic habitués of the capital, scandalising many, whilst amusing, indeed entertaining, considerably many more. The officers thus nodded knowingly, fully aware that the remainder of her time at the school would be spent with the young Irish cadet.

As soon as Lamballe and her escorts entered the coach, the driver gently smacked the reins, and it lurched away from the imposing main gate of the École, briskly rounding the buildings and the south wall of the eastern of a pair of Cours de l'Etat Major, following the eastern walls and building until it reached the imposing entrance of the Cuisine, the massive structure used for the storage, preparation and cooking of the significant amounts of food necessary to sustain the school's officers, other-ranks and civilian instructors, not to mention the corps of cadets, which averaged approximately two hundred in number. Hearty meals were served in the adjoining Refectoire, the men at long, gleaming, dark-stained tables, all but the most senior officers seated in the same high-backed, hard chairs.

Once again exiting her coach, and wholly inconsistent with the prim, indeed eccentrically prudish reputation she had maintained for herself at court and out in society prior to meeting Hugh, the princess flirtatiously linked her arms with each young officer's, the trio entering the building as she laughed with her companions, both of whom were young, handsome, Irish and flattered, though they were clearly aware it was only Hugh O'Connell for whom she cared, in the background the plodding supply wagons creaked softly as they continued on the gravelled drive towards the delivery entrance.

Once inside the large, high-ceilinged kitchen wing, the princess again took note of the vast, impressively displayed array of gleaming pots, pans and utensils hanging from the smoke-darkened beams above, as well as from numerous, well-placed, wrought-iron hooks drilled into the kitchen's dazzling, whitewashed brick walls. The scrumptious aroma of roasting beef—which she concluded correctly would be the meal she would share with Hugh before returning home—filling the space, once she had effusively gathered the chefs, butchers, cooks and scullery boys about her, with the help of some of the more animated culinary staff, she related in detail the massive amounts of fresh meats, fish and fowl, along with difficult-to-obtain fresh vegetables and fruits she had provided, ". . . not to mention the pastries and breads . . . and, as occasionally before, Monsieur Chef, by midweek the supplies of breads and pastries shall be replenished, *oui*?" She flashed another brilliant smile to the already-beamingly delighted chef de cuisine.

Her business now largely accomplished, she waited with her escorts as the wine and brandy delivery was finalised, the chief steward bowing gracefully as he reported its accomplishment to Lamballe, with effusive expressions of gratitude, including multiple kisses and bows.

This having been done, the more senior—a full lieutenant, named O'Malley—of the pair then escorted her out through the intricate entrance to the Cuisine and towards the obverse of the school's massive Chapelle, an impressive church built in the same baroque style as the rest of the École, which fronted on the sprawling Cour des Exercices, the space used for dress parades and cavalry displays, as well as the grinding daily marching in formation performed by all but the most senior cadets. The princess smiled as she saw that directly in front of the church, a freshly bathed and, although it was not yet a daily necessity, shaven, impeccably uniformed Hugh O'Connell awaited her, his long, heavy, black cloak blown to one side by a gust of wind, his face already wreathed in a broad, toothy smile. Noticing the tall, young cadet, Lieutenant O'Malley immediately halted and bowed to the princess, then kissed her hand and stepped backwards as he took his leave, making a half bow to her before he turned and walked crisply away.

Hugh's boots were silent on the grassy surface of the Cour as he strode briskly towards the young woman whom he had, to her delight, just recently come to address in Irish as Laoise, his now-ungloved hands extended, smiling as her arasaid flapped about her, revealing more of the deep, green-velvet robe beneath. Lamballe's steps quickened as the pair met, stepping effortlessly into each other's embrace. "Leesha, my darling," Hugh murmured, Marie Thérèse Louise managing a delicate, "Ah, *mon cher* Hugh, *mon plus cher*" as their lips met.

As the couple finally, reluctantly separated, Lamballe almost primly took her friend's arm. Feeling the sudden welcome warmth of the mid-afternoon sun on their faces, they began to stroll directly across the vast parade ground, through a small, almost-elegant gate onto the Cour Royale and thence through the school's main building, the residence and office of the *surintendant,* the institution's administrator. Turning right, they passed one of the subtly constructed entrances, which, at strategic intervals in several places, punctuated the depth of what could be said to be, in effect, a single huge building, strung about the periphery of the parade and towards the Seine, talking, laughing, teasing, the sun-gentled breeze rustling both Hugh's cloak and Lamballe's long woollen cape as they walked, by now simply holding hands.

As had become their practise, they spoke in English of news from Ireland—or "home," as the princess had come to refer to it—as well as of Vienna, of Lamballe's life at court, about how the object of Hugh's youthful

Viennese infatuation, the dauphine of France, was faring—seemingly, quite unhappily—and, for the longest part of the conversation, about their own lives, especially and most importantly, of their love: its uniqueness, as well as its still-chaste pleasures and complexities.

After following the Seine for some distance along its wild, overgrown, gravelly, ofttimes muddy banks, they turned and slowly traversed a corner of the Champ de Mars—still a rough, grassy field of sorts.

The breeze now-gentle, the sun seeming even warmer. Tugging Hugh to a halt, "My darling," Louise smiled at Hugh, "you may perhaps have heard the term '*La Princesse du Sang*' in reference to *my good self*." They both laughed at her use of the Irish idiom in her uniquely accented English, even more so as she appended, "Have you not?"

Hugh nodded, advising that he had first heard her referenced as such by quite unintentionally overhearing one incredulous French officer exclaiming to his equally so companion, both men seemingly unaware of Hugh's proximity, much less his identity, "How is it, indeed why is it, indeed *how can it even be*, that a woman who is ranked and regarded as being a Princess of the Blood could *possibly* have an attraction for a penniless, untitled Irish cadet?"

At that, Lamballe burst out in unusually hearty laughter, which caught Hugh in midsentence of his response, preventing him from immediately relating that, having learnt this, his ever-curious nature had led him to seek out some basic information about the status and the reasons behind it, to the extent that when he was finally able to continue, he coyly, and playfully, indicated to "Louise," as he also, albeit rarely, addressed her, as she'd advised him in no uncertain terms that she clearly preferred the singularity of the Irish version, that as he had indeed on several additional occasions heard her being referred to by this title, her eyes now twinkling up at him as she listened intently. "From what I have learnt, it would appear that you most clearly outrank me, my darling! Indeed, as best as I am able to determine, you outrank most in this kingdom, aye?" he said affectionately.

Lamballe lowered her soft blue eyes and nodded, almost whispering, speaking now in her Franco-Italian version of the brogue, "Aye, 'tis true, my darling, my rank is indeed high—dizzyingly so, I fear, my love . . . this . . . and . . ." she lowered her voice even further, sighing very softly, "this and my wealth, I trust that knowledge of these . . . that it will not alter your feelings . . ."

"For certain, not at all, darling girl" Hugh responded firmly, his tone serious. "I am quite confident now that I was in love with you by the time I departed Versailles the day we first met. At that time, I knew only your name and title, and of that only that you were a princess. I had no idea of the nature or meaning of your being the Princess de Lamballe or anything else—certainly not of your wealth. Had you been the dauphine's most humble servant, I would have felt no different. All of this—what you are, how rich you are—they matter not, my darling. I would feel the same standing here were you a scullery maid."

The princess lowered her eyes and almost whispered, "Though that I am not."

Pausing at that, he confessed, "Indeed from what I have heard, I have already concluded that very rich you may be," he teased gently.

At this, again almost whispering, the young princess gently shook her head. "In truth, you must know that the wealth, it is indeed beyond all reason, my darling." She stepped into his embrace and rested her lightly dressed golden locks against his chest, revelling more than anything in the moment, in the closeness, the feeling of security, of the love she experienced in his encirclement.

And they spoke no more of status or wealth, at least not this day

What Hugh had discovered and had at least begun to more fully understand, sifting through the various rumours and speculations about her, to which he had begun to pay attention, all of which were greatly augmented by what the princess would over a period of time continue to share with him in some considerable detail, was that by virtue of her brief and by all accounts horrific marriage to Louis Alexandre de Bourbon Penthièvre, whose numerous titles included that of the prince of Lamballe, she had become and remained titled and ranked as a Princess of the Blood, a designation reserved solely for a woman wed to a direct descendant of a king of France, in this case Louis XIV, who had legitimised her late husband's grandfather, originally born a bastard to the Sun King and his long-time mistress, Madame de Montespan.

As a result of this, the striking young woman with whom Hugh found himself in love would eventually share equal rank with the wives of the two as-yet unmarried brothers of the current dauphin, Louis Auguste, who would one day be king and no one else.

Indeed though she finally admitted to Hugh that she initially relished— *"Who would not?"* she had laughingly exclaimed—her near-singular status, over time, to the princess's own chagrin, she had come to appreciate the reality that she outranked everyone in France save for the members of the immediate royal family itself: at the moment, King Louis XV and his three unmarried daughters, as well as Louis Auguste, Marie Antoinette and his brothers. "'Tis all rather complex," Hugh would note, in gross understatement, writing to Eileen several days following Louise's most recent visit to him at school.

The most significant complexity the couple continued to discuss in minute detail was that, technically at least, Louise was unable to wed Hugh. In an effort to put the issue into context, she had explained that, sometime following her husband's death, more than a few senior persons at court had spoken strongly in favour of her wedding the by then widowed Louis XV. She quickly added that the prospect had both disgusted and angered, as well as terrified her, given not only the king's highly public profligate behaviour, even to the maintaining of a harem of young girls—some said to be *very* young girls—at a small building in Versailles solely for his pleasure, but also because of the manner in which her own spouse had lived and died: as, she had finally said to Hugh, a "pox-ridden libertine."

It having been determined that there was no man other than Louis XV himself of suitable rank to wed a Princess of the Blood, Lamballe had largely to her relief remained unmarried.

"Though now, darling, deeply in love with you, and enamoured of the prospects of our being wed, we must together confront the reality that it will require the consent, indeed the full permission, of the king himself for us to do so," she finally explained to Hugh.

Quite unabashed, Hugh calmly, almost casually reminded her that he and Louis XV had met, ". . . and indeed since our doing so, and to the great discomfort of my superiors, I have had any number," he exaggerated, "of more than merely amicable visits with His Majesty. Indeed I believe 'tis fair to say that rather good friends we are become." He smiled complacently and, Louise correctly concluded, not at all in jest.

Smiling softly, marvelling at her intended's confidence—and gently amused by his guilelessness—Lamballe could only say, "So, my darling, it shall then merely be a simple matter of when might be the most optimum time for us to approach His Majesty . . . or . . . perhaps more correctly, my love . . . *ton très bon ami*, Louis," she said affectionately.

County Cork, Ireland—Spring and Summer 1771

The early May sun was warm, not hot, the wind steady but gentle and, this very morning, Eileen O'Leary had thought as she awakened in the massive Hofburg bed she normally shared with her since-January absent husband, that she was a very contented woman, this despite Art O'Leary's return to Vienna. *How desperately I miss you, my darling!* Each of her many letters since his departure had ended with roughly the same thought, as did his more abbreviated ones. Of her contentment, she had so advised Mistress Anna Collins—she laughed joyously, a sense of fulfilment at the thought of Anna achieving what she had—as her former servant and long-time dear friend, now wed just a month and a bit more to the quiet, gracious Squire John Collins of Derryleigh, had stopped in for a surprise visit in midmorning.

The mid-April wedding had been a joyful occasion, only O'Leary's absence making it ever so slightly bittersweet for Eileen and Anna.

The women sat in chairs on the lawn, the pungently sweet smells of both Anna and Eileen's very first West Cork springtime being a heady mixture of wet grass, newly turned earth, a recent explosion of trees and flowers and the inevitable dung and seaweed being spread by the men in the fields. Anna pronounced herself as being "very nicely married, I think yes! Thank you!" as she had yet again merrily flashed her simple gold wedding band for her friend. Leaning conspiratorially towards the taller, older woman, the Austrian girl, her blond hair brilliant in the May sunshine, as the wind gently played with it, rested her palms on her knees and smiled. "I must tell you how I agree with you, *Mistress*—" they both laughed at the use of the once-required form of address for Eileen— "as to the *'wonder of it all,'* it is wonderful indeed!" and her cheeks blushed beneath their healthy tan glow.

Eileen laughed and feigned shock at her friend's mention of sex, only to add, "As I told you it would be, *ja?*" and Anna shook her head vigorously.

"Up you go now, my little man!" Eileen said to Conor as, later in the day, she lifted the laughing little blond boy onto a chubby grey, as yet unnamed Kerry Bog pony, such as the ones at Derrynane, brought to Rathleigh just the day before by one of Squire MacCarthy's stable lads.

Even as the squire's young groom was departing back down the Rathleigh House lane, Conor appeared immediately fascinated with, seemingly in his own small eyes, the wonder of a horse being so little! Eileen had walked him around the shy, obviously sweet-natured little pony, repeating "*Your* pony!" and then, leaning to the little boy, she told him, "Now, you say it, darling boy, '*my* pony'!"

Very quickly, the clearly bright, not quite three-year-old boy had managed something that sounded a reasonable approximation, close enough for his doting grandfather to declare, indeed to pronounce that, "The wee lad is brilliant, is he not?"

Eileen laughingly responded, "He is indeed, *Grand-dah!*"

The elder O'Leary stood at Eileen's side as she'd lifted the little boy onto the miniature saddle—proudly, as he had acquired it for his grandson, his namesake—and together, one on each side, Eileen holding the pony's bridle, the squire resting his hand at one point gently on Conor's left thigh, at another just beneath his left foot, in neither case holding the boy but rather permitting him even now to be able to shift his weight, to experience balancing himself. For better than an hour, they walked about the yard, down and back up the lane, across and around several close-in open fields and finally into the stable, where awaiting them was young Seamus, the lad who had formerly worked for the Baldwins. "By spiriting young Seamus away from them, I have assured him a better life and us a soundly run barn," Art had announced to his wife and father the day he'd brought the lad and his few belongings to Rathleigh House.

As Eileen began to lift him off, Conor wriggled his strong, little-boy legs and announced in no uncertain terms, "Noooooooo! More 'ide ohhhhhhhhhhneeeeeeeeee . . . nowwwwwwwwww!"

Eileen stood her maternal ground, finishing lifting the boy off and setting him down on his feet; she knelt on the hay-strewn, packed-earth barn floor, placing her fingers on his shoulders and looking steadily into his brimming eyes. "Tomorrow we shall ride again, *tomorrow*," something in his mother's expression or perhaps her voice causing Conor to unscrew his face and, rather than weepingly protesting, at least on this occasion he meekly took his mother's hand, and they walked together back to the house, the pony's soft eyes following his new wee master as he departed the barn.

That night, Eileen wrote breathlessly to O'Leary of the pony's arrival and their little boy's first day in the saddle, on his very own horse, describing the Kerry pony and his gentle nature . . . and confided that Anna had pronounced herself *very nicely married, I think—yes!* Eileen appending her belief that "From this and other things that she has said, it thus appears to me that Squire and Mistress Collins are happy indeed ... abed and otherwise!!" and she laughed as she inserted the second exclamation point.

Though she had remained in regular written communication with family and friends since first she had returned to Ireland the previous May, beginning with O'Leary's departure for Vienna and continuing on into spring and the sunny but often cool summer of 1771 that followed, Eileen found that almost every day she wrote or began at least one letter and frequently continued another that she had not yet finished. Her correspondents were varied, each occupying a special place in her life, her heart. She wrote to Abigail and O'Leary most frequently and was pleased that both of them had proven to be faithful letter writers, providing her with news-filled and insightful missives on a regular basis; to her mother at least once a month; Daniel Charles perhaps twice a month; Hugh the same, although his responses had proven to be quite terse, "as were someone standing over him as he wrote, counting the allotted minutes," she had written to Abby.

Eileen had begun to carry on separate correspondence with General O'Connell and Aunt Maria, the countess. She found that the general was a frustratingly uneven correspondent; sometimes his letters ran on for many clever, enjoyable pages, whilst others, more frequently, were brief, almost militarily direct. Countess von Graffenreit-O'Connell, on the other hand, was an accomplished and avid letter writer; indeed Eileen had told Squire O'Leary, whom, she knew had been quite taken with the warmly elegant countess, that "her letters, they are like reading fine literature; she tells stories rather than simply relating news, events!" As a result, other than those in her husband's familiar crisp, almost rigid hand Eileen found herself most anticipating and being truly excited on the arrival of letters in Maria von Graffenreit's graceful hand, to which she now always affixed the O'Connell stag, be he strutting or prancing, in the familiar green sealing wax.

Countess Trautmannsdorf and Colonel Wolfgang Klaus had both become dependable occasional correspondents, and Eileen found it interesting to hear each of their unique impressions, written from two diverse perspectives—the countess was now contentedly serving quietly under Abigail in the empress's household, writing that she found her duties, though limited, to be genteel and pleasant, whilst the colonel, happily permanently returned from St. Petersburg, was military attaché to the Emperor Joseph himself—of life at the Viennese court and the news and activities of the many people she knew there. Von Klaus frequently contrasted—with rare exceptions, favourably—the Viennese court with that of Catherine the Great's in St Petersburg, assuring her that "We have no madmen or women here of the calibre the Russians seemingly have!" in one memorable, extremely gossipy letter. Eileen could almost hear his booming laugh.

Most surprising to Eileen was the fact that, beginning in late June 1770, at least once, and, occasionally, twice or even three times a month thereafter had arrived at Rathleigh letters contained in envelopes that had obviously been addressed by, written in the predictably flawless hand of a secretary, a professional scrivener, bearing the at first unfamiliar, now totally understood and joyfully welcomed cipher composed of delicately intertwined, flowery, complex versions of the letters M and A impressed into a substantial splodge of light blue wax. The letters enclosed were sometimes brief, more frequently not, and perhaps more than anyone, Eileen realised and appreciated the time and effort Marie Antoinette had devoted to writing each one. "I am certain she still struggles to write, though her feelings, they do come through," she shared with Squire O'Leary at breakfast one morning.

The well-travelled, worldly man was enthralled that his daughter-in-law now regularly received letters from the dauphine of France, written at and dispatched from Versailles, a place he had actually visited once, in the company of the elder, now deceased General Arthur Dillon. "'Tis hard to believe, is it not?" he wondered aloud to Eileen one particularly dazzling June morning, "that she has proven to be such a regular correspondent."

Eileen thought a moment, then nodded. "In one way, yes; one would think that the dauphine of France would have better things to do than to write to her former governess, yet . . ." She paused, looking quietly into the soft blue eyes of her dear father-in-law, in which she daily saw the genesis of much of who her beloved horseman of the bright eyes had become, only then continuing. "Without violating her confidence . . . even to you, my dearest Father . . . I am able to say that her life, 'tis not wholly satisfactory, her marriage, not yet . . . not yet as satisfying as I am certain it will ultimately prove to be. . . . Versailles, she has quickly learnt, is very different from Vienna."

In truth, the young dauphine, who appeared to still occasionally struggle to sign her letters as *Antoinette*, had written yet again, in painful, graphic detail in her most recent one of the continuing problem of the dauphin's seeming unwillingness, or, Eileen wondered, perhaps his inability, to consummate their marriage, a topic she had first touched on during the summer of 1770, and of her genuine fear both as to whether it would ever be accomplished and of the empress's increasing unhappiness at what she still apparently believed to be her daughter's failings in the bedroom, writing, *I must tell you that the empress is sorely displeased with me, and even now expresses her fears for the alliance.* . . . She also wrote of what she called a "clique-ridden court," in reference to Versailles, listing what Eileen found to be a dizzying array of individuals and describing things said to and about as well as numerous acts done to her, virtually all of which Eileen viewed as being cruel and heartless, vicious even.

Do these vacuous courtiers—these bitches of women—have nothing else to occupy their time, such as they are able to spend their days in crafting and circulating malicious gossip? . . . Is there no power there who can bring these people and their actions up short? What does this king do? Is there no high chamberlain as in Vienna? Comparing Versailles to the court of Maria Theresa, Eileen could only shake her head at what she perceived as being the chasm like difference in attitude, behaviour and practices between the two courts. *My wee little archduchess, she deserves better. Has she been dispatched into a snake pit?*

Turning back to her letter, after one lengthy litany of cruelties, the young dauphine had added, *I know not where or to whom to turn other than you, my darling, my beloved Eileen; would that you were here, together I believe we could perhaps resolve all of my complicated difficulties. . . .*

Amongst the more puzzling aspects of her former charge's correspondence Eileen felt was the dauphine's failure to mention even in passing that she had succeeded in inviting Hugh to Versailles. It was only after receiving Hugh's own letter, in which he disclosed his June visit and described, in not insignificant detail, both the changed circumstances of his relationship with Antoinette, as well as his introduction to and his seemingly near-immediate fascination with the young widowed Princess de Lamballe, that Eileen finally raised the topic in a subsequent letter.

Marie Antoinette's response was terse: *As you say, Hugh indeed did come and spent much of a day and evening here. I introduced him to the king, to my husband, the dauphin; and to she who has been my closest companion, with whom, I understand, he has become quite friendly*, at which point she enumerated, without comment, the princess's apparently frequent visits to Hugh at school in Paris, about which Hugh had already made her aware. Eileen was tempted to pursue the topic but concluded that the tone, not to mention the brevity, of the dauphine's reply were both such that she ultimately decided against doing so. This being the case, she nevertheless reflected on more than one occasion that her youngest brother had treated his one-time "dearest friend" rather shabbily.

Indeed, Eileen generally found herself being more circumspect than she felt in her heart in a number of her responses. Whilst he was still in St. Petersburg, when he learnt that Eileen was to depart Vienna, and prior to learning that he himself was shortly to return there, Wolfgang von Klaus had reminded her that virtually every letter she would write from Ireland, whether to him in Russia or to others in Vienna or elsewhere—and most especially to the dauphine—and even to Daniel and Hugh—in France stood an excellent chance of being read, . . . *and not only by our adversaries, but by some we would consider to be our friends as well!* It was because of this cautionary, passed to the dauphine by Countess von Graffenreit, that the salutation in Marie Antoinette's letters to her was "Eileen" as opposed to "Mama."

As enjoyable as Eileen had come to find her varied correspondence to be, as avidly as she awaited each of the irregular mail deliveries that found their way to Rathleigh at least twice or occasionally more times a week, perhaps more than any letter she had written or would write for quite some time, she enjoyed the one she wrote to Art, dated 12 May, 1771. It began lovingly and progressed mundanely enough, consisting mainly of reports on both Conors, the weather, updates on the Rathleigh farm and the arrival just the day before of a beautiful new foal, neighbourhood news and gossip and an odd note she had just received from Catherine, in which she had raised the possibility of Eileen journeying to Cork City . . . *and here to remain awhile with me . . . so that I may introduce you to some friends, and thus possibly expand your horizons . . . to more approximate my own much broader ones. . . .* Eileen told Art that she was mildly bemused, but that she had gently dismissed Catherine's advances: *After all, I am a traditional Irish girl, I do not wish to become an iconoclastic anti-monarchist, do I now   . . .?* she inquired of her husband across most of Europe.

As she continued, her mood and the tone of the letter now became reflective, even a bit wistful: *I have yet more to tell you, husband, but whisper it softly I must, as I would were we not separated thus. . . .* She nodded her head, indicating the letter in process and, as she whisperingly read her words aloud, she suddenly surprised herself and paused a moment so as not to weep . . . yet . . .

For a time I have known this in my heart, but before I told you, husband . . . more certain I wished to be . . . as a wife should be at such a time . . . so, you see, Arthur, to Sally Fitzgerald's cottage I stopped last evening, because . . . because, if anyone could assist me, in being certain . . . 'tis Sally ~~as you know she has~~ *. . .*

Eileen frowned at her imperfect attempt to obliterate the words she had just written, but, rather than start the letter anew, continued on:

The fact of the matter is, my darling horseman of the bright eyes, for all you have taken from me with your return to Vienna . . . 'tis something wondrous that you have left behind, have given me, have given us both actually, my darling, and to Conor, as well . . . for 'tis a baby—your son, I know, Captain O'Leary, it will be a son, another little boy, of this I am certain . . . he is, I know . . . he rests quietly within me—the palm of her left hand touched her abdomen gently, almost reverently—*and your second son I shall bear by Samhain next, Sally says.*

Silent, joyous tears now streaming, she smiled as she leaned into her chair, resting her head against the high back as she read what she had written thus far and, finished, again sitting forward and dipping her quill, she wrote:

Would that I could see your face, my darling—She smiled and closed her eyes, and still smiling, opened them after a bit. *I have! Your expression is one of joy and wonder, truly the wonder of it, husband . . . 'tis a wonder, is it not, sir? The night just prior to your departure, I sensed as I lay next to you afterwards . . . I seemed to feel "something" was a bit different, and yet again, my darling, it is that I still sometimes just sense things, do I not?*

After pausing yet again briefly to read what she had just written, she went on, an expression of radiant joy and wonder now on her own face.

Sally is to have yet another wee one prior to Christmas next and has four, so 'twas to her I went . . . I felt I could not tell Anna before I did your good self, and I cannot speak to anyone here but you, husband . . . so 'twas Sally, who talked and felt and prodded . . . and I knew then 'twas time to tell you . . . so now I have, so . . . thank you, sir. . . .

With a flourish, she closed in her singularly swirling elegant script, *Now, forever and always, your loving and devoted, Eileen* . . . and, with a nod, she gently folded the pages, slipped them into an already addressed envelope and, as she walked down the hall to leave her letter near the door, her hands gathered at her expanding waist.

County Cork, Ireland—Autumn 1771

The hours each day Eileen spent with Conor, whether riding with or reading to him; her letter writing and receiving, especially from Arthur; visits with Anna and her increasing circle of women friends in the neighbourhood, as well as the gentle, warm relationship she shared with Squire O'Leary—all continued to contribute to her feeling of contentment as an uneventful summer passed quietly at Rathleigh.

As the wee life within her continued to thrive and her movements became more restricted, she gradually and reluctantly curtailed her time aboard Bull, until by late July she had given his daily exercising over to Seamus, otherwise leaving the ever-gentle stallion to frolic with his barn mates as they saw fit during the long Irish summer days.

Eileen would long recall that the most startling event of the warmer months had begun quietly, with an unexpected visit from Dr. Baldwin one afternoon in late August.

After showing him into the smaller, more intimate family sitting room, Ann quickly fetched Eileen, who was in the stables with Conor and the pony, now named Fionn.

"Why, brother, what a surprise to see you, sir!" Eileen smiled as she rustled, significantly more slowly than her customary stride, into the comfortable room. Baldwin, standing quickly, silently noted that her hair was flecked with hay and that she was even more pregnantly rotund than she had been when last he had seen her, perhaps three weeks prior.

As they sat, Eileen saw a troubled and, as it was directed at her, took it also to be an immediately troubling look on his face.

"I apologise for any intrusion. . . . I have just seen a patient, and what I have learnt whilst in his vicinage, and most definitely not of his medical condition, has brought me here with some urgency. Indeed I felt an immediate need to see you, Eileen," the physician said, his expression now grave.

Eileen gestured for him to continue. As well he did, his familiar soft, droning voice—the voice he used to soothe ill or troubled patients, the one she sometimes found unnerving, with its absence of inflection—telling her a troubling tale of an event that had occurred the week before.

". . . and as there in the wee little pub at Dorgan's Cross, just a table away from where I sat, a quiet pint in my hand, little of note on my mind, was the high sheriff himself, seemingly deep in his cups, who, within earshot of my good self, loudly declared himself satisfied, indeed very well satisfied with an undertaking that had seemingly been well accomplished by his three companions, whose backs were to me. I must confess even when I did see their faces, their identities remained unknown . . ."

Eileen sat quietly, her hands folded in her lap, still wondering why this should be of any interest or import to her, as he continued, his voice now animated to an unusual degree. "Amongst what had been achieved, I was able to easily learn from their lengthy and detailed talk, was the interception of several letters sent, incredible as it may seem, to you, ones I surmise you received in recent weeks, the sheriff, he . . ."

"Letters, you say . . . *my* letters?" Eileen asked incredulously, her cheeks suddenly ablaze.

As the physician nodded and gently raised a hand, she grew quiet.

"Morris spoke of the letters being from, I recall him saying, 'the courts of accursed Catholic Europe,' from people he referred to as your 'dammed bloody traitorous relations' and others, including your former charge, the young woman now in France—though he seems aware of her status, he does not appear to know the basis or the nature of your relationship. . . ."

As Dr. Baldwin spoke, Eileen's mind raced silently, concluding that she had, in the weeks prior, indeed received a letter from Marie Antoinette, as well as ones from the countess and Abby in Vienna and from both Daniel Charles and Hugh in Paris—all in addition to several from her husband; *they must have enjoyed his "playfulness,"* she thought bitterly.

Eileen then stood, with the awkwardness of an athletic, normally active woman in the final month of pregnancy, her hands resting on the high back of the wing chair in which she had been seated, obviously shaken by what she had just learnt. She glared down at her brother-in-law and said, "Did the *good high sheriff . . .*" she scoffed, "did he perhaps indicate *why* he felt the need to intercept . . . and read . . . *my* letters . . . and his supposed authority for doing so? *Did he?*"

As Dr. Baldwin did not take the patent hostility voiced in Eileen's questions as being directed towards himself, he calmly and dispassionately told her, "He spoke of learning of your as I believe he phrased it 'intentionally treasonable liaisons.' He seemed quite certain that you and she whom he called 'this French girl' are now plotting an invasion of Ireland . . . and of England after she becomes queen!"

Eileen laughed aloud, adding in a bitter tone, "The man is indeed mad to conjure, much less to actually believe, such utter nonsense!" Baldwin could not help but laugh as well, the inanity of the theories, the fears ridiculous.

As she strode heavily about the small, comfortable room, she then grew grave, in silent rage, until from across the room Dr. Baldwin heard, "How *dare* he? *How dare they?*" as she finally demanded, her husky voice shaking, though, yet again, not of her mild brother-in-law, who could do little more than shake his head in shared disbelief.

The grim tale now having been told, it was only as they continued to speak briefly over tea did Eileen recall and so inform Baldwin that in her most recent letter from either the general or the countess, she could not recall which, the O'Connell stag had appeared to have been cracked, and that—even more troubling—the last letter from Versailles had actually lacked the hard, thick, light blue wax depiction of the dauphine's cipher, "Though it was apparent that it had at one point been there affixed, the outline of the originally molten wax visible on the reverse of the envelope."

As she was seeing him out the door, her mind already whirring, Dr. Baldwin recalled, "Ah, forgive me, sister. One final item, so that you will know all that I do: One of the other men at the table with Morris said, as they were ending their conversation, words to the effect that, '. . . the arrogant and pretentious *Mistress O'Leary* received her letters, did she not . . . just a bit tardy,' and I observed that they all guffawed as they departed the public house." He shrugged.

Then, with a nod to her, in seemingly a single motion, he mounted his quiet bay, turned the animal's head and, gently touching its sides, began to head up the Rathleigh lane. Waving matter-of-factly to her visitor, Eileen seethed in the quiet warmth of the late afternoon, murmuring aloud, through gritted teeth, "So they 'guffawed,' did they? I shall be most interested to see who of them shall be in any mood to *guffaw* after I . . ."

Windsor Castle, Berkshire, England—late October 1771

A wet fog draped the hulking ramparts of the massive, much of it ancient, structure that was Windsor Castle, early this Wednesday, 24 October. Prime minister barely a year, Frederick, Lord North, accompanied only by a young clerk, approached the palace slowly, pondering—was it with some sense of awe?—that it was William the Conqueror himself who had chosen this site, high above the placid Thames, recalling that in 1070 Windsor was originally intended to guard the western approaches to London.

As the statesman dismounted, he recalled that the outer walls of the structure were in virtually the same position as those of the original castle built by William. "Much *his'try* in this place, a great deal, a great deal indeed," he commented to the young man in his company, gesturing to the ramparts as grooms led their horses away, the royal standard drooping wet and still in the soggy air.

Lord North, who was thirty-nine, and the thirty-three-year-old King George III had developed a cautiously cordial relationship, and the prime minister and the sovereign typically met at least once every month. The king set the agenda, to which his first minister was permitted to add a limited number of items of significance to him, though whether they were discussed or not was at the king's discretion. Their conversation was precise, mutually respectful and business-like but not devoid of humour.

One trait they most uniquely shared was a striking physical resemblance of one to the other; though neither had ever spoken of it, assuredly both men were aware of the court gossip that their appearance was so shockingly similar because Prince Frederick, the late Prince of Wales, was said by many to be father to both men, a possibility that comported with the prince's reputation, though not with that of North's mother. Nevertheless, as they faced each other that afternoon, as always, both were full of face, with large eyes and prominent noses; neither handsome, but neither wholly unattractive.

From the list of agreed-upon topics to be discussed, appearing on the single piece of paper folded in his coat pocket, it appeared to North that today's meeting would be largely unremarkable, the recent news from the American colonies being mixed, but overall of little event, as it had been since July, when Virginia had become the last of the colonies to resume trade with England, virtually all of the provisions of the Townshend Acts, save for those providing for a tax on tea, having been repealed.

Within moments of entering the castle, Lord North had been received by the sovereign and, with North's clerk and the king's young secretary sitting unobtrusively, slightly apart from the two, just within earshot of their masters and thus able to take down cryptic notes, sovereign and first minister began their conversation, the king pointedly ticking off the items on his list as discussion of each topic was, in his mind, concluded, Lord North having come to understand it thus being so, even if the prime minister had perhaps an additional thought on the subject.

The final agenda item having been ticked by the royal pen and duly noted by the young men with their pads, North exhaled and sat ever so slightly back in his chair. Just as he did, whilst gesturing for both clerks to leave them, George III leaned wordlessly forward, handing him a compact sheaf of rough-feeling paper, upon which Lord North quickly noted writing, most likely that of a woman, in a flowing, he would later reflect, quite beautiful hand.

"Sir, you will please read this, which we have just passed to you, slowly, and with thought. It is rather quite a remarkable document . . . given as much as to the fact that its author sent it directly to the king, indeed, it was carried here from Ireland by a single messenger, we are told . . . as in its disquieting subject, which we have found to be startling, sir . . . indeed quite troubling."

Having heard the word *Ireland,* Lord North sighed quietly to himself as his eyes began to move slowly across the coarse pages:

Rathleigh House
Co. Cork, Ireland
27 September 1771

Your Majesty—
I have given this letter much thought prior to writing, much less dispatching, it to the king.
Please be assured that whilst I write most reluctantly, it concerns a matter of great import
to me and, well beyond that, I believe so should it be to Your Majesty.

Lord North's eyes grew wide, as in the paragraphs that followed, after briefly introducing herself, Mistress Eileen O'Leary of Rathleigh House, near Macroom in County Cork, Ireland, had described, in minute, precise detail, the apparently successful scheme undertaken by the high sheriff of Cork and some of his men to intercept and read her mail.

Whilst I accept the reality of espionage amongst nations, regrettable though this may be, this type of invasion . . . absent a compelling reason, of which I can think of there being none in this instance, Sire! of a private person's confidential correspondence has no place in the civilisation as we know it of Your Majesty's (truly) Great Britain.

As a loyal subject of the king, living in peace in a remote part of Your Majesty's realm, I believe that I should be free of this type of intrusive behaviour.

Indeed whilst the wife of the late Squire John O'Connor of Ballyhar, Co. Kerry, an individual I am quite aware well-known to Your Majesty, I enjoyed only the most satisfactory of relationships with the king's good servants and true, loyal men in north Kerry, and indeed I remain in periodic contact with and most fond to this day of the Earl and Countess of Moyvane, in that vicinage.

Sadly, it appears that a number of the king's servants here in Cork in 1771 are of a nature and character far different from those in Kerry of years past . . . here and now, they are for the most part small, crude men, patently ill bred, seemingly ill-educated and lacking in even the most basic of social graces. Indeed, the high sheriff of whom I herein write, one Abraham Morris, accosted my husband and myself at an otherwise most enjoyable occasion, a Christmas ball held in Macroom, making the most dastardly of accusations . . . the tenor and substance of which I am certain those gathered there dismissed, as the man was so deeply into his cups that he could barely stand—the shame of it all!

I fear there is a—highly inaccurate, I would respectfully say to Your Majesty—assumption amongst these small, ill-mannered men here that, as my husband and a number of individuals from families such as ours, have—as Your Majesty would agree, I am certain—there being limited opportunities for advancement in this part of Your Majesty's realm, availed themselves of certain opportunities outside of Great Britain, they and we are of questionable loyalty to Your Majesty. Please permit me to disabuse this notion, Sire . . . indeed despite my own service of some years in Vienna, never have I expressed myself or in any way behaved as one other than a loyal subject of Your Majesty, nor have any of my relations.

Indeed, Sire, save in those unfortunate times of conflict between Great Britain and France, Austria and Spain, the House of Hanover has both honoured and respected the rights and privileges of those Irishmen who have availed themselves of the opportunities provided under the Treaty of Dingle, it often affording them the only realistic opportunity of providing for their families.

I would respectfully point out to Your Majesty that my uncle, General the Count Moritz O'Connell; my husband, Captain Arthur O'Leary and my brother-in-law, Major Denis O'Sullivan—whose spouse is my dearest sister, Abigail, who presently serves as lady-in-waiting to your own "sister," Her Imperial Majesty, the Empress Maria Theresa—all of these gentlemen hold commissions in the imperial armies of Austria and Hungary, have each, at one time or another, appeared in full uniform on the streets of London, and have, to my knowledge on their information, been treated with the utmost of respect. Sadly, Sire, such is not the case here in County Cork.

The titles of the individuals with whom I correspond notwithstanding—the majority of my correspondents are members of my family, the others close friends and colleagues of many years and one, Sire, a young woman for whom I cared from childhood until her relatively recent departure for the court of Versailles—this, too, is the most intimate of close personal friendships, nothing more and of absolutely no public import, of this I assure Your Majesty, without reservation!

I would respectfully emphasise that I lead a quiet, near reclusive life, with my father-in-law and little boy, whilst I await the arrival of a second child, due within weeks of writing, and the return of my husband, I pray sometime after the new year. Being a mere woman, I neither hold nor am I able to aspire to a position of any importance. I thus only desire to lead my life in peace and privacy, as I am sure do all of the good people of Great Britain, all of us fellow subjects of a great and good king.

Being nothing more than a retiring country woman, I am unable to begin to suggest what, if any, action may be indicated in a situation such as this, though I do recall my late and still beloved husband, the Squire O'Connor, saying on more than one occasion that the House of Hanover, at that time in the person of Your Majesty's august grandfather, "rules nobly and justly, rewards goodness and disdains—and, when and as may be necessary, punishes—venality, corruption and disregard for the rule of law." I would humbly suggest, Your Majesty, that this may be one of those rare occasions when the most basic of rights belonging to a British subject have, unbeknownst to the king, Sire, in Your Majesty's name, been violated in an utter and, to me, Sire, incomprehensible disregard for the rule of law by the king's servants here in Ireland. Whilst they have caused a grave injustice to be done to me, in serving Your Majesty so poorly, they have done to the king a far graver one.

Eileen proceeded, as Lord North read, the king watching him, as he had throughout his reading, to finish with a respectful and suitably humble, almost obsequious, conclusion, at the end of which he again looked up at an unusually reflective king, and observed, "The woman is nothing if not well written, Your Majesty."

The king nodded in agreement, adding, "We have inquired briefly of the lord lieutenant. You are of course well acquainted with General Townshend, yes?" Though he knew his more prominent relative well, the general less so, as he was his lord lieutenant in Ireland and a member of his cabinet, the prime minister nodded respectfully. "Who by mere coincidence has been fortuitously in London of late, though now returned to Dublin, and he advises much."

Lord North now tried unsuccessfully to suppress a sigh, fearing embroilment in what immediately seemed to him to be an altogether uniquely Irish type of controversy, which, because of the inimitable nature of the place and of the types of disputes that, perhaps because of the rain and the bogs and the beliefs in fantasy by so many there, it seemed to generate, had cost the career of many a true and loyal British public servant, elected or otherwise.

The king nodded again, perhaps understandingly. "According to Townshend, the woman is of the O'Connells of a place called Derrynane, said, again by Townshend, to be a rather remarkable family, dwelling in the remote fastness of far southwest County Kerry, who have somehow managed to convey the appearance of loyalty to the crown whilst, aside from being practicing Papists, have long engaged in what we are told is one of the most successful of smuggling operations in the history of Great Britain." He could not help but laugh at the irony. "Perhaps of the world!" Shaking his head, he added, "The Irish, you know."

North nodded.

The king noted he had also rolled his eyes but let it pass, continuing, "In the event, this aside, she was indeed married briefly. . . the poor man died less than a year after the nuptials, leaving her a child widow. . . to this O'Connor of whom she writes, an extremely wealthy and powerful, and quite loyal, despite his own Popish beliefs, man, well-known at court . . . I am certain to our predecessor, as she indicates, and as a memory to yourself . . . as well as at Whitehall. Her own reputation, such as is reported to Townshend, is generally of good character. . . . Her current husband, the absent subaltern, a more colourful individual, seemingly favouring his magnificent uniforms as dress whilst in Ireland and given to broad pronouncements of his supposed rights under this Treaty of Dingle, but other than by these petty local officials in Cork, including this Morris, he is viewed, whilst with some degree of annoyance, as being relatively harmless in the scheme of things overall."

The prime minister gently cleared his throat. "If I may observe, Your Majesty, these people . . . they serve sovereigns other than yourself, Sire; it appears half of her relatives serve the Hapsburgs, the other, the Bourbons; they . . ."

The king gently raised his left hand. "Though you know well that we certainly have no fondness for the Papists and their dastardly idolatrous religion, not to mention their disloyalty to the crown, we believe, Minister— and, sir, we would caution that we are saying this to you alone—that *these people* choose to do what they do out of, at least it seems they have convinced themselves, some degree of necessity," the king himself now sighed, "rather than outright conscious disloyalty. The men she mentions are said, yet again by Townshend, to be well educated, contrary to law of course at Louvain, we are told, and even this woman is obviously by some means well-schooled. We are aware of what they do and where. These officers of whom she writes, and many, many dozens of others, indeed do move freely back and forth across Europe, across the Channel . . . probably on the O'Connells' ships"—he shook his head and laughed ironically—". . . quietly, making no trouble. As she says, in 'times of conflict' they of course stay put in Europe, and, yes, they fight us . . . and indeed they, these Irish soldiers, they fight better than anyone else does . . . but in times of peace, as now, they cause no significant worry, little trouble, especially when one considers with what we are dealing in America, eh? Indeed, we believe that there exist in North America far greater challenges, indeed more significant potential threats to the peace and stability of Great Britain than those possibly posed by a small group of overeducated native Irish Papists in the far southwest fastness of the kingdom.

"Also, my dear Minister, we are compelled to admit that we are intrigued by the tale of a girl such as this one, who appears to be rather well-educated . . . wed at perhaps fifteen or sixteen, widowed almost immediately, who avails herself of an opportunity to serve at the Viennese court and there cares for a child upon whose head will, I am quite certain very soon, rest the crown of the queen of France . . . and the governess then returns to *Ireland* . . . to live on a *farm*," he grimaced, "and produce babies for a mostly absent young officer. What an extraordinary individual! Or perhaps Ireland is a more compelling place than we think of it as being."

Lord North frowned, saying nothing, but thinking rather that Eileen O'Connell must be an extraordinarily bold, indeed arrogant individual, that her beautiful handwriting and elegant, obsequious language skilfully cloaked yet another clever, disingenuous and duplicitous Irish intellect. He knew these types of men were thus, but   . . . now a woman of similar traits!

"My good man," the king continued, "we have detained you and we shall now dismiss you, sir, with, as always, our gratitude and, in this regard, with the understanding that we shall permit the lord lieutenant in Dublin to take such measures as he, in his sole discretion and acting alone, shall deem appropriate, in dealing with this Morris, this sheriff."

The prime minister relaxed, taking a breath.

The king then rose, as did Lord North, bowing immediately, a powerful sense of relief coursing through his very being, thinking, *one less Irish morass . . . praise God Almighty!*

Within a week of the conversation at Windsor, additional investigation, which had begun previously, conducted by the lord lieutenant's men, had uncovered that the high sheriff of Cork had targeted the correspondence of individuals other than Eileen O'Leary for similar scrutiny, including, inexplicably, a group of high-ranking military officers, a vicar of the Church of Ireland and several lesser nobles.

Though none of the individuals would learn of this, it was discovered that the interception by the sheriff's men of their letters was relatively easily accomplished, facilitated by the haphazard delivery of mail in Cork, indeed in most of the island of Ireland. Whilst there had been regular intercity mail delivery amongst Cork City, Dublin, Belfast and Derry since 1638, once a letter intended for an individual in County Cork reached the City, there was only a largely informal, at best semi-official mechanism for accomplishing deliveries beyond Cork City itself.

Thus, through the use of bribery and informers, the high sheriff and his henchmen were, with very little effort, able to pluck especially Eileen's letters, given their places of origin and the various ways they had reached Ireland out of what little local mail delivery system there existed.

As for Ireland's lord lieutenant, General Townshend, albeit shocked at the extent of what he, too, viewed as being serious, and quite pointless, wrongdoing, he was otherwise most pleased both with the investigation and with what he characterised as a "most positive turn of events," as the latter fit well within his ongoing efforts to limit the reach and break what he felt was the excessive power of the Irish gentry, including the "undertakers," as well as officials such as Abraham Morris. He had largely accomplished his purpose by February of that year of 1771, by shamelessly, overtly corrupting the Irish Parliament so that a party effectively controlled by himself and, he had virtually assured, by his successors at Dublin Castle now held the majority position in Dublin.

Harshly and publicly disciplining a sitting high sheriff of Cork for malfeasance seemed a wholly logical extension of the significant change his policy had already wrought: The ultimate power in Ireland rested now at Dublin Castle, whilst the Irish Parliament, the gentry, those local office-holders now were and henceforth would remain under the direct control of the Castle, of himself and his successors; the timing of this foolish escapade by Morris could not have been better for his purposes.

Before month's end, dispatched by and with detailed instructions from the lord lieutenant, preceded and accompanied by suitable pomp, Joseph Grimsby, the deputy lord lieutenant of Ireland, sailed into Cork and was immediately taken to Cork City Hall, where there awaited him a clearly discomforted but by no means contrite Abraham Morris.

The absence of even the slightest bit of remorse on Morris's part having been anticipated, during the course of less than one half-hour, Morris was by a suitably irate deputy lord lieutenant summarily impeached and removed as high sheriff, compelled to and did immediately turn over all seals and symbols of that office and—to his chagrined surprise—was required to stand in humiliation as news of his disgrace was cried out to a large crowd, the members of which had been carefully selected and summoned for that sole purpose, the lord lieutenant's clear intention being to assure that there would be no doubt left in the peoples' minds as to the gravity of the nature of the offenses—the identities of Eileen and the other victims not being made public—causing his removal and the significance of the removal itself.

By the time Eileen learnt of Morris's fall, and weeks before she received a brief, courteous but inconclusive acknowledgement in the elegant hand of some court factotum of her original letter to the king, she had herself been happily delivered of Fiach Morgan O'Leary, born safely though not uneventfully at Rathleigh, the day prior to Samhain, consistent with Sally Fitzgerald's softly spoken prediction.

Dr. Baldwin had, as planned, been summoned as soon as it was apparent that the birth process had begun, but so quickly had Eileen's labours progressed that it was she and Anna Collins who collaborated in the baby's safe and sound arrival in early evening. By the time the physician arrived, the women were sitting together on the Hofburg bed with the infant's wide-eyed elder brother and equally wide-eyed grandfather in attendance, as Eileen quietly nursed her second son.

Versailles—late January 1772

The countless clocks in the château and throughout the bustling town of Versailles had most likely all completed striking the second hour of a cold, still, but sunny Tuesday afternoon. The courtyard of the immense palace, constructed for Louis XIV on an east–west axis, such that the sun would always rise and set in alignment with his home, and the areas beyond were already streaked with stark, lengthening shadows as the sun moved precisely as it was, in the mind of the Sun King, supposed to.

A trio of horsemen approaching the palace, their destination, following an uneventful ride of some eight miles from Paris, through the stark winter landscape of the Île de France – did so at an even, almost leisurely walk. Their horses were handsome—two chestnuts and a grey—and the riders' uniforms even more so. The officer at the centre as the men rode abreast, Captain Arthur O'Leary, was by far the most strikingly attired: His magnificent red uniform coat, a short dolman jacket, featured horizontally paralleled rows of heavy gold bullion-laced braid covering the front from neck to high waist, occasionally glinting, as his horse's steps carried him into the retreating sunshine; a pelisse of similar colour and fabric—though with its collar and cuffs handsomely trimmed in fur— which, as per regulations, he wore elegantly loose, draped almost casually on his left shoulder. His buff breeches were snug, his knee-high black boots lustrous. As did one of his companions, despite that it was not the customary rather quite singular fur shako worn by an officer of the Hungarian Hussars of the Imperial

Armies of Austria, the soldier sported a simple black, gold-trimmed, tricorne hat.

O'Leary's cohorts this day were also his brothers-in-law, Major Daniel Charles and Hugh O'Connell.

Daniel, who had been in Paris almost ten years now, had begun his service to the king of France in the Royal Swedish Brigade, though he had since transferred to Lord Clare's Regiment of the Irish Brigade. Unexpectedly finding himself intrigued by the concept of military engineering, he had become skilled in the various, some complex, methods of constructing fortifications and roads on the battlefield, as well as in the strategic placing of heavy artillery. In the process, already regarded as being a strong, solid leader, he was viewed as having significant potential as a combat officer, as well, his precise mind and deliberate manner lending themselves to his success in all these areas. The tall, athletic twenty-seven-year-old Kerryman wore the long, full red coat of Lord Clare's officers, the heavy, padded cuffs extending, both stylishly and protectively, to his elbows; his breeches were yellow, his hose white. His sword was worn at his back, suspended from a heavy leather belt, configured in the pattern which, some centuries later, would be referred to as a Sam Browne. A soft black slouch hat was perched rakishly atop thick, dirty blond hair, carefully tied in a red queue.

Hugh, still completing his studies at the École Militaire, wore a simpler, short-jacketed redcoat cadet version of the uniform of Dillon's Brigade, with yellow facings, white breeches and gleaming, high black boots. His headgear was similar to O'Leary's.

As the threesome passed though the massive, always-open gates to the palace itself, O'Leary's first impression of the immense structure was of its magnificent church, located on the far right of the palace, as they faced it, noting that prominently displayed on the wing was proclaimed, in quite large, dark lettering, "A TOUTES LES GLOIRES DE LA FRANCE," musing to himself that *perhaps this provides an insight into the occupants' view of the purpose of the place . . . or perhaps 'tis a justification to themselves of its supposed excesses!* That he chuckled softly went unnoticed by the O'Connells.

Looking straight ahead now, they noted that apparently awaiting them was a solitary woman, as well as—separated from her by perhaps fifteen feet—a trio of boys, most likely young grooms.

As they drew closer, they, or at least Daniel O'Connell and O'Leary were, surprised that the woman, who appeared to be tall, young and blonde, was already waving effusively, gaily out calling, "Bienvenue, Monsieurs O'Connell . . . O'Leary!"

Hugh O'Connell smiled broadly at the animated Princess Marie Thérèse Louise de Savoie Carignan, the young woman about whom he had spent the bulk of the brief journey from Paris telling his uncles all he could, especially as he saw suggestions of what he knew was a magnificent, heavy red brocade afternoon dress peeking out from within and beneath the folds of a dense heather-and-brown-hued wool Scottish arasaid, in which she was enveloped against the January chill.

As they both, Daniel and O'Leary, took note of her unusual—definitely for a French Princess of the Blood, most certainly for the court of Versailles—choice for a cloak. Even to that about her hips, she wore the heavy leather belt designed to maintain the bulky garment secure against a woman's body, especially whilst mounted, they laughed affectionately, Daniel observing, "I have heard that Her Royal Highness was now favouring an arasaid over a more shall we say *conventional* cloak, though not yet had I seen so . . . I must say she wears it rather well, aye?"

O'Leary nodded in the affirmative. "Fetching, the girl certainly is."

As the trio dismounted almost as one, mere feet from the princess, the young grooms stepped quickly, so as to remove each rider's reins from the man's gloved hands before he had a chance to drop them, hustling the animals away before any of them had removed their gloves.

His uncles reflexively holding themselves back, Hugh stepped slightly forward, into the princess's open arms and a warm embrace.

His face bright red, he turned, gesturing wordlessly to O'Leary, who stepped forward, exchanging warm smiles with Lamballe, who proffered him her hand, which he took and delicately kissed, at which point she curtsied and he bowed in a singularly fluid, shared gesture. As they rose, they exchanged double-cheek kisses, as if they were old friends.

Having regained his composure, Hugh began to introduce the pair, which proved unnecessary, as the words "I have heard much about you . . ." spoken in English, by her, laced with her singular, soft Franco-Italian accent, whilst by O'Leary in his deep, elegant voice, echoed at almost precisely the same moment, such that the three of them, as well as Daniel O'Connell, burst into spontaneously hearty laughter. Louise, her hands held up, finally managed, "Well, monsieurs, I *have* indeed!" and they laughed again.

As Lamballe indicated her desire to have the men join her for coffee or tea in her apartments, Daniel quietly excused himself. "I must now see Monsieur Louis François, Marquis de Montagnard—"who was just this month completing his first year of service as Louis XV's Secretary of State of War—"but I shall most assuredly join you, Highness, and—" he gestured with a smile—"your intended for dinner, if I may."

She beamed. "But of course, monsieur," and with a bow, the soldier withdrew, taking several respectful steps backwards before he turned away.

"So, now, my dears, if you would . . ." She slipped between uncle and nephew, playfully taking their arms. "Let us now finally visit."

They entered the palace by a small side door, away from which she led them down an elegant hall, gesturing to the doors of the residence that belonged to her father-in-law, the Duke de Penthièvre, adjacent to which was her own less-opulent but still comfortably large, elegant quarters.

As they entered the small audience room, she faux-grandly gestured with her open arms. "Bienvenue *a ma maison*," she said and laughed.

As she turned to O'Leary, he smiled and gestured approvingly at her outer garment. "'Tis lovely and certainly warm it is . . . your arasaid, madame."

Beaming, she hugged the bulky fabric about her trim frame. "*Je l'adore*," then gently placing her forefinger on the striking brooch, she added, ". . . and the O'Connell stag, I love *this* even more!" O'Leary nodded, smiling.

She proceeded to conduct her guests farther into her suite, the door to what proved to be a sumptuous parlour being opened by a young female servant who blushed as Hugh and O'Leary acknowledged her. As the girl quickly extricated the princess from the folds of her heavy cloak, slipping the brooch into the pocket of her apron, Lamballe gestured the men to take seats on a comfortably sized camel-backed sofa, covered in thick brocade with alternating white and Bourbon blue stripes. Almost as soon as she took her own place across from them, in a matching high-backed, winged chair, a tea and coffee service, with ample pastries and croissants, was laid before them.

As the coffee was being poured into a trio of delicately elegant Sèvres cups, O'Leary spoke first. Just as he began, "If I may, Your Highness . . ." she rose sharply from her seat, took a step, perhaps two, such that she stood over O'Leary, slightly lifting his chin.

She immediately placed her right forefinger softly on his slightly cold-and-wind-chapped lips. "My dear Monsieur Captain O'Leary . . . if you would please do me the honour, sir, of addressing me only and in any setting as Laoise, you will, for certain, know this to be the Irish version of my Christian name, which your nephew has lovingly bestowed on me. . . . I have come to treasure and embrace it, and all it means, sir, such that I even say to those of the French to whom I feel closest, '*Je m'appelle* Laoise.'"

Looking up at her, O'Leary saw her eyes moist and said softly, "And so 'tis Laoise you shall henceforth be, my darling girl."

As they drank the thick, dark Viennese coffee Lamballe favoured, which both of the men appreciated and partook heartily of the pastry offerings, Hugh found himself quite gently but most definitely marginalised in terms of much of the ensuing conversation, something he had both fully anticipated and hoped would prove to be the case.

Indeed, the discussion that unfolded was a detailed and wide-ranging one, during which the princess addressed all of O'Leary's carefully phrased questions, as well as anticipating most of his unspoken queries and concerns, elaborating on them as well.

As she spoke, at several points standing and walking about, gesturing for emphasis, her long train following, at times lifted and *swished* by a delicate gesture of her slender-fingered right hand, mindful that Eileen would desire every possible minute detail of the visit, O'Leary committed to memory his impressions. *She is indeed tall, very blonde and truly beautiful, albeit in a soft, perhaps even delicate way. Her eyes are, as Hugh wrote us, very blue, and most of the time she appears to have them only for him! Her manner of speech is most delightful to experience; she speaks English very well, much as does our dear Anna and, as is Anna's, it is with the rich flavour of her native tongue, though in her case, it seems a combination of Italian as well as French.*

Lamballe expounded at length on a number of themes, indeed, in such detail that at several junctures, each time quietly excusing himself, Hugh had stepped out of the room. O'Leary listened intently as she related to him her background, how she'd come to the French court from Savoy—the king of Sardinia having long favoured an alliance with France, secured by a high-ranking female Savoyard noble's marriage into the French royal family— her brief, unpleasant and ill-fated marriage to the prince of Lamballe—his expression evidencing both his shock and surprise as she scoffed, *this detestable man, you will know that he was nothing other than a pox-ridden libertine,* about which union Hugh would quietly advise O'Leary that it was unconsummated—as well as the import of her position as a Princess of the Blood, the details of the latter which he found fascinating. She also explained the exercise, which had not yet begun, involved in obtaining Louis XV's permission and consent for them to wed. "Though wedded we shall be, sir! Of *this* you may be certain!"

Our—Eileen's and mine—surmise of some time ago was and, more importantly, remains wholly incorrect, O'Leary reflected. *This princess, she seemingly cares not at all about Hugh's station or lack thereof in life and society, thinks nothing of that he is obviously untitled and indeed quite penniless,* he laughed to himself, *but, rather, she appears and sounds as animated and excited by his forthcoming commissioning as the most junior of officers as were he being ennobled and becoming a Marechal de France! Indeed, as to anything regarding Hugh's humble station, she characterised it as being "little more than an annoyance, trivial, indeed, of no consequence at all!"*

As if to emphasise this, she is very much secure in her own apparently grand positions, both her titled one and her role as companion to the dauphine, such that her response to my not-at-all-subtly-posed suggestion of the, in most ways significant, vast differences between her and Hugh was several times to the effect that "Truly, none of this matters. I am, after all, a Princesse du Sang!"

At that point, in response to O'Leary's inquiry, she elaborated on the bases for her unique status, explaining, as she had not previously done, that her late husband's family was descended from Louis XIV himself. He would recall refraining from smiling as she lowered her eyes in what seemed to O'Leary a playful gesture, qualifying the nature of the heritage, *"only by virtue of the prince's grandfather's being 'recognised' . . . therefore shall we speak plainly and indeed more correctly say he was legitimised by his most gracious Majesty!"* She laughed, almost cruelly.

That evening, as planned, Daniel joined Louise and Hugh for dinner in her apartments whilst O'Leary dined alone with Louis Auguste and Marie Antoinette in the dauphine's apartments.

When he arrived, he was shown into her audience room, an ornately done, rectangular chamber, clearly meant to awe, to impress, rather than to welcome the visitor, with a profusion of gilt, carved mouldings and a number of sombre renderings of various Bourbons, mostly deceased. O'Leary found the settee as stiff and hard as were one seated on a crate.

It was only as a side door was opened, and through it burst an animated Marie Antoinette, that the mood in the space changed—and changed markedly.

"Papa! Papa," cried the future queen of France as she literally raced across the room towards him, O'Leary bemused to note that she was barefoot. She threw herself into his widely open arms, with which he immediately embraced her. "Papa, Papa . . ." she sobbed, "I never thought I would see you here, not for a long, long time, and here you are, my darling papa, come to me." She buried her face against his right upper arm, and wept, until she finally stopped. As she cried, O'Leary held and gently rocked her, gently stroking her hair, saying nothing.

Her face red, her eyes moist and weary, she took his hand in her own as, with the absence of bowing and hand-kissing, of curtseying, disregarding as well the prim taking of his arm, and led him into a small, elegant, but considerably more welcoming and comfortable room. She gestured O'Leary to one of a pair of closely set, English-style wing-backed armchairs. As she directed that he sit first, for a moment he thought she might actually sit on his lap—indeed she seemed to have been considering doing just that—and instead took her own seat, and they sat quietly for a moment, facing each other.

To O'Leary, she appeared generally well, *more a woman than the girl from whom Eileen separated at the Rhine nearly two years prior. She is fuller of figure and of face but remains youthfully beautiful.*

As he continued to gaze upon this pretty, sweet young woman whom he and Eileen would always consider to be their first child, their daughter, and sat back as, leaning forward slightly, she began to speak in a soft, almost conspiratorial tone. "Papa, my husband, the dauphin, he will join us shortly, but I must speak with you first, and I must do so quickly, my darling Papa."

His expression calm, gentle—*loving*, she thought—he gestured for her to proceed.

Taking a breath, she began in a normal tone, advising him with a smile that, thanks to a recent letter from Eileen, she was "aware of things at home in Cork," though she inquired briefly of the O'Sullivans, as well as the von Graffenreit-O'Connells, still enthralled that the countess, affectionally known to the O'Connell family—including, Antoinette—as "Aunt Maria," had given birth the year before to a baby girl, *"and at her age!* . . . such a blessing, a *miracle!*" she exclaimed. Pausing momentarily, she continued. "Though I am curious, I did want to inquire, Papa, when dearest Aunt Maria wrote me of her safe delivery, she said initially that the little girl is called 'Katrina' . . . a lovely German, indeed Austrian name, *ja?*" she laughed, " . . . but the spelling!" she feigned shock. "It appears almost unpronounceable . . . 'Caitríona' . . . Is this Irish, or . . ." She laughed again.

O'Leary nodded. "You are correct, it is that . . . it came originally from the Scots. It means 'pure,' and like the German Katrine, 'tis another variant of Katherine."

With an impish grin, she suddenly leaned forward. "And did you know, her second name, her saint's name, is Antoinette?" She sat back up, tears in her eyes. "It moved me so very much. . . . I love that we—little Caitríona and I—that we shall forever share St. Anthony's Day as our name day." O'Leary smiled contentedly, as she quietly advised that she fairly regularly corresponded with both Eileen and Countess von Graffenreit, thanking him for his own less-frequent but equally welcome letters.

She then momentarily again sat quietly, growing pensive, her expression, her manner reflecting what O'Leary correctly sensed was a sudden, profound shift to sadness. When she did again speak, her tone was emotional. It was apparent that she had been waiting to talk to this dear man who she had come to regard as her Papa, with whom she shared a father-daughter relationship much deeper, significantly closer and certainly more intimate than the one she had had with her actual father, the Emperor Francis Stephen I, dead now these not-quite-seven years.

As he did with his conversation with Princess de Lamballe and for the same reason, O'Leary listened carefully, at times saying very little, committing his observations and reflections to memory.

"I am," she began brightly, "completely enthralled that Mama is the mother of two sons, my dear, sweet little brothers. . . ." Having said that, her expression almost instantly became sad, her eyes misty as she continued, ". . . though *I* am of none, not even a daughter . . ." This she said most softly, as, to her surrogate father, she appeared deeply troubled concerning her childlessness. "I have opened my heart to Mama, in ways"—she lowered her eyes, then her voice—"in ways that I of course cannot do to you, my dearest Papa, but she knows all of what I speak." He nodded wordlessly.

Her small voice audibly shaking, she said, "The empress, she is so angry, livid, Papa, she is positively *furious!* She is so displeased with me. She scolds me in her numerous letters, reminding me over and over again what I already know . . . that the *alliance"*—the close union of the Bourbons and the Habsburgs, the sole reason for and behind her marriage—" . . . it is not secure . . . and, and . . ." Her trim shoulders began to shake. "It is *all my fault!"* As she dissolved in tears, O'Leary rose, immediately kneeling before where she sat, reaching, embracing, holding her as she wept bitterly.

Though it was several moments, even as she was still daubing her eyes, sipping a glass of tepid, sugary water, the door to the parlour swung open and Louis Auguste's stolid form filled the room. After taking a deep breath, as if to steel himself against what for him might be a difficult act, and O'Leary rose, the husky young man extended his hand. "Captain O'Leary, sir, welcome!" he managed as he offered O'Leary what the young officer felt was a limp, almost weak handshake.

By then Antoinette, who had subtly wriggled her feet into a pair of silk slippers that had been beneath her chair, stood between the two men, smiling softly. She was in fact relieved that her spouse had returned from his almost-daily hunting expedition sufficiently early so as to wash and change from his ofttimes muddy, frequently bloody hunting clothing, such that he made a far more favourable impression on O'Leary than he did on his first meeting with Hugh O'Connell, now some two years past.

As to his impressions of the dauphin, O'Leary would reflect that *he is a tall, heavy, blond young man. At first he appeared quite ill at ease, but as we spoke a time he grew less so. Though destined to become king of France, he is a self-conscious lad, part of the reason I sense being that his eyesight is not good; he squints quite obviously; equally so, I fear he cannot see much about him. The poor boy should wear spectacles, but I sense this is not done at this court, so the world a few feet beyond himself is ofttimes a blur, a daunting prospect for a king of France, especially in contrast to Louis XV, whose manner is commanding. What is said of this king being "the handsomest man in*

Europe," may well be true; a striking man indeed he is, according to brother Daniel and Hugh. Suffice it to say, the dauphin is quite unlike his grandfather.

Though awkward he may be, Louis Auguste nevertheless appears a bright fellow. He has strong mechanical interests; quite unusual, I feel, for one such as he, he is fascinated with lock-making and forging!

Of more compelling interest to me is that his knowledge of world geography is quite extraordinary. He spoke of Cork and Kerry as if he had visited both, though never beyond the confines of the Île de France he says he has been. When I asked him of his knowledge of Ireland, he indicated that the dauphine had told him much of Eileen, of both of us and of her fascination with the places from which we had come, and he apparently took it upon himself to become thus knowledgeable, for her sake as well as his own edification.

As the pleasant meal progressed, the young officer was amazed—shocked actually, truth be told—by the volume and variety of food the presumptive king of France consumed, such that, as it was close to ending, he looked aside diplomatically as the young wife quietly nudged her husband, gesturing that he should limit his intake of the incredible display of pastries set on a half-dozen multitiered servers.

O'Leary had found the conversation during the relatively informal meal to be extremely pleasant, though in personal terms, compared to the one he'd had with Antoinette, of little consequence. In addition to discussing Ireland in greater detail. the dauphin asked several excellent questions about the Austrian military, expressed admiration for General the Count O'Connell, expressing his interest in the fact that O'Leary and O'Sullivan were brother officers in the Hungarian Hussars, as were Daniel and Hugh in the Irish Brigade and conducted much of his conversation with O'Leary in English. At one point the dauphine held up her hands in mock distress. "All my years with my beloved Eileen and yet my spoken English . . . it is still so limited." Despite her comment, O'Leary noted that her comprehension had nevertheless improved significantly; she appeared to follow the men's conversation in English with relative ease, joining in a sometimes refreshingly comical combination of both languages.

Several times she wistfully, warmly reminisced about her time with O'Leary and Eileen at Laxenburg, at one point telling her husband, as she seemingly had many times before, "Those what seemed many weeks before Conor was born . . . a very special *petite famille* we had become. The Captain—" she reached for O'Leary's hand and took it in her own— "Lady Eileen and I, the 'little archduchess,' as I had come to learn was how she affectionately referred to me!" Though she laughed softly, O'Leary could see that tears glistened in her eyes. "Even after the wee one came, we remained thus."

As she looked at O'Leary, he nodded warmly, adding softly, "Conor, your wee little brother he shall always be."

The one-time little archduchess smiled through her tears, her husband taking her free hand in his own and nodding warmly at O'Leary, of whom he would frequently speak to Marie Antoinette as being a "very unique man."

The dauphin having almost shyly risen, O'Leary and Antoinette rose almost as one. Touching his arm, she gently confirmed, "Papa . . . I shall join you for breakfast, prior to your leaving for home," she said softly, a faraway expression on what O'Leary felt was her weary face.

Having taken his leave of the royal couple, as O'Leary was being escorted to his quarters for the night, a slender young page in a simple, elegant black velvet suit and white hose, shod in soft, padded silk slippers that apparently enabled him to move speedily and silently about the vast interior confines of Versailles, had been hastening to intercept the long-striding cavalryman, finally catching up with him and his guide just as they reached the entrance to O'Leary's rooms. Bowing gracefully, from that position, with his right, white-gloved hand, the boy proffered to O'Leary a small, square envelope. As soon as O'Leary gently plucked it from his fingers, he was quickly away, presumably on another nocturnal errand.

Excusing himself momentarily, O'Leary tore open the envelope. *Please meet me at the Place d'Armes, which you will know leads from the Courtyard of Honour, within the chateau's main golden gates towards the stables beyond the high fence*, Daniel O'Connell had written. O'Leary explained the change of direction to his escort, who adroitly turned them down and back the way they had just come. Within moments, he was pointing the soldier in the direction of the pair of stables.

The night was delicately moonlit and chilly, the air about the massive palace pungent with woodsmoke, as O'Leary's gleaming boots crunched on the crushed white rocks of the footpath crossing the Place d'Armes, leading, as Daniel had explained, from the Courtyard of Honour, within the chateau's main golden gates, to the Small Stables, which appeared to him to be almost precisely the same size as the Main Stables, both buildings being constructed of gleaming Parisian limestone and situated just opposite on his left as he walked. Raising his arms in greeting to his brothers-in-law, a sudden, stiff breeze caught the hem of his elegant pelisse, seeing which Hugh O'Connell thought again momentarily, as he frequently had, that the fur-trimmed garment was perhaps the most striking component of any uniform he had ever seen. All three men quickened their pace, coming together at the ornate stable entrance.

"Ah, brother, I am grateful for a word with you before we are off for Paris; the lad, he must return to barracks," Daniel Charles grandiloquently called out, half-bowing as he did, Hugh remaining upright, smiling but slightly puzzled.

"I should say that there are far less-pleasant places to be than at this august chateau," Hugh volunteered, and the others nodded as he added guilelessly, "and our dinner with Louise; it was quite good, was it not?"

Daniel rocked with laughter and clapped his youngest brother on his back. "A dozen courses, half that many appetizers and desserts, wines and brandies, mountains of pastries, coffee: indeed I would say it was quite good, indeed!"

The older brother grew quickly serious. "Monsieur Cadet d'O'Connell," he said, "might I trouble you to see to our mounts whilst a moment of Captain O'Leary's time I take?"

Hugh nodded reflexively, appending a clipped, albeit smiling, "Oui, monsieur!" as he turned sharply towards the Small Stables.

As he did, Daniel shifted back towards O'Leary. "So, Captain, as I have seen her most infrequently this year and some months since her arrival, becoming known to her primarily as Eileen's brother, and have not had until this moment the opportunity to inquire of you: How fares Madame la Dauphine, as best you are able to tell, from your visit with her today, this evening? . . . I ask this of you of course without suggesting that you violate any confidences."

O'Leary nodded, his expression sombre. "What is the obvious, that neither a son nor at the very least a daughter has arrived at Versailles, is seemingly the principal source of her unhappiness here, indeed her quite genuine distress. Whilst she indicates that Eileen is made very aware of the details of the situation, of them I know nothing, of the issue itself no more than I have just related, sir."

Daniel Charles nodded gently, thoughtfully, lowering his voice several octaves. "Ah, oui . . . *La Situation*, 'tis the talk of the court, indeed of much of Paris itself, from the glittering salons to the tanneries, the fish stalls, the charnel houses of the *poissards*—at times, it seems that people speak of nothing else. I am barely able to imagine what the problem is. . . . If I may, was the archduchess not . . ."

O'Leary laid a gentle hand on his brother-in-law's right arm and sighed. "As I know I am free to speak openly and in confidence to you, brother, I can advise only that—and this itself being based solely upon remarks she made to me whilst we were still in Vienna and as she was preparing the archduchess for her life here," he gestured about, "Eileen surmised that the archduchess was, more likely than not, made to understand the, shall we say, *mechanics* of the . . . *activities*, whose frequent consequence is . . . in this instance 't'woud be the eventual arrival of a Son or Daughter of France— though given the current state of affairs here, I fear *she* based this solely on a rather graphic conversation on the topic she had with her other charge, the dauphine's slightly older sister, now the Queen of Naples."

"Did Eileen not raise . . ." Daniel began, somewhat incredulously.

O'Leary shook his head. "The Archduchess Maria Antonia seemingly showed no interest in the topic, and Eileen may or may not have provided her adequate opportunity, so 'tis fair to say that we do not know for certain the adequacy or lack thereof of Her Royal Highness, the dauphine's preparation."

Daniel then heaved a sigh. "I can only speak as to the dauphin, whom I have seen frequently, as he seems, for reasons unbeknownst to me and to others of whom I have inquired, to have taken a bit of a liking to me, appears frequently juvenile, his behaviour at times, I have both seen and am told, rather inane: playing silly practical jokes, as one would expect in a nursery. I fear perhaps that an adequate understanding of the *mechanics,* as you say, may very well be in *him* lacking . . . the sad family situation growing up, his parents and elder brother's early deaths, the lad and his two younger brothers and the wee Princess Elisabeth left with a variety of servants and *Mesdames Tantes,* the king's three rather peculiar, seemingly by-design spinster daughters, becoming paramount in their lives, the attention of the king, the grandfather of them all, obviously and for some time fixed almost solely on his own pleasure; 'tis not been the most favourable of circumstances for the proper rearing of a dauphin of France."

The young officer shook his head dismissively, but then, as he quickly looked about, touched O'Leary's arm. "As our lad is not yet returned . . . if I may," Daniel began, and O'Leary immediately nodded.

"Thank you, brother, as the time for this discourse may be brief. . . . I would advise you, as I have been until this moment unable, that the last time Hugh and I journeyed out here . . . ah, perhaps three weeks past . . . I to visit with the king- and queen-in-waiting, young Hugh of course to see his princess, obviously not considering that he might be coming with me, the lad and I were greeted by Louis . . . and Antoinette," he rolled his eyes, "and indeed as soon as we drew close to them, I noticed on the part of the dauphine, clear indication of, might I say, feelings for Hugh. . . ."

". . . ah, Dear God, brother," O'Leary said softly, "If your observation is correct, indeed certain that this is the case, despite the obvious and effusive degree of affection between the lad and the stunning princess, this being known to Antoinette, I genuinely fear . . ."

". . . and despite that as well, I share your fear," interjected Daniel, then elaborated "Whilst Hugh was briefly in her presence, and even as he was departing to meet his princess, the dauphine, she exhibited a wistfulness, perhaps even a degree of sadness that, to me, could evidence some pining for the lad, which could impact her . . ."

O'Leary effortlessly completed his brother-in-law's thought, ". . . her 'interest,' shall we say, in her husband, perhaps even her 'performance' or lack thereof in their marital bed."

Nodding his concurrence, Daniel gently raised his hand, gesturing towards Hugh, approaching at a distance, leading the brothers' saddle horses. His expression quickly serious, O'Leary spoke quickly. "So, aye, it would appear that our concerns are identical: The thought that they, Louis and Antoinette, may both quite possibly be inadequately prepared in the ways of the bedroom aside, is it also not possible that the girl rejects her husband's advances, if any there have been . . . and indeed as she is quite lovely, comely, one must in all candour observe, such interest, such advances would be wholly understandable . . . because of some misplaced notion of affection or longing for our lad?"

"Precisely!" exclaimed Daniel.

"I shall surely discuss this with Eileen," O'Leary managed, just as Hugh stepped up and offered his brother the reins to his horse.

"You will share your findings, if any there be, brother?" he asked, hurriedly adding, "as I shall, in the same manner, attempt to engage the lad and see . . ." Then stripping his gauntlet from his right hand, he extended it to O'Leary, who was ungloved. O'Leary nodded in silent response as the men shook hands, and then extended his to Hugh as he arrived, leading the men's horses. O'Leary then stepped back as both O'Connells effortlessly swung up into their saddles, adjusting their heavy cloaks about themselves and, with nods and waves of gauntleted right hands, turned the horses' heads away from Versailles and toward Paris, the night cold, still and softly moonlit.

O'Leary was awakened even before a chill, raw dawn had broken over Versailles by a French cavalry lieutenant of approximately his own age, who, on introducing himself, indicated he had been sent by the dauphin and that he would be accompanying the captain on his journey to the coast. "If you would please join Her Royal Highness *pour petit déjeuner*, I shall see to it that your belongings are taken care of, and I shall await you at the Court of Honour. We are fully provisioned for our journey, sir," he added with a firm nod.

O'Leary completed his toilette, drew on his uniform coat and stepped out of his room, his boots resounding in some of the more cavernous passageways of the château. He was directed towards the dauphine's apartments, where he was greeted by the unmistakable Princess Lamballe, she of the flawless complexion and gracious manner, this morning wearing a full-skirted, deep purple velvet robe.

"I trust that you will recall me, Captain," Marie Thérèse Louise of Savoy said coyly in the softest of tones as she curtseyed playfully, continuing in what this morning seemed to be her strongly Italian-flavoured English. "I was so honoured, and it was such a joy, to finally meet you in person last evening, from whence we first began to speak of our families, Hugh has spoken so highly of you, sir, and of your raven-haired wife." She smiled at O'Leary's slight surprise upon hearing the level of personal detail of which she was already knowledgeable.

"This morning, however, I am additionally honoured to greet you officially, as it is my privilege to, albeit informally, be in occasional charge of the dauphine's household. Please …" she gestured O'Leary into the comfortable dining room, where he had supped with the prospective rulers of France the evening before. "You will please await Madame la Dauphine, sir."

After taking a few steps, the stunning young woman turned and walked back to O'Leary as he was pouring himself a cup of coffee, from a magnificent silver service atop an elegant walnut sideboard. As she approached, he smiled broadly. *She is indeed a singularly beautiful girl*, he could not help but think again. *No wonder our Hugh was smitten from the very first moment.*

"Captain, I am of course aware of your—and your wife's—close and fond relationship with the dauphine, so I feel I am not being inappropriate to advise you, sir, that *this*," she gestured at the breakfast table, "is indeed a singular occasion." Her smile was almost impish.

The princess noted that O'Leary's expression was clearly one of curiosity.

"The hour, sir, it is barely six thirty. Her Royal Highness usually rises at ten, and often then most reluctantly. She cares deeply for you, sir, and for your, as I am told she is, most beautiful wife." She nodded and turned.

When she returned, she was following the dauphine, who, attired far more simply than the princess, wore the French court equivalent of a simple afternoon dress and looked ever so slightly sleepy. Indeed, O'Leary chuckled as she daintily covered one, no, actually two yawns as he bowed her into the room.

As she positioned herself to take her seat, O'Leary waved off a slender young footman and held her chair himself. "The dauphin, he rises even earlier than this, so . . . I do not see him until much later in the day," she said as she delicately picked at a bowl of fresh fruit and some bread. Lifting a delicate, gold-rimmed Sèvres cup, she added, "I drink hot chocolate still, as I did each morning with Mama for all of our years in Vienna. . . ." Her voice trailed off softly and, O'Leary sensed, again wistfully.

It was when the pastries, croissants and coffee—and more chocolate for Antoinette—were again served that O'Leary looked softly at the young woman for whom he indeed felt a powerful paternal affection and inquired,

"My darling girl, if I may ask . . . in addition to that of which we spoke last evening, how *is* your life here?"

Evidencing some measure of shock—*I had somehow forgotten how direct the Irish can be*, she would later tell Lamballe—her cheeks immediately pink, her eyes filling, the dauphine sat quietly, looking at the man she called Papa. She daubed her glistening light blue eyes with her stiff linen napkin, took a deep breath and, her voice softer than usual, slightly tremulous, she began to speak. "Oh, Papa . . . were that I could tell you I was as happy as I was when we . . ."—she gestured with open arms—"when we were *la petite famille* in Vienna, but, regretfully, that is not the case, it never has been the case. Since first I arrived here . . . I have been generally sad."

O'Leary said nothing, his gaze resting warmly on her, as she continued. "You have met the dauphin . . . he is . . . I feel he is a nice boy, yes . . . but . . . but we see little of each other, we have no shared interests, none at all. . . . I fear I may bore him, for he is, as you have seen, quite bright, and he is kind, but . . ." O'Leary did not expect her to speak of her marriage and, given what he already knew, he was just as happy that she abruptly changed the subject, at least until she resumed speaking.

"The worst of the many things which daily prevent my experiencing virtually any happiness is Versailles itself. . . . This court, it is one of *malice!* They are horrid—*all of them*, these vacuous little people possessed of many titles. I do not understand why there are so many of them or what virtually any of them do but preen and strut, drink and eat and gamble. And *we*—the royal family—*we* appear to have to pay for *all* of them: pay them to do nothing! It is *nothing* like Vienna, Papa, *nothing at all!* . . .

"And Papa, what is even worse is that they hate me, they *loathe* me! They are cruel, merciless, vicious and vindictive. They detest Austria . . . and . . . and they criticise my clothes, my speech, my appearance. They hate even little Mops!" O'Leary's eyes softened even more as hers again teared up. "Old prunes like the Countess de Noailles and her dottering clique, as well as the flocks of younger parvenus, all with too much money . . . *our money!* . . . and too little to productively do . . . they turn their malicious tongues on *me* . . . and on my few friends.

"Indeed I must say that behaviour exists here, conduct is tolerated here, that in Vienna would result in one's permanent banishment from court! I have written to Aunt Maria, describing some of these things, and . . . and, she says, 'With a flick of my hand, such a person would be gone!' . . . from Vienna, yes, but alas not here, not at *Versailles!*"

O'Leary toyed with his now-cold eggs as Antoinette seemed to wind down, expressing her gratitude for the Princess de Lamballe, albeit qualifying this relationship as well, adding "Even she, as kind, as sweet even as she is much of the time . . . or at least some of the time, she, too, is frequently enmeshed in the tattling, the gossiping. It is as common here as breathing!"

Reluctantly, dreading what demons he might be releasing, O'Leary nevertheless took the opportunity, probing, "And Hugh . . . we . . . your Mama and I, Uncle Daniel, we have come to understand . . ."

"*And Hugh?*" Her eyes flashed as she looked up sharply. "He . . . she . . . she   . . ." Antoinette stumbled, at first pale, ashen even, her face then flamed red as her tone turned angry and became harshly dismissive. "*She and Hugh, they are become friends* . . . seemingly close, *very close* friends. . . Is it *this* that all of you understand?" she snapped. O'Leary purposely remaining mute, she paused, and when she did speak again her tone was apologetic, her voice and her eyes softened, grown misty, her expression suddenly distant. Before O'Leary could say or do anything—he was going to take her hand—she took a deep breath, and in doing so, it appeared to him that she'd seemingly shaken herself free of the thought, until she added that her hurt was because of what she termed the "betrayal of it all."

The room then grew silent; after a long moment, the dauphine smiled weakly and managed, "All of this said, Papa, I assure you that, at least as to this 'betrayal,' I am improving each day that passes. My life, as I imagine you have concluded, it is far too complex and challenging for me to continue to dwell on what I have referred to others as being *memories of a pleasant time with an Irish boy in Vienna* . . . which now seems a long time ago and very far from France."

O'Leary gently nodded his understanding, though his expression was pained.

Noting that O'Leary had eaten virtually nothing, she requested of a footman another full breakfast for him, and more fruit and croissants for them both, fresh coffee and chocolate, as well, all of which, to O'Leary's unexpressed amazement, arrived almost immediately. During the remainder of the meal—as he ate, and she nibbled, and as they both drank—they spoke much of Eileen and of the "wee lads, my dear little brothers, though only Conor have I held in my arms," as the dauphine referred to the O'Leary sons, in precise English, with a warm smile. She expressed yet again her gratitude to O'Leary for coming to see her and, her eyes brimming, "for remaining my papa."

Noting that he had not as yet held Fiach either, O'Leary in return thanked her for joining him so early. Once she determined her guest had completed his meal, she rose, requesting of the small bevy of servants that had formed around the Princess de Lamballe, visible at the apartments' main doors, "My cloak, please. I shall accompany the captain to the Court of Honour."

In a breach of protocol by all three of them, O'Leary immediately extended his hand to the princess; receiving the garment, he draped it over Antoinette's trim shoulders and squeezing them gently, causing her to turn, look up and smile warmly at him, after which she then took his right hand in her left.

It was just at that moment that Lamballe—acting as if the dauphine were not in the room, much less holding her papa's hand—availing herself of what she saw as perhaps her final opportunity to do so in private, gently curtseyed and smiled her goodbyes to O'Leary, gently adding, " . . . and you will please, *my dearest brother-to-be*, please do convey my love to the Lady Eileen," she lowered her eyes, "*my dearest sister-to-be* . . . and to the *wee lads;* I already feel them to be *my dear little nephews.*" By the time she'd finished speaking, Antoinette's nails had dug into her papa's palm as she gripped it ever more tightly.

Still holding his daughter's hand, O'Leary nevertheless managed a partial bow, and softly kissed the back of the young royal's proffered hand, delightfully scented and smooth. *This girl will, it surely appears and as incredible as that may seem, become an O'Connell . . . in addition to all else that she is. I truly like her, she adores Hugh and he her, so . . . I cannot, I shall not immerse myself in my dear daughter's emotional tumult involving her.*

At that, Lamballe quickly gathered her arasaid about herself, disregarding the O'Connell stag brooch, which rested on a small, ivory-inlaid side table by the apartments' doors, casually flipping part of it over her left shoulder as if it were a Highlander's plaid, letting the garment drape her.

Trailed by the princess, who remained a considerable distance behind them, and several lesser ladies-in-waiting, they—papa and daughter—walked slowly through the vast palace and outside, with obvious reluctance on Marie Antoinette's part, to where the young French soldier awaited with his own mount, two packhorses and O'Leary's horse, a striking young chestnut brown mare, large for a female, with a white star on her forehead and, the dauphine noted, a dramatic black mane and tail, very much like Eileen's beloved Bull's.

Without releasing O'Leary's hand, Antoinette was immediately drawn to his horse. "How beautiful she is, sir! Magnificent, and her eyes so soft," she said, stroking the mare's head and gently kissing her nose, "Hello, pretty girl," she said softly as she looked deeply into the animal's huge, kind eyes.

O'Leary smiled. "She is new," he began, "and you should know she is indeed a most special animal: A gift upon my departure from Vienna she was, bestowed upon me by the empress herself!"

Marie Antoinette smiled knowingly and gently rested her head against that of the mare, who, in obvious contentment, whinnied softly.

"The empress has always been virtually without equal at selecting the finest of animals," she correctly observed. "Has this special lady been gifted with a name yet, sir?"

O'Leary's smile was customarily dazzling as he leaned back his head just a bit. "Ah, indeed she has, Your Highness. She is called Banrían," he said, not with a French accent.

Marie Antoinette's expression was quizzical. *"Bonnerion,* Papa? It appears a strange-sounding French name," she observed, puzzled because O'Leary's French was superb.

"Ah, my dearest girl, that is because it is not French at all, but rather Irish. It translates as *queen* or, in this case, *empress.*"

The dauphine smiled, nodding effusively. "Then it is most assuredly a superb name for her!"

Casting a glance at the weak sun and the patiently waiting young soldier, the dauphine grew sombre. She stepped closely to O'Leary, taking his right hand in both of her own, speaking in the softest of voices. "I know you must depart, Papa," she managed weakly, her eyes brimming with tears, releasing his hand. "My mama and my wee little brothers," she said in English, "they all await you in Ireland, sir, so hasten!" She gestured with a flick of her left hand. She then dipped into a deep curtsey, her head bowed. O'Leary intuitively took both of her hands in his, raising her, and—yet again contrary to all protocol—embraced her, as the dauphine of France buried her face in his uniform coat and wept softly for a long moment. Her tears ebbed, she finally stood back, gently brushing her eyes, her wet cheeks, struggling to finally offer a weak smile.

"I shall miss you, my dearest Papa, indeed I miss all of you, but now . . ." She gestured with her delicate fingers and stood regally as O'Leary bowed formally and deeply. The French officer then skilfully draped O'Leary's pelisse over his shoulder and fastened it. Swinging up onto Banrían's trim back, O'Leary said, "Adieu, Madame." Looking down at her crestfallen expression, he corrected himself. "I should say *au revoir,* my darling daughter!" Her face brightening somewhat, he then sharply turned the magnificent mare's head away from Versailles.

The dauphine stood in tearful silence, solitary, the nearness of her ladies notwithstanding.

Not having walked out with the small group, as she joined them, Lamballe stepped to Antoinette's right side, reflexively, unthinkingly offering her hand, evidencing no surprise that she'd taken it. The cluster of elegant, mostly young women watched until the two men and their horses were out of sight. Finally, turning away, the dauphine, now gripping Lamballe's hand tightly, led her companions back into the palace.

County Cork, Ireland—February 1772

It was mid-afternoon on the fifth day following his departure from Versailles when a previously road weary, now suddenly elated Art O'Leary turned Banrían's head off the coach road and cantered the frisky mare onto the lane leading to Rathleigh. As he reached the simple open gate, he slowed her to a walk and then halted, looking at the vividly white house with the gleaming black shutters that always appeared to him to have just been freshly painted.

The young officer, who, as he had throughout his journey, was wearing his striking uniform, the dazzling red coat, with its vibrant gold-braided front, the fur-trimmed pelisse gracefully draping his left shoulder—sat for a long moment, absorbing the sight before him, savouring the hint of warmth in a spring day—St. Brigid's Day having been the first of February—in West Cork. The pleasing dissonance of returning birds and migrating geese sounded distantly; as he walked his horse, her hoofs crunching almost delicately on the broken stones and sandy dirt of the lane, he heard a single bark, and then another, and instantly the cacophony of those Eileen had named collectively the *Rathleigh hounds* filled the air, causing the young mare to shy slightly as O'Leary gently touched her sides with his heels, propelling them the final yards home.

As the gleaming black front door was flung open, O'Leary gasped audibly, abruptly halting the horse some twenty feet from the house, deciding immediately, *This vision I wish to remember always and forever,* as Eileen, regal in a dress of heavy, dark-grey Scottish wool, a subtle, not-quite-purple, heather-blue plaid visible on the full skirts, much of her thick black hair gathered to her right side and falling over her breast to below her waist in the front, a small object loosely wrapped in a traditionally knitted, natural-coloured sheep's wool coverlet crooked gently in her arms, stepped out into the afternoon sunlight.

A little boy with dirty blond hair immediately rounded her and raced towards him, and then stopped suddenly, his mouth opened wide, evidencing wonder and, O'Leary suddenly realised, uncertainty, despite his distinctive uniform until he heard Eileen call out, "It is your *papa*, Conor. Your papa is *home!*" and the boy darted forward. O'Leary reached down as he flew by, hoisting him up onto the saddle in front of him, hugging his son tightly against him the remaining few feet.

He halted and looked down at Eileen, and she up at him. After first easing Conor off the horse, as he dismounted, he immediately felt a wave of warmth, hearing the words spoken by a familiar, husky voice: "So, Captain O'Leary, it is you now, is it not, sir?"

Conor standing between them, "*Aye*, it is indeed myself, Mistress O'Leary; home I have returned, madame," he said, and they stood in silence, a long moment of wordless wonder and brief, gentle tears, finally broken only by Conor, tugging at the pelisse.

"Papa, Papa, we have a brother, see. . . ." He pointed.

Silently, his eyes fixed on his wife, O'Leary stepped to her and then by her right shoulder, gazing down over it with a degree of awe at his second-born son, as his fuzzy blond head rested securely in the crook of his mother's left arm. "And to you, Master Fiach, when you shall awake, I shall properly introduce myself. . . ."

Eileen was taking note of Banrían. "'Twould appear you have an introduction to make here, Captain O'Leary, of your stunning lady friend!" She laughed, then smiled, lifting her left hand, rubbing the white star on the mare's forehead, stroking her soft nose. "She is beautiful, she . . ."

". . . is a gift from the empress herself, thus her name, Banrían."

"Ah, sir, 'tis a lovely and most fitting name for such an eye-catching young lady, from an as-always gracious lady. May you journey in health and safety upon her back wherever she may take you, near or . . . I pray, only rarely, if at all . . . far away, for many, many years, my darling." Eileen added teasingly, "Glad it is I am to hear that the empress still favours you, my love." O'Leary's cheeks reddened, and she laughed playfully.

Eileen then turned to her husband, and they shared as powerful, as lengthy and as awkward a kiss as one could imagine in the presence of one boisterously precocious child, who giggled as he made kissing sounds, the second one slowly waking in his mother's arms. Smiling, O'Leary stepped back, tousling Conor's hair with his fingers as he suggested, "Perhaps we should continue this later, Mistress O'Leary?"

Eileen lowered her eyes coyly. "I believe that would be quite . . . lovely, Captain O'Leary . . . especially as *Squire* O'Leary, he remains with your dear sister in Cork until at least week's end," she purred wickedly.

The day passed in a pleasantly chaotic way, with the servants off-loading the packhorses, sorting O'Leary's not-many belongings and prioritising washing and otherwise laundering his clothing. Dinner was a simple roast with potatoes and vegetables from the house's larder, though Art and Eileen shared a bottle of champagne he'd brought from France for the occasion and with O'Leary cutting Conor's meat and Eileen nursing Fiach until the infant nodded back off to sleep. The couple laughingly waved off the servants' assistance with bedding down the wee lads, after which they settled by the fire with some glasses of Richard Hennessey's cognac. As the house began to grow silent, O'Leary and Eileen checked each boy again, Conor in his own small room, adjacent to their own, in which the baby lay in his cradle in a corner. "I shall walk the place, the house once and join you shortly," O'Leary advised his wife, smiling back at Eileen as she was unfastening her stays, an impish expression on her face.

Clad in a heavy blue waistcoat, O'Leary strode briskly about the exterior of the house and its few small outbuildings, especially the stables, leaning in his head when he noticed a candle still burning in Seamus's cosy quarters located in the latter, poking in his head there, and chatting briefly, after having learnt that he was engrossed in *Hamlet*. O'Leary bid the young stablemaster a soft, *"Oíche mhaith"* before closing his door with a gentle click.

Once inside the main house, he walked quietly amongst the ground-floor rooms, re-banking one of the trio of fires burning.

As he mounted the stairs, he looked down and about, seeing into the large parlour, but one thought came to mind . . . *home.*

Reaching the second-floor landing, he smiled at the slender line of dim light beneath their bedroom door, walking softly to it, grateful as he cleared the thick Chinese carpet runner that he had removed his high boots as he'd entered the house. He leaned forward, turning the brass opener gently, as quietly as possible.

As he stepped inside, he smiled again: on the far side of the bed—customarily safely away from the door, O'Leary's body would lie between his wife and any danger—snuggled an apparently sleeping Eileen's long body, cosy under several puffy, down-filled Austrian quilts or eiderdowns , her hair gathered in a long, black rope, some of which was dark against the white linen of the pillows. The room was illuminated by a substantial single candle, barely flickering in its high, fine glass chimney.

He was unfastening his stock when the form in the bed stirred, Eileen's face popping up from under the mound of covers. "Ah, 'tis your first night at home, sir . . . please permit me, sir. . . ." She smiled, sitting up, her bare, broad shoulders appearing first. She gradually emerged, quickly standing, shamelessly naked. O'Leary's instantly flashing eyes fixed on her, as she fully intended, hoped they would be, and she slowly, seductively, albeit laughingly, untied and shook loose her mane, her hair blue-black in the candlelight tumbling over her shoulders. As she walked slowly towards her husband, she pushed it all to one side, so that some of the mass of it hung over but only partially covered her full right breast, her left one, her stomach, her body otherwise bare.

O'Leary smiled broadly, then chuckled, gesturing towards the smooth, hairless spot between her thighs. "The ways of Imperial Vienna, of

Versailles . . . thanks to the wax of the fine candles we have, they continue in use in the remote Kingdom of Ireland, sir." She laughed playfully.

"Indeed they do, my Lady Eileen, indeed they do," he managed as he embraced his wife, the linen of his shirt rough against her smooth, still-warm skin.

Eileen nudged him to sit on the bed. "Think me a humble harem slave, and ye the sultan himself," she said, kneeling at his feet, her eyes up to him, wordlessly removing his stockings, then his breeches, smoothing his long shirttails over his thighs before precisely folding and placing his other garments on a chair. At her direction, O'Leary then rested against his mound of goose down-filled pillows, piled against the headboard of the high, magnificent mahogany bed that has been in their apartments in the Hofburg in Vienna. Climbing up onto it, she wriggled slowly on her knees, her breasts jiggling just slightly as she moved between his long, slender, bare legs.

Kneeling up, her breasts at his eye level, Eileen finished unwinding his stock, playfully tossing its balled-up fabric over her shoulder and then slowly, deliberately unbuttoned his shirt, opening it, slipping it off his shoulders, leaving O'Leary as naked as she. Her hands behind his neck, Eileen leaned to her husband, her lover, and kissed him powerfully, their heads moving gently as their mouths found each other, and as O'Leary's cold hands—Eileen ignored the feeling—rested first on her hips, then beneath her firm, ample bottom.

They held each other, kissing and touching, murmuring softly for neither knew how long, until O'Leary eased Eileen's head onto her pillows, onto her back and knelt between her long, slender legs, bending to her, his blond-fuzzed chest pressing against her bosom. He kissed her, then they kissed long, languidly, soft moans in the chill, tranquil air of the room, until he began to lick her throat and shoulders, her breasts, his tongue teasing her hard nipples, twirling, circling them, lingering for a time, softly kissing, sucking her left breast, momentarily sensing the aroma, the taste of her milk, drawing his tongue, his lips over her flat, smooth stomach, licking her thigh creases and kissing, then licking, her bare, only slightly fuzzed mound. Her giggle was quickly silenced as her legs reflexively fell open, his tongue finding her warm wetness, her gasped silence quickly becoming long, soft moans as he slid his tongue into her, his hands—warmer now—resting on, gently squeezing her firm, athletic thighs . . . his tongue licking, darting, flicking into Eileen's depths, her scent powerful, her nectar intoxicating to her long-absent lover. His hands firm, his head and mouth moving slowly, almost imperceptively, Eileen arched and moaned, at one point gasping, "Ahhhhh—stop!" only to have O'Leary do precisely that. Her eyes wide, chest heaving, she sat bolt upright, her hands sharply reached forward, roughly grasping his head, pushing his mouth back down to her, as, lying back, she arched up to him, her head back into the pillows, lifting, writhing against his mouth, his face, moaning softly and then not softly, until a long *ahhhhhhhhhhhhhhhhgawwwwwwwwwd* began to rise from deep within her, as her body rose up and thrashed, her long arms stretched above her pillows, toward the bed's intricately carved headboard, the *ahhhhhhhhhhhhhhgawwwwwwwwwd* finally filling the room, undoubtedly echoing throughout the silent, sleeping house until O'Leary covered her mouth with his own. The room suddenly stilled, save for their breathing and the soft rustling of the fine cotton sheets and Austrian covers.

Moving gently, O'Leary drew the stacked, puffy quilts over them as he snuggled next to his still slightly panting wife, his left arm gently draped over her, his palm resting on her rising, then falling right breast. Thus, there they lay for a time, whispering—Fiach had stirred briefly—softly, teasing, joking, touching, kissing and then in silence, perhaps one of them, perhaps both had nodded off.

The tall, massively, intricately cabinetted clock in the front hall bonged twice, or so Eileen would recall: *perhaps 'twas only a single bonnnnng . . . or perhaps 'twas three*, she would laugh over their breakfast coffee.

Whatever time deep in the night it was, Eileen stirred, stretched and wriggled to her husband, kissing him softly, then not so softly, her lips moving over his throat and neck, teasing his hard nipples until he sleepily laughed aloud.

"I desire you . . . *I shall have you, soldier*," she growled, uncovering his nakedness . . . then almost immediately covering it with her own. She threw her long right leg over him and was quickly astride her husband, instinctively, reflexively impaling herself upon him. She bent forward, her breasts full and warm on his chest. "Fuck me, soldier . . . 'tis been too long, sir!" she smiled.

O'Leary answered, "*Too bloody long indeed, woman!*" and he did, and she did, and they did; he arched, and she rode, her fine, long fingers resting on his chest, his shoulders, – both of them demanding, giving, demanding, taking . . . until O'Leary reared up, shocking Eileen as he tumbled her onto her back, her legs open, knees up as she reached for him, pulling him roughly towards her even as he was entering her. . . .

"Mmhhhhh, yes, yes! Like *that*!" she practically snarled in her husky voice, O'Leary responding with a sharper thrust of his loins, wondering aloud, ". . . or perhaps like *this*?" Her eyes burnt and her sharp, albeit clipped nails tore down his smooth back; the tiny rivulets of blood that flowed would become minute gossamer, threadlike scabs.

They thrashed and rolled and tore at each other, kissing, biting, an almost violent mutual ravishing, until Eileen finally rumbled a singular profundity, "Fuck!" as her body arched and shuddered upwards and then lay flat. Momentarily, O'Leary thrusted deep into her darkness—once, twice, again and again . . . *ahhhhhhhgawwdfuck*, finally releasing, flooding her, *yesssssssssssssssssssssfuckkkkkkk.*

They lay silent, breathing hard, skin moist, their bodies sprawled, at first uncovered, then burrowing, finally nestling, entwined beneath the luxuriously warm quilts against the chill of the room. Spent, with scant conversation, they finally dozed off in the soft depths of the night, Eileen's hair pulled to one side and away, her bare back and bottom snuggled up against her husband, O'Leary's arm draped lovingly, protectively about his wife.

O'Leary slept soundly through the night, whilst at some point Eileen was sufficiently awake that she reflected drowsily that, as he had arrived the previous day, she'd immediately thought how very much he appeared as he did that day in the Market Square more than five years prior, "How magnificent you were, how grand you remain . . . my darling, my husband, father of our sons. . . ."

Paris and Versailles—Spring 1772

Hugh was en route to what he feared might prove to be an exceptionally dull lecture on something referred to simply as "mobile fortifications" one surprisingly chilly early May morning, when he was intercepted on a stairway by a very junior cadet, whom he did not know well, whose name he continued to forget; Jean Claude *Someone* came to mind. "Your brother is here, *sir,* to speak on some topic," the younger boy announced, "I have just learned of this, *sir.*" Late, as he still frequently was despite his efforts to be more prompt, not bothering to yet again remind the young man that he should never address another cadet as "sir." Hugh nodded his thanks, taking the remaining stairs two and then three at a time, his boots clicking on the marble floors as he approached the small lecture hall.

Mindful of the early hour, that the usually vibrant building was just now awakening, as quietly as possible he closed the massive high, dark wooden door behind him. As he did, Hugh smiled as, leaning casually against the ornately carved podium, the only attempt at elegance in the otherwise-stark hall, was indeed Captain Daniel Charles O'Connell, in the distinctive long red coat of Lord Clare's Regiment of the Irish Brigade. Hugh gestured a greeting and looked to join his fellows when Daniel crooked several fingers, beckoning him to step in his direction, moving in Hugh's as he did.

Halting, then standing in front of the first row of seats, the brothers smiled and quickly shook hands, Daniel at the same time lifting his other one in the familiar upraised palm gesture he used when he wished to speak.

"Maintain a straight face, say nothing, lad," he said softly. Hugh visibly stiffened—he loathed surprises, feeling they were invariably bad news— though his brother then smiled. "I am just come from a quick word—at his behest—from Monsieur Colonel Registrar Depuis." His smile grew even broader. "The old boy advises that you will indeed be commissioned in a matter of weeks. They have been vetting a number of you lads to determine if they had a sufficient group of new sub-lieutenants to foist on the active service." He laughed. "I have not seen any list, and I know of only the 'foreign regiments,' but O'Connor from Galway . . . he's to be with Lord Clare and my good self," he laughed again, "and, for the Royal Suédois, a very tall, almost gaunt Swede with dark hair . . ."

"Nielsen!" Hugh interrupted. "He is Lars; he says he is the only black-haired Swede *ever*! A good fellow, an impressive marksman . . . "

Daniel's palm was again upraised. "They complete the complement of a dozen or so of you lads, so . . . well done, brother!" They shook hands, and Hugh saluted him crisply. "Just do not fall bloody asleep during my talk, Cadet!" Daniel whispered.

Though he noted several of his classmates nodding, neither they nor Hugh actually dozed off. He would later on admit to his brother that he'd found it difficult to remain alert as the topic was indeed, and as he had feared it would be, "dreadfully boring." He did not bother to mention that he found his brother's usually lyrical, pleasantly lilting voice, reduced to a dull monotone whenever he lectured, whether it was in French or English.

On the brilliantly sunny morning of 18 May, Hugh, along with an even dozen of his fellow soon-to-be-officers—the three Irishmen jested aloud that the full complement constituted a "baker's dozen," necessitating an explanation, provided hastily by Hugh, to their puzzled fellows—strolled from their barracks for the last time as cadets. Each young man was wearing for the first time the officer's uniform of his individual regiment. Save for the Irishmen and the lone Swede, the new sub-lieutenants were native Frenchmen, being commissioned into a variety of regular French regiments, divided by geography as well as purpose, their duties ranging from infantry and cavalry, to artillery and engineering.

In terms of the foreign brigades, Hugh was the only new officer being commissioned into the Dillons' prestigious regiment, whilst two other men—the O'Connor, one Joseph, of whom Daniel had previously spoken, along with Charles O'Neill, both from County Clare,—would be entering Lord Clare's Regiment. Commissioned into the Royal Swedish would indeed be Hugh's virtually singular black-haired friend, Lars Nielsen.

Without forethought, Nielsen and Hugh had ambled ahead of the rest of the group, each admiring the other's new raiment, the Swede's uniform consisting of a striking dark-blue coat with buff collar and cuffs, a white ruffled shirt, a blue waistcoat and snug buff breeches. Over a belted white waistcoat, Hugh wore a high, stiff-collared, brilliantly red-tailed coat, with gleaming brass buttons, yellow facings and cuffs and tightly fitting white breeches. Both sported well-made black tricorn hats, Hugh's being the more ornate with gold braid trim as well as being topped by a regimental badge and a small, smart-looking feather, their nearly identical high black boots shone in the bright May sun as they strode across the Cour des Exercises. Their destination was the Chapelle Saint-Louis, the military academy's magnificent church, just completed the year before, its foundation stone having been laid by Louis XV himself in June of 1769, where the simple ceremony would be held.

Having already been advised that the event would be brief, and its attendance limited—it was commonly referred to as being little more than *une petite affaire de famille*—the young men were surprised, shocked actually, by the large—by a quick count, several dozen men—contingent of mounted troops, a sextet arrayed about the entrance to the church, the remainder largely circling the perimeter of the open space. As they drew closer, they took further note of a pair of elegant closed coaches, each with its own contingent of civilian mounted outriders, the much larger group of horsemen bedecked in the by-now largely unmistakable red-white-and-blue livery of the King of France himself, the use of the tricolour first begun only in 1770.

The other, smaller cluster of horsemen, whom Hugh instantly recognised, were themselves clothed in the distinctive soft blue and gold hues of the eminent Bourbon-Penthièvre family, together indicating to the stunned young Irishman the probable and wholly unexpected presence of the sovereign and his bride-to-be.

Stopping abruptly, reflexively grabbing Nielsen's upper arm, Hugh gasped, "Bloody hell, man, *Louise*. She is here!"

Before he could say anything about the king, smiling through his own shock, the Swede exclaimed, "Bloody hell to *ye!*" laughing aloud at how his attempt to employ the Irish idiom sounded with a Swedish accent. "Look closer, see . . . *there* . . . the tricolour . . . unless he loans out his conveyances . . . and his outriders, and his cavalry . . . His Majesty, the King of France *himself*, he graces *notre petite affaire de famille* as well!" He laughed again, this time clapping his soon-to-be brother officer on the back. "*And* I do believe that *both* of them are here solely on your account, brother!" Hugh's cheeks flamed.

Having shocked themselves into silence, straightening their backs, heads held high, both young men strode quickly towards and up the steps of the magnificent church, where they were joined by their fellows as well as by a well-known, highly officious lieutenant named Desautels, a young man small in stature and large in ego who announced grandly that for this "auspicious occasion of your commissioning," he would be acting as *maître des cérémonies*. "You shall thus follow my every direction, monsieurs! Each and every one, oui? . . . oui!"

Save for Hugh, who stared somewhat blankly across the school's well-kept grounds, each of the other twelve young men displayed some measure of mirth, nudging one another, rolling their eyes; whilst one laughed, several chuckled. Lieutenant Desautels ignored them. The source of their humour was that the occasion was so simply done, they'd been told that all they had to do was line up in a single file; they knew the order to follow. It being by height, Hugh O'Connell would be the last cadet to enter, walk slowly up the church's centre aisle and, alternatingly, from left to right, stand shoulder to shoulder at the altar rail of the impressive church.

To Desautels's frustration, having formed their order of march themselves, the young men knowingly awaited what would be a resoundingly powerful blare of brass from within, the hornsmen having formed in the gallery at the rear of the church, running its full width, supported by four ionic columns. The joyous noise blaring, the two main doors of the church were flung open by a pair of very young other-ranks, their eyes wide at the sight of boys not much older than they, knowing that they were to become officers of the king! And, as if on Desautels's order, tout de suite! *immédiatement!* the column processed into the magnificent church. As they entered slowly, their headgear now tucked under their arms in some fashion, the young men in the column appeared to their seniors suitably solemn, there were no expressions of wonder. They regularly attended Mass here, it was their church.

Their walk was neither a short nor a lengthy one, the brilliantly white-walled church measuring not quite 150 feet from the gleaming mahogany main doors to the striking, larger-than-life portrait of St. Louis, whom Hugh had always felt appeared to be floating amidst the clouds of Heaven, above the main altar, the building's width slightly more than forty feet. A profusion of intricate Corinthian columns provided support to an arched vault as well as grace to the interior. The church consisted of a unique rectangular nave divided into eight equal spans, the last of which forming the chancel.

As he walked at the end of the line, Hugh yet again took in the stark white brilliance of the interior, which made the dazzling array of various shades of red and blue, as well as the black uniforms of the seated officers, including the commanding officers of the regiments into which the new officers were being commissioned, all the more striking. His eyes straight ahead, he gazed at the chancel, especially at a pair of doors on either side wall, which permitted entrance to the sacristy, above which were galleries where guests of importance were seated for Mass. As he drew closer to the front, his eyes went first to the left, then to the right gallery; both were unoccupied.

It was only as Hugh reached the altar rail, his position being almost at the centre of the gleaming brass barrier, that the music ceased, instantly replaced by a profound silence.

After several long moments, the left door, and then the right, were opened very slowly.

Almost immediately, through the one to the left stepped King Louis XV, festive in a bright red, heavily gold-brocaded coat, snug white breeches and hose, wearing gleaming, slightly high-heeled, gold-buckled black shoes. For the occasion, the only decoration he had chosen was the magnificent Cross of the Holy Spirit, the insignia of the Ordre du Saint-Esprit, the highest order of chivalry in France, which, according to their custom, was suspended from his neck on *le cordon bleu.*

His deep black eyes and lashes contrasted sharply with his flawlessly powdered hair, the difference all the more marked by his broad forehead. The assembled officers rose, and then immediately dropped to their right knees almost as one, heads bowed, until, with a smile, the king almost casually gestured to them to rise.

At that moment, perhaps even more dramatically, the young woman known to virtually all the assembled as the Princess de Lamballe appeared through the right-hand door, on the arm of the eminent, elegant Louis Jean Marie de Bourbon, the Duke of Penthièvre. Releasing herself from her father-in-law's arm, the duke then being escorted to a seat in the first row of pews, Lamballe immediately performed a deep curtsey to the king. As their eyes met, the sovereign gestured for her to rise, a gentle smile on his still-handsome face.

Hugh could not help but admire Louise's stunning, long-trained robe of deep Kerry green, the gold brocade delicate and subtle, with full sleeves, featuring ample décolletage beneath a sparkling, multitiered diamond choker. Her deep golden hair was, save for several dazzling, well-placed large diamond stickpins, loose, resting on her trim shoulders.

As she rose from her curtsey, her eyes went immediately to Hugh, and she smiled softly.

The king having taken his seat on a small, gilded throne, Lamballe likewise did so on a smaller, plainer, albeit still gilded, high-backed chair on the other side of the sacristy, directly across from the monarch, the assembled now sitting as well.

As they did, a hush again fell over the church, as Lieutenant General Jacques René Croismare, governor of the school since 1768, stepped slowly to the open gate in the altar rail. As he approached it, the distinguished officer, the sash and badge of the Grand Cross of the Order of St. Louis, one of the highest honours in France, splayed across his chest, turned back and bowed gently to both royals. He then turned to face the group, consisting of perhaps fifty officers, professors, teachers and staff, as well as the more senior cadets, numbering perhaps some sixty young men.

It was at the conclusion of the general's brief, almost perfunctionary remarks that the to-be-commissioned officers were called up by name in the order of march. Each young man received a brisk handshake from the governor, whilst junior officers from their respective regiments pinned subtle indications of their rank, depending on the individual regiment's custom, on their lower sleeves, cuffs or collars.

When it was finally Hugh's turn, his fellow graduates by now standing at attention lining the walls of the sacristy, six on each side, he stepped forward, facing General Croismare who, after a firm handshake, with a nod of his head, joined by the now-standing monarch doing likewise, gestured for the princess to approach them.

Rising dramatically, arranging her vast skirts, she crossed the sacristy slowly, deliberately, her train reaching from where she had been seated to where she stood, as she dipped into a demi-curtsey to the king. A clearly awed Captain Desautels, who had been standing behind General Croismare, bowed and offered her a small silver tray, upon which, on a cloth of red velvet, rested a pair of simple bronze oval chevrons, each subtly engraved with a spray of shamrocks. Her hands shaking ever so slightly, with the thumb and long, slender forefinger of her right hand, she retrieved one and then the other, slowly, precisely affixing them in sequence, first to the right side, then to the left of Hugh's high, rigid collar.

Her task completed, her soft blue eyes moist, resting on Hugh's, she momentarily stood still. She turned her eyes to the king, who nodded almost imperceptibly. At that, she formally kissed Hugh on both cheeks, whilst holding his hands. "I am so proud of you, my darling," she whispered, "so very proud!" Hugh's eyes suddenly misty, he managed only to mouth an unspoken, "Merci."

The ceremony completed, as ordered and led by Captain Desautels, the now-commissioned officers of the armies of Louis XV withdrew from the church in double file, marching slowly down the steps to the approximate centre of the Cour des Exercises, thence taking a sharply ordered, precisely executed right turn, they then faced a secondary entrance to the Refectoire, where a bountiful feast of hearty foods and fine wines awaited them and their commanders and a select group of fellow junior officers.

The small contingent was immediately followed by the assembled officers, a small number of whom proceeded at almost march step, others striding briskly, most strolling casually, many of them in animated conversation.

Well to the rear of all the soldiers slowly sauntered Louis XV and the princess, who had gathered her voluminous train and draped much of it over her right shoulder, as she had learnt from Hugh the manner in which Highlanders wore their plaid, chatting amiably, the king jesting as he invariably did, at least when in Louise's company, of "how very close"—although it actually had not been at all—the two had come to marrying, following the death of Queen Marie Leszczynska, the sovereign's long-suffering wife. Indeed, Lamballe had done all she could to avoid the marriage, experiencing vast relief when it became clear the king had no desire to wed anyone. He still occasionally, including this afternoon, playfully addressed her as "my queen," which never failed to make the princess exceedingly uncomfortable. Other than this, however, today had been rather pleasant, the king, having been made familiar with her and Hugh's romance, recalled for her how very much he'd liked the young Irishman the first time he'd met him, when he was introduced by Marie Antoinette. When he unsubtly observed, "We assume that you and your dashing new officer will be paying your most benevolent king a visit . . . sometime soon, Your Highness. We shall look forward to seeing you both." Lamballe blushed, laughed somewhat uneasily and changed the subject, nevertheless pleased both that his words were positive as well as that the entrance was now but a few more steps ahead.

The enjoyable gathering that followed the brief ceremony was indeed sufficiently informal to seem much like a family occasion, with the usual formalities being dispensed with. The young, newly commissioned men mingled easily with both the more junior officers as well as those of lofty rank, most of whom appeared to go out of their way to be both approachable and convivial. The food, set out on the dining room's long tables, proved to be quite superb, as did the selection of fine wines.

Louis XV ate and imbibed freely, atypically moving about the large hall alone, as casually as anyone in attendance. He sought out his newest officers and made a point of speaking with each more-than-slightly awed young man individually. It was only as he joined Hugh and Louise, who were visiting with the also-young—he was but twenty-three—Colonel Arthur Dillon, now and since 1767 the hereditary commander and proprietor of the proud regiment that had borne his family's name since 1653, that a number of people stopped to take notice.

The conversation amongst the four was informal, even light, and there was considerable laughter. At one point, the monarch referred to Louise again as "my queen," causing Hugh to playfully take her hand and, kissing the back of it, smiling guilelessly, said, "*Mais non, Majesté* . . . my hope, my prayer is that Her Highness will soon become *my* queen!" Though Louis smiled playfully, there had been an inevitable moment of awkward silence until the king, first feigning a sad expression, then the weeping of a dejected suitor, caused them all to laugh heartily.

After light-heartedly clapping Hugh on the shoulder and taking his hand, Louis shook it firmly and then, cocking his head, tugged him aside momentarily, speaking quietly to the new sub-lieutenant. "I recall when first we met, I concluded then you were, shall we say, *different*. And so you are. I understand from Crossmaire that you are both bright and talented, that you ride better than the best and your marksmanship is impressive, that you have the makings of an excellent officer . . . oh, and *oui*, your taste in women, it is *obviously* superb!" He laughed genuinely. His face serious again, he added, "I shall expect much from you, O'Connell, *much indeed!*" As the king turned away, Hugh's face was red, his heart pounding.

After having visited with many of his senior officers and all of his most junior ones, Louis made a gracious and—save for the polite applause of those gathered—gracefully quiet exit, General Crossmaire escorting him to his coach.

As senior as well as junior officers and guests observed, throughout the rest of the afternoon, Hugh effortlessly—and unintentionally—overshadowed his fellows, and in truth, as soon as the king departed, he and Louise in many ways dominated the proceedings. Both taller by some inches than most in attendance, the princess, obviously well-known, though pleasantly surprising virtually all by her ebullient manner, so different from her reputation, whilst Hugh was clearly more at ease than any of his new fellow officers . . . indeed, Louise reflected that never had he been more graceful in any setting, certainly not one as daunting as this. He was neither casual nor in any way familiar but simply altogether at ease, as was she.

Later, having taken their leave of General Crossmaire, the attractive couple walked arm in arm to the Penthièvre coach. "So, my love, you were surprised, *non*?" Louise playfully inquired. Hugh stopped, turned her to him almost brusquely and kissed her firmly.

"I was surprised, yes!" He laughed.

Patting his arm, she smiled. "Good . . . that was my intent, and once having decided to come, I could not resist inviting *ton très bon ami*, Louis to join us." Hugh's eyes became wide.

"You did not tell him . . . you did not share with him what I had said about . . ."

Her right hand behind his head, Louise kissed her future husband as forcefully as he had her but did not answer his question.

Within a week of the event, Hugh and Louise hosted Colonel Dillon and his wife, Thérèse-Lucie, at an intimate dinner at the magnificent Hôtel de Toulouse. Originally acquired in 1712 by the Duc de Penthièvre's father, Louis Alexandre de Bourbon, who had become the Count of Toulouse in 1681, upon his legitimisation at the age of three by his father, Louis XIV, the mansion, not far from the Louvre, had undergone significant renovations. Louise had continued to maintain it as her Paris residence after joining the dauphine's household. Whether, once wed, she and Hugh would retain the living arrangement as their own was one reason for dining with the Dillons.

Without advising Louise that he'd planned to do so, Hugh had guilelessly mentioned in a brief, respectful note to his commanding officer that they would like to pay a call on the Dillons at the imposing residence of Lucie's mother, Madame de Rothe, in the relatively new, fashionable Faubourg Saint-Germain, on the left bank of the Seine, where the couple lived with their three-month-old daughter.

Reading his newest sub-lieutenant's carefully written message, Arthur Dillon could only laugh affectionately, remembering his own level of naivete as to many protocol-related matters not all that long ago, and made a point to seek out young O'Connell, which he did the following morning, as Hugh strode from an early breakfast.

"O'Connell!" Dillon had merrily called out, quickening his step as Hugh had halted, standing at attention. Smiling, the shorter, less-handsome—a friend at one time had observed that "he resembled a parrot eating a cherry"—Dillon smiled. "At ease, Monsieur," and Hugh relaxed. "We— Thérèse-Lucie and I—should love to welcome you to our home, but, Hugh, my dear man, *c'est impossible!*" Hugh's shock was evident; *dear Lord, what type of breach of protocol have I committed* now? until Dillon clapped him reassuringly on the shoulder. "Ah, 'tis no great worry, man . . . just something you are not yet used to." Hugh breathed easily again as the colonel reminded him, "You must be ever mindful that your future spouse . . . your very own *Princess of the Blood* . . . 'tis *she* who requests the presence of any individuals she might deign to host, or *commands* anyone whom she might wish to be hosted by, when and where she chooses to do either!"

Hugh finally managed an unspoken "O," his mouth forming the letter, causing Dillon to laugh and clap him on his left arm playfully.

Colonel Dillon advised Hugh that he and his wife would "be honoured to dine with you, either as your humble hosts or most-honoured guests," offhandedly suggesting that Hugh discuss it with the princess and "let me know her pleasure—and yours, sir!" He then smiled and walked away.

As it was, it worked out well for both couples to dine at the Hôtel de Toulouse, approximately a week later. Just having completed a week of field training exercises for a number of new recruits recently arrived from Ireland, both officers were in Paris, whilst Louise had already planned several days in the city and, as Hugh and Louise would learn, it was especially pleasant for the Dillons to be out of their home for an evening, as they related to their host and hostess that the tumultuous household at 91 rue de Bac was in an even more advanced state of interfamilial turmoil than was usually the case.

Louise was especially taken by Lady Dillon; Thérèse-Lucie was tall and slender, almost too thin, albeit very pretty in a wispy, delicate way. Only very recently a mother, she appeared weary but had a sweet, gentle way about her, to which Louise was drawn. Away from the men, the princess posed a flurry of questions about love, marriage and "babies," causing Lucie to blush on several occasions, though the younger woman listened patiently and was candid and open, "Arthur and I, we are actually cousins and, despite our French birth, we are both of County Roscommon stock."

She paused, uncertain of the princess's knowledge of Ireland, but smiling, and pleasantly surprised, when Louise easily interjected, " . . . whilst cousins Hugh and I most definitely are not; *we* when we do become a *we*"— she laughed joyfully—"we will be said to be of County Kerry stock!"

Lucie then asked her own questions of how the two had met, the circumstances and particulars; after Louise related their story in some detail, Lucie seemed to become slightly wistful. "Ah, a true love match you have, Highness ... how lovely, how special and how very rare, especially at Versailles and in Paris." Sensing that her new friend's own tale was perhaps less of a love story than her own, Louise smiled softly and, she would tell Hugh later, "felt truly blest."

As their conversation continued, the princess emphasised that, " *Laoise* would be my preferred form of address, *Lucie*." She smiled, as did the young Madame Dillon.

During the course of the relatively simple, albeit elegantly presented meal, when the would-be O'Connells first mentioned what Hugh referred to as being their "complex situation," Arthur laughed aloud, though his quiet wife did not. "Few are more 'complex' than ..." He gestured to her and himself, then in the general direction of the Left Bank, the location of the majestic residence where they dwelt with Lucie's seemingly autocratically domineering grandmother, the widowed Madame de Rothe, along with, much of the time, an apparently much more docile Archbishop Richard Dillon of Toulouse and Narbonne, long reputed to be her lover. "Complex indeed," laughed the youthful colonel. Noting that Thérèse-Lucie's smile was forced, Louise reached out to squeeze her hand.

As coffee and pastries were served, Louise peeked at a small card upon which she'd made some notes. Addressing her questions to Lucie, she wondered, "Is it possible for us, without ruffling any royal or regimental feathers," she said, "to 'reside' at Toulouse, whilst Hugh is not with the regiment, especially given the flexibility of my arrangement with the dauphine?"

Lucie nodded softly. "I believe so, *oui*, Highness." She instantly blushed, as if she remembered that the princess had made it clear she wished a friendship with her. Louise having smiled warmly, with a soft smile, Lucie finished, "That you, my dear, are indeed a Princesse du Sang ... this makes these concerns somewhat less delicate."

Hugh expounded very briefly about his sisters' living arrangements at the Habsburgs' palaces, " . . . and these comfortable quarters and their lives there, they seemed quite pleasant."

Dillon nodded, qualifying, "Of this I have little doubt, but based on what I have heard from you and others, relatively certain also am I that life in Vienna and with the Habsburgs is far simpler and less stressful than 'tis here with the Bourbons. One example being that, as you say, Maria Theresa has 'simplified' protocol, whilst here, 'tis as cumbersome, indeed perhaps more so than it has *ever* been!"

Lucie sighed deeply and shook her head sardonically.

Hearing that their living arrangements would prove not to be an issue, especially considering the stifling atmosphere at court, Louise and Hugh had smiled with relief. And the atmosphere became even lighter as, with both Dillons' thoughtful advice, they decided that very evening to have a relatively small wedding at the chapel at Toulouse. "You would of course invite the king, the royal family and others of your choice," Arthur said, and volunteered to be his newest officer's best man. The offer was instantly accepted with a clink of brandy glasses, and laughter all around.

Indeed when the young couple ultimately wed, in the ornate chapel at the Hôtel Toulouse the Sunday following Christmas 1772, Arthur Dillon was at O'Connell's right side, whilst Thérèse-Lucie was Louise's matron-of-honour. In addition to a scattering of Bourbon-Penthièvre relatives and Daniel O'Connell, in attendance would be the king of France, sans Madame Du Barry, and the dauphin and dauphine of France. Both the guests and the newly wed O'Connells would all agree that it was a lovely, elegant and beautiful wedding. Whilst it and the luncheon following were underway, Hugh's clothing—military and civilian—as well as his numerous books and other belongings, which had been in his small apartment at the far end of the sprawling mansion would be moved into Louise's sumptuous quarters.

The question of whether Lamballe's seemingly vast independent wealth could prove problematic was dismissed as not presenting any significant issue, as Lucie quietly observed, "Everyone at Versailles behaves and lives as if they were all fantastically wealthy when, in truth, most are deeply in debt and many exist—it cannot be said that under such circumstances they 'live'—in constant dread of bankruptcy," her husband adding, "The difference is that you, my dear Laoise"—he gestured to the princess—"you are understood to be quite wealthy, so 'tis no issue. The lieutenant's pay will of course 'help' at least a wee bit anyway!" He laughed, as did they all.

The last small bit of advice, distilled from a series of comments made by both Dillons, was perhaps the wisest of all: Spend as little time as possible at Versailles, avoid the internal strife that always seemed to be rife at, as Arthur put it, "the bloody dammed place" and to be extremely careful in choosing one's friends.

It was late June, little more than a month after Hugh's commissioning, when the Duke of Penthièvre succeeded in interceding with Louis XV on the young couple's behalf, arranging for them what he was assured would be a carefully, well-crafted audience with the sovereign, which would occur in the king's private apartments.

By the grace and favour of the duke, Hugh had only just recently been given his own small suite of apartments, located discreetly two floors above and at the opposite end of the massive Hôtel de Toulouse from Louise's own much-larger, considerably more ornate quarters, thus avoiding any whiff of scandal in the gossip-prone household and city.

On the morning of their meeting with the king, having breakfasted together in the duke's small, intimate personal dining room, as the couple strolled down the majestic, multifloored main staircase of the Hôtel, Hugh's uniform was impeccable, his elegant, gold-braided tricorn hat slipped under his arm. For the occasion, Louise had selected a simple forest-green, gossamer, light-muslin afternoon dress with a less dramatic train than she normally favoured. Both were unusually subdued as they stepped outside into the brilliantly warm late June sunshine, the horses' hoofs and the black wheels of the coach crunching on the well-groomed gravel. Hugh smiled when he noticed that Louise had ordered 'her' coach: the one she had always taken to visit him at the military academy. He liked the cosy, deep-leather cushioned interior.

As the elegant conveyance clattered out into the midmorning streets of Paris, the young couple held hands, each quietly gazing out the windows at the bustling scenes about them. "I . . ." began Hugh, just as Louise started, "Do you . . ." and their laughter eased the tension, but only slightly.

"I am," Hugh tried again, "just a wee bit anxious," he admitted.

Squeezing his ungloved hand with her own, the princess inquired softly, "Why, darling? Of what are you apprehensive? After all, are we not simply journeying out to visit *ton très bon ami*, Louis?" she said affectionately.

His hand resting gently on her thigh, his face suddenly hot, the young officer smiled weakly, silently wishing he'd never spoken so casually of his "close, even intimate"—he rolled his eyes—relationship with the sovereign. "What if he says 'no'?" he asked softly.

Taking his hand into both of her own, as she had when first they met in the gardens of Versailles, Lamballe laughed genuinely, warmly. "He will *not* refuse us, darling, he *cannot* refuse *me*!" she answered firmly, "I believe the old roué may actually have some fondness for me . . . and the duke advises he looks very kindly on you, my love. Also, I am fairly certain that somewhere in his complex make-up remains a small measure of decency that virtually compels him to grant such a request. Indeed, darling, to permit us to be wed, and to be happy, costs him nothing and provides him with at least two more people who . . . who at least do not loathe him, as so many do these days." They both laughed tentatively.

After a few moments of silence, the creaking of the wheels, the thudding of the horses' hoofs on the rough road the only sounds, the princess queried mischievously, "So, Monsieur Lieutenant, my darling, would it matter to you if our first child were not a 'wee lad'?" As her husband-to-be's cheeks flamed an even brighter red, and Louise laughed heartily and hugged him tightly. In the embrace, Hugh whispered in her ear, "A pair of twin girls would be no less welcome than a 'wee lad,' my love."

Their moods lightened even more, as did their conversation as they progressed on the gentle coach ride out to Versailles, joking about the current minor scandals of the court, the princess trying to recollect when she was last in the company of Madame Du Barry, Hugh recalling Arthur Dillon's cautions avoiding the "dammed place," as he referred to Versailles, which they agreed they would, at least to the extent possible.

The elegant coach, its sextet of outriders in near-perfect formation, two in front of the team, one on each side of the coach and two behind it, after a bit more than an hour finally turned briskly off the Paris road, the handsome animals' hoofs clattering on the paving stones, the bulk that was Versailles looming closer and closer. The massive chapel dramatically on their right, a far-less-so parallel wing to its left, jutting into the massive entry courtyard.

The coach slowed as it approached the recessed Marble Courtyard, which Louise told Hugh had been the entrance court to the original chateau, built by Louis XIII, smilingly lowering her eyes. "Though I know not the year, my love." The expanse was paved in black-and-white-marble squares, laid in a geometric pattern. As the coach halted at the edge of the marble, the footmen immediately stepped off their perch at the rear of the conveyance and opened both doors so the couple could exit at the same time, Hugh stepping out on the side away from the palace.

Hugh came around the rear of the coach, and as soon as Louise slipped her arm in his, the couple traversed the striking space in long, youthful strides.

As they approached the entrance, they were greeted by the king's own footmen, two bowing deeply to the princess whilst one less-senior boy hastened ahead to open the door.

Just above where they'd crossed the courtyard and to the right was that part of the king's rambling, commodious apartments known formally as the Privé Cabinet, though more frequently referred to simply as the "corner room." Entering a large, open vestibule, Hugh's boots clicked sharply as he strode across the marble floor, whilst the princess, now employing as she rarely did the idiosyncratic Versailles glide, which involved a woman taking dainty, bouncing steps beneath the volumes of her skirts, so she appeared to float at his side.

Having scaled a relatively simple staircase, they threaded their way through a labyrinth of short halls and several rooms until they arrived at a massive, dark mahogany door, which was immediately opened from within. "How did . . . ?" Hugh began, though the princess silenced him with a wink.

Admitted by a bewigged, magnificently liveried older servant, his coat a rich, deep-blue velvet, his breeches and stockings dazzlingly white, he conducted the couple deeper into the king's rooms, indicating they should stop some feet behind him as they reached a simple door, which, as he opened it, his voice strong as he announced, "*Votre Majesté, Son Altesse Royal, la Princesse de Lamballe . . . et . . .*" he hesitated, as if he found it difficult to announce Hugh at the same time as he was announcing a Princess of the Blood, and lowering his voice by several octaves, he finally concluded, " . . . et *sous*-Lieutenant O'Connell, *de la Brigade Irlandaise de Votre Majesté!*"

The room they entered was spoken of as being one of Louis XV's favourites amongst the collection that made up his apartments. The couple took note of the elegant, eye-catching wooden panels, sculpted on-site by the artist Jacques Verbeckt in the mid-1750s. Hugh also glanced at the sovereign's celebrated cylinder desk, the singular design of which was said to enable the monarch to quickly shield his papers from the prying eyes of ministers and servants.

From the far side of the room, seated before a large window, Louis gestured for them to approach. Louise dipped into a deep curtsey as Hugh executed a similarly profound one-kneed bow, lowering his head but noticing the king was casually dressed, in a light tan cotton suit and a nondescript linen shirt, his shoeless, white-stockinged feet incongruously stretched out on the floor before his high-backed chair. The monarch neither rose nor did he extend his hand to the young couple but simply gestured for them to "*Asseyez-vous s'il vous plait,*" indicating a pair of nondescript cushioned armchairs, obviously positioned opposite his own for this occasion.

Even as they'd entered the room, the princess and Hugh were surprised, shocked even, to find the woman they both knew was the du Barry perched on the left arm of Louis's chair, massaging his neck, whispering in his ear, being very familiar with him even as they—the monarch, as well as his genteel supplicants—began to speak, the trio being very proper and suitably serious, given the nature of the conversation.

"*Majesté*," Hugh began, "*Nous vous remercions de prendre le temps de nous voir ce matin.*"

Louis smiled and gestured at the two of them. "It is always a pleasure to spend time with such a delightful young couple.

"I am also aware, O'Connell, of the purpose of our conversation. I alluded to this in speaking with she who would be *your* bride," he smiled at Louise, "when we were at École Militaire for your commissioning." He appeared relaxed and, contrary to how he often was, genuine.

"Indeed let us make this easier, my children: The King," smiling broadly, Louis playfully sat up straighter, "The King most graciously decrees and grants," he stretched out his right arm grandly "to you, both individually and collectively, all rights and privileges and powers such as are or may be necessary in order for you to wed, this, despite the, shall we say, not insignificant disparity in your respective positions at court and in life." He paused dramatically, finishing with a gracious flourish, "We also happily bestow our blessings on you and on your now-forthcoming marriage." He laughed affectionately.

Louise held Hugh's hand tightly, her eyes bright, her cheeks glowing. Hugh smiled gently, an expression of relief as much as anything else on his face.

The momentary calm was almost instantly shattered. "*The King* is indeed most kind, most gracious, is he not, *children*!" interjected du Barry loudly in her rough-edged voice, causing Louis to sigh and remove her arm from his.

Appearing impatient, he hissed, "*Shhhhhhhhhhh*, woman."

Seemingly oblivious to her lover, du Barry prattled on, inquiring, "I have been wondering, why should you even wish to wed, children? You are so young. You are so handsome." She practically leered at them. "Do you not wish to savour the pleasures of, shall I say, others. . . perhaps many others?" She laughed wickedly, almost caustically; indeed as Louise would later observe, "most crudely!" especially as she then patted the monarch's thigh and added, "Though, I will tell you, I—*I* who have savoured much and many—now feast on only one! As does my lover on me!"

A chilling, powerful, beyond-awkward silence filled the room. Louis's face was enflamed, his hands forming a pair of fists, as du Barry remained perched on the chair arm, a guileless—or was it merely a stupid—expression on her heavily powdered and overly rouged face. Hugh and Louise sat in shocked silence until the king stood abruptly, almost displacing his mistress from her perch, and

Noting a semi dazed expression on his handsome face, the princess, looking directly at the monarch, began softly, "Your Majesty, we have taken so much of your time . . . for which we are so grateful, as well as for your blessings upon us, we . . ."

Seemingly grateful for her lapse in etiquette, the sovereign managed, in almost a whisper, "Both were my pleasure, my dear, dear children." After kissing his hand, the couple beat as hasty a retreat as was possible, speaking hardly at all until they were back in what they suddenly felt was the sanctuary of their coach.

"I have never . . ." Louise sputtered, but stopped herself, Hugh merely shaking his head, though once they had moved beyond the confines of the palace, the coach clattering through the massive gates, past the stables and other functionary buildings and onto the road back to Paris, he told his fiancée of when he was first at Versailles as Marie Antoinette's guest. "When first we met!" the princess smiled, dazzlingly, any thoughts of misbehaviour towards the dauphine on her part on that occasion seemingly banished from her mind as he related that he'd taken silent note of the young woman who had arrived though not exited the carriage with the king,

"When I mentioned her, Antoinette actually sneered as she told me, '*She* is *called Madame du Barry* and *she* is a stupid, crude and ill-bred courtesan, a commoner of the basest kind, who has seemingly captured the king's attention.' She said further that du Barry was '*nothing* . . . she is *no one!*'" He related how the dauphine had continued haughtily, flicking her dainty fingers in a dismissive, trivialising gesture. She then explained that she had already developed a deep animus towards "the du Barry," refusing even to speak to her.

Louise listened in silence, finally relating, "Well then, Madame la Dauphine was true to her word, my darling. . . . She did not utter a single syllable to the woman until the first day of this very year, when, at a ball, and it is said as a result of having been virtually ordered to do so by Maria Theresa's ambassador himself, while looking generally in du Barry's direction, she casually observed aloud something to the effect that, 'There are many people at Versailles today.' This was apparently satisfactory to both du Barry and Count Mercy, so yet another trivial rupture at court was resolved . . . absent bloodshed." he laughed.

The couple sat quietly for a long moment.

"Which is *why* . . ." Louise eyed her fiancé playfully, as in response, as she'd anticipated, he spoke some of the words of Arthur Dillon's sage advice, ". . . which is why we shall avoid the 'bloody dammed place' to the extent that we are able!"

As the coachman quickened the team's pace just a bit as the horses perhaps realised their stalls and feed buckets awaited them at Toulouse, the carriage's speed was greater moving towards Paris than it was to Versailles. The happy young couple chattered away: about their own life and lives, with no concern about the king or anyone else, Louise's head resting gently against Hugh's shoulder as the still rather sparsely settled suburbs on the Left Bank began to appear in the distance.

County Cork, Ireland—Spring–Summer 1772

The weeks following O'Leary's return were largely gentle, witnessing, in part, a resumption of the prior family routine, though they also adjusted to significant changes, occasioned not only by the relatively recent arrival of a second child but by the fact that, as he advised Eileen, O'Leary's return was to be semi-permanent. He had requested and been granted a general leave of absence, which by its terms permitted him to retain his commission on half-pay. Thus, he could remain indefinitely at home, waiving any right to promotion during his absence and subject only to being recalled, he explained, "in the event of a political and/or military occurrence, the magnitude of which, in the judgment of Her Imperial Majesty, would require the recall of all commissioned officers."

They had discussed the arrangement further whilst at breakfast the morning after his arrival, Eileen, warmly tousled and comfortably relaxed in a soft dressing gown, her feet bare, smiled softly, her eyes bright, then brimming. "My darling, to not have to share you with the empress, not to mention with her son, the emperor, their entire empire and the imperial armies of Austria and Hungary . . . 'tis a gift beyond all imagination, sir! 'Tis a second beginning of our life together." She unexpectedly burst into tears of joy.

Their first weeks of readjustment to what Eileen was calling "this glorious reality," were pleasantly punctuated by visits from neighbours and relatives, the first of which being Squire and Mistress Collins of Derryleigh. O'Leary was overjoyed by Anna Collins's pregnancy, her chubby face and body, and amused by the ever-proper John Collins's almost sheepish acknowledgement of congratulations on what he blushingly characterised as being "the Lady Anna's most delicate condition."

As the spring progressed slowly into summer, the O'Learys also happily resumed the active social life they had enjoyed prior to his return to Vienna. Eileen had generally withdrawn from appearing at most events during his months away, but they again enjoyed the feasting, the music and the dance of many of the occasions and were quickly re-establishing themselves as active and largely well-regarded members of the community.

Art easily slipped into what he called a *countryman's routine*: He both oversaw and laboured alongside the men in the fields, also working with James in the barns, journeyed into Macroom several times a week to meet with friends to collect any mail that may have arrived; following Eileen's unpleasant experience, they took their mail at the small inn, located on the edge of Macroom, not far from Macroom Castle, in which Squire John Collins had an ownership interest. It was between the inn's public house and the town's principal one on the market square that O'Leary alternated gathering with his circle of friends for drinks and, at least once a week, a meal.

Art found the local political scene considerably less contentious than it had been prior to his departure. The removal of Abraham Morris as high sheriff, arising out of the scandalous intrusions into the mail of a number of people in addition to Eileen, appeared, at least to the Catholics, to have had a positive impact on the local Protestant gentry, in that their attitude now seemed more deferential to the powers at Dublin Castle.

"This lord lieutenant, he has bribed and otherwise bought, cajoled and threatened the Irish Parliament into submission," John Collins told O'Leary over dinner one night at his inn, "and with this, so too has he, to a great degree, subverted much of the local officialdom, at least here in Cork, which is encouraging."

Collins advised his friend that he agreed that removing Morris from the local power structure had been a good development, "though he has wheedled . . . or should I say 'weaselled' his way back into the fringes of officialdom as a magistrate now, so some degree of power he will again accrue. . . . He and his fellow magistrates in something they formed last July, which they call the Muskerry Constitutional Society, a grand-sounding name for a group of bloviated dolts!"

More than anything, O'Leary had quickly come to appreciate the quality of life he, Eileen and their young family had. Squire O'Leary remained in his various business activities and relished being a grandfather now to two little boys. The relationship with Catherine had become relatively stable, largely pleasant and surprisingly noncontroversial, the woman's occasional colourful expressions of her still highly unorthodox social, political and religious views notwithstanding. A June visit from the eldest O'Leary son, Conor, who, having nominally publicly accepted the Church of Ireland, whilst covertly hearing Sunday Mass each week, was now a well-established barrister in Dublin and had strengthened the familial ties amongst the

O'Learys and provided Eileen with a strong sense of security, which her life since John O'Connor's demise more than a decade before she felt she had largely lacked. Though Art's brother was reserved and genteel in the manner of Squire O'Leary, she enjoyed seeing the brothers together, talking, joking and roughhousing like her own.

As to her "relations beyond the Kenmare," as she collectively referred to the O'Connells at or in the general vicinity of Derrynane, they remained to a degree strained, significantly with Maurice and to a lesser extent her younger sisters. This being the case, she remained in written communication primarily with Morgan, himself now wed and running a thriving commercial establishment at Carhen, some ten miles west of Derrynane, and, though less frequently, with her mother.

Her mother, Maire Ni Dhuibh, she sensed, was growing weary as she aged—Eileen was certain she was now approaching ninety—and most likely largely deferred to the eldest O'Connell male, Maurice, in terms of what Morgan, the brother to whom Eileen remained closest, stiffly referred to as "familial governance matters." It was clear that Maurice and Maire ran Derrynane and the far-flung O'Connell operations in tandem and had grown even closer, Maire seeming to have become significantly more conservative during Eileen's years in Vienna. Morgan had advised that unless and until Eileen sought and received permission to return to Derrynane and, once there, "to grovellingly seek forgiveness and absolution" for eloping with O'Leary, "and for whatever other sins they deem you to have committed," that she would remain estranged.

"So be it then!" she had declared to Art as she finished reading Morgan's most recent letter aloud. Nothing more was to be said about the topic for a number of months.

Eileen clearly revelled in being Mistress O'Leary; she continually applied the many lessons she had learned and practices she had developed in what now seemed her far-distant, long-ago time at the O'Connors' Ballyhar to her duties on the smaller but still significant and prosperous estate that was Rathleigh. As it had when she was Mistress O'Connor, her long stride took her about the farm daily, climbing onto Bull's back to more quickly access the farther reaches of the place. As the tenants were fewer, she quickly grew close to the women, and continued to foster literacy amongst the families.

She had written Abby that "daily, the Captain and I grow closer, and—were it even possible—I believe more deeply in love!" She treasured the fact that, despite the huge distance between Cork and Vienna, and the two sisters' now radically different lives, she and Abigail shared the still-rare experience of being wed to men they truly loved, and by whom they were loved. "Now that we live not under some set of orders by which he must return to active service, I truly feel we shall thrive and grow old together on this happy place in Cork," she had wept softly as she'd continued her letter to her sister.

O'Leary, too, seemed to grow more settled, more content, though he still regularly wore his full uniform, including his silver-hilted sword, as he believed himself to be fully entitled to do, whether for a special occasion or simply to attend to business matters in Macroom as well as, infrequently, in Cork City. In whatever setting, thus attired, O'Leary, especially when mounted on Banrían—who, Eileen had come to silently observe, carried herself regally, as befitting her name—was a striking figure, and together they, whether it was to the beholder's admiration or disfavour, rarely went unnoticed.

Perhaps, she reflected, it had been their year-long separation, but Eileen felt him even more handsome, even more striking, especially when uniformed, though she would jest, "You have yet again drunk deeply of the elixir of the Continental officer, have you not, my darling?" in response to which O'Leary would smile or nod, though once he grew serious.

"Perhaps yes, yet no longer intoxicated by the elixir do I feel myself to be; in years prior, I believed it necessary to loudly proclaim much. . . . Now I believe in making *silent proclamations.*" He smiled, gesturing to his raiment, gently patting the hilt of his sword.

Thus, though the young aristocrat continued to maintain strongly held views and obviously remained conscious of his relatively unique status as a Continental officer, it seemed to a number of their friends that he had become less contentious and significantly less outspoken. "'Tis a good thing indeed," pronounced John Collins as he noted that Art occasionally now appeared to reach out to, even to cultivate a degree of relationships with some of the local Protestant squirearchy.

"By the actions of the lord lieutenant in subverting the Irish Parliament, for whose members we are unable to vote, but no matter that, at least for now, he has also succeeded in clipping the arrogantly flapping wings of the local officialdom in the counties," O'Leary observed one evening to Eileen and his father as they took brandy after dinner. "Dublin Castle controls much more than prior, the independence of these 'little men' in Cork as a result also significantly reduced."

Summer arrived in late May and remained, many days tropically sultry, the winds blowing steadily off the Atlantic and across West Cork frequently heavy with moisture. The activities at Rathleigh continued pleasantly; little Fiach was thriving and Conor many days amazing as he approached his fourth birthday in August. O'Leary blossomed as a father, frequently taking the little boy riding along on Fionn on his various rounds and errands, including his periodic visits to Derryleigh, as he continued a subtly paternal relationship with Anna, who was delivered in May of a flaxen-haired little girl whom she and the squire had named Maria Theresa Collins, Art and Eileen standing godparents for the baby.

O'Leary also enjoyed John Collins's company immeasurably. Though the men shared a common background, they were quite different in terms of experience and personality; that said, they nevertheless shared a love of literature, similar social, political and religious views, as well as the farmer's strongly conservative beliefs in personal and property rights, loved their families and recognised the significance of their continuing participation in the small Gaelic aristocracy in the neighbourhood. Collins, who had known him casually for a number of years, and had thus been fully aware of O'Leary's brash, contentious behaviour and resultant reputation, had by now come to admire what he viewed as the younger man's maturation, though he at times, as he told Anna, still wished to see "less of the uniform and sword." Perhaps as much as anything else, O'Leary had come to hold John Collins in his highest respect and esteem.

Such was O'Leary's admiration for his relatively new friend, and for the man's sound judgment, that, after they had talked the matter through thoroughly, it was on John Collins's considered advice—"As you have sought out some of the others, Arthur, 'twoud be well if you could similarly do so of the loathsome Morris. Whilst ne'er a friend he will be, I believe that at least a neutral person he could possibly be made to become"—that O'Leary had surprised—shocked actually!—Eileen, one airless early July afternoon, when on his return from Derryleigh, he told her that he planned to seek out Abraham Morris and attempt a rapprochement with his seemingly long-time adversary.

As Eileen protested—"What could you possibly hope to achieve by attempting to engage this nasty little man in a civilised manner?"—whilst he unsaddled Banrían, O'Leary quietly advised that Morris's ongoing behaviour towards and continuing dislike of him—and through him, of her—may well have had its roots in what seemed an insignificant event of some years prior, thus possibly being the result of a long-held feeling of resentment. Slightly intrigued, Eileen agreed to hear him out, "here and now, in the barn . . ." she laughed.

Within moments, comfortably perched on, then leaning back in the driver's seat of the family's trap, her soft French slippers playfully dangling from and then slipping off her toes like a little girl would, her expression grew into one of mild bemusement as Eileen listened whilst O'Leary told her what he characterised as a tale of a "sad, though all too common Irish country grudge, one involving a young woman." As she occasionally shook her head, rolling her eyes several times and laughing softly once or twice, he related almost sheepishly that it was at a dance in Millstreet, held some months before Art had first gone to Vienna, that he had taken an instant, inexplicable and wholly unintended fancy to a "sweet, winsome though somewhat plain lass" named Eliza Sherlock: petite, fair, trim—and *Protestant*. Ignoring her repeated assertions that she was attending the dance specifically to see one Abraham Morris, O'Leary admitted that he had monopolised her time as much as he could, swept her about the dance floor as frequently as he was able—she apparently did not resist the opportunity to dance, as Morris either could or would not—and delivered food and drink to her throughout the evening, all despite her supposed focus on the short, not terribly attractive squire of Hanover Hall, who had visibly seethed each time O'Leary appeared during the evening.

O'Leary acknowledged to Eileen that the apparent, and "wholly unintended" result of what he called his "immature, rather loutish behaviour" was that whatever Eliza Sherlock's interest in Abraham Morris had been, had quickly evaporated and, with it, seemingly any hopes the not-handsome, somewhat-older man had of capturing an attractive young wife; in his mind, his dreams cruelly dashed. Though the girl had no interest in the brash, young *Catholic* boy O'Leary, the attention the elegantly handsome lad from Rathleigh had paid to her had seemingly led her to believe she could aspire to a significantly better match than what Morris offered her and indeed it was within the ensuing three months that she was betrothed to and by year's end had wed a tall, handsome young Protestant squire from beyond the hills in County Tipperary.

"... and you saw the ultimate Mistress Morris at the Christmas ball," O'Leary said softly, not in a cruel or mean way, though immediately causing Eileen to reflexively wince as she recalled the unfortunately, almost shockingly plain, dour wife, uncomfortably seated in a dark corner of the glittering hall and, before evening's end, there cowering as well.

Judging Art's apologia complete, Eileen slid off the trap, brushing some random hay from her light-blue, cotton dress, plucking several stray strands out of her hair, and eased her bare feet back into her slippers. "So, husband, what—if anything—is it that you propose to do in this regard, sir? What is it that you can possibly accomplish, Arthur?"

Lifting Banrían's saddle from where he'd set it on the floor, finally placing it on its rack, O'Leary straightened. "I believe there is little if anything I could do that could fully rectify these circumstances, but, as a gentleman, an officer and . . . because we reside here now, because should I ever be compelled to return to full-time active service, you and the children would be here, alone . . . and, perhaps most significantly, because this is our home . . . I believe I must, and I shall attempt to speak with the man. . . . No matter the outcome, I nevertheless believe 'tis the correct, the proper thing to be done."

Hanover Hall, County Cork, Ireland—13 July 1772

Within a matter of days, in a hand-delivered message to Abraham Morris, O'Leary had, after briefly outlining the reasons behind his request, written, "Thus it is, I seek audience with your honour at a time and place of your convenience, sir," in response to which Morris had, as O'Leary "most respectfully" requested that he do, immediately scribbled a reply, with which Seamus hastened back to Rathleigh, Morris advising, in his spidery hand, that "I shall receive you at my home, Hanover Hall, with which location I believe you are familiar on 13 July, this year at one thirty o'clock in the afternoon. You will be prompt; I remain—as I have always been—an extremely busy man."

On that day, O'Leary, dressed unassumingly in a simple grey suit, white shirt and stockings and, covering the hose, simple civilian black boots, his appearance devoid of any military decoration or indeed of any ornament that could be misinterpreted as pretence of aristocracy; even his queue was tied with a plain black ribbon instead of the colourful hues he ofttimes favoured.

As he was preparing to leave, Eileen kissed him softly and cautioned, "Please be watchful and guarded, my darling. I believe strongly that this is an evil little man with whom you are trying to reach some accord."

O'Leary nodded as he mounted Banrían and, after clattering up the Rathleigh lane, Eileen still watching, pointed the pretty mare's head in the general direction of Doneraile and, his apprehension aside, proceeded to largely enjoy the not-quite-two-hour ride through the pleasantly undulating, vividly green countryside between Rathleigh and Hanover Hall, his mind calm, thoughtful, even reflective. *'Tis weary of conflict with this—what did Eileen call him?—this "evil little man" I have indeed grown. My sincere hope,* he thought several times during his ride, *is that we are somehow able to arrive at a mutual peace. What is it that Spinoza spoke? Something akin to peace not being merely an absence of war, but . . . but what? Oh, bloody hell, 'tis something like "a virtue . . . a disposition for benevolence" . . . and . . . and other bloody things, aye, but perhaps we can at least arrive at some bloody "disposition for benevolence,"* he sighed.

Eventually, fairly certain of where he was, O'Leary finally turned into a narrow, unkempt, largely dirt lane—a rough boreen, in fact—its irregular borders overgrown, itself overhung in places by untrimmed sapling branches.

As he approached the hulking, grim, rather menacing dwelling that was Hanover Hall, O'Leary was intercepted, rather than greeted, by a young lad, wearing rough clothes. Instead of being escorted and, as he anticipated, then admitted to the residence, he was told to remain with his horse in what the young man had referred to as "the yard," this at a distance of some hundred, perhaps even one hundred fifty or more feet away from a broken hedgerow that fronted the house, perhaps a dozen feet from the dwelling's main entrance. Puzzled but determined to remain unperturbed, O'Leary withdrew slightly as he was directed, releasing Banrían and permitting her to graze the thick, high summer grass.

Morris emerged from the house several minutes later. As he strutted the distance towards O'Leary, he, too, was dressed simply, in a plain black suit and shoes, white shirt and hose, the only addition one appearing to have just been donned, being an ill-fitting wig, the queue ribbon of which needed retying. As he finally drew closer to O'Leary, breathing heavily, he seemed a significantly older man than when last they had faced each other, appearing now much more worn, his features devoid of any positive animation.

The elder man halted perhaps eight feet from where O'Leary waited, his expression a mixture of disdain and puzzlement, his unremarkable green eyes dreary and sad, obviously waiting for his visitor to approach him, which O'Leary did.

Formally wishing Morris the time of day, appending a precise, ". . . to you, sir," with a nod, O'Leary extended his hand, which Morris did not take, his own hands remaining pointedly at his sides.

Rather, he spoke in a dry voice, his tone instantly edgy, impatient. "You wished to see me, sir," being his response to O'Leary's gesture, adding condescendingly, "You must understand that my time is quite limited, as I am a very important man." At that point he began strolling away from the immediate vicinity of the house, Art falling in step with him as Morris repeated, " . . . *a very important man, you understand . . .*"

Stifling a sigh, Art looked at Morris for a moment before beginning. "Aye, I did, as I wished to speak with you, sir, to address the unfortunate occasional history we have shared, and indeed to apologise to you for a wrong I have come to believe I may have perhaps committed against you . . . *sir.*"

Stopping abruptly, Morris eyed O'Leary warily, after a moment evidencing patent suspicion, but said nothing, as O'Leary continued. "I fear, sir, that some years ago I intruded on an occasion in Millstreet at which you were to meet and not for the first time, a young lady . . . one, emm . . . Eliza Sherlock."

At the mention of the name, Morris's eyes narrowed, his face immediately flushed, his breathing more pronounced; though he said nothing as O'Leary continued, he gritted his teeth.

"Then and there, by my actions—wholly out of thoughtlessness, I assure you, sir, rather than by any design—I believe that I may have damaged the nascent relationship I have since learnt that you and the young lady had commenced sometime prior, and . . ."

Morris's dull eyes suddenly flashed, and his right fist struck first the heavy air, then his left palm, quite hard. ". . . *and* so it was that within *a matter of days* of that evening, I was informed by Squire Sherlock that his daughter no longer wished to have me call; indeed that I was never again to call at their home, her interests having . . ." He grew silent, quietly but obviously seething, enraged.

"Thus, most assuredly, *sir,* by your actions you did not merely 'damage' but rather you *destroyed utterly,* you *catastrophically ruined* in a matter of hours what I had for some time believed to be a most promising . . . indeed perhaps my only opportunity to . . ."

"I was impulsive, impetuous; I . . ." attempted O'Leary.

"So it is that you remain."

"I behaved in an arrogant fashion," O'Leary admitted.

"As you continue to this very day to act; by your very presence here this is evidenced."

O'Leary stepped back slightly, folded his arms and cast his eyes briefly at the dull grey sky overhead. He sighed softly before speaking equally so, "*Nevertheless, sir*, I am truly, *truly* sorry for what I did, and indeed I *most sincerely* regret any residual sense of dissatisfaction, of unhappiness you may have experienced as a result of . . ."

Morris's hands were now knotted into a pair of rounded fists. "'*Residual dissatisfaction,*' you say? '*Unhappiness,*' you suggest? What do *you* think, O'Leary?"

He stepped close to the significantly taller, younger man, looking up at O'Leary and markedly lowering his voice. "Do you even recall the attractive appearance of Eliza Sherlock? Do you remember her clear, white skin, her thick, brown hair, which shone? Her fine, soft, brown eyes, her carriage, her smile, her . . ." As the older man's expression became momentarily distant, O'Leary sensed perhaps a vision of Eliza Sherlock appearing to Morris.

The men had continued to walk away from the close of the manor house.

Abruptly stopping, shaking his head one time sharply, Morris's appearance again turned grim, now speaking even more quietly yet, so softly that O'Leary bent slightly towards him. As he seethed, Morris hissingly sputtered, "When, when . . . compared to the . . . the . . . that *sour, wretched, miserable, barren bitch of a woman* who dwells with me within that house"—his hand, and his voice, shaking violently, gesturing bitterly back towards his home. "She . . . she . . . there is *no* comparison . . . no possible comparison! So I say yet again, *what do you think*, O'Leary?" His expression abruptly became empty, and then simply very sad.

As O'Leary gazed down at the obviously miserable, resentful man, he experienced a powerful sense of remorse and perhaps an even greater degree of pity, prompting him to say gently, "For this result of my untoward behaviour that long-ago evening I most sincerely apologise, sir," and he extended his hand. As earlier, Morris did not take it, the expression on his face yet again being one of malign anger.

"So you say, though you continue, *to this very day*, O'Leary, to disrespect me . . . to hold me up to contempt, even ridicule, by *your people* and indeed, sir, by even some of my own," he whined, now wagging his left forefinger at O'Leary.

"With respect, Squire Morris," O'Leary attempted, speaking evenly, "for much of the recent time I have been absent from here on my military duties abroad. I have not—"

"I speak more precisely of certain happenings at Christmas, almost two years now past, sir!" Morris snapped.

The tension hung profoundly in the wet afternoon air, thick, moisture-heavy clouds limping by above them, some appearing to barely clear the widely scattered treetops.

O'Leary paused, saying nothing, thinking quickly. Finally, having formed his thoughts and the resultant words with care, he spoke slowly and precisely. "If it is indeed of those events that occurred at the gathering held in Macroom during the week of Christmas 1770 that you speak, then I shall say that, *aye*, I profoundly regret . . . as I most assuredly do . . . *all* of what occurred between us there on that occasion, but as *for* any of this I am unable to apologise, sir, as . . ."

Morris glared up at O'Leary, again wagging his finger, whining, "You caused me there and afterwards to suffer scorn, sir, to be ridiculed . . . to . . . to experience a degree of humiliation that no man of my position in life and society should *ever* . . ."

". . . Yet again, 'tis *of* or *about* this that I have genuine regret, but *for* this occurrence and any results afterwards, sir, I was in *no way* responsible," O'Leary began, his tone still level, though it became firmer, more commanding than contrite, as he continued. "Indeed, sir, you must remember that 'twas you yourself who confronted Mistress O'Leary and myself as we walked about the hall, it being patently obvious to all that you were even then well into your cups. That being the case, I would strongly, albeit *most respectfully* suggest you accept that it was *you*, sir, in your abject state of inebriation, who brought, if indeed this has proven to be the case, what you say was 'scorn and humiliation' on yourself. Thus, for this I am unable to . . . in all honesty, I cannot . . . thus, I do not . . . indeed, sir, I *shall not* apologise!"

Morris's expression was now unmistakably one of scorn and rage, though, as he spoke only after an obvious hesitation, O'Leary sensed a degree of fear as well. "Why, why, then . . . then, you, *sir*, you are not a gentleman! You—along with *your people*, especially your *wife*—if indeed you even bothered to marry a woman like *that*; indeed why would you? A woman who would steal away with you from her home and family in the middle of the night. You are an arrogant, conceited and disloyal Papist, as have you always been, *as shall you remain!*" As it frequently did in times of stress, his dry voice now screeched. "Indeed I have long felt that you . . . perhaps even more so your pretentious bitch of a wife, or, should I say, perhaps more accurately, your *pretentious whore*, had much to do with my, yet again, my *public humiliation* in Cork City. . . ."

By now, Morris had begun slowly, almost imperceptibly, moving back towards the house, though the broken row of shrubbery still lay well in excess of at least one hundred feet away. To O'Leary, it seemed that perhaps it was closer to two hundred feet distant from where the men stood.

O'Leary's face flamed. His eyes, his voice both vivid expressions of contempt and loathing, of ire, quickly approaching rage, he took purposeful steps towards Morris such that in a moment he was looking down on the man, compelling Morris to lift his eyes to him. His voice frighteningly icy, cutting, the young officer roared, "How dare you, *how dare you!* You ill-bred, barely literate, feckless little sack of shit . . . !"

Visibly shaken, his eyes wide and sweat trickling down his pasty cheeks, Morris continued to withdraw from the open space.

As he did, O'Leary, by design having remained some distance from him, the younger man's voice now filled the sultry atmosphere. "If by your 'public humiliation in Cork City,' you are referring to your formal impeachment and dismissal from the office of high sheriff, I am informed that the deputy lord lieutenant of Ireland himself described in detail the numerous illegal acts that led to your removal from office, as well as making clear the reasons behind the highly public manner in which your dismissal was conducted, *sir!*" O'Leary raged from some distance away.

Still withdrawing, gradually moving backwards, Morris cast his eyes repeatedly towards the dwelling, his only possible refuge from what he had long conjured in his mind as being O'Leary's uncontrollably violent temper. For his part, despite maintaining his distance, as Morris quickened his pace, so too now did O'Leary.

As they moved in an awkward minuet, O'Leary snarled loudly, swinging his fist through the oppressive air, though nowhere near Morris. "So as to what you allege about *that*, to you I say *bah!* . . . rather at that time, 'twas made clear beyond any doubt that you were being removed from office as a result of . . ."

Morris suddenly stumbled, almost falling; unwittingly halted, he found himself, equally so, facing his nemesis as O'Leary stepped sharply forward. An arm's length, perhaps less separating the two, the tip of his right forefinger jabbing punctuatingly at Morris's heaving chest, ". . . as a *direct* result of your *unwarranted . . . illegal . . . cowardly . . .* and *purposeless* intrusions into the personal and confidential correspondence of a number of citizens of this county, included amongst those being, as *you know full well, she is,* my wife, you disgusting, spineless little snot!" O'Leary's resonant voice now melded into the hot, wet, still air enveloping both men.

Instantly regretting touching the man, O'Leary stepped sharply several steps back, his arms rigidly at his sides, his fingers closed into his palms. Reminding himself of his reason for coming, he was now desperately trying to avoid a physical confrontation.

Suddenly, apparently having fully realised the furies he may well have unleashed, his near terror on experiencing O'Leary's reaction obvious, Morris abruptly bolted and ran towards his home. As he did, O'Leary stood, momentarily frozen, his mind whirring until he finally roared out, "Bastard! . . . stop, you cowardly little bastard! *Stop!*"

Morris did not hear him, running as quickly as he was able to on his short, bowed legs, casting a single swift, frightened look back over his shoulder as he bounced almost girlishly across the remaining distance to the front door, in the process entangling himself in the row of scruffy, unkempt hedges. Struggling in their prickly embrace, having last seen O'Leary standing in place, Morris was horrified as he looked back again to find him by then racing towards him. Finally wriggling himself free from the bushes, the smaller man reached the house with barely sufficient time in which to slam the heavy door behind him, just as O'Leary arrived at the entryway. Morris realised that but for O'Leary himself being forced to weave between or around—he hadn't taken the time to notice which—the hedges as well, he most likely would not have made it safely inside.

As the thick, iron-banded oak door slammed shut, O'Leary's right fist pounded on its exterior. "Morris, *Morris!* For *your remarks,* sir, *you* shall apologise!" Having heard the unmistakable sound of a bolt being slammed into place, he hit the massive door again, with such force that, despite its size and bulk, it moved imperceptibly within its iron hinges.

Standing silent for what seemed to be several long minutes, O'Leary finally called out, "I await you, Morris! I do not intend departing here anytime soon," and he banged on the door yet again and, after a few more moments, even harder. He finally retreated closer to the hedgerow than the dwelling; turning away from the house, seriously considering departing, he was trying to determine how far away Banrían was.

Unexpectedly, the door opened, at first tentatively, then instantly it was flung, swinging wide, and, as O'Leary turned in response to the sound of the door hitting the stone house's obverse, a sweating, red-faced Morris suddenly appeared, his chest heaving, his wig askew. The barrel of a smallish, single-shot pistol flashed dully, Morris holding it unsteadily, upraised in his left hand, as he stepped back into the open area between the door and the hedgerow, where O'Leary stood, his arms folded.

"Apologise! *Ha!* Shoot you I should, you conceited, disloyal, treacherous, fucking Romish bastard!" he shrieked as he approached O'Leary, pointing the weapon directly at him. When he finally stopped, he spread his legs, planting himself little more than a foot in front of the younger man.

O'Leary, seeing that the pistol was fully cocked and, assuming it was loaded, thus a deadly weapon being waved in his face, stepped back slightly. But before he did, he noticed a potent suggestion of obviously just consumed *uisce beatha* on Morris's breath.

Pausing, and reflexively holding up his hands, palms open, as he had been trained to do if ever he were to be confronted in close quarters by an armed foe and he himself unarmed, O'Leary, his tone unexpectedly, deliberately gentle, conciliatory, probed deftly. "Abraham, lower your weapon. Indeed, sir, please put it down. I believe, sir, we are both gentlemen . . . and, as gentlemen, I believe that we should be able to—"

A manic smile on his gleaming, whiskey-flushed face, his eyes wide, his jowls dripping with sweat, Morris instead dangerously poked the fully cocked pistol he held in his now-trembling left hand at O'Leary's face, the end of the barrel grazing the officer's right cheek and chin, before he returned it to a shakily upright position, squinting at O'Leary.

Again, similarly by well-trained reflex and without redirecting his steady gaze from Morris's sweat-sheened face, wordlessly, the young cavalryman's right hand shot up sharply, skilfully gripping Morris's left, pushing the gun's barrel upwards and then away from them. By further twisting the smaller man's wrist, forcing the pistol and Morris's outstretched hand to the side and down, he caused Morris's trigger finger to involuntarily move and the weapon to thus loudly but harmlessly discharge into the soft midsummer grass and weeds at their feet, the heavy air nevertheless filling with thick, bitter, black powder smoke, the unpleasantly pungent cloud looming in the searing afternoon heat.

Though O'Leary was coughing, his eyes smarting, he nevertheless now firmly grasped the still-smoking barrel of the gun in his own right hand. Casting a quick, disdainful look at Morris, he almost casually arched the empty pistol high into the air and well aside of the spot where they stood. His mouth hanging open, Morris followed the gun's trajectory, staring as it hit the ground with a soft thud. Looking back at O'Leary, he said nothing, still slack-jawed.

Apparently deeming the matter closed, his mission a failure, O'Leary turned sharply and took a step to walk away, calling over his shoulder, without looking back, "I have attempted, sir . . . 'twas in good faith that I have come . . . I . . ."

At that moment, Morris awkwardly lunged forward, almost falling as he did so. With the thick, stubby fingers of his left hand, he attempted—and failed—to grab O'Leary's coat collar, the hand rather only clumsily glancing off his shoulder.

Barely halting, in a crisp, fluid motion, O'Leary swung around, his right fist coming up from alongside his body, connecting solidly with the smaller man's jaw; the blow, after first lifting Morris up off his feet, propelled him heavily to the ground, where he landed on his back, his arms and legs spread wide.

Breathing hard now, his own face glistening with sweat, the fire of battle fully upon him, O'Leary nevertheless stood motionless, his still-fisted right hand cupped in his left—silently watching, waiting—until some minutes later Morris sat up unsteadily, glaring at his opponent, albeit loudly mumbling, his jaw barely moving. "I *am* going to kill—"

Silencing Morris with a smile and a derisive, "Perhaps so, little man . . . though not this day!" O'Leary laughed mockingly as, with a sudden though almost gentle thrust of the sole of his right boot to the man's chest, he rendered a shocked Morris again on his back. This time, O'Leary turned once more towards Banrían, his long, quick strides even, again not looking behind.

Struggling unsteadily to sit up, then again to get on his feet, a now nearly hysterical Morris squealed, albeit not loudly, "Did you not hear me?! I *said* I was going to . . . *kill you* . . . O'Leary, kill you I shall . . . O'Leary . . . halt, I say, *halt* . . . O'Leary!"

Ignoring what were for the most part disjointed ravings—though he did make out the word "kill—made even more incoherent by the whiskey that was by now taking full effect on the small man, as well as that his blow had seriously damaged, perhaps even broken his jaw, O'Leary continued walking almost diffidently towards his horse, sarcastically, exaggeratingly shaking his head from side to side, similarly waving both of his upraised hands. It was only then that he noticed that the untethered, curious mare had wandered—that indeed Banrían was still in motion some distance away. He whistled for her.

Stumbling forward, Morris was barely able to withdraw a partially cocked pistol from the deep left pocket of his coat; despite that his feet were again spread wide, his body now perceptively swayed, his hands shaking, he struggled to fully cock the weapon, which was considerably larger than the one O'Leary had but a short while before disarmed him.

Banrían seemingly treating his whistles as part of a game, quickening his own pace, a frustrated O'Leary ultimately reached his still-ambling horse that had finally begun to, though even-then playfully tossing her head, walk towards him, reaching up, gripping the pommel, O'Leary mounted effortlessly, turning Banrían in the process, even as he slipped his toes into the stirrups. Once seated, he briefly fixed his eyes on the unsteady, still-screeching man whose arms were gesturing wildly over his head, for the first time becoming aware of the outsized pistol, fully cocked and being waved treacherously in Morris's left hand as the older man unsteadily approached.

Despite his shock and unspoken reaction, *Bloody goddammed hell!* displaying no evidence of surprise, he slowly drew closer and faced Morris. His expression now rather one of haughty disdain, from his saddle—as Banrían walked him slowly towards the man—O'Leary called out mockingly, "You are *indeed* a weak, snivelling, scrawny little coward! No courage is required to shoot an unarmed man." Momentarily releasing the horse's reins. he opened his arms wide, palms up and open. Shaking his head at Morris, he again gathered the reins in his right hand.

Anticipating an immediate escape, with his now-gloved left hand he sharply smacked the mare's side, at the same time tightening the reins, attempting to turn her head with his right. Shockingly, the rarely before skittish young horse shied and hesitated uncertainly, seemingly distracted by

Morris's continued incoherent shrieking, despite O'Leary tightening her turning rein and pressing his left leg hard into her side.

With wildly trembling hands, Morris levelled the pistol as best as he was able, both of his forefingers on the stiff trigger.

Only as it exploded, belching a heavy cloud of smoke and a burst of flame not dissimilar to a small cannon's, the blast resounding thunderously in the oppressively still air, had Banrían, finally responding to O'Leary's direction, turned and bolted sharply away. His back to his attacker, O'Leary heard the blast but neither saw the gunfire nor heard the fabric rip as the pistol ball tore through the right shoulder of his coat. He did, however, feel an immediate sharp pain in his upper right arm.

Enraged, "*Bloody hell, you worthless little bastard! Bloodyfucking coward!*" he roared, as, with agonising difficulty, O'Leary was able to rein in a confused, now very frightened Banrían. Letting a long moment elapse, he deftly turned the, to his relief, again responsive horse, and streaked back towards Morris, who was awkwardly retreating, impotently waving the smoking, discharged weapon, his eyes streaming, his chest heaving, his wig wholly, comically lopsided to the right.

As he stumbled in the general direction of his house, he was shrieking unintelligibly, "Finally, shot . . . killed, yes! I killed! . . . I executed him! My ultimate victory . . . God save the . . ."

O'Leary quickly reached and at least twice circled a shocked, terrified Morris. Pulling back hard at her reins, he drew Banrían up sharply in front of the frozen, wide-eyed little man. As O'Leary had hoped she would, the young mare whinnied loudly as she reared dramatically, her forelegs pawing the air. Though the theatrical gesture had caused him severe pain in his wounded arm, and had he not at the last moment grabbed the pommel of his saddle with his left hand, could well have unhorsed him, after witnessing Morris's horror at the spectacle, O'Leary nevertheless triumphantly cried out, his momentarily commanding voice again dominating the place: "*As the feeble, pathetic, craven coward you are,* you have shot me from behind . . . but you have not killed me, *you gutless, spineless, worthless little bucket of piss!*"

A trancelike Morris remained in place and stared blankly up at him, now holding the weakly smoking pistol at his side.

His right boot already out of the stirrup, sharply moving the horse closer alongside the swaying, open-mouthed man, with a supreme effort, O'Leary drew back his leg and violently propelled the toe into a stunned, rheumy-eyed Morris's upraised jaw, exultantly sending him sprawling unconscious, spread-eagled into the dirt and a few broken rocks of the rough lane.

After permitting himself to fleetingly savour the triumph, not caring if Morris was alive or dead—though he would have been pleased if Morris's already damaged jaw was indeed quite shattered—O'Leary wordlessly gave Banrían her head, and together they finally raced away from Hanover Hall.

He did not gallop for long. Once he believed them out of sight, O'Leary slowed the flying young horse, his upper arm now throbbing, sensing small amounts of blood seeming to spurt at each pulsation, his shirt and coat sleeve quickly soaked and stained red. At best, he maintained Banrían at a canter; more frequently, she trotted. Quickly discovering that virtually any movement of the young horse caused him significant pain, O'Leary slowed her to what became an agonizingly slow but mercifully gentle walk.

As a result, for O'Leary the plodding miles they travelled from Hanover Hall passed as if horse and rider were moving in a dull pantomime of their normal actions. He eventually lost all sense of time and began to feel feverish. He was certain only that he was shot, wounded, though most likely—*so I hope, please God!*—not seriously, and, most significantly, that he was headed home.

By the time, several tedious hours later, he was suddenly surprised to find himself a mile, or perhaps it was two—at the most two—from Rathleigh, O'Leary, woozily conscious of how unsteady in the saddle he was as, having dropped the reins, he gripped the pommel as tightly as he could with his uninjured left hand, came upon a mounted man whose identity he could not immediately discern riding slowly in the same direction as he. "Sir!" he called out weakly, then again, but, with some effort, louder: "*Sir!*

Please, sir!" which the man then heard and abruptly stopped and turned his horse.

As the riders drew closer to, and were then facing each other, O'Leary managed, his voice weak, raspy, "Are you familiar with Dr. Baldwin, near Clohina, sir?"

The horseman, an adolescent boy, shock evident on his face, nevertheless nodded affirmatively as he walked his horse yet a few steps more towards O'Leary. "Captain O'Leary, sir, I am the youngest son of Squire James Fitzgerald, sir. I am Joseph!"

O'Leary shook his head and smiled weakly in recognition at the flaming redhead. "Ah indeed you are . . . grown you certainly have, lad, whilst in France, aye? I beg your pardon for greeting you in this condition, dear boy, but I must pray you to hasten to Dr. Baldwin, and that you will please request that he meet me at Rathleigh. Also . . . you will please advise him that I am shot, shot by Abraham Morris . . . be certain to tell him that, lad! . . . 'Tis with a degree of urgency I ask all this of you!"

His eyes wide, the boy nodded, wondering aloud, "Aye, sir, I most certainly shall. . . but Captain, should I not first see you safely home?"

O'Leary shook his head weakly. "No, dear lad, the doctor, please! Go!" Young Joseph Fitzgerald nodded, then wordlessly and immediately turned his horse's head, digging his heels into the gelding's sides, and was quickly out of O'Leary's sight.

Finally reaching the Rathleigh lane, O'Leary through the as-always open gates, moaning aloud even as he gently turned Banrían's head towards the house; such was the level of his discomfort by this point that he was grateful that the young mare had been able to maintain an even, steady walking gait on the more level coach road, as even her gentle steps on the groomed but broken rocks of Rathleigh's entry lurched him painfully in the saddle.

Reaching the house's striking black front door, greeted by the usual canine dissonance, he admitted to himself that he was too weak to safely dismount unaided and so reluctantly remained insecurely in his saddle, despite that the fingers of his left hand still gripped the pommel tightly. He was visibly weaving, his expression wan, his breathing heavy, as, on the dogs' heels, Conor appeared. Instantly wide-eyed, the little boy happily exclaimed, "Papa! Papa!"

O'Leary could only manage a weak, "Aye, lad, 'tis I."

Seconds later, an equally wide-eyed, albeit shocked, Eileen's "*Holy Mother of God in Heaven!*" echoed as soon as she saw her ashen-faced husband. Immediately shooing Conor back inside, though the lad peered out the open door from the hall, she stood close to the horse's left side, reflexively opening her arms. "Lean to me, Arthur," she commanded softly and, lifting her arms, as she stretched her body up to meet him, O'Leary turned and, his arms somewhat extended, toppled in some controlled fashion towards her, the strong woman tightly grasping him, her arms about him, his hands weakly behind her neck. Together, they went to the ground, almost softly.

"Seamus! Ann!" she cried, her husky voice shaking.

As she wriggled up and onto her knees, O'Leary, weakened by loss of blood but fully conscious, looked up at his grey-wool-clad wife, noticing streaks of his blood on her skirts, spatters on her white apron. "The visit with Morris, it did not go as I had hoped." He managed an ironic smile. "Indeed it did not go at all well, madame." He sighed deeply, shaking his head, and closed his eyes.

Ann having quickly gone to remove Conor from the house, to have him play with the children, his best little friends, at the nearest cottage, Seamus, along with a stout, strong young lad new to the household named Henry, and Eileen half-walked, half-carried O'Leary into the small family parlour. They instinctively positioned him on the wide, multicoloured, striped-velvet, camel-back sofa, so that his wounded right arm faced the room and, for the moment, extended over the bare floor.

"A knife!" Seamus requested sharply. "We must cut the captain's coat!" Ann quickly returned with a sabre-sharp kitchen knife, Henry at the same time trundling a pot of hot water, a bunch of clean rags in the pocket of his rough leather breeches. As Eileen held him, Ann and Henry quickly draped the rags and some other heavy cloth over the sofa where they had settled O'Leary, after which Eileen rolled back the thick Indian rug.

As Seamus began to cut and tear the fabric at his shoulder, as evenly as possible, O'Leary moaned softly and stirred; his voice sounding somewhat breathless now, he managed, "Met the youngest Fitzgerald boy, the redhead like his mama . . . on the road, sent him . . . retrieving brother Baldwin, I hope . . . soon," and Eileen knelt next to him. With her long fingers, she gently brushed his hair out of his eyes, wiping away the beads of sweat now thick on O'Leary's sunburnt forehead.

"Was it Morris himself? Did *he* do *this?*" she finally managed.

"Shot me . . . indeed he did, woman . . . to be sure, the fucking little bastard did!" O'Leary muttered bitterly and, sighing, again closed his eyes.

Within the hour, there was heard the welcome sound of hoofbeats of two horses bearing a grim-looking, sweating James Baldwin and young Joseph Fitzgerald, his expression anxious, apparently fearful that by now O'Leary might have expired.

The physician flung open the door, shedding his tan suit coat onto the floor as he entered; within seconds he stood by his patient. O'Leary stirred. "Brother Baldwin, how good of you to come so quickly . . . you have met young Master Fitzgerald." He looked up and smiled at the wide-eyed boy. "I am not dead, Joseph, and I hope Dr. Baldwin will see to it that I remain thus." He smiled wanly and again closed his eyes.

Whilst Eileen hastily advised him that, according to Arthur, it was a pistol ball, seemingly shot from a distance. Baldwin set a leather satchel at his feet, from which he withdrew and quickly draped a long white apron— faint bloodstains still visible despite repeated lye-soap washings—over his head, tying it at the back of his waist. He knelt heavily, then wriggled on his knees so as to quickly, closely examine O'Leary's now bared right arm and shoulder, Seamus having carefully cut and torn away the sleeves of his coat and shirt, skilfully using the shirtsleeve as a tourniquet, largely stanching the blood.

The physician nodded several times, at the wound and the situation and, as he stood, managed a weak smile. "You have done well, you three," he said softly, rising slowly. Shaking her head, Eileen wordlessly gestured towards Seamus, and the physician, understanding, acknowledged him. "Well done indeed, lad."

Stepping closer to and looking directly at a now-standing Eileen, he sighed with some measure of relief in his voice. "Whilst nasty in appearance, the wound is nothing approaching fatal. . . . The ball has lodged in the fleshy part of his upper arm—" He gestured, patting his left hand on his own right arm, near the shoulder. "Arthur is quite fortunate that Morris is an inept marksman, and indeed clearly a man not knowledgeable in the use of firearms. A rifle fired thus and in a true manner could well have . . ." He coughed, the import of what he had begun to say nevertheless searing into Eileen's mind.

She briefly closed her eyes, then, exhaling, folded her hands at her bosom, as if in prayer. "Thank God, brother Baldwin, but . . ."

The lanky physician gently raised his fingers. "But I of course must still excise the pistol ball. By stanching the flow of blood, young Seamus here has helped preserve Arthur's strength; the cutting, the pain, the ball being well embedded, they shall not be so horrid for him," he said almost matter-of-factly.

Within moments, he had ticked off a series of orders: brandy, more hot water and clean rags, ". . . and, if at all possible, a thin but sturdy, flat piece of wood, clean," he said softly.

Seamus brightened. "Shims; I have cut new birchwood shims in the barn," he said softly as he scurried out.

Eileen looked silently at her brother-in-law, her expression still one of concern, and quizzical as well.

"For Arthur to bite on as I cut; it helps . . . as will copious amounts of brandy," he said softly.

Eileen, who was not a typically squeamish person, winced and went to retrieve the crystal brandy decanter and a tray of pewter tumblers.

Shortly thereafter, O'Leary, already amply plied with brandy, and the requisite supplies in place, Dr. Baldwin withdrew a series of instruments from his physician's bag.

After first pouring brandy and some hot water over the wound—*"Holy Mother of God!"* O'Leary cried out—the doctor then poured brandy over his tools, dipping them also into the cauldron of hot water. Noticing Eileen watching him, and sensing her characteristic curiosity, even in this moment, without pausing, he explained, "I am using the brandy and the hot water on Arthur's wound as an *antiseptic*, a term that first appeared in an English medical pamphlet perhaps fifty years ago, in a brief treatise on how to prevent the putrification —*sepsis* in Greek," he added, "of flesh." He gestured to O'Leary's wound. "As I have read discussions in more current medical papers, opining that cleaning of surgical instruments is being *antiseptic* as well, I subscribe to the practise.... I have even heard of surgeons in Europe washing their hands," he shook his head in some measure of disbelief, "the reasons for which I cannot imagine," though he nevertheless then quickly plunged his own fingers several times into the near-boiling water.

O'Leary, conscious though not especially talkative, began to grow a bit giddy from the amount of brandy he had consumed, Eileen holding the pewter tumbler to his lips as he drank, each time just a bit more deeply.

Dr. Baldwin sat on a milking stool Henry had brought in from the barns, his instruments—a pair of scalpels, as well as of forceps to extract the pistol ball from the wound—now on a tray on the floor by his feet.

"Arthur—" he began.

O'Leary cast his weary, slightly glazed eyes towards him, smiling weakly and sighing. "Yes, James? I assume 'tis time, sir . . . for the cutting, aye?"

His brother-in-law nodded. "Aye, Arthur. . . . I am going to place this bit of wood between your teeth and you will bite down as I cut; such I have found 'twill be a natural reflex."

With a degree of uncertainty, O'Leary took the shim, now wrapped in a small cloth, and looked at Eileen, who squeezed his left hand gently.

Picking up a narrow-tipped scalpel that appeared to Eileen and the others like a small, very sharp, pointy knife, Baldwin placed it at the top of the wound and gently but firmly cut into O'Leary's upper arm.

The patient bit hard into the birch shim, his moan muffled into a *mffffffffffffff*, and he squeezed Eileen's hand hard enough that she grimaced slightly.

Dr. Baldwin gestured to Ann, to, as he had previously explained to her, daub the wound, where a light, fine flow of blood trickled from where he had just cut. "I shall do this three times more—" he gestured with the scalpel— "like the quarter-hours of a clock," he explained to the small group, which still included young Joseph Fitzgerald, in some state of awe as he stood aside watching, listening, absorbing all that was going on about him.

And he did, each time O'Leary biting, *mffffffffffffff*'ing and Eileen grimacing.

Wiping the blade off on his apron, Baldwin placed the instrument on the plate at his feet and took a smaller, even sharper scalpel and cut just a bit more at each of the four incisions. As he completed the last one, O'Leary struggled and pulled the wood out from between his teeth. "Good God, Baldwin! You have inflicted more pain than did Morris!" he exclaimed, adding, "a wee bit more, Eileen, please?" gesturing with his eyes towards the brandy decanter, "as I sense the wretched ball remains in me."

Nodding, Baldwin indicated to Eileen that she was to give her husband another deep dram, and he himself now took one, before trading his second scalpel for some small forceps. "We are almost now completed, Arthur," he said softly as, without hesitation, Eileen having replaced the shim in Art's mouth, he deftly plunged the edge of the tool into the now gaping wound and, with a final *mffffffffffffff* from O'Leary, quickly extracted what was a nasty-looking, irregularly round, lead pistol ball, dropping it onto the plate on the floor with a *ping*.

Looking down at the ball, momentarily releasing her husband's hand, then bending and picking it up, Eileen shook her head in disgust. "Even the man's ammunition is badly made and of poor quality." Baldwin could only smile gently, evidencing no surprise that his sister-in-law could, and even in this moment, would judge the quality of a spent pistol ball.

Dr. Baldwin gently tugged at the shim and O'Leary opened his mouth. "Are we now concluded, Dr. Baldwin?" He smiled weakly.

"We are indeed now concluded, Captain O'Leary, *sir*," the fervently civilian physician responded with a smile, in what was his best attempt at the precision of military communication.

"More brandy, then!" O'Leary weakly laughed.

The atmosphere in the room relaxed significantly as Eileen poured drams for Baldwin, the others and then one for herself, jesting, ". . . and no more for *you*, sir!" as O'Leary weakly raised his empty tumbler, playfully jiggling it; only then did she smilingly relent with a partial pour, to be followed shortly by another, more substantial one.

The doctor informed his patient and the others what he was doing and why: "As this is a relatively small wound, not gaping, I shall not stitch it closed." He raised his right hand, gesturing to what he was holding. "Whilst 'tis to a certain degree porous, packed into the wound, this soft lint absorbs some measure of drainage from it and thus prevents the bandages from becoming soaked. The lint shall be changed as the bandages are, until the draining ceases, at which point only the bandaging shall be used. Ultimately, the wound will scab over, and complete healing will be in the open air." Dr. Baldwin packed the wound with the lint, indicating he would leave a supply of the batting and bandages with Eileen, but that he would himself return in the morning to examine the wound and "repack it," he said. He then wound a bandage and adhesive around the wound.

"He shall require the use of a sling for a time to immobilise his arm," he advised Eileen. O'Leary's convalescence would be remembered, in part, by his use of colourful scarves for the requisite immobilising slings.

After permitting O'Leary to doze for perhaps an hour, during which time they all quaffed brandy, Dr. Baldwin, Eileen and the three strapping young men managed to trundle the patient upstairs, Eileen insisting that he be settled into his side of the massive bed they shared, "for 'tis only right for a wounded man to recover in his own bed, even if that bed be shared by those who subscribe to the traditional German custom of the marital bed, as we do in Vienna." She smiled playfully at her brother-in-law, well aware that the good doctor and Mary O'Connell Baldwin had always maintained separate sleeping quarters.

County Cork, Ireland—late July–August 1772

O'Leary being the healthy and athletic cavalry officer he was significantly aided and considerably shortened his period of recovery. Though for the first few days he was a generally pliant patient, as he improved he suffered neither pain—though daily it decreased— nor inconvenience well. Eileen managed to humour him through the time, the little boys providing him with welcome distractions, and John and Anna Collins came frequently with books, good conversation and little Maria Theresa, who had already interested both O'Learys in the possibility of perhaps having a wee baby girl next time.

One breezy though still very hot Tuesday afternoon, the second of August, Squire Collins surprised O'Leary by bringing the relatively young Magistrate Andrew Baggot by to see him at Rathleigh.

As the two men joined O'Leary at his afternoon perch on the long back porch, even as he was taking a seat, the tall, fair, thirty-three-year-old Protestant aristocrat, heir to considerable properties surrounding Doneraile, was highly animated, first explaining that the Muskerry Constitutional Society, established in August 1771, was at present composed of approximately fifty Protestant gentlemen, all large landowners, of whom perhaps twenty were sworn magistrates.

"Squire Collins and I have spoken at length," the young man began, "concerning the vicious armed attack on you by Abraham Morris; his status as one of these magistrates notwithstanding, I believe the nature of the charges to be preferred by your good self against him should be discussed."

Correctly sensing O'Leary's expression to be at least to some degree questioning, Baggot continued, "I shall of course recuse myself from any consideration of your charges," and O'Leary nodded, though he wondered aloud if Morris would similarly act in terms of his own against O'Leary, which he felt certain would be brought. Baggot only shook his head, his expression evidencing his thoughts: *One can never tell with any degree of certainty what Morris will do . . . in any situation.*

Baggot posed and O'Leary answered a number of probing questions. In response to some of them, O'Leary spoke at length, his anger becoming patent. By the time the rambling conversation was winding down some two hours later, Baggot had, in the form of the careful notes he had taken, a detailed statement of what had transpired at Hanover Hall and, in his mind, a list of offenses, including multiple counts of assault and battery and one of attempted murder.

"I shall see that the charges are properly set out in legal form and bring them before as many of my fellow magistrates as quickly as I am able," Baggot advised O'Leary as he began to stand, slipping the papers into the pocket of his brown suit coat.

Still with some difficulty, O'Leary stood as well, his left hand half-raised. "I am most deeply grateful for your time and efforts, sir, but I am inclined to wait a bit to see what Morris does. You see, whilst an obvious coward he clearly is, I nevertheless believe that, as so they should, the facts shame him. Were he to bring charges against me, in doing so he must surely know I would allege in my defence what I have just now narrated to you . . . this being the only way the fact of his abject spinelessness on July thirteenth were to become public. So, you see, nothing may come of this." Both Collins and Baggot looked at him askance and shook their heads in unison.

"Ah, gentlemen, please permit me to say that I approach this from a station different from either of you: As a trained soldier, indeed a cavalryman, I have learnt in studying tactics that when, with good reason, one believes one's defence to be superior to that of one's opponent's probable offense, 'tis far better to await the other's first move   . . ."

Indicating their understanding of his rationale whilst, after again expressing their collegial disagreement, they laughingly exchanged somewhat awkward handshakes, with O'Leary's proffered backwards-facing left hand, and the visitors departed.

Wearied, as he still frequently found himself becoming later on in the day, O'Leary sank slowly, heaving back down into his chair, his eyes fixing on Bull, whom he suddenly felt was looking directly at him from across the enclosed field. "Ah, large fellow, is it that you know something I do not?" he said aloud, then laughed and closed his eyes.

Having waited a time after the men departed, Eileen's curiosity finally propelled her to the porch, her footfalls gently awakening her husband from his nap, and they began to chat softly, O'Leary summarising the conversation and explaining his strategic reasons for having Morris take the next step.

"Are we to believe that the Muskerry Constitutional Society would act so as not to somehow quash charges against one of their own?" Eileen asked, expressing some measure of disbelief as he disclosed the identity of Squire Collins's companion and explained the purpose of the visit.

"The young magistrate concludes the actions of Morris constitute grave legal mischief, and that he should be charged and may well be convicted of all the offenses alleged," he advised.

"I am less sanguine, my darling, though I am heartened that there even exists a young Protestant magistrate in this vicinage. Perhaps there is reason to hope for an improving future after all," she said.

"Of that I am uncertain, my darling. I do, however, feel that in this instance 'tis better to wait rather than plunge ahead."

In this, Eileen—recalling Donal Mór's seemingly very long ago similar-sounding admonition in favour of acting cautiously in uncertain situations—concurred. "Very well then, Captain, wait we shall."

They did not have long to do so.

Almost to the day, on a suddenly cool, misty afternoon the following week, young Squire Baggot returned alone to Rathleigh. Now knowing his identity, Eileen greeted him, and the young man smiled effusively. "How terribly pleased I am to formally make your acquaintance, Mistress O'Leary." He bowed. "I have heard much about you, my lady."

"Of what I can only imagine!" She laughed as she gestured him into the small parlour where O'Leary was reading to Conor.

As soon as Eileen and their little boy withdrew, Baggot sat heavily in the chair opposite O'Leary's. "Captain, your foe has indeed made the first move, sir; he has arrived on the field—in force," he said, equally heavily, handing O'Leary a sheaf of papers. The younger man's eyes quickly scanned down the first page and flipped to the second and did the same again . . . to that one and those that followed, finally looking up and shaking his head, his expression incredulous.

"He alleges sundry offenses, truth there being in but two or three of them," he finally said.

"*Some* degree of truth, perhaps, yes." Baggot nodded quietly. "So minute a measure indeed, such that I believe this may be the reason why he has caused these to be delivered to the magistrates rather than publicly publishing them in the newspaper, as is, you are aware, more typically the case."

O'Leary nodded, then volunteered, "He was armed with two loaded pistols, keeping the one with which he ultimately shot me secreted even as I had disarmed him of the first . . . and yet he has the audacity to make an allegation of attempted murder . . . *against me?* I being unarmed!" O'Leary's expression was now one of disbelief, his voice sharp, angry, echoing in the elegant, high-ceilinged room.

"Audacious indeed to level the charges . . . yet gutless, pusillanimous, both consistent with his character, to not bring them publicly."

"It is I, then, who shall bring it all into the public eye," O'Leary informed Baggot as he slowly walked him to his horse.

On 19 August 1772, there appeared a lengthy notice in the *Corke Evening Post*, in which O'Leary acknowledged that "Incredibly, given the facts as set forth herein," he had been charged by Morris with "significant various and sundry crimes," arising out of the events at Hanover Hall on 13 July.

O'Leary had no fear of any of the facts and was perhaps more willing than was his opponent to pay the per-word costs charged by the *Corke Evening Post* for such postings, so he outlined in detail what he characterised as his "wholly well-intentioned visit" to Hanover Hall, including an explanation of the reasons behind it, noting that he had "in writing, requested and received the said Morris's permission to enter upon his lands." He proceeded then to set out that "despite his good intentions," his "most civil conversation" with Morris had drawn "a most unwarranted response" from the man, who, O'Leary contended, had addressed him "in the most vile, the most foul of language." Not bothering to mention his own colourful exercise of the English tongue, O'Leary then narrated the steps that he had taken to withdraw, finally alleging that "the said O'Leary was pursued by Morris," who, he emphasised, "was armed with two loaded pistols, with one of which he shot O'Leary, who, though wounded, was fortunate to escape with his life."

The young officer also acknowledged the "various and sundry measures" by which he had sought to defend himself against the "wholly unprovoked armed violence, which was, despite such measures, ultimately visited upon him." He set out in specific detail what he had done to both defuse the situation—by requesting that Morris lay down what O'Leary had believed at the time was his only weapon—and to defend himself (by physically, forcibly disarming Morris), as well as the nature and extent of his gunshot wound, adding, with a customary flourish, that "O'Leary fled not in cowardice but, rather, retired only after vigorously defending himself, as would any gentleman finding himself in such circumstances, and, notwithstanding Morris's pistol ball being lodged in his upper arm, departing only after rendering his attacker unconscious."

O'Leary closed his notice by stating categorically that he was prepared to stand trial at the next Assizes at Cork, "then and there to offer a vigorous defence to the baseless and unwarranted charges levelled against me, confident in my full vindication," requesting only that in the interim "the public and the authorities suspend judgement," until such a trial may be held.

County Cork, Ireland—October 1772

The rest of the summer passed largely uneventfully. Conor's fourth birthday had been marked amidst his father's convalescence. Little Fiach had begun to make attempts at walking. Morgan O'Connell had journeyed from Derrynane in mid-September for a pleasant multiday visit. As autumn came on, the various harvest-related activities had gotten underway, two foals had been birthed—both fillies—and letters from Vienna, from Abigail, the countess and Colonel von Klaus, had all brought Eileen current on their various lives and activities.

The eighth of October fell on a dreary, chill Wednesday; late in the afternoon, John Collins arrived unannounced at Rathleigh, indicating to Ann as she opened the door that it was urgent that he see O'Leary immediately. She gestured for him to proceed directly to the stables. "The Lady Eileen is breaking a horse; she has *an audience*," she said, rolling her eyes. Collins smiled in reply.

Eileen, in breeches and with her hair tightly tied back, was indeed aboard a significantly unhappy young stallion, experiencing his first time under a saddle and doing all he possibly could to rid himself of this annoying person, who was equally determined to remain where she was. As Collins approached the paddock, it appeared to him that the battle was winding down and that Eileen O'Leary would be the ultimate victor.

Noticing his friend, O'Leary walked over to him, calling, "Come! Witness a grand war of wills!"

Collins smiled but rather gestured for O'Leary to step aside with him, immediately handing him the day prior's edition of the *Corke Evening Post*, already folded to an inside page.

His eyes quickly moving across the page, O'Leary frowned as he read of the "dastardly acts" Abraham Morris claimed had been committed "by the said O'Leary against my person and property," specifically alleging that, ". . . then and there O'Leary did . . . attack . . . repeatedly threaten . . . and from both the ground and from the security of his ferocious warhorse kick me to the ground."

O'Leary's hands were shaking with rage by the time he finished reading, learning that ". . . only after exhausting all of my pleas for reason, them falling on the deaf ears of the violent, aggressive and vicious O'Leary and finally succeeding in my attempt to reach the security of my home did I then, *and only then,* resort to the use of a small, virtually harmless pistol, firing it in an effort to frighten my attacker, in which effort I succeeded, the said O'Leary cowardly fleeing my property."

"The little bastard is creative, if nothing else. He has elaborated on the original charges, made without publication, and though his language is more colourful, little of this is new or of any greater concern to me than what I first saw in August," O'Leary muttered bitterly to his friend, who draped an arm over his shoulder.

"I agree, but I shall nevertheless seek out our friend, Baggot, and endeavour to obtain some advice," Collins said, with which course of action O'Leary agreed.

A fact of which neither Collins nor O'Leary was aware was that young Squire Baggot was at present in Dublin, called there just two days before on family business.

His absence, and indeed that of a second magistrate, Alexander Cameron, who had been in London for several weeks now, had removed two of the more thoughtful and least anti-Catholic of the membership of the Muskerry Constitutional Society from a meeting of fewer than half of the sitting magistrates, which was occurring even as Collins was learning of Baggot's journey to Dublin. The fact that these two men were out of the area had become known to Abraham Morris and his allies in the Society, the network of informers and spies he had developed over the years remaining active.

The rules for the Society's proceedings were few and ironically did not require that formal notice of any meeting be given; thus, Cameron and Baggot being absent, no effort had been felt necessary to alert any magistrates other than Morris and his allies, generally all rough-hewn in the

Cromwellian mould, each possessed of limited education but all maintaining to a powerful degree a full and utter detestation of Catholics, a uniquely virulent level of abhorrence being reserved for those they viewed as being amongst the highly pretentious, so-called Gaelic Aristocracy.

The proceedings this day, conducted in a corner of the public house in Macroom, were brief. With virtually no discernment, before they had drained their first flagons of the day, the men reached their collective decision. "So ordered!" cackled Wilfred Noble, thought to be one of Morris's few genuine friends, and his strongest ally amongst the magistrates, as he slammed his flagon on the rough tabletop. "We are now adjourned and, as always, gentleman, justice has been done. God Save the King!"

Even before the proceedings had occurred, the text of a notice of the magistrates' findings had been delivered to the offices of the *Corke Evening Post* and appeared the day following, 10 October, informing readers that "overwhelming evidence" had been produced, "sufficient so as to permit us to find and, acting in concert, we do so find and declare that the self-professed 'Captain' Arthur O'Leary be and the same is hereby found guilty of all charges brought against him by the Honourable Abraham Morris, save that of attempted murder, arising out of an incident on 13 July, this year. The single charge of attempted murder, constituting a felony, shall be tried by the court of Assize for the County of Cork, when next the same shall sit."

In bold lettering, the notice concluded that "***In light of the aforegoing findings made and verdict rendered, we further adjudicate that the said O'LEARY, having been lawfully convicted of multiple misdemeanours, be and the same is hereby declared to be an OUTLAW in our midst, liable to capture, dead or alive, by any loyal subject of His Majesty, good and true of this jurisdiction, said citizen, upon the production prescribed for in law, of the person of O'Leary, whether he then be living or dead, to be awarded forthwith the sum of 20 Guineas Sterling.***"

County Cork's most recently decreed outlaw first became aware of his new status whilst scanning the rough-paper pages of the newspaper some five days later, seated comfortably before a crackling fire, Conor playing with small metal soldiers at his feet, the thick Indian carpet apparently serving as a suitable battlefield, save that a troop advance over the rear legs of one of the family's massive Irish wolfhounds had just been repelled by the dog.

O'Leary read it once and then at least once again, shaking his head in disbelief, then laughing, genuinely and heartily, before he called, "Eileen!"

As she was just descending the stairs, a freshly napped Fiach O'Leary in her arms, she called cheerfully, "Coming I am, my darling!" just as she smilingly entered the room, immediately setting him down on the finely woven Chinese carpet, the smaller boy instantly knocking over Conor's carefully set battle line formation. As the inevitable protest began, O'Leary swept up his youngest son and plopped him onto his lap, allowing Conor to resume playing.

"You wished to see me, my love?" Eileen said as she sat. "Or perhaps . . ." She gestured at the paper, draped over the high arm of the winged chair in which O'Leary sat.

"Indeed!" groaned her husband, passing her the paper.

Eileen's deep-blue eyes went wide, and her lips parted as she shook her head vigorously, as if she had just been struck. "If this were not so horrible in print, much less in reality," she began hesitantly, "'twould be laughable, but . . ."

"But" O'Leary said sharply, "I shall consult with Collins and Baggot, the latter of whom I am quite certain will have great interest in this judgment having been rendered in his absence . . . and in the meantime, I shall respond briefly and in a restrained fashion."

As he did, in a 19 October advert in the Cork newspaper, saying simply that he "respectfully calls the attention of all interested persons to the allegations appearing over the said O'Leary's name" in the 19 August 1772 edition of the paper, concluding by saying that he "most humbly and respectfully requests that judgment of all charges against him be stayed until such time as O'Leary shall be afforded a trial on the merits of *all misdemeanours*, as well as the still-pending felony, by the court of Assize for the County of Cork, when next the same shall sit, at which time O'Leary, maintaining his oft-times expressed high regard for and trust in such Court, remains confident of his full and complete exoneration."

"It is done!" O'Leary called out as he dropped the Cork paper at the edge of the desk at which Squire O'Leary sat writing. "'Tis published and 'tis now done," he added more softly.

The older man gazed benevolently at his tall, trim son. "All I would request, my dear boy, for the sake of your beloved wife and children— indeed for all of us—is that you move carefully about, avoid public or indeed even private confrontation or disputation with any of those people and pray that reason prevails."

O'Leary placed his right hand on his father's shoulder. "I shall, Father, all of what you say. I would also say that, if 'tis any comfort to you, sir, Squire Baggot, the magistrate of whom I have spoken to you, advises that rarely if ever has any common person taken it upon himself to attempt to collect the price on the head of an *outlaw* such as myself . . . and that, in this instance, the legitimacy of the actions of Morris and his cohorts is so widely questioned that no one in authority would dare act in accordance with their decision."

The older man nodded thoughtfully. "But, my boy . . ." and O'Leary replaced his hand firmly on his father's shoulder, his gaze on the older man steady, sure—yet gentle and respectful.

". . . *but*, Father, I shall nevertheless conduct myself with the utmost circumspection and act only in total decorum, whatever the setting, whatever is said to me." He nodded firmly in emphasis and quietly walked out of the room, in search of his wife.

It was several weeks later, that, once again, yet another irregular gathering of the Muskerry Constitutional Society would convene, this time only Baggot and, interestingly enough, Abraham Morris himself not being in attendance. The sometimes-thoughtful George Davidson, the rough-edged master of a small horse farm just east of Macroom, as well as several men viewed as being perhaps more pro-Ascendancy than simply anti-Catholic in their beliefs and actions were present, along with Wilfred Noble and Morris's staunch allies from the 9 October session in Macroom.

Davidson had called the meeting and convened it. "The topic before us, my reason for bringing us together, is Captain O'Leary's most recent missive in the newspaper, most significantly his request that . . ." spreading the text out before him and adjusting his glasses, he proceeded to read O'Leary's words aloud. "I must admit I am impressed by the man's turn of phrase. . . . It would appear there is something to be said for obtaining an illegal Continental education." Davidson laughed softly. "I believe at Louvain, yes, as I was told by Baggot. I also believe he makes a somewhat compelling case."

"How so?" whined Wilfred Noble. "He is now a declared outlaw, subject to being shot on sight. I would . . ."

"When is the last time an outlaw has been shot on sight in County Cork, Wilfred?" Josiah Watson, owner of a small but successful dry goods store in Millstreet, demanded.

The response came not from Wilfred Noble but rather from James Aiken, a quite elderly—he would celebrate his ninetieth birthday in the autumn—squire, who had at one time served as high sheriff. "I believe in the late thirties, perhaps the early forties," he chirped. "The man then shot's name was Morrissey; he had killed his landlord in an ambush. Deserved killing, *both* of them did!" he rasped and leaned back in his chair.

"Precisely," said Davidson. "O'Leary is many things, but he is not a murderer."

"Not yet!" snapped Noble. "Poor Morris, he . . ."

"Poor Morris, my hat," Aiken joined in again. "He brought the violence that apparently occurred at his home on to himself, as I interpret the accounts."

Davidson smacked the tabletop with his palm. "Gentlemen, *please!* Please permit me to suggest that we make no ruling on O'Leary's plea, and I shall see to it that the Assize judges do not as well. Thus, an outlaw he shall remain, but free and at large . . . at least to the extent that no one desperate enough to try for the money gets off a lucky shot. Should that occur . . . it would be too bad for O'Leary but would leave us one less arrogant Papist traitor in our midst, eh?"

"In the event that he should not behave, or that he and Abraham . . ." began Watson.

"In that instance, should Abraham find himself aggrieved by the noxious O'Leary, I would suggest that we might then permit Abraham to, shall we say, do the king's work, eh? In the meantime, I suggest we let this matter rest."

"So then, are we agreed, gentlemen?" queried Davidson

"Agreed!" the group responded.

"God save the King?" enquired Aiken. ". . . *God save the King!*" they spoke as one.

County Cork, Ireland—Spring 1773

Though O'Leary had engaged in any number of private conversations, including ones with each of the men with whom he was this evening gathered, it was well into the winter, whilst at table in the public house partly owned by John Collins, with whom he was dining, Andrew Baggot, Squire MacCarthy, his equine partner and several others, that O'Leary for the first time openly, publicly discussed how he viewed his ongoing situation, and how he proposed to continue to deal with it, over what it now appeared would be at least several more months.

As the men gathered comfortably, seated in high-backed, rush-seated armchairs around one of a number of smooth, stained plank tables in a small side room, they began with pewter tankards of stout or porter and settled with ease into the dark, walnut-panelled, brass-fixtured elegance that Collins and his partners had created, the wood and the brass being dramatically highlighted by the flames of several dozen candles and the steady glow of the turf fire.

"Whilst technically 'outlawed' I am compelled to concede I indeed am, I maintain sufficient faith in the integrity, if not of the government then at least of several of the Assizes judges and the properly constituted courts they conduct, such that I do not intend to hide away or skulk about in the shadows as a result of the acts of a ragtag group of ill-educated, vindictive, make-believe judges!"

Seeing Andrew Baggot's wry grin, O'Leary's face reddened and remained so until his friend called out, "*That bunch*, they *are* 'make-believe'— *Hear! Hear!*" and the men all laughed heartily.

Later, in response to an earnest question from stout, sombre Squire MacCarthy, O'Leary elaborated. "As I have since October, I believe that I shall continue to be permitted to move about the County of Cork, and wherever else in Ireland, as I may see fit, as a free man. I have in good faith requested that this obviously illegal judgment be stayed—and such request has thus far been by no one, including those men who handed down the original decree, denied. Thus, I hold that the mantel of the king's justice rests lightly, protectively on me, as it does on all law-abiding men, and that it will protect me from all but the most venial of men, being those who would take another man's life—indeed the live of a stranger to them—for twenty guineas."

Leaning back in his chair, O'Leary raised his right hand for emphasis, concluding, "To those who *would* consider doing so, I would say that I shall protect myself from them, and that—fear not!—any attempt to capture or kill me will be met with violence, men will die in the attempt and I do not intend to be amongst them!"

Now it was John Collins who proclaimed, *"Hear, hear!"*

The year 1773 had begun quietly, and an uneventful, largely snowless winter had ended abruptly in a series of warm March days, as Cork once again began to quickly don its emerald-green cloak, the distant, blue-hued, warm ocean current dispatching gently moist breezes to mix and mingle with the near-daily, ever-increasing warmth of a benign sun.

"This day," Eileen had proclaimed poetically one Tuesday morning in mid-March as she tossed her heavy wool shawl onto the porch railing, "'tis one on which one must be grateful to be alive!"

"Indeed! *Ja!*" laughingly agreed Mistress Anna Collins as the two women watched and marvelled at the antics of both Maria Theresa and Fiach as, fully upright and walking wildly about, the two toddlers chased chickens and geese and, on Conor's heels, were now heading to the paddock fence to see the new foals.

With the arrival of spring, the winter-dormant social life of the neighbourhood had returned, the largest and most significant events the O'Learys, Collinses and much of the landed squirearchy—predominantly Protestant Ascendancy, as well as the much smaller number of Catholics— would attend revolved about the melded traditions of horses and hounds, all very much an intricate part of the social fabric, indeed of the culture of West Cork, and one in which the O'Learys especially revelled.

On 17 March, attired in the magnificent scarlet hunting coat Eileen had had made for him in London and given to him for Christmas, as he had done over the years whenever he was at home for the occasion, O'Leary, now aboard Banrían, joined in the annual St. Patrick's Day hunt of the Muskerry Fox Hounds.

As the O'Learys rode from Rathleigh, the early morning air was chilly, heavy with the aromas of turf fires, and, as they drew closer to the gathering place for the hunt, the cooking and the boiling of coffee and tea, all of the scents being carried on a gentle breeze.

As she had in previous years, Eileen, who appeared in breeches, high boots and an elegant tweed riding coat, her hair tied into a gleaming rope caused more than a bit of a stir. As a woman, she was of course not permitted to hunt, but she enjoyed the social aspects of the occasion, sampling the excellent array of spirits and food assembled for the hunt, both before and once the riders had departed. Then she mingled with those wives who had similarly come along with their husbands for much the same reasons, although, as Anna Collins observed to her friend in a playfully prim voice, accompanied by a saucy smile, "I note that Mistress O'Leary is the only lady attired in breeches."

Pewter tumblers of whiskey punch in their right hands, Eileen gently gripping Bull's bridle with her left, she and Anna were making their way through the small but animated group of women, moving from one conversation to, they hoped, a more interesting one, when Eileen felt a gentle touch on her left elbow and halted.

She found herself looking down onto the unfortunately unpretty indeed the pinched and sad-looking face of Mistress Morris, as, with a nod, she had correctly greeted the woman who had sought her attention.

The much-smaller woman, her complexion pale and slightly sallow, her tightly done hair a dull, grey-flecked brown, was visibly shaking as she gazed up at the imposing equestrienne whom she, in turn, had respectfully addressed as Mistress O'Leary in a dry, expressionless tone.

Eileen stood silently, Anna remaining at her side.

"Your husband, madam," Hannah Morris, despite her wispy, tremulous appearance, began in a suddenly steely voice, "as he stands convicted of numerous criminal offenses against my own, as the result of which he has been *outlawed* . . . as well as remaining charged with the attempted murder of *my* husband . . . I find it remarkable that he dares to show himself in public, and even more so that you would appear, especially dressed as you . . ." She gestured, a look of disdain on her plain little face.

Anna touched Eileen's arm, and she nodded wordlessly before saying, "Mistress Morris, I am of course uncertain as to what of this unpleasant affair your husband has spoken to you, but it is my understanding, as well as it is of the many people I know, that what actually occurred at Hanover Hall in July last is a subject of much debate, such that it remains for a court of law alone to properly decide. Nevertheless, as you are at least generally aware of the matter, you will remember that Captain O'Leary—and, if I may, that designation being his military rank, granted to him by commission of Her Imperial Majesty, the Empress Maria Theresa of Austria, Hungary and the Holy Roman Empire," she purred, "and in no way 'styled' by himself—has not only unequivocally denied all allegations against him but, as he remains free, at large and obviously quite alive, he having early on formally requested that the highly questionable judgment made by and the decree of a significant minority of magistrates be stayed. As his request has not been denied by any judicial body with authority to do so, I must say that he is, and indeed for that matter, we *both* are quite free to appear where and when we choose—as are you and your good husband." Eileen smiled, deliberately cloyingly.

Saying nothing further, Mistress Morris had turned to walk away when Eileen softly called, "Oh, and . . . *Hannah*, how I choose to dress and in what type of array I may decide to appear at a particular occasion is for me alone to decide . . .would you not agree?"

Wordlessly, Hannah Morris stiffly retreated to a distant corner of the distaff gathering, rejoining a pair of equally plain, seemingly equally unhappy, indeed similarly sad-looking women. As she did, Anna found herself staring at the woman, for whom she felt a fleeting pang of pity.

Anna and Eileen, who finally relinquished Bull to a young groom, rejoined the body of the group, and both were soon regaling a number of the other women with their versions of what the countess had always referred to as *Tales of Vienna*, to which Eileen now added some second-hand stories from Versailles, and Anna provided the always humorous, ongoing chronicles of her still-in-progress transition from life at the Viennese court to life in West Cork.

Whilst the ladies chatted and visited, ate and imbibed and strolled about for much of the pleasantly, neither overly cool nor excessively warm day, a gentle breeze rising at midmorning and continuing, their husbands traversed a broad, rolling cross section of the barony of Muskerry West, walking or gently trotting their horses until, as soon as the hounds had come upon the scent of a fox and raced off in pursuit, so, too, did the men accelerate their steeds, sending them racing across open country and flying—or, in some cases, attempting to, occasionally without success over a variety of obstacles —small creeks and larger streams, fallen trees, outcroppings of rock, the chase requiring skilled riders on sturdy, healthy mounts. The continuing cry was "over or through; never around!"

No fox had been run to ground, but most of the men were in high spirits, sweaty, mud-spattered and, more than a few, sore, several of those bruised or even bloodied from meeting with the ground or an inconvenient tree whilst no longer mounted. Both O'Leary and Collins had successfully cleared a daunting assortment of obstructions, largely natural in origin, though O'Leary had also come upon and Banrían had impressively taken at least two random fences,

Having heard what she correctly identified as being the long, mournful wail of "Blowing for Home," sounded distantly by the huntsman's horn in the still afternoon air, Anna had hurried to where the men were to arrive; she loved the excitement of the splendid horses and the elegant appearance of the mostly red-coated riders. By the time she heard the pounding of hoofs, Eileen and some of the other women had joined her, in time to witness O'Leary—strikingly alone and well ahead of his fellows—appear on the crest of the hill, his profile made sharp by the angle of the sun, Banrían's mane and tail starkly black against her chestnut coat, gleaming magnificently in the not-quite-late-afternoon light, as she and her master led the hunters home, the good-natured hoots and cheers of most of the men echoing along with the horses' thundering hoofs over and down the emerald-carpeted hill.

O'Leary and his by-now beloved mare were so far ahead of the others that he had raced almost to the bottom of the hill, near the level ground where the women awaited them, causing Banrían to rear up theatrically in greeting, and then to dramatically turn and streak back up towards the gentle crest, so as to re-join and arrive amidst his fellows.

As it was then, they all thundered and pounded and, as they slowed, thudded and jangled to a gregariously noisy halt, the sight causing Anna and Eileen and most of the women to laugh, cheer and applaud.

Eileen was enjoying just listening to the good-natured cheers and banter of the largely Protestant group, at the moment directed primary towards O'Leary and his prowess in the saddle: "Some good I see has resulted from your Hungarian Hussar-ship, Captain O'Leary!" . . . "You are a magnificent horseman, O'Leary, for a Catholic" . . . "Ah, for a Protestant, I feel myself compelled to say, you would be as well!" . . . "So, would my youngest lad have to become a bloody Papist to go, to where is it, Vienna? to learn to ride like that?" As well as lauding Banrían's appearance and performance: "Gawd, an extrord'nry animal she is, indeed!" . . . "Funny name; what's it mean, old boy? Ah, *queen* like an empress, you say. There, that makes sense!" . . . "The old girl actually gifted you with her? I doubt the third King Geordie gives away horses to junior cavalry officers!" . . . "Oh yes, right, how true indeed, the Lady Eileen, she was governess to the little whatever they call princesses there, was she not?" . . . "Perfectly magnificent mare, O'Leary" . . . "I have a stallion to stand stud to her" . . . "Bloody hell, no, you do not, sir, I have a far, far better one" . . . "She may be the most superlative mare in Ireland! . . . Never have I seen a mare of the quality of yours. . . ."

Eileen and Anna shared smiles and broke into laughter as, after a sweating, muddy John Collins slipped his arm through his wife's, then kissing her forehead, informed them both, "What none of this gaggle is aware of is that Banrían is promised first to our Lightning!"

In response, Anna cried out, "Upon the birth of a foal, we should then all be related, would we not . . . at least perhaps in some fashion, *ja?*"

The laughter continued as O'Leary joined them, kissing Eileen and pronouncing it "a gloriously good time!" Collins immediately and enthusiastically agreeing.

It was as the four of them were seeking out, as O'Leary exclaimed, "food and beverages!" that they heard what, as the noise of two men's voices grew closer, Collins instantly characterised as being "a slight rumble," leading the foursome away from the direction of the verbal discord.

"Morris! Morris . . . why do that? Why must you . . . ?" Andrew Baggot was demanding.

Then Alexander Cameron, who had been an officer in the King's Own Loyal Regiment of Foot, joined in. "Goddammit, Morris, 'tis been a good day, a grand day. . . . We all are enjoying . . . Who the bloody hell gives a goddamme who led the charge home? . . . You annoying little sod, the man is a trained cavalryman, riding perhaps the most magnificent animal . . . mare, at least . . . ever I have seen in Ireland in my lifetime! . . . *Morris!*"

It was to no avail.

Abraham Morris, his face nearly as red as his mud-spattered coat, had stalked away from Cameron, who nevertheless followed quickly on his heels. Obviously enraged, Morris suddenly grabbed O'Leary's left arm, his wrath only increasing as, without even a glance at him, the younger, stronger man effortlessly shook him off. "Like," one of the older gentlemen stage-whispered to everyone, "a bloody, stinking, nasty wee bug!" causing immediate laughter and outspoken derision of the stubby, former high sheriff of Cork.

Disregarding both, his small hands gripped into a pair of fists, the little man screeched loudly, "O'Leary, a word with you *I shall have*!"

Whirling about, O'Leary snapped, "*No!* You shall have not one bloody damned syllable with me," as most, men and women alike, who had heard the exchange, laughed, some of the men even whooping mercilessly.

O'Leary himself was not amused; his hands now on his hips, glaring down at Morris, he raged, "How *dare* you? How dare you deign to address me, much less to touch me, you worthless little sack of . . ." He paused, took a breath. "Do not ever attempt to touch me again. Do not ever speak to me again."

He then raised his voice, so as to assure that those of the gathered who wanted to would clearly hear what he next spoke. "Though you repeatedly deny that any of it occurred, you know full well what I did to you in July, following your unsuccessful attempt *to kill me, by shooting me in the back:* I rendered you senseless, your pistol ball lodged, if not embedded, in my arm notwithstanding. Know full well, sir, of what I am capable!" he dismissively commanded Morris, who froze in place as the group slowly dispersed, moving towards the plank tables of food and beverages and leaving a visibly shaken Morris standing mute, alone.

Later, unknown to the O'Learys, who, following drinks and a light supper, having said their goodbyes to their numerous friends, even as they were mounting Bull and Banrían, on the fringe of the gathering, retired Major Alexander Cameron's right forefinger was poking Morris's still pounding chest. "You are without credibility, sir, and your standing is virtually nil. If you are not careful, Morris, you will soon be a dead man, of this I am certain, and—now, hear me well, sir—it may well *not* be by Arthur O'Leary's hand that you forfeit your life," he sneered. "Disregard what I am saying at your own peril, Morris . . . you are bringing this cataclysm on yourself, sir!"

Shaking his head, the distinguished former British army officer stalked away, muttering, "Fool, bloody fool! May he get what he deserves!" as he rejoined his wife in the scattering crowd.

Dunisky Racecourse, near Macroom, County Cork—10 April 1773

At the early urging of Alexander Cameron and, after their witnessing her performance on St. Patrick's Day, the virtual insistence of a number of other gentlemen in the general neighbourhood, including virtually all of the men against whose horses she would race, O'Leary had entered Banrían in the annual race, run over the Dunisky racecourse, some four miles southeast of Macroom.

On race day, it was a beautiful, verdantly green setting, part of the course meandering gently along the south bank of the River Lee.

With the main race due to be run at noon, O'Leary and Eileen had set out from Rathleigh relatively early, "As I do not wish to tire our girl," explained O'Leary, again attired in his scarlet riding coat and, today, also in dazzlingly white breeches and his gleaming black, knee-high cavalry boots. Eileen, again riding Bull, was more conventionally attired in a simple, dark-blue wool robe, a traditional hooded Cork cloak draped over her shoulders.

O'Leary was bemused by the fact that she was riding sidesaddle, which she rarely did. "Given the prominence of our beautiful girl here"—she reached over to touch the chestnut mare, who, but for the distinctive white star on her forehead, had come to appear to many as being a smaller version of Bull—"and that, due to her excellent chances today, I feel she and we may briefly be the centre of attention, and I thus wish to be the *very soul of conventionality!*" She laughed heartily.

As they traversed the rolling, late-spring-green countryside between Rathleigh and Dunisky, swinging wide around Macroom itself, their conversation relaxed and wide-ranging, O'Leary inquired playfully at one point, "Are you aware, my darling, that the very first steeplechase ever took place *right here* in 1752?"

Instantly genuinely intrigued, Eileen nevertheless shook her head playfully. "No, sir, I was not . . . *do tell!*"

"Ah, 'twas from the steeple of St. John's Church in Buttevant to that of St. Mary's in Doneraile." O'Leary gestured generally north, referring to two Church of Ireland parishes with a gloved left hand. "Some four miles, and 'twas between a Blake and an O'Callaghan, the latter fellow I believe perhaps being my dear friend since childhood Johnny O'Callaghan's uncle, or perhaps grand-uncle, though never have I inquired.

"The rules were and remain simple: The riders must clear whatever fences and natural obstacles they may encounter on the most direct route between the two steeples . . . and thus was born an exciting form of racing," he pronounced, and they both smiled.

As they rode on, their talk turned to today's race, O'Leary sharing that it would be a relatively large—"At least two dozen, I am told by Cameron"—field and that, also according to Cameron and confirmed by John Collins, approximately half of the horses would be ridden by their owners, and many of the leading local Catholic and Protestant landowners would be represented. "I admit I enjoy the chase," he told Eileen, "and she is such a joy to ride, 'twill be as much fun as anything else." The rest of the field would be ridden by a variety of family, friends, trainers and itinerant professional riders.

"My darling, you must admit you also enjoy winning!" Eileen laughed playfully, "and with herself, I believe you stand a fine chance of doing so."

"I do indeed and I fully intend to ride to win today," he concluded, patting Banrían firmly.

As they arrived at Dunisky, the sounds of pipes, whistles and bodhrán echoing in the warm, gentle breeze, they immediately began to savour the fairylike atmosphere. Scattered about the sunswept field were clusters of tents and wagons from which a variety of foods and beverages were being hawked. They knew many and appeared to be known to a great many more people, with all of whom they exchanged greetings. They were both pleased to see that townspeople, small farmers and tenants, including virtually all of Rathleigh's population, as well as visitors from outside of the immediate area had gathered in sufficiently large numbers to make of it a truly festive occasion.

Shortly before their arrival, preliminary races had begun, including several for younger equestrians, one of them for girls, for which they were present. In her enthusiasm, Eileen spontaneously rushed over to personally congratulate all the girls who rode.

Taking her gently aside, she then quietly slipped a gold coin to the young winner. A hum of female adolescent conversation sounded behind Eileen's brief repartee with Ann Flanagan, a beaming, petite girl of perhaps fourteen years, with wild cascades of brilliant red hair tumbling below her shoulders and bright green eyes, who had won what had been a very close race:

"Do you not know who that tall lady is? She is the wife of O'Leary, *the outlaw!*" . . . "'Tis said she rides a huge stallion!" . . . "Aye, yes, see it there, he is tacked with her sidesaddle! What a handsome horse he is!" . . . "My mama says that she was for many years in Vienna, serving at the royal court" . . . "I knew that as well, for 'tis said that there she cared for the girl, a princess I believe she must have been, who is now the dauphine of France!" . . . "Yes, so 'tis *she* who one day will be queen of France. Can one imagine? Queen of France! . . . Can one even imagine actually *knowing* the queen of France!"

As time for the featured event drew closer, whilst O'Leary took Banrian to the makeshift paddock that had been assembled for the participating horses, Eileen joined Anna and several other women who awaited their husbands' return from the paddock. Collins and two of the other gentlemen had horses entered in the race, but, unlike O'Leary, other men were riding for them. As soon as he arrived, one of the owners, Arthur McGee, a spare, balding, almost severe-looking, middle-aged Church of Ireland minister said to be one of the very few local churchmen of significant independent means whose true personality lay in the constant twinkling of his large, green eyes set between crinkled lines, and whose parish included the area about Dunisky, leaned towards Eileen and in a playfully conspiratorial tone admitted—"confessed," as he laughingly described it—that "many of us owners are quietly hoping that your good husband and the magnificent young mare he rides will prevail. Whilst he is a most impressive rider, your horse is even more splendid!"

Eileen smiled her thanks, casting an eye towards the horses and riders as they continued to mill about. It was then that she was the first of the group to spy a wildly gesticulating Abraham Morris.

When she asked him, John Collins confirmed that Morris indeed had a horse entered. "The animal even appears much like him: small, not at all graceful, sad-looking and unpleasant." He laughed, though he quickly, unsmilingly, qualified his jest by adding, "The animal is also a strong, sound one; a skilled rider could propel him to victory."

Eileen had not laughed but rather sidled up closer to him, the tone of her familiar, husky voice an almost urgent one. "I just now noted Morris being present amongst the owners. Is Arthur aware of the fact, do you know?"

Collins sighed. "Whilst he may be, he said nothing of it to us"—he gestured to McGee—"and indeed, my dear, even were he, unless the good captain knew the hired riders, few of whom I have ever seen prior to today, and their masters, once the horses leave the start he shall be far too occupied to focus on the ownership of any of his competitors' mounts. Worry not then, Eileen." He smiled.

Try as she might, Eileen found herself unable to fully comply with his admonition.

In the paddock, the overall mood was light, almost festive. "'Tis for bragging rights at best that we race, for entertainment." O'Leary had gestured expansively at the crowd as he chatted with young Joseph Fitzgerald, recalling that "Both my father and I have had the privilege of competing against your good father, my boy, and if I recall correctly, on those occasions he was twice the victor." He clapped the young man's shoulder as he smiled proudly, laughing aloud when O'Leary turned back and announced, "But not today, lad!"

At the opposite corner of the enclosure, men nearby had, with no effort, overheard Abraham Morris, as one man characterised it, "haranguing the poor lad," the master of Hanover Hall gesturing wildly as he continued lecturing Martin McDaniel, a tall, lean, itinerant rider and groom of perhaps twenty years whom he had engaged to pilot his dapple-grey stallion.

"I was told you were a fierce competitor, boy; that best be true . . . for your own bloody good sake," Morris growled coldly through gritted teeth. "You see that smug-looking, yellow-haired fop over there, the tall one in the red coat? The one *holding audience?*" he sneered, gesturing bitterly towards O'Leary, who was surrounded by a mixed coterie of owners and riders. The young man nodded affirmatively, his jaw set. "You are to and you *shall* do all that is required to see to it that he does not complete the race . . . that would be the ideal. . . . Barring that, as loathe him I do, I concede he is a fine horseman; you shall similarly do everything necessary to defeat him. I do not care as much for winning the race as for your making certain that he does not prevail. In any case, he is *not* to finish the race ahead of you. Do you understand?" he hissed, gripping the younger man's lapel and physically shaking him.

His expression now grim, McDaniel nodded. "I understand completely, sir!"

Morris glared up at his rider and began to leave; abruptly turning back, his face ashen, he declared, "You best be certain, and ride as if you do. Should you not, the consequences for you . . . not good at all." He stalked away, leaving McDaniel momentarily alone as the eddying crowd of men and horses closed back around him.

Almost all of the nonriding owners having by now departed the paddock, there still being perhaps a quarter of an hour left until race time, loosely leading Banrían by her reins, O'Leary continued to stroll casually about, engaging in playful banter with those of the other riders he knew, or attempting to with those he did not, amongst the latter being Martin McDaniel, whom O'Leary had noted had been carefully studying him and his mare. As O'Leary attempted to engage the stranger, McDaniel only managed an obviously uncomfortably mumbled, "A fine animal, sir," before moving awkwardly away. Thinking nothing more of it, noticing movement towards the starting line, O'Leary reached for Banrían's bridle and led her in that direction.

Shortly after noon, the familiar command, "Riders—up!" was given, loudly enough so that even some of the spectators heard it, and the—for West Cork—vast throng was drawn inevitably closer to the course. Those who would first be at the starting line knew they would have to scramble for a good view once the horses were off. Others had already determinately marched directly to their chosen piece of higher ground, yet others held back, more interested in the finish than the start itself.

Her own heart thumping in a way it had not since O'Leary's wounding several months before, Eileen stood next to Anna and Margaret McGee, a chirpy, trim woman with an open, merry demeanour. Eileen had liked her immediately and was enjoying the minister's wife's story of a time when her husband was new to a parish elsewhere in Cork when they found themselves sheltering a Catholic priest from the local authorities.

"We believed him to be a groom—as so he said he was, and a fine one he was at that!—and over time we had both grown most fond of him," Mistress McGee was relating. "At one point in conversation the Reverend McGee questioned his frequent absence from service on Sundays. It was then that he related his tale and made known to us his true identity. Though he asked only for sufficient time to make good his escape before we advised the authorities, so fond of him we had become that we sheltered him, keeping safe his true identity and purpose until such time as our own period of service there was ended. We learned that he departed the vicinage shortly after we did, and that he is now ministering in Dublin."

Eileen had just said, "What a grand story . . . and, if I may, truly Christian behaviour on the part of your good husband and your good self, Margaret!" when, over the shorter woman's shoulder, she saw a familiar pair moving through the crowd.

A sharp, almost shrill, "Sister! Sister, *we are here!*" reverberated as Mary O'Connell Baldwin and her husband hurried towards them.

The disparate twins embraced, amidst much laughter and conversation, Reverend McGee looking at them standing side by side and pronouncing, "Sisters perhaps, but *twins . . . never!*"

Dr. Baldwin explained, though sharing no details, that 'twas the setting of a broken leg right in Clohina that had delayed their planned much-earlier arrival.

"Ah, the vagaries of a life in medicine!" exclaimed John Collins, handing the physician a tumbler of punch and pointing out O'Leary and Banrían in the paddock.

"We are *so* excited to see Arthur race," chirped Mary.

"Indeed!" added Baldwin, accepting a refill from Reverend McGee, as the cleric gave him a hasty overview of the field. "Unfortunately, we hear your brother-in-law's nemesis, the always-angry Morris, has a horse entered," he mentioned, "though at least he is not himself riding."

Dr. Baldwin's expression tightened somewhat. "Well, then, we can only hope that whomever the nasty little fellow has engaged behaves himself, eh?" and both men nodded.

Along with the others, they then turned their gaze towards the racecourse itself, as officials walked back and forth across the wide line of horses and riders, barking final commands, restating a brief description of the two-mile racecourse, one of the local minor nobility then reminding the riders, "You are either gentlemen or men who know how to behave as such whilst mounted. In either case—" he loudly exhorted—"you shall all conduct yourselves accordingly!"

O'Leary's battle spirit was by now up, his heart beating, rather than racing, at a steady thump, as he spoke softly to his beautiful mare. "You know who you are, from whence you have come and what you can do. Do your best, dear girl!" He reached over, tousling her mane.

Within seconds, an ancient blunderbuss was fired up into the air, the *boom* filling the moment, the heavy cloud of smoke drifting slowly over the spectators, as to many it appeared the horses themselves had been shot forward.

O'Leary nudged Banrían right, and then immediately left, then right again, playfully gesturing to Joseph Fitzgerald as he shot past the boy, who, in turn, pulled his own mount to the outside, passing O'Leary momentarily before he himself was passed by a magnificent black stallion on the far outside, its owner and rider, the elegant, prematurely white-haired Squire James Walker, gesturing to them both as he shot ahead.

Banrían was running as if she knew it was to be a long race, and that even though she was young and strong, she needed to hold herself back now. O'Leary sensed the mare's innate instinctive wisdom and gave the horse her head, permitting her to set her own pace, at least until he sensed they were slipping into the second pounding group of competitors, at which point, calling out to the mare, gently booting her, he reassumed control and, pulling sharply right, they streaked ahead, nearly along the outside, at the first-mile mark leading all but six or seven entrants.

They were now well away from the spectators and the officials, under a vividly blue, wide-open Cork sky. Having completed a series of irregularly placed, fencelike obstructions, the field was thundering across verdant, flat country, virtually all of the riders being aware that a series of ravines lay ahead in the second mile. O'Leary calculated they were in fifth or perhaps even fourth place, there being much jockeying ahead, and felt himself still unable to comfortably and safely break loose on either the right or left. Banrían was nevertheless running a strong, beautiful race; he loved her, adored the elation he was experiencing, causing him to spontaneously call out to the mare for the first time, "*Win,* girl, by Heaven, we shall win!"

Just at that moment, sensing pressure on his left stirrup and boot, he shot a glance at the surly, terse young man aboard the dapple grey he had been holding in the paddock. O'Leary gestured—*Watch yourself there!*—with a cock of his head, a flick of his left gloved hand, only then to realise the contact had been deliberate.

The stranger's right boot was now out of his stirrup. Momentarily drawing even with O'Leary, he shot a hard but glancing kick at his left leg, just as O'Leary accelerated. The grey's rider wildly striking—"beating him," other riders would say afterwards—with his crop, the horse again briefly caught up with the brown mare, McDaniel then slashing madly at O'Leary with his horsewhip, catching Arthur's left cheek at least once. O'Leary glared at the younger man, considered returning the violent gesture with one perfected in his cavalry training—which would, properly executed, have unhorsed McDaniel—but concentrated rather on urging Banrían forward.

"Faster, girl, forward!" he cried, using his voice and his heels, not his crop. The mare bolted ahead.

The dappled grey was charging to O'Leary's left, its rider now clearly attempting to cause a potentially deadly collision by forcing his own horse's right shoulder hard into the left hindquarters of a now-slowing silver-grey gelding. Whilst the desperate manoeuvre failed, it caused an abrupt bunch up to form before O'Leary could safely move Banrían almost fully to the far right outside, that being his desired position at this juncture.

As he slowed, the grey made another sudden charge on his left, a wild, *insane* expression on his rider's face now, as O'Leary would advise the officials afterwards.

Martin McDaniel desperately slashed once, then again and again, repeatedly striking mostly the air now, though several times glancing off of, once hitting O'Leary's back and thighs. Art O'Leary, clearly having had enough, abruptly and with uncharacteristically reckless abandon, pulled Banrían sharply left, immediately then to the right, only narrowly missing a collision but now fully on the far right outside, and leaned forward, his vision limited by what he could see through the mare's ears, his focus solely on the open space ahead, reminding himself to be aware of the oncoming ravines.

Shoulder to shoulder with Squire Walker aboard his reenergised black stallion, O'Leary cleared the first ravine effortlessly. The black, having done the same, then shot past, heading straight for the second, only to have O'Leary fly by on its right. At the next ravine, the handsome stallion inexplicably shied, abruptly, momentarily freezing, nearly unseating his highly skilled master, whilst Banrían took the final rift with graceful ease.

"Go, go, Banrían, *go* . . . fly, my darling, girl, *fly!*" O'Leary cried out, his body indeed his mind both seemingly now one with the majestic chestnut's as horse and rider then did fly, at times almost effortlessly, or so it appeared from a distance, especially to the few mesmerised men who held spyglasses to their eyes.

They were approaching the banks of the river, perhaps a half mile from the finish line, O'Leary now in the lead but not by much distance. Out of his left eye, he caught a glimpse of the gleaming black stallion, despite his mishap at the ravine now making a sudden, heroic charge on the far left outside. Some seven or eight horses bunched closely about Squire Walker and behind the chestnut mare; that group did not include the dapple grey and his desperate rider.

O'Leary could clearly see the throng a quarter mile ahead on his right.

For the second time, just as she sensed a lessening on her reins, Banrían felt O'Leary's heels sharply in her sides and must have heard him cry out, "All right . . . now, my darling girl, 'tis time! *Now!*" It was then as if Banrían understood: Summoning from deep within her the strength to support her determination, drawing on the spirit she shared with many of Maria Theresa's finest Thoroughbreds, from whom she had come, she once again shot forward.

Intense spectators now correctly sensed that Walker's gallant stallion was fading; much more thrilling, however, was their realisation that the beautiful chestnut was herself actually accelerating.

Banrían and O'Leary together now clearly saw the finish line; jointly, they heard the near-deafening roar of the throng as now seven, almost eight lengths ahead of the magnificent black, they triumphantly flew past the line, O'Leary letting his darling girl run herself out, finally pulling her up almost a quarter mile beyond, cantering back, then trotting, finally walking, slowly, precisely, deliberately as the crowd roared. With at first nothing more than elegant nods of his head and a gleaming smile, O'Leary gently acknowledged the raucous acclaim.

As they neared the crowd and the officials, O'Leary bent and affectionately embraced a gleaming Banrían's neck, and it seemed they cheered even louder. O'Leary finally stood in his stirrups, raising his right arm in triumph.

Eileen could no longer contain herself; gathering her skirts, she burst forward from where she had been standing between Anna and Margaret McGee. Her hair flying, she ran to a now-standing horse and rider, waving with both arms, laughing, crying. O'Leary dramatically bent and kissed her passionately from the saddle, and, if that were possible, it seemed that the people cheered louder still.

The race officials quickly moved forward. Even as O'Leary was dismounting and quickly embracing Eileen, they bombarded the victor with a series of rapid-fire questions about irregularities during the race, O'Leary's answers being sharp, blunt and, despite or perhaps because they were liberally spiced with the words *bloody* and *fucking . . . bastard* and *cheat,* as well as variants of the latter, apparently sufficient for the officials as, several of them bowing slightly to Eileen, the men stepped away. The couple, now arm in arm, acknowledged the crowd, smiling as Banrían suddenly found herself bedecked with a garland of wildflowers.

One surprise of the afternoon was the unexpected, and, most were certain, unprecedented, attendance of Lord Hamilton Boyle, sixth Earl of Cork and Orrery, believed to be the first of his line to ever have spent any time at all in Ireland. As the tall, spare, and always elegant noble, a bachelor in his early forties, stepped forward, O'Leary—one of the stewards having gestured towards Boyle, quickly whispering his identity—reflexively bowed, whilst Eileen, following suit, curtseyed deeply and flawlessly, the two rising to unexpectedly warm handshakes and kind comments from the severe-looking man, who had once served as the high steward of Oxford University, and who was perhaps best known by reputation in Ireland for his outspokenly virulent anti-Catholicism. It appeared to many surprised onlookers that he was at one point briefly joking with O'Leary, who later commented to Eileen, "He was quite friendly indeed, was he not?" Later, turning to John Collins, he advised that Lord Boyle had observed something along the lines that "'tis a genuine tragedy we—Eileen and myself—are 'disloyal, heretical Papists' . . . he said that, he did indeed and with a smile! . . . as what we have learnt of proper etiquette in Vienna, 'tis far superior to what he typically experiences in these islands!" O'Leary laughed, as did Collins, who, after reflecting a moment, told O'Leary, "If we have reached a point where a nobleman of long heritage, one who is seen as being amongst the most outspokenly bigoted of anti-Catholics, can speak and behave in the manner you have just described, I feel there may actually be hope for our troubled, still-contested island." He clapped his friend on his left shoulder and they strolled towards and quickly rejoined their wives.

Before it had begun and whilst the brief ceremony continued, the unsuccessful entrants were ridden or walked slowly off the course. It was then that a few of those not fully focused on O'Leary and Banrían sensed that some other form of tumult had erupted.

"You bastard! You lout! *Worthless son of a cheap whore*! You useless . . . fucking . . ." Abraham Morris shrieked as he repeatedly struck at a cowering Martin McDaniel with a coachman's whip; before he had caused any serious harm to the young man, just as he was screaming, "Not a fucking ha'penny to you, you fucking . . . " a group of men had disarmed him of the whip, leaving Morris to express himself solely through a barrage of incoherent verbal fury, at which point McDaniel finally grabbed the older man by both lapels, his right hand instantly forming a fist, which then solidly crashed into Morris's jaw, knocking him to the ground. McDaniel was immediately bent, seemingly reaching to draw Morris upright so as to again punish him when he himself was pulled off by several race officials.

A strikingly composed, professionally detached—such that he had almost ambled into the fray—Deputy Under High Sheriff Harry McCain then turned first to McDaniel, gesturing with a clenched left fist.

"*You* are a cheat . . . and, from what I could see from a distance and am just now told, not even a very good one. You will forthwith depart County Cork, never to return! I shall see to it that information as to the manner in which you have conducted yourself whilst racing here today will be circulated widely enough so that you may be safely assured that you will *never* again race anywhere on this island. Should you be found in Cork any time after the setting of the sun this day, you shall at once be jailed . . . to be held indefinitely. Now," he gestured with his gauntleted hands, "be gone!"

As the shaken young man then scrambled for his own horse, and kicking and whipping the animal wildly, did indeed depart, Harry McCain, flanked by a semicircle of grim-faced officials, turned coldly to Abraham Morris.

"Mr. Magistrate, sir, as I am at present only able to speculate as to whether or not you knew what your man was doing out there in the race, though from what I have just heard, just observed, I have a fairly good idea of your culpability, I nevertheless am uncertain as to what steps to take insofar as your own conduct this day, sir, or the manner in which they might be accomplished. On your undertaking that you will not leave the county, I shall take no measures against you until such time as I am able to obtain orders from the high sheriff. Should you flee, you shall be regarded as being and therefore shall be pursued and dealt with as a common criminal having broken bond, your status notwithstanding."

Without anything further, the young law enforcement officer turned away, an expression of severe disappointment, at, he thought, *this kind of behaviour, on the part of one of our own, no wonder we suffer the disrespect of the Papists,* on his round, open face.

As the young lawman finished, Alexander Cameron grabbed Morris by the left lapel, the still-rugged, former infantryman literally lifting the much smaller Morris off his feet. "I *know* what *I* saw and heard, and I deem the men from whom I learnt more to be honourable, unlike you, Morris, you cheat, you bloodyfucking fraud!

"We," he gestured at the other officials, "we shall see to it that you and any horse that is ever possessed by you shall never—do you understand, you poor excuse for a gentleman, *never!—ever* again participate in any sanctioned race in this county, you disgusting little snot. Now, be gone! Out of my sight!" Led by Cameron, the group of men turned and stalked away, melting into the eddying crowd.

As if the result of the race and being knocked to the ground by his own rider were not enough, the brief conversations with the young sheriff's deputy and Cameron, coupled with the thunderous cheering he had no choice but to conclude was for O'Leary and his horse, had only further enraged an already livid Morris.

Within moments, having retrieved his coachman's whip, he was stalking to where the joyous festivities continued. There, Eileen, by now radiantly clutching a small silver cup, was in animated conversation with Lord Clancarty, one of the very few remaining Catholic peers in Ireland, whose domains embraced Muskerry and a broad swath of the area beyond. Having only been in his company on one prior occasion, she now learnt that he had known John O'Connor at the time of their brief marriage. "All he spoke of you then is as true now, my Lady Eileen," he finished softly, only then excusing himself with a partial bow.

It seemed by then that everyone—which included John and Anna Collins and the Baldwins—gathered around the O'Learys and the still-flower-draped young mare, who appeared to be revelling in the attention being paid to her, was talking at the same time. Some men sang, whilst a piper, a bodhrán-player and two men with whistles had begun a raucous serenade.

Towards this joyful furore stalked a red-faced, sweating Abraham Morris, two men, sensing possible trouble, instantly swooped down on him. As he flailed about with his whip, striking one of them across his face and leaving a nasty welt, the men stepped back, shaking their heads. "Mad he is. I truly believe him to be a lunatic," said one to the other.

As O'Leary and Eileen stood flanking Banrían, a young artist was quickly sketching the occasion. John Collins observed to no one in particular, "Sometime in the future, man will have devised some contrivance that will instantly record a scene such as this."

"Squire Collins," laughed one of the day's beverage purveyors, "in light of that remark, I would respectfully say that your honour might wish to switch to water!"

The immediate crowd roared as Collins cried out, a raised goblet in his hand, "Never, sir, never!" and more so as he posed. "And, sir, is that any way to speak to a *prophet*!" Anna laughed so hard, tears came to her eyes.

At that moment, spreading his legs, holding up his coachman's whip in his left hand, as if it were a battle standard, a sweating, red-faced Morris fixed himself directly in front of a surprised, an almost bemused O'Leary, who had not, at first, even noticed him stalking into the gathering. His unabated rage obvious, arms waving, Morris started to shriek, obviously at O'Leary, and was immediately hooted and shouted down by more than a few men.

O'Leary stepped forward, Eileen reflexively taking the horse's bridle on the side where she stood, moved away, as did their friends, Anna tugging a wary Collins's sleeve.

"Please, let the magistrate speak!" O'Leary requested of those closest, over his shoulder. Annoyed as some hooted then at him, he turned fully back to the crowd, his expression unmistakably serious. *"Permit the man to speak and be heard!"* he ordered loudly, and the crowd was silenced.

O'Leary stepped to within three feet of Morris, eyeing the whip gripped in the smaller man's right hand, and gestured, his voice elevated, saying then, "Sir, speak if you will. . . ."

Morris cleared his throat, attempting, despite his generally dishevelled appearance, to appear as distinguished as possible. Now looking up at O'Leary, his dry, raspy burr gratingly sounded, loudly enough to be heard by many of those gathered.

"Under and as provided for in the *Act for Better Securing the Government By Disarming Papists*," he proclaimed ostentatiously, the crowd beginning to grow silent as people came to understand the drama that was unfolding, "I hereby tender you the sum of five pounds, five shillings, in return for which I demand that you forthwith turn over to me possession, full title to and ownership of that horse"—he swung his right arm towards Banrían, Eileen's head resting against hers. With his left hand, in which he held a small purse that presumably contained the statutorily required five pounds, five, he gestured at Banrían. Those people nearest to them noted that his hand trembled. An audible gasp was heard, and the crowd then quieted almost completely, word of what was occurring being passed to those further back.

O'Leary stood still, his cheeks ablaze, his eyes piercing, but said not a word.

"Now!" Morris screeched, "I demand of you, hand over that horse! *Now!*" his shriek piercing, gesturing wildly whilst dangling the small purse towards O'Leary.

Standing quietly, O'Leary dramatically, slowly folded his arms. Looking archly, scoffingly down at him, he nodded and then laughed . . . a loud, hearty, derisive, bitter, totally dismissive laugh, in which more than a few men joined.

Taking a step forward, his hands now on his hips, he snapped, "You? *You* demand Banrían? How dare you!"

"How dare I? How dare *you* flaunt a law of . . ."

"Silence!" O'Leary roared, leaning towards the smaller man. Morris immediately fell mute, stepping backwards to more than a few snickers and hoots from the crowd.

"This magnificent horse . . ." his voice remaining theatrically loud, O'Leary gestured grandly towards where Eileen held Banrían, ". . . was gifted to me personally by Her Imperial Majesty, the Empress Maria Theresa . . . of *Austria . . . Hungary . . .* and . . . *the Holy Roman Empire.*" He raised his voice dramatically at each geographic reference.

"The bloodlines of this horse," he gestured again, with a broad sweep of his right arm, "are amongst the oldest and finest in Europe. Despite your man's disingenuous efforts to have it be otherwise, along with all present"—

he spread his arms—"you witnessed yet again today, for yourself, her brilliance.

"So I say to you, *sir* . . . and I now declare publicly that I employ this form of address with grave reservations: You may put your wee purse with its pitifully wee pittance away, as were you to offer me one hundred times, indeed one thousand times, indeed *ten* thousand times five pounds, the same would be woefully inadequate for my horse, and would still constitute an affront, *Mister* Morris!

"So there can be no doubt in the mind of any person, whether present here or nay, please permit me to say, *I formally refuse your demand*," he said, the last words having been spoken slowly and precisely—and loudly.

As applause, even some shouts emanated from the gathered—*Oh, Arthur*, reflected Dr. James Baldwin, his wife's small hand gripping his own larger, much rougher one as they anxiously watched and listened to the drama unfolding before them, *if you could but somehow see fit to surrender the damned horse . . . magnificent as she may be . . . what I now foresee as being much difficulty could possibly be avoided*, though he kept his thoughts to himself, as, despite the number of people gathered, barely a sound was now heard; a cough, another one, the barking of a dog, someone beginning to speak and a *sssssh* . . . hissed by Lord Boyle himself, standing quietly with several acquaintances, his arms crossed.

O'Leary leaned ever so slightly down towards his foe. "So if I may, I shall now re-join my—" his words trailing off as incautiously he turned away, moving briskly towards Eileen and Banrían.

As he did, slipping the purse into and suddenly withdrawing a pistol from his left coat pocket, the coachman's whip still upraised in his right hand, at that moment, with an odd, high-pitched cry, Morris charged towards O'Leary, who was now striding a dozen, perhaps a bit more, feet from him.

The crowd erupted, as with one voice, "He has a gun!" . . . "O'Leary, turn about!" . . . "Oh my God, the little bastard . . . !" . . . "O'Leary, a gun, a pistol, that sack of dung, that bag of shit . . . he has a . . . !"

Almost immediately taking heed, O'Leary swung about, a pair of strides sufficient to put him directly in Morris's path, thus causing the little man to instantly halt, O'Leary effortlessly, or so it seemed to all who were watching, with an almost graceful motion of his right hand, seized the barrel and swept the uncocked pistol from a gape-mouthed Morris's apparently weak grasp, tossing it high and to one side.

This accomplished, using both hands O'Leary then proceeded to disarm his adversary of the long coachman's whip he was attempting to flail. With his right hand, theatrically but—the *whoosh* of the lash audible to those nearby—still sharply, O'Leary struck Morris, several times quite smartly, on both shoulders and thighs, at least twice across his chest, the smaller man coweringly covering his face as best he could, with his arms—"*Look at the little bastard, like a frightened wee child he is!*" someone in the crowd loudly observed, sparking a roared chorus of scornful laughter and words—even that to no avail, as O'Leary succeeded in striking Morris's cheeks and ears, then his neck, leaving his wig laughingly cockeyed, the ribbon of what had been its badly done bow hanging loose. Before the young soldier abruptly halted the thrashing, a number of sharp, red welts had appeared on each of Morris's cheeks, a smart one across his glistening forehead and a number on the backs of both his hands. Deeming himself finished, shaking his head dismissively, the young officer flipped the whip up into the air and over his right shoulder. A number in the crowd cheered, others applauded. They all then grew hushed as O'Leary faced his opponent.

Seeing Morris's uncovered face and wide eyes—the little man's hands gripped in tight fists, an incongruously yet pointedly grinning O'Leary, his own hands on his hips, suddenly stretched his neck—comically and rooster-like, stared at him, then feinting so as to appear to be springing forward at him. The lithe young officer then immediately leant back and quickly again lurched forward, the ploy causing a much-less-agile Morris to lose his balance and fall backwards, landing hard on the soiled, well-trampled ground.

Another booming-voiced man in the throng could not contain himself. "*Sitting in horseshite you appear to be, your honour, Mr. Magistrate, sir!*" he called out loudly, to which even more raucous, harshly derisive laughter was again heard, and hoots and boos as well, the mockery continuing. *Aye, in horseshite ye are . . . right where ye belong! . . . Would your honour like a shovel, sir? So you can do right here what you do every time you speak!* The crowd roared with more hoots, whoops and laughter.

Grimly serious now, without taking his eyes off a partially sitting, then kneeling Morris, O'Leary strode over to where the pistol had landed and picked it up from the ground. Turning sideways to the gathered, he dramatically fully cocked it.

As the crowd murmured, he continued walking towards where Morris had struggled to finally stand. Facing him, two arms' lengths between them, O'Leary offered the now fully cocked and loaded weapon—stock first, the barrel pointed at O'Leary's chest—to his adversary.

Speaking precisely in an even, clear, noncombative but loud voice, O'Leary ordered, "Here, take your weapon!"

Morris stood mute, his eyes wide, his mouth agape; his small hands occupied, still attempting to right his cheap, poorly dressed wig, he did not reach for the pistol's stock.

The silence profound, the tension palpable, O'Leary then formally challenged Morris to a duel, ". . . at this very moment, if you wish; I am certain a pistol I shall be able to obtain from someone here and now, or at another time and location of your choosing, here and now or then and there, for you to *perhaps* achieve what you have *yet again* failed to accomplish."

Morris eyed O'Leary disdainfully. "You well know that a duel between a Protestant and a Catholic is illegal, forbidden by the laws of Ireland!" he tried weakly, his voice shaking.

O'Leary laughed aloud and immediately postured, also loudly, "So say ye . . . how convenient! When, however, you attempted to kill me at Hanover Hall last July—I unarmed, and that fact fully known to you—you had no such qualms about shooting a Catholic *then.*"

Dramatically turning to the now-murmuring crowd, the pistol barrel still in his hand, O'Leary spread his arms wide. "Hear and witness the fact, all of ye! The magistrate has refused my challenge!" he cried. "He pleads the law!"

The crowd was momentarily silenced, and then sporadic booing ensued. O'Leary, who had turned towards Morris, silenced it by again facing the throng.

Recocking the pistol, transferring it to his right hand, O'Leary now theatrically whirled about so as to again face Morris. As he did so, pointing the pistol skyward, the young cavalryman discharged it—a powerful *boom* and heavy smoke filling the space—and simply dropped the weapon at his feet, the crowd, if anything, more silent than before.

"*No!*" O'Leary's voice now thundered dramatically, "no, you decline my challenge for but one reason, and one reason alone: You are, as I have always known you to be"—O'Leary's right forefinger now aimed accusingly at Morris—"a *coward!*"

His head snapping back as if he had been physically struck, Morris stood, stunned, mute. His jaw slack, he whispered weakly, "How dare you . . ." but stopped, realising no one could hear him. O'Leary's powerful voice was fully in command now, speaking so all could hear him, the utter silence a background for his words.

"Above all of your many other failings, by your own words and actions, anyone–as I do now, Morris—could only adjudge you a *coward*—" the repeated word hanging in the air—"as the pathetic, snivelling *coward* you indeed are! You are an utter disgrace to yourself . . . you are clearly no gentleman! . . . to your family, to *your people*, upon both of whom you now bring yet even more dishonour . . . and *you people* wonder why so little regard is paid . . ." Shaking his head, his voice drifted. O'Leary now spectacularly extended his right arm, his forefinger aimed at Morris as if it were resting on a pistol's trigger, preparing to deliver a final, mortal wound. "As I have said, I say again to you, Morris: a *coward* you are!" O'Leary roared, "A *coward, I say!* Shame! Shame!"

As O'Leary turned sharply and quickly walked back towards Eileen, her normally calm face ashen, her left hand clenched about Banrían's bridle, her right still gripping the winner's silver cup, a strident, harsh chorus of "Coward! Coward! Coward!" began spontaneously, alternating with "Shame! Shame! Shame!" Ever increasing in volume, accentuated by a sea of accusing fingers and fists, it followed Morris as he bent to retrieve his weapon, which rested atop a mound of horse manure, and even as he stumbled away, alone.

County Cork, Ireland—17–30 April 1773

The days following the race proved to be largely unremarkable, though just a week after the confrontation there between O'Leary and Morris, John Collins passed on to his friends chatter overheard in his public house, to the effect, without further elaboration, that Morris was planning "some type of armed response."

To which O'Leary felt he could only respond, "Should he do so, I shall then defend my family, our home and myself."

As she served the men tea, Eileen softly added, "We are all watchful and vigilant here; we can be nothing else."

So, too, in his own way, was Abraham Morris being vigilant, his own, however, being more concrete, taking the form of a request that the Muskerry Constitutional Society support him in obtaining the issuance by the high sheriff of Cork of a warrant for the arrest of Arthur O'Leary.

Given what many of them viewed as the ever-increasing gravity of the situation, virtually all of the member magistrates—except Morris, who had been requested to absent himself from the proceedings, in order to permit a free exchange of views and a vigorous debate—attended a meeting at the residence of the elderly James Aiken one evening several days after the race, and following receipt of Morris's written request.

Within minutes of George Davidson calling the meeting to order, Andrew Baggot had begun to speak. "My concern, gentlemen, is that, should we proceed in any way to now vary the Society's prior decision in favour of permitting O'Leary to remain at large, pending final adjudication by the Assizes, we would be perceived as being biased, and that—"

"*Biased?* Biased in favour of whom . . . or of what, Baggot?" barked Wilfred Noble.

Before Baggot could speak in answer, Josiah Watson smacked down both of his palms hard on the table around which the men were gathered, looking hard at Baggot. "With all due respect, sir, I believe what could perhaps be said to be your own bias, in favour of your apparent new friend, Captain O'Leary, may be clouding your own judgment, sir. . . ."

"But sir," interjected Alexander Cameron, only to have Watson sharply interrupt him.

"You, also, sir, appear to have become quite, *congenial* shall we say, with the outlaw O'Leary." He smiled, a nasty, cutting smile, silencing the quiet retired military officer.

Davidson then directed an accusing right forefinger, aimed, as he spoke, in a back-and- forth motion, at both Baggot and Cameron. "I would respectfully suggest that both of you gentlemen remind yourselves that we are charged with assisting to assure peace, security and the inviolability of the king's writ in this vicinage, and that in order to do so, we must at all times be vigilant to the reality that we—the king's loyal servants, good and true, and Protestant, which I would say includes both of you—remain a distinct minority here and, as such, that we must present a strong, cohesive defence against disloyal, seditious and dangerous Papists, such as your friend O'Leary."

"But, sir . . ." attempted Baggot again, his effort ignored by Josiah Watson, who continued Davidson's unsubtle diatribe, beginning with an audible sigh.

"It is clear that both of you have permitted the fact that O'Leary is—or at least we hear that many of his coreligionists believe him to be—witty and bright and charming, that the Lady Eileen is, in addition to being, shall we say, quite *fetching* in her own right, perhaps also witty and charming, to disabuse yourselves of the reality that both *are*, and, despite their appearance and even occasional behaviour to the contrary, *remain* disloyal, seditious and boldly arrogant Papists!"

Wilfred Noble, one of Morris's few friends, and viewed as his strongest ally, coughed and, for effect, rose. "Indeed, if I may, the fact is, gentleman, that this man O'Leary is a well-known, violent Papist. He traitorously serves—indeed he is a commissioned officer—in the Catholic Army of Europe, the full force of its power and vengeance of which is aimed at the heart of Great Britain, at *our* heart."

Alexander Cameron then stood rigidly, as if at attention. "Speaking now as a long-serving commissioned officer in the 4th (King's Own) Regiment of Foot—" he began proudly—"*I* wish to be certain that you realise, sir, that there never has been and there is now no such milit'ry organisation, no such fighting force, as the 'Catholic Army of Europe.' Am I correct, sir, you *do* understand this, do you not?"

Ignoring the pointed question, Noble continued dismissively, "One can only imagine the dark skills and deadly abilities in which he is trained. O'Leary is quite capable of killing a man with his bare hands, of that I am certain."

Cameron snapped back, "Bah! Nonsense—all of this! *Delusional*, it is that you are!" and he sat down abruptly.

Clearing his throat in punctuation, Davidson resumed, his volume increased. "Nevertheless . . . I am certain that we are able to agree that the uniform he wears . . . I might add, all too frequently . . . is the uniform of a commissioned officer of the army of a foreign Catholic power, whose interests always have been, remain and forever shall be contrary to those of Great Britain, of which Ireland—of which *we*—are an intrinsic, permanent and wholly subject part!"

A chorus of "Hear! Hear!" accompanied by much table pounding followed, silencing both Cameron and Baggot for the balance of the discussion. Cameron raised his hands in exasperated surrender, while Baggot wearily shook his head.

"Now, then, gentlemen, let us proceed," suggested Davidson. "In light of O'Leary's just days ago very public assault on a magistrate of the Crown, not to mention his refusal to comply with the five pounds for a Catholic Horse Law"—at the mention of the obscure, in recent years rarely enforced early Penal Law statute, several of the men chuckled—"I would suggest we consider how we might assist in maintaining peace and order here, absent the issuance of a formal warrant of arrest of O'Leary by the high sheriff."

"Might I suggest," began James Aiken, cracking a wry, bitter smile, "continuing in the spirit of not formally responding to O'Leary's request to stay judgment, that given his recent infractions, committed whilst nevertheless having been previously declared to be an outlaw . . . and there existing at least on the part of some individuals, I believe, concern both as to the validity and issuance of that original declaration, though I myself take no issue with either—remember, *remember*, we are dealing with a native Irish Papist here!—that we perhaps 'suggest' to Morris that it would not be seen as being inappropriate were he to informally assemble a small . . . at least for now, civilian . . . force of armed men," nodding his head, he smiled again his bitter smile, "with which he could then attempt to capture—or, we could only hope, kill!—the outlaw O'Leary, eh?"

Several men appeared quizzical, perhaps even doubting, and Davidson, his expression grim, demanded of all of them, "Why should we not permit this course of action?"

"Because it is con'try to the law and its workings, you fool!" roared Alexander Cameron, again standing.

"Hah!" scoffed Davidson. "The law in Ireland is, as it must be, sir, *flexible*, as we—the king's loyal Protestant servants, along with all of the king's loyal Protestant subjects on this island—remain a *besieged* people . . . the views of *you*," he pointed at Cameron, "and *you* . . ." he pointed with the other hand at Baggot, "and your weak-kneed ilk notwithstanding!"

Gesturing with his hand, giving what he was about to say an air of finality, Davidson spoke firmly. "To permit it to be thus done—by Morris and a posse—could serve our purpose of ridding ourselves, our county— indeed ridding Ireland itself—of a notorious Papist traitor, either by death or lengthy incarceration, whilst at the same time shielding His Majesty and the crown, should there be any public outcry from . . ." he gestured broadly at the two men in dissent, "those whom I understand are, in certain quarters, now being referred to as so-called 'enlightened Protestants' . . .

'enlightened,' I interpret, as meaning *feeble, foolish and naïve.*" He laughed dismissively. "Such as our misguided friends here, eh?" he finished, a number of palms, even knuckles and a fist pounding yet again on the tabletop in response.

"If I may," cackled the ancient James Aiken, "with any providence, such a confrontation could prove to be doubly beneficial . . ."

Puzzled expressions now appeared all around the table.

"Should Morris, in the process of capturing or killing O'Leary, somehow get *himself* killed, we would thus have rid ourselves of *him* as well!" He laughed caustically, cruelly. "I myself have long found Abraham Morris to be as troublesome as virtually any bloody Papist bastard!" He laughed again, as did most of the others, the ironic truth of what he had expressed not being lost on any of them.

Aware that he would inevitably be delegated the task, "I shall thus advise Morris," volunteered a partially standing Wilfred Noble, "that, should he so choose, a party of men he may then assemble."

"But no arrest warrant!" qualified Davidson, continuing, "none! Thus, should he choose to act, and remember," he gestured broadly, "Morris indeed may well not thus act . . . as what O'Leary apparently expressed in no uncertain terms at Dunisky, about the little bastard being a coward, as I have always felt him to be! But should he act, and should it go badly, if then pressed, we would be able to opine that, though the actions may have been done under some measurable 'colour of law,' he possessed no actual authority to do so, eh?"

"Whatever the hell *any* of that means!" rasped James Aiken, his creased face glowing.

"Indeed! Brilliant!" echoed about the table.

Andrew Baggot and Alexander Cameron then rose to depart in disgust, and left in some degree of apprehension, as well, the snarled words of Josiah Watson chilling. "You two, you will keep the confidence of this Society, of this meeting! Should it come to our attention that you have failed to do so, either or both of you will pay . . . with your standing, your fortunes, your lands . . . or anything else deemed appropriate . . . *anything* at all, gentlemen."

Seeing Baggot and Cameron exit, the door again closed, the final response was spoken. "Indeed, yes! . . . and we are adjourned," declared John Davidson. "God save the king?"

"*God save the king!*" so said all of them.

Anna had raised the possibility of Eileen and the little boys staying for a time at Derryleigh, but Eileen told her, "In no vainglorious way, my darling, I believe my place at a time like this is with Arthur."

Even when O'Leary urged that she at least consider a temporary removal, Eileen resisted strongly, and indeed it was she who had quietly gone about checking and loading the house's various weapons, assuring herself that there was adequate shot and powder at Rathleigh, should they be required. She reported her activities to her husband, who thanked her most sincerely, and suggested they resume their lives, though they consciously decided to remain at home for an indefinite period, also attempting, though with little success, to discourage visitors, including Alexander Cameron and Andrew Baggot, who appeared shortly after dusk one evening, briefly sharing the substance of the most recent meeting of the Muskerry Constitutional Society and, at both O'Learys' insistence, quickly departing into the unnervingly still night.

So, it came as little surprise to either Arthur or Eileen when, about half past six on the warm, otherwise quiet morning of the seventeenth of April, a breathless Seamus burst through the main entrance and raced to the dining room as the couple were breakfasting with their little boys. "*Men!*" the young groom cried. "A large group of mounted men has just been seen on the coach road! One of the lads from the fields," he pointed, "spied them and raced cross-country."

O'Leary, already dressed for the day in a rough white shirt, grey breeches and black boots, lowered his half-drunk teacup, daubing his lips with a napkin. "The wee ones, and all of you girls, to the cellar, please, now," he requested almost matter-of-factly, of Mary, one of the younger girls who shared a variety of household duties, who half-curtseyed and offered her hands to both boys. "Toys . . . as well as food and drink for you all will be brought down," O'Leary added as, rising, he gestured to the other serving girls to gather and deliver the items, telling them to then remain in the cellar, then saying quietly, "And to you, my darling, my gratitude for seeing to our arsenal." He smiled.

Eileen was already standing, in a crisp, grey wool dress. "To our positions, then, Captain?" she asked with a brave smile, for they had quietly, between themselves, and with Seamus, Henry and Ann, and Squire O'Leary—who, at their request, now remained with Catherine, in Cork—discussed the possibility of an armed confrontation occurring at their home since the previous summer. They were fully prepared to an extent that not even John and Anna Collins knew: Once, as planned, Seamus and Henry would join the couple, amongst the four of them, upstairs and down, they would have over a dozen rifles, each a brace of pistols, as well as the extraordinary volume of powder and shot Eileen had laid in, on both floors.

"Indeed, Mistress O'Leary, to our positions we shall now proceed." He pointed his finger up, indicating that, as planned, Eileen would be upstairs, whilst, taking two rifles out of the gun cabinet in the long corridor, he positioned himself at the as-always-gleaming black front door.

It was there that he was, and upstairs at the grouping of three front windows in the middle of the second-storey façade that Eileen was, both already heavily armed, as a mounted group of perhaps a dozen men, with, not surprisingly, Abraham Morris in the vanguard, clattered up the Rathleigh lane, with some effort finally arraying themselves across, and some twenty feet back from the front of the stately, starkly white house. Quickly looking out through a parlour window on what appeared to be a largely ragtag posse, O'Leary swung open the front door and stepped just outside, cradling a fully cocked rifle, at the moment Morris was awkwardly dismounting.

"Arthur O'Leary, you have been outlawed, and I have come to arrest you!" Morris cried out dramatically, his left hand, drawn across his ample stomach, now resting incongruously on the hilt of what appeared to be a very old sword. "Or, should it prove to be the case, to deliver your dead body to the authorities."

O'Leary stood quietly, studying Morris closely, considering, weighing the reality of the situation, and then, speaking in a calm, firm tone, "Very well . . . but as to which I must first ask of you, if I may:

"Since you say there is to be an 'arrest' . . . which I should think would be considered an 'official' act, pray, please where is the high sheriff or perhaps the under high sheriff . . . or at the very least, even a *deputy* under high sheriff?" he asked, then, walking forward and along the irregular line, he began gesturing at random men, each of whom lowered his eyes uncomfortably. "Are *you* he?" he asked a lad of perhaps seventeen. "Have *you* today been so deputised?" he inquired of an older man, awkwardly cradling a dirty, battered rifle, which was not even partially cocked, the man quickly averting his eyes. "Or perhaps you?" O'Leary pointed at another mere lad, who never did look up.

O'Leary stepped back from the mounted men, mere feet from Morris and, his rifle now clutched in his right hand, spread his arms wide, theatrically: "I ask of you, then: Is there no man here empowered, whether by His Majesty, the King, or by act of Parliament or by the lord lieutenant of Ireland or by the high sheriff of Cork, to enforce the king's writ at this time and place, absent an extremely questionable resort to the use of force of arms, eh?"

With a disdainful look down, O'Leary then stepped past Morris, who appeared confused, and finally stood again at the entryway of the house, facing them all. He laughed ironically at a visibly discomfited, though increasingly angry Morris, and as he did so, O'Leary approached him yet again.

"I then demand of *you*, Mr. Morris, as your men have all stood before me mute; I conclude that 'tis you who most assuredly possesses the authority to have come here thus . . . so I demand that you now hand to me *your* commission . . . hand to me as well the properly prepared warrant of arrest by and under which you claim to legally act." Switching the rifle to his left hand, O'Leary held out his open right one.

Morris stood mutely; at first fingering the sword hilt, he then clumsily, awkwardly withdrew the dull-looking weapon from the scabbard, grasping it tightly, its tip resting on the broken stones. He never looked directly at O'Leary.

Finally, stepping back, O'Leary once again cradled the rifle across his body, his finger resting gently on the front of the trigger guard.

"I thought thus," O'Leary said sharply, dismissively to Morris. "Nevertheless, hear me now." His eyes then scanned the line of mounted men and boys. "Hear me, *all of you!* Had you appeared here as or in the company of a properly, legitimately constituted individual, possessing the authority to lawfully arrest me, I should have—though most unhappily, I assure you—immediately submitted and departed with you." He gestured at the band of men, several of whom nodded to one another, as if to say, *I believe he would have.*

Turning to Morris, addressing him directly, "This obviously not being the case, you have no right to be here, none at all! I order you now to leave. Depart from here at this moment, you and your henchmen . . . from this my family home, in which at this moment there be solely my wedded wife and two small children and our domestic and outside servants . . . all innocent people."

O'Leary waited a long moment and then levelled his rifle at Morris. "You and your little army shall now retreat," he said flatly.

Several of the men immediately began to turn their horses' heads.

At that moment, Morris, now wielding, or attempting to, his abruptly upraised sword, with the use of which he appeared utterly unfamiliar, unexpectedly, ineptly and with a piercing screech, charged O'Leary, whose face reflected simultaneously felt surprise, and perhaps even more than a bit of mirth.

A rifle shot shattered the deathly silence of the moment, the ball lifting Morris's fine beaver hat up and off his head before ricocheting off a tree or some rocks. Dropping his sword with a clatter of stones, stopped in his tracks, the little man then stood with his left hand incongruously and unsuccessfully attempting to straighten his now comically lopsided wig.

Eileen, who had fired the weapon from her second-story perch, leaned out of the middle of the group of three windows, peering through a slowly clearing veil of smoke that lingered in the still morning air. "I would most strongly suggest you comply with Captain O'Leary's orders," she called out as the horsemen sat stunned, none yet with a weapon raised, "and depart from our home now, Mr. Morris . . . before someone is injured or . . ." She quickly, dramatically, reached down and, with the assistance of an unseen Henry, deftly switched weapons, immediately raising a loaded, fully cocked rifle, pointing it directly at the yet-again-reduced little man, standing awkwardly alone, his hat gone, his wig, despite his efforts, still laughably off centre, his sword lying in the gravel where he had dropped it. ". . . *killed*," she finished without lowering the weapon.

Shaking his head, O'Leary flicked his hand dismissively at Morris, calling out, "So I order you yet again: Be gone, then!" After waiting a long moment, unchallenged, he turned only to halt abruptly and turned again to face Morris and his men.

"On second thought, rather than arrest me, why do you not simply shoot me? It is permitted under the law, under which I believe that I am *liable to capture, dead or alive, by any loyal subject of His Majesty* . . . or words to that effect."

The silence hung heavily in the yard.

Still grasping his rifle— "So you can say that I was armed and dangerous," he advised—O'Leary spread his arms wide. "Shoot me! Mr. Morris? Any of your brave men? Shoot this 'outlaw'!" he laughed. After several long moment, he lowered his arms, turned and withdrew into the house, closing the black door with a gentle click.

Turning towards his passive group of men, Morris cried, "*Fire!* Fire, you worthless scum . . . as you were ordered to do, should this occur! *Fire*, I say!" Scrambling for his hat and his sword, perhaps half of the men now cocking and levelling their rifles as, waving his sword frantically above his head, he rushed to rejoin them.

"For the final time, before I shoot one of you sons of bitches, *fire!*" Morris yelped, finally cocking his own firearm, the large pistol with which he had shot O'Leary at Hanover Hall and waving it in the air. Only then did an uneven burst of gunfire hit both the entry and Rathleigh's façade, accompanied by loudly whining ricochets, the balls pockmarking the gleaming black door, the spotlessly whitewashed obverse of the lovely house, whose defenders immediately answered from within with a spew of smoke, fire and lead.

Seemingly unprepared for any armed resistance, the men—all of them shocked, some obviously horrified—quickly dismounted and scattered, seeking sparse cover behind the few random trees that stood between the house and the coach road, as a withering fire blazed at them from the house, upstairs and down, virtually and, to them, terrifyingly uninterrupted.

Morris, who had not taken a shot, raced towards the thin cover, dramatically threw himself facedown on the ground, then crawled towards a wispy birch and knelt, from which position he fired his pistol impotently at the house.

"Remember, as with our first volley we shall not shoot to kill, my darling, as this could possibly strengthen his already weak legal position," O'Leary called up the stairs during a lull in the uncoordinated incoming volleys, hearing only a firm, husky, "Aye!" before Eileen immediately fired again, joined by Henry and Seamus.

From upstairs and down, O'Leary and Eileen's, as well as the young men's rifles and pistols, steadily belched gunfire, Seamus reloading Eileen's weapons, whilst young Henry did O'Leary's, both lads firing their own guns sporadically, so that the house's firepower quickly overwhelmed the ostensibly inexpert posse. O'Leary and Eileen had now wounded at least three of the company, including one man who lay on the dew-wet grass screaming, "I am kilt! Dying it is I am!" though this not being the case, Eileen concluded, primarily from having taken careful note of the small amount of blood on his shirtsleeve; she saw it as most likely being a superficial flesh wound.

From their different perspectives, she and O'Leary both then noticed some movement, apparently responding to the wounded man's cry; first one and then another figure timidly appeared.

Eileen, who had the better view, called out first, "Come, rescue your fellows! And please assure *him*"—leaning out of the window, she gestured with the delicately smoking barrel of her rifle to the vocal, middle-aged man lying in the open—"that he is most likely *nay kilt*!"

O'Leary echoed his wife: "We shall not fire on you; come get your men . . ." he ordered.

During this pause, serious old Ann appeared defiantly in the parlour, lugging a loaded, gleamingly polished rifle, which O'Leary did not recognise and, after assuring him that his sons were safe "with the girls below stairs," demanded politely but firmly of him ". . . to be given my rightful place, in defence of this, my home, sir," which—although they had attempted, unsuccessfully, to prevent Seamus and Henry from actually firing, lest the young men possibly be later charged—O'Leary immediately did, the woman taking a position in a window of the large, more formal front parlour, across the entry hall from where O'Leary crouched in the smaller one.

As soon as a seemingly tentative fire resumed from outside, levelling her rifle, to O'Leary's amazement, Ann expertly sighted and squeezed the trigger, screaming, "Take that, you bloody cowards!" A loud cry, "I am shot!" immediately reverberated from behind a spruce. She stood and smiled, gesturing with the smoking tip of her rifle's barrel. "Got me one, 'twould appear I did, Captain sir!" she called smugly to an open-mouthed O'Leary, who had been unaware that Ann even knew how to fire a weapon, which was why he'd permitted her to shoot. Staring for the moment at the uncharacteristically animated woman, he looked again out the window where he knelt, sincerely hoping she had not killed the man.

Sporadic firing, with Ann, to O'Leary's bemused surprise, skilfully reloading her own rifle, continued for approximately thirty minutes more, both O'Learys and the others concluding, correctly, that Morris and his men were close to running out of ammunition.

"Show yourself, Morris!" O'Leary finally called out. "I shall not shoot you, you have my pledge," he said as he opened the front door and, unarmed, his hands palms up, at his sides, stepped into the sun-drenched entryway.

There was no response.

"Be gone then . . . with your wounded," he ordered. "Be gone now!"

Turning to and for the first time seeing the bullet-scarred front door and the façade of his home, he stood for a moment and appended a muttered, "You bloody common bastard!"

O'Leary's pledge notwithstanding, Morris and his men remained huddled in fear and uncertainty on either side of the lane for another quarter hour. Ultimately concluding that they would not be fired upon further, they skulked out of the woods carrying their four wounded men, all of whom would recover, and were soon mounted and away.

County Cork, Ireland—the Final Week of April–the First Week of May 1773

The hours following the armed attack on Rathleigh House witnessed the descent of a dreamlike atmosphere about both the place and its people.

Once the departure of Morris and his henchmen from Rathleigh was confirmed, Eileen permitted the servants—Mary, to whose care the little boys had been entrusted, as well as the four other serving girls—to emerge from the safety of the cellar.

As they—Mary carrying little Fiach, Conor clinging to her right hand— did, they entered a profoundly changed atmosphere, one reeking with the bitter aroma of burnt black powder, sacks of random, stray, dirty grey lead pistol balls scattered about the floor, a delicate haze stubbornly floating through much of the usually elegantly, comfortable house, accentuating the discomfiting image of rifles leaning against chair-railed, crown-moulded walls, pistols resting on fine mahogany tables, granules of gunpowder spilt by several windows.

Eileen and Art, not to mention, Seamus, Henry and Ann, all appeared as none of them had ever before been seen: sweat-soaked and dishevelled, their faces and hands, especially their fingers, smeared with powder residue and dust.

The little boys, especially Conor, seemed equally bemused and confused by their parents' unusual appearance. Eileen tried as best she could to make light of how they looked and of the situation in general, but, as O'Leary said wearily, "Even the wee ones, they know *something* has happened here."

It was Monday evening of the last week of April when, just before nine o'clock, an ashen-faced John Collins rapped sharply at Rathleigh's bullet-damaged front door, just beginning to say, in his familiar, chest-deep voice, "'Tis I, 'tis Collins, 'tis most urgent I see . . . " as the door was pulled open by O'Leary.

"Arthur, we must speak . . . alone and immediately."

Without a word, O'Leary led him to Squire O'Leary's small study, closing and locking the door.

"My friend John, were you to have seen a banshee I do not believe you would look thus," said O'Leary, gesturing as, with a flick of his hand, he silently offered Collins brandy from the sideboard, his visitor's response a vigorous, wordless *yes*.

Pouring two deep snifters, O'Leary leaned back in his father's chair, waiting for Collins to take a deep draught of the warming liquid. "Speak, my dear friend; tell me now by what it is you are so troubled."

For the next half hour, a grave John Collins spoke—angry, at times enraged and animated as O'Leary had never before seen him—and a shocked O'Leary listened, saying literally nothing, as Collins related what he had been told by one of his barmen, who this evening had worked not for Collins but in the public house on the Market Square in Macroom. "The lad, who is fully trustworthy and thoroughly loyal, came directly to Derryleigh from there, and I from Derryleigh to you, Arthur, after he spoke with me . . ."

The news Collins shared began in a mundane enough manner; this night Abraham Morris was drinking at the public house with, amongst others, Wilfred Noble. Collins's man related that it appeared they had been there for a time when he arrived to work but even then were into their cups, emphasising that, as the evening progressed, so, too, did their intoxication.

The snippets of conversation the young man had at first caught were meaningless; he did not begin to focus his attention until he heard "that bloody bastard O'Leary" mentioned. He then began to listen carefully.

"After so long," Morris had slurred only slightly, "no longer do I desire the bastard dead."

This apparently surprised his companion, who inquired, "Why this change . . . why now?"

"O'Leary fears not death. . . . He is a bloody fool, a fanatic of sorts, he thinks himself brave, or the Auz-rians they have made him b'lieve he is . . . but . . . of little matter that . . . or he actually b'lieves that Papist heaven shit, wi' fucking angels an' a Blesht Virgin, hah! . . . and whatnot . . . No, death, it does not frighten him . . ." He laughed uneasily. "It bloody fucking terrifies me," he managed to add quite seriously.

Alternating between porter and whiskey, as he downed swallow after swallow, between gulps, he sat sullenly, silent, continuing only when his tankard was empty of porter, his tumbler drained of whiskey, both being promptly refilled by Collins's man.

"What he fears . . . what would destroy the great O'Leary . . . would be if that woman . . . that tall, black-haired bitch, his fucking wife . . . were killed . . . The Lah-Lah La-dee Eye-Leen," he cackled, ". . . now *her* death—" he knocked heavily on the rough plank tabletop—"now *that*—" he struck the table again, this time with his fist—"*that* is what would devastate the bastard, of that I am now certain. . . . No more strutting . . . no more fancy uniforms, no more fucking sword . . . or horse-racing or fox-hunting or dancing. . . . It would ravage him . . . her bloody well fucking dead, yes, it will! . . . *and so it shall!*" As he again slammed his fist on the tabletop, his face became illuminated with a frightening light, a terrifying grin.

Whilst a rambling, desultory conversation in which he did not participate continued for a time, and as his companions, other than Wilfred Noble, drifted slowly away, Morris drank considerably more, and was hunched over his arms, which were folded on the table by the time Noble attempted to resume their own talk.

"So . . ?" Noble had finally asked, apparently trying to lead Morris back to the previous topic and, receiving no response, asked again, "So? Wha'bout O'Leary? Wha'bout O'Leary's woman?"

"So?" Morris flared. "So?" and drained his glass, slamming on the table.

"So! . . . the p'sumptious . . . arr-gunt Papis' bisch, I kill . . ." Swaying in his seat, drooling now, he stared at Noble . . . "will kill . . . fuck, I . . . I . . ."

He paused, forcing himself to sit straighter and, wagging a finger at Noble, Morris announced, ". . . I wan get zis crec't," then, taking a breath, he struggled, "I . . . will . . . I will have . . . her . . . killed," finally finishing with a manic hoot and a call for yet more drink, which Collins's man quickly brought, then took his time to yet again wipe the surrounding tables thoroughly.

"Yeh . . . tha's it . . . *I . . . will . . . have . . . her . . . killed!*" He pounded his fists on the table as he spoke again each of the last five words.

"Wen?" A by-now equally very drunk Noble managed to ask. "Wen . . . d'ye . . . do this?"

"You soupid fuck." Morris waved his hand dismissively. "Wen you t'ink? Soon . . ." He slammed both palms flat on the table. "Fuckin' soon, fuckin' now. . . fuckin' nest week . . . th'latest . . . nest week . . . have this fool'sh, soupid bas-sard my place . . . will do it . . . he haste Caf-licks . . . prolly haste Papis' bischess, like tall bisch O'Leary even more." He leered. "Yes!" He pounded his fist on the table. "He fuckin' shoots fuckin' Eye . . . Leen . . . in 'er fuckin' 'ed—" he laughed hysterically—"an' . . . an' *I wan t'tell O'Leary* that . . . Eye-leen's fuckin' 'ed blown off . . . then see O'Leary's arr-gunt face, then . . ." He rapped again and paused for long moments, as if to think; then he began wagging his left forefinger at Noble.

"Y'know, annnn, may-bee not zhust uh bisch . . . but his fucking sons . . . I—" Morris thumped his chest—"I . . . n'er had sons . . . that barren, useless, fucking bisch o'mine—" he cackled bitterly—"none! . . . but O'Leary, two!" He struggled to hold up two fingers, laughing when he finally did so. "My man, maybe . . . should kill fucking two sons, too, yes? *Yes!* Kill the bisch . . . kill the sons of a bisch! *Yes oh fuck yes!*" He pounded on the table, laughing hysterically.

Even Noble, as intoxicated he was by then, appeared to Collins's man to be shocked, frightened even, not only at his scheme, though that was sufficiently horrifying in itself, but perhaps even more so at the expression, the manner, the tone of Morris's voice, not to mention the unsettling glow of his face, the terrifying fire in his eyes, as were Morris a man possessed.

"My man related that he then left, Morris and Noble remaining, as he himself could take no more; sickened he was, but said that he knew immediately to come to me." Collins nodded, his expression a combination of worry and rage.

O'Leary then sat silent, as he had for the duration of his friend's terrifying narrative, his face gleaming with sweat in the candlelight, his fists clenched tightly, undried tears on his own cheeks.

He took a long swallow of brandy and, as his cheeks flushed, sat reflectively for another moment, finally speaking in an even, weary voice. "Morris . . . in his drunkenness, his rage, perhaps, yes, his madness . . . he has yet spoken the truth. I do not fear death. I cannot remember when . . . perhaps as a lad? . . . whence last I did. Perhaps it is foolishness, perhaps bravery . . . whatever *that* may be . . . or faith?" He nodded. "Perhaps *'tis* faith, *and* the angels." He smiled weakly, gesturing towards heaven with his fingers.

"But . . . were I to lose Eileen . . . yes, he is wholly correct, 'twould indeed destroy me . . . a condemnation to lifelong grief, never ending . . . until I joined her in the grave and in God's heaven . . . but *this I shall not permit to happen*, not by Morris's hand, not by that of any man. . .

"For him at this time to threaten Eileen . . . not to mention the wee lads . . . He has now crossed a line . . . he has gone too far . . . he has brought us

. . . Morris and myself . . . to a place from which only one will emerge," O'Leary concluded, his expression one of determination, his voice quiet, calm even. Collins sat, staring, a sudden chill causing him to shudder.

"Whilst nothing can be done this night, friend John," O'Leary said as he led Collins to the door, waving a lantern for Seamus to bring up his horse and, awaiting the animal's arrival, he continued, "I shall speak with you soon, as early as tomorrow perhaps. Say nothing of this to Anna, please?"

Collins nodded, and, as O'Leary watched, he thundered off into the soft, moonlit April night.

It was at that moment, standing alone in the moonlight in front of his home, that O'Leary irrevocably decided that he would kill Morris, certain that, without question, he had no doubt it was the right thing to do, indeed the only thing he could do. And, as he snuffed out the various candles on the first floor and, carrying a small, still-lit one, slowly climbed the stairs, he for the first time began to seriously consider returning to Vienna with Eileen and the little boys. *As I promised General O'Connell I would, should circumstances here deteriorate*—he shook his head—*as it would appear they now have.* Once he had slain Morris, *who truly deserves to die, not solely because he now dares to threaten Eileen and our sons, though this alone is reason enough . . . no, because he is indeed the human embodiment of Loyola's "malignant enemy"* . . .

Once upstairs, O'Leary stopped first in the nursery, looking for a moment on his sleeping wee lads, recalling what his father had written when he had learned of Conor's birth at Laxenburg, almost five years earlier, that "a son secures for him a father's immortality"; now, seeing both of his treasured sons, tucked in securely, sleeping soundly, the gentle moonlight but a shaft in a corner of their room, he stepped out noiselessly.

In the bedroom he and Eileen shared, as he shed his clothing and slipped under the light covers with her in their massive bed, O'Leary knew now that his determination had become steel. Resting up on his elbow, looking down on Eileen, also sleeping soundly, the soft blush of the late April moon on her cheek, delicately reflected in the tumble of blue-black hair, now wonderfully tousled across the pillows, silent tears streaked his nighttime lightly blond-bearded cheeks. *Nothing shall happen to you, my darling Eileen of the Raven Locks . . . that I promise you.*

Wednesday morning of the final week of April, O'Leary softly but firmly advised Eileen that "I fear we have reached that point in time when *something* must be done to stop Morris in his crazed, vindictive madness," but said nothing more.

By Wednesday afternoon, as his wife returned from the outdoor kitchen, O'Leary seemed to her unusually quiet, pensive, distant even. "You appear to be yet again far away, my darling love," Eileen said softly as she drew her hands about his neck, beneath his carefully tied queue. She was pleased to see that he had reverted to a bright red ribbon with which to secure it.

"I am very much here present, darling, but, aye, my thoughts they are many and conflicting and, yes, indeed distant. Whilst I admit I have, over time, brought much of this wrath on myself, there being a variety of causes . . . I fear not for myself, for my own life. . . . Not that I ever did, but 'tis no longer fair for you and the wee lads, as well as my father to be in harm's way; and Ann and the young girls and Seamus and Henry, even the men in the fields, the tenants and their families—I fear we all are now potential targets. When next he comes, will it be then somehow he will manage it will be with the king's own troops?"

Though he had indeed made up his mind what the *something* was to be, he purposely did not tell his wife, or, other than John Collins, anyone else. Nor did she ask.

By early evening on Wednesday, O'Leary had made several critical decisions and, during the course of a solitary ride on Banrían through the gently gathering dusk, he had already begun to put his general plan into action.

In accomplishing the actual killing of Morris, he would act alone: His honour demanded it; his love for his family, his affection and care for the people about them required that he involve no one else directly. In obtaining necessary information as to the man's movements, his whereabouts, he would rely on but a few people, and even with these individuals, he would avoid asking direct questions, making pointed requests; this O'Leary had already begun, during the course of his ride, by posing indirect, indeed highly circumlocutory inquiries of some of the older, most-trusted tenants, all of whom, in truth being his friends, men who would, he knew, as each had nodded or otherwise gestured, in turn, do the same, in most likely an even more oblique manner, of similarly trusted acquaintances farther afield.

Thus, even as the dusk of Wednesday evening finally descended over West Cork, murmurs and rumours had nevertheless begun to float through the moist, inconsistent May zephyr.

By midmorning on Friday, from Rathleigh to Derryleigh to Macroom, and as far as Doneraile and back towards Millstreet and Carriganima, the words were yet again on the wind; it was, they said, to be a time of resolution, a moment of conclusion, of finality . . . *all were at hand*, the words on the wind said.

Not only, as intended, had Abraham Morris heard the words; he had also felt the eyes, sensed them upon him . . . and with barely a word of explanation to Hannah Morris, he fled Hanover Hall, such that Saturday morning, after a restless night, he had awakened at lodgings in Macroom and by late morning had most urgently requested of a perceived friend, Major James MacAteer, military protection and support; this, he had said, "being required in light of my perilous position—a matter of life and death as I am attempting to apprehend, indeed to kill an enemy of the crown, a violent declared outlaw who remains at-large in our very midst." He had told MacAteer a most creative version of his unsuccessful attempt at Rathleigh, attributing its failure solely to the fact that he had been compelled to gather a civilian posse, "when it is only trained soldiers of the king who shall be able to rid Cork of this disloyal and seditious Papist vermin."

MacAteer had listened patiently to what he believed were Morris's rantings but refused his request.

Morris did not relent; undaunted, early Monday morning he resumed hectoring the beleaguered officer. So it was that Morris's ongoing entreaties proved such and his pestering persistence sufficient, that by Monday evening, a worn-down though still hesitant Major MacAteer had nevertheless, albeit reluctantly, assigned a detachment of a dozen mounted other-ranks only to Morris, justifying it to his superiors in Cork City by describing Morris's official capacity as "a magistrate of this vicinage, who has been and remains engaged in armed pursuit of a notorious outlaw and traitor, who, despite the gallant and heroic efforts of the said magistrate, remains at-large, threatening the peace and order."

As a result, on Tuesday morning, 4 May, as Morris travelled to Millstreet on a distinctly non-military mission of acquiring and selling several horses, he did so at the head of what someone had catcalled from a window as he departed Macroom, "his own itty-bitty little army."

From several directions, the eddying Cork winds, from which O'Leary had earlier learnt it was this day that would bring Morris to Millstreet, had also brought word that Morris was attempting to obtain military support but nothing more, to Art O'Leary, who at early afternoon dressed in a fresh, white linen shirt, grey breeches and a striking brown tweed riding coat, his workaday boots also brown but shined, entered the smaller family parlour at Rathleigh, where Eileen was kneeling on the floor, playing at toy soldiers with Conor and Fiach. Smiling as he overheard her even huskier voice say, as she advanced several hand-painted lead figures of mounted cavalry across the thick rug, ". . . Ah, all is well, have no fears, O'Leary's men of the Hungarian Hussars are arriving. . . . See, they approach yonder . . . the battle, it shall now be ours!"

After watching wordlessly for a moment longer, he gently, almost casually bent and kissed Eileen's forehead softly and, lifting her right hand, her fingertips equally so. "'Tis good that your work is completed and aside, Eileen, and all is right here," he said, and she looked up and smiled, his voice powerful but gentle. "For 'tis time, I must now proceed. . . ."

She looked up wordlessly, saying nothing in response, though she knew, as he began, "As I depart now, perhaps never to return . . ."

Hearing this, she shook her head, though her expression remained nevertheless unchanged, for, since they were first wed and she having then allowed that she may perhaps have been a wee bit insecure, he would always in jest say something similar upon departing and, as she did now, she had come to say, "I shall here await you, my darling, for return to me you shall, as return to me you always have." She smiled and sat back on her heels, her elegant hands folded in her lap as she had done at Derrynane, as well as in the imperial palaces of Austria, and watched O'Leary depart.

As he looked back at his wife and sons once again at play, O'Leary whisperingly repeated, "Perhaps never to return . . ." and shook his head sharply, dispelling the notion.

When O'Leary entered the barn, precisely as he was supposed not to have been, Seamus was nowhere to be found, but Banrían was saddled, and to her customary tack had been added hand-tooled Spanish leather holsters, in the right one of which now rested O'Leary's silver-hilted sword, whilst the one at his left knee held his loaded rifle, as well as, draped over the horse behind and affixed to the saddle, a pair of saddlebags containing ample powder and shot.

Mounting the mare, O'Leary walked her out into the sunlight, his eyes briefly drawn to the brilliant white house, the unimaginably dazzling emerald green of its setting, he then trotted up the boreen, the horse's hoofs crunching and clicking on the broken stones, heading thence out onto the coach road, following which he pointed Banrían briefly in the direction of Macroom and then sharply due north towards Carriganima, where—basing his estimate on what he had heard on the wind and thus believed—O'Leary would intercept a still presumably solitary Morris as he returned from his horse-trading expedition at Millstreet. *I need not confront him; I require no dramatic altercation. I shall simply kill him . . . and be done with it,* he mused.

As O'Leary cantered into a quiet mid-afternoon in sleepy Carriganima, unbeknownst to him, Morris and his mounted force were approximately five miles north, moving south at a steady pace. Seeing nothing unusual afoot, O'Leary slipped quietly into the afternoon coolness of Cornelius Duggan's small, nondescript country pub. Nodding to the half-dozen patrons and the barman, he requested ale. As he was standing at the corner of the room, sipping quietly, an older farmer approached, his hand extended. "Michael O'Riordan I am, Captain O'Leary, sir, and a fine race you and your brown mare ran at Dunisky." He smiled, O'Leary taking his hand and his compliment, and they chatted for perhaps twenty minutes.

They discussed horses and the weather. O'Leary laughed as the man wondered aloud if Eileen were "the tallest young woman in Cork." Immersed in their equine-centred conversation, neither man appeared to have taken particular note of the arrival by the front door, shortly after O'Riordan had introduced himself, of a dark-haired, nervous-looking adolescent boy, who, after exchanging brief words with the barman, hastily departed by the rear one. As he did, O'Riordan nodded imperceptibly.

Finishing his drink and his conversation, O'Leary took his leave of Squire O'Riordan and returned to Banrían, beginning then to wonder if the quality of the words, the information that had reached him on the wind was as strong as he had believed it to be. He rode slowly perhaps a mile farther north in the direction of Millstreet, quietly, unobtrusively and somewhat impatiently; there was no sign of Morris, and no indication from either of the wordless exchanges he had on the road that Morris's precise whereabouts had become known, beyond that he was to have been in Millstreet.

Frustrated, with a deep sigh, O'Leary finally turned the mare's head south again. *Ah, loathsome Morris, perhaps it is that today is not the day on which you shall die*, he thought as he again neared Carriganima, riding cross-country on a back road and from a slightly different direction; judging from the arc of the sun it was perhaps four o'clock.

Circling to one side of Carriganima, O'Leary approached and crossed the rough footbridge over what he knew was a narrow part of the gentle River Keel. A few birds chirped, and he caught sight of the tip of a fox's tail as the animal darted into the cover on the stream's far bank. As he came nearer to the coach road, alongside of which meandered the river, he reined his horse left, onto a low ridge, just above and parallel to the road, and clicked gently to her, urging her into a trot. The empty road travelled down a bit and just ahead; after that, a jaunt of perhaps six miles to Rathleigh, during which he would ponder his next moves, in this strange, evil game of chess he was playing with this malevolent man. . . .

O'Leary heard the sound of a gun being fired at the same moment he felt the pain of the musket ball violently tearing into his chest. Proceeding forward perhaps another hundred feet, finally, reluctantly, he toppled heavily from Banrían and found himself lying on his side on the warm ground, the sun having managed to filter some of its light through the trees. He vaguely sensed distant sounds and movement . . . and lay quietly, *assessing the situation*, he would have said were he in combat, then reflecting that, ironically indeed he had been, *though this enemy refused to show himself but rather has stalked me instead of meeting me on a field of battle.* He shook his head. The pain in his chest was extraordinary. He pursed his lips and closed his eyes for a moment, taking a deep breath, sighing.

The old woman—she was certain she was at least ninety; recently, she had begun to think she was perhaps even older still, as she had heard people speak of distant events, a number of which she remembered first-hand, or nearly so—her shawl drawn loosely about her late-afternoon-weary shoulders, had heard the resonance of gunfire as she struggled up the slight incline of the riverbank. Her basket full of nettles, she shook her uncovered grey head, thinking in Irish, her only language, *Shooting? At this time of day, in this place?* She had heard a single shot at first, and then others. . . .

As she ambled through the cover, she briefly heard the distant thud of horses' hoofs moving away quickly, and then, but for the softest May breeze, silence.

It was not until she was almost upon a single large, brilliantly yellow-blossomed gorse bush, the flowers thick, the distinctive coconut aroma heavy in the still afternoon air, that she startled and then gasped, kneeling as quickly as she was able. She was immediately at the side of a *handsome . . . ah, beautiful even*, she thought, she would always remember, young man, inexplicably lying on his side, attempting to raise himself up on his elbow, near to the bush.

As she approached, a horse—a striking, chestnut-brown mare, though she did not take note of it, with a white star on her forehead—which had been standing over the man, who was seemingly its rider, looked at her with wide, terrified eyes, perhaps even nodded abruptly, whinnied and then, turning her head, sharply bolted. From where she knelt, the woman could see the animal swiftly heading south on the coach road, reins trailing, stirrups flailing, her coal-black mane and tail flying.

As the woman knelt, his eyes—she would never forget his eyes—*'twas of the gentlest blue, they were*—fluttered and opened, looking at her plaintively. Then she saw the blood spreading, staining, already soaking the young man's very fine white linen shirt, pooling ever so slightly in the thin soil from which had sprung the gorse bush.

"I am shot," the beautiful young man said softly in Irish, and she silently, right away nodded, to show she understood. He continued, "I saw no one, heard but one shot . . . and immediately felt its effect as it entered my body and forced me off my horse . . . and I heard then a volley." He breathed deeply. "I fear my wound, it may be a mortal one," he added calmly.

The old woman tenderly moved him so that he was lying flat; she lifted his head, pillowing it with a thick, folded, bright-red kerchief, smoothing his blond hair, shining golden in the sun. She gently moved back his coat and looked more carefully at his wound; she had lived many years, and she had seen and come to know much about many things. Judging by the blood flowing from the musket ball's ragged point of entry on his chest, she was sadly certain that the beautiful young man was correct.

She held the young man's hand and nodded, and so did he. So now they both knew. She had smiled forlornly at his strong Irish voice; so finely dressed he was, she at first had thought he might have been a young Protestant squire, but *no, too handsome, an Irishman he is to be that!* She shook her head sadly in silent reflection.

O'Leary had closed his eyes, and as he opened them, the woman squeezed his hand. "Save your strength, sir, perhaps someone . . ."

O'Leary knew from his training and experience that *someone* would make little difference in what he knew to be virtually inevitable and closed his eyes again. He felt himself breathe, sensed the laboured beating of his heart, the unevenness, the growing weakness of his pulses; perhaps he was sufficiently prescient, adequately aware such that he realised he was feeling his life ebb, gently, slowly, but ebbing nonetheless away.

As the woman held his hand, she noticed a very gentle smile on his lips, his eyes half-closed.

O'Leary felt his hand was in Eileen O'Connell's, in the square fronting the Market House in Macroom, and he was smiling, for now he saw Eileen—*ah, elegantly arrogant, daunting was she not?*—and he gently shook his head. *From that moment, I have loved you,* "Eileen of the Raven Locks. . . ." He was not aware that he had whispered the last words softly aloud.

The old woman, whose eyes had been focused on heaven, in silent prayer, queried softly, "Please forgive me, sir, but who is Eileen? May I try to get word to . . .?"

O'Leary's eyes opened, and he smiled softly. "Eileen is my wife, old woman, my Eileen of the Raven Locks. . . ." She nodded; those were the words she had thought she had heard him say. He paused, taking as deep a breath as he could. ". . . she will come, she . . . she . . ."

The woman held his hand a bit tighter. O'Leary, understanding her puzzled expression, insisted, "She *is* coming . . . indeed, of this I am certain. . . ."

"But, gentle sir, how so?"

"My horse . . . the mare that departed as your good self arrived . . . 'tis she who will bring Eileen . . . Eileen will see the blood, which I am certain is on the horse and saddle, the reins . . . and she will know . . . and Banrían . . . she will bring Eileen here . . . to me. . . . Soon, I pray," he said weakly. "They are both wise girls." He nodded firmly, the tiniest trace of a smile again on his colourless lips. He then rested quietly for several minutes, his eyes closed. The woman repositioned herself slightly and gently lifted his head into her lap, his eyes briefly open, looking directly up at hers, his expression one of gentle gratitude. He closed them again.

In the brief, silent moments of solitary darkness, O'Leary sensed it again, rejected the thought, pondered it and then of it he was certain, and he opened his eyes. "Old woman," he whispered firmly, "dying it is that I am." His beautiful eyes looked up at her weary ones and the two nodded at each other, the woman sighing softly.

"Whilst 'tis I who have lived in two centuries, it is indeed you, sir, who will not be alive at the sun's next rising," she whispered, her chapped lips quivering.

Holding her hand still tighter, O'Leary gazed at the sky. ". . . nor, I fear, at its setting."

Tears now streamed down the old women's rough, tanned cheeks.

O'Leary shook his head, saying, "I am a soldier, old woman, though 'tis not on a battlefield, this death it is . . .'tis fine . . ." With only the slightest tremor, his voice trailed off, and he breathed and opened his eyes wide now.

"Should Eileen not arrive before . . . before . . . before I die," he said the last word firmly, "if you are able, will you tell her I died well, old woman?"

The woman's expression—and her voice—became resolute. "To your Eileen I shall speak only of what I have witnessed, of what I know to be true: that you died a brave soldier, sir, that you died the death of a Gaelic gentleman, at, I am now thinking, the hands of the Sassenach." She hissed the word, looked again deeply into his eyes. She knew not yet who he was, but she was now in her own mind certain indeed of *what* he was: *a handsome young aristocratic Irish Catholic . . . a soldier, he says, so a Wild Geese soldier, for sure an officer he must be . . . well-dressed, well-spoken, so wealthy he must be . . . and, being all of these . . . proud he is, of this I have no doubt. . . . The Sassenach does not like proud Irish people; the Sassenach kills them. . . .*

O'Leary was struggling now. "Old woman!" His voice was weak but urgent. "Please, *please* also say 'twas of her that I spoke last, that 'twas her face I saw . . ." He gathered himself, continuing, "*Tell her*—" as he squeezed her hand almost firmly, the woman then heard the unmistakable sound of command in his voice, "that it was of the market square in Macroom, almost six years past . . . and of Rathleigh, that Christmas . . . when we wed . . . and *Vienna*, please tell her I spoke of Vienna." He smiled weakly, speaking a bit faster now, as were he seeing images passing before his eyes ever more quickly. ". . . and of the Hofburg and Schönbrunn and Laxenburg . . . of our—" he gasped softly, as a breath refused to come when he summoned it—"our little archduchess," he smiled again, ". . . and especially of the wee lads, of Conor, of Fiach . . . she will know, I know they will always remember their papa, of this she will make certain . . ." At the mention of his sons, tears trickled out of the sides of both eyes. Gasping audibly, struggling, he managed ". . . and that I love her . . . have always . . . shall always . . . love her . . ."

O'Leary's eyes were closed now. Her eyes fixed on his face, the old woman saw a soft, beautiful, almost peaceful smile, for he was now smiling at Eileen. They were both smiling sadly, through their tears.

I know you must depart, Arthur, but, as you do, you must know, you must always remember, must never forget—as I spoke to you the night we fled Derrynane, "I shall never love another as I love you, Arthur O'Leary," . . . he clearly heard her say.

He nodded. *I have, with gratitude, known that since even before that moment, and . . . and you, my darling love, you must know that I shall love you forever, that my spirit, it shall remain always with you, loving you, watching over you . . . and the wee lads . . . I so regret that I . . ."*

Eileen appeared to him loving, steadfast, but suddenly very strong . . . *Regret as you may, my darling . . . but know I love you, now and forever, my Horseman of the Bright Eyes. Take with you my love, my heart, my very soul, my darling . . .*

Eileen's image began to slowly fade from his sight.

". . . and I you, Eileen . . . my *Eileen* . . . *my Eileen of* . . . *my* . . ."

She was gone.

He was very soon gone himself.

Arthur O'Leary died, his head cradled in the old woman's lap, her voice softly murmuring simple prayers spoken in Irish. Even as she sensed his passing, she remained awhile thus, smoothing his golden hair, smiling sadly at the rakish red ribbon still holding his queue. *How . . . whoever it was who did this to you . . . how he, how they must have hated you . . . you, who I now know dared to stand tall and to wear a red ribbon.* Finally, reluctantly moving, she gently rested him on the warm spring earth, again pillowing her kerchief behind his head, and covered him very tenderly with her shawl, smoothing it over him, her gnarled hands gentle, almost reverent.

She then sat on the ground with him, and she waited with him . . . for Eileen to come.

As O'Leary had lain near and in death, and as Banrían was streaking towards Rathleigh, Abraham Morris slumped alone in a creaky seat at a dirty corner table at Cornelius Duggan's pub, and as he began his third refill of Duggan's clear, gasp-producing poteen, how he wished he could get quickly drunk! His heart was pounding, his shirt soaked with sweat, his legs and hands trembled, yet outside waited a dozen English soldiers *under his command.* He shook his head, his trembling hands gripping a battered, already half-emptied tankard.

He stared into the semidarkness of the pub's dim interior, where it always seemed it was early evening. Art O'Leary was dead; he had to be. Morris had seen the ball from Greene's musket strike O'Leary in the chest, was certain he had immediately seen the blood spurt even before his enemy toppled from his horse. When Morris had given the command to withdraw and the soldiers had turned their horses so sharply, he had to struggle to assume the lead of *his* troops.

His first command of the afternoon had not gone as well.

On the information of the dark, shifty-looking stable boy . . . *imagine, the little bastard, him thinking a reward he would be given! As were he the only loyal one . . . ah, that son of a whore, O'Riordan, now he was worth . . . Hell, I shouldn't even have paid fucking O'Riordan; I required no help at all, I . . .* who had seen O'Leary at Duggan's earlier and raced to locate Morris's detachment. They had, unbeknownst to O'Leary, left the coach road from Millstreet and hurried around Carriganima and lain in wait behind the wispy, scraggly cover of thin trees just off the road.

Morris knew only that no matter where he had been or which route—the road, footpaths or cross-country he followed—O'Leary would ultimately most likely access the road to return home; were they fortunate, their position would permit them to fire at him should he come onto or even near the coach road from any one of several directions. *Brilliant field strategy, hah!* Morris congratulated himself as he sat and drank. As it was, they were roughly arrayed on the far side of the not-broad River Keel as O'Leary emerged opposite their position, on a low ridge up the road several hundred feet, after crossing the footbridge.

When O'Leary had first appeared in the distance, Morris immediately gave the order: "Prepare to fire!" No man but one had even lifted a rifle; the opportunity would shortly be lost. "You will fire when I say so or you shall be brought up on charges, you cowards!"

O'Leary being perhaps seventy-five, maybe as much as one hundred feet away, Morris shrieked, "Fire!" and along with a few of the others, a corporal named Greene's musket roared and Art O'Leary was struck. The remainder of the men's shots were wide or high. . . . He was certain several were not taken at all.

Morris drank deeply now. He no longer cared about *his* men: Arthur O'Leary was dead or soon would be; that was all that mattered.

Following O'Leary's departure, Eileen had spent a largely unremarkable day consisting largely of household matters and chores, reading to her little boys and, sometime after three o'clock, a ride on Bull. She and her old friend bounded cross-country for at least an hour at a healthy clip, such that as Eileen pulled him up and turned the stallion's head toward home, horse and rider were drawing deeper breaths, and both shone with sweat.

Heading back at a much gentler pace, Eileen breathed in the perfume of early May, the coconut aroma of the gorse and the incense of yet again rapidly growing grass. The sun was warm on her face, on her shoulders, which made the sudden chill that coursed up her spine all the more intense. She drew Bull to a halt and sat, the chirping of myriad birds in the distant trees and on the wing—and Bull's heavy, comforting breathing—the only sounds. She cast her eyes about: The sun filled the space in which she sat; she was near no trees, in no shadows. The chill was nevertheless sharp, profound, and she cast her eyes to heaven. "I sometimes sense things, is all," she heard herself say. What *chilling* thing had she sensed? She thought a moment longer and shook her head almost violently, seeking to dispel the only thing that immediately had come to mind. "No, no, *no . . . that* it cannot be," she whispered as she gently booted her horse and pointed his head towards home.

After her ride and a quick change of clothes, Eileen O'Leary was slowly descending the main stairs at Rathleigh, following Fiach as the little boy purposefully took each step, placing one chubby hand over the other on the banister, first placing one foot and then the other on each step, as both his parents had shown him.

As mother and son approached the last steps, the sudden pounding from outside the massive, now always bolted front door of the house was thunderously powerful, like nothing she had ever before heard before, sounding first at the door's top, then its centre, sounding as if the sturdy oak could shatter: *'Tis as if it were a sledgehammer, a post maul pounding*, she thought, though when she drew the bolt aside and pulled the door open it was upon a gleaming, panting, dusty Banrían that her eyes fell, on a Banrían whose hoofs had caused the powerful sound as she crashed them against the door—and her eyes went wide as they fell on a riderless animal.

Eileen's heart stopped—*as it did on our wedding day*, she would always recall—forgetting her toddling little boy, who remained standing in the hall and watching as she practically leapt out of the now-open entryway, her right hand instinctively stroking the beautiful, road-weary mare's face, the animal's eyes wide with terror, as if she had experienced some unimaginable horror.

Then Eileen saw the reins trailing the ground, the magnificently tooled Spanish leather saddle, the mare's back itself; they streamed, indeed were already stained, a deep red, *blood red*. She immediately knew. . . *the chill* . . . her face flushed, her breasts heaving, her fists clenched and her eyes closed at first, she raised her face to Heaven, whether it was pleadingly or in anger, in rage . . . and then she screamed, an unearthly, primitive scream, the Gaelic cry of total, inconceivable loss, of unimaginable grief, of an anguish beyond belief . . . then a long, deathly silence, followed, in English, by a wrenching cry, "Arthur! Noooooooo! Ohhhhhh myyyyy Gawddddddd . . . Arthurrrrr! . . .

". . . noooo . . . ohhh, noooo . . ." she whispered as, her hands crossed over her breasts, she sank slowly, almost gently to her knees, the echoes of her wails alive in the still air, as, lowering her face to the broken rocks, she murmured softly, now in Irish, *"Ó, mo Dhia, ó, mo ghrá - le do thoil, a Dhia, uimh . . ."* "Oh, my God; oh, my love—please God, no . . . . NO!"

At the first of the crashing sounds made by the horse's hoofs on the front door, young Mary, bringing Conor with her, ran from the tiny kitchen house towards the back of the main house, hearing Eileen's violent screams as she came. Racing into the hall, immediately scooping Fiach up in one arm, her other on Conor, now hugging her waist, she and they then saw Eileen bent to the ground, her forehead on the broken rocks, sobbing, speaking softly, incoherently. Mary knew then as well and, crossing herself, she knelt and immediately gathered both frightened little boys to herself.

Eileen stood abruptly, trembling, silently looking at her sons, then at Mary but seeing them not. Mary's tear-dimmed eyes momentarily focused on a strange, faraway look on her mistress's anguished face until suddenly, as Eileen saw the mare begin to move towards the gate, wordlessly, her eyes flashing, even wild, she bounded towards the horse and, propelled by her muscular thighs and calves, leapt onto the mare's back, clapping her hands. As the horse lurched forward as if in response, immediately scrambling to gather the blood-dampened reins, Eileen O'Leary and Banrían became as one and together they hurtled up the lane and out the gate, heading north on the coach road, north towards Carriganima.

Eileen understood that the horse somehow instinctively knew where she was headed, where she had to go, to the place where she had to carry Eileen, and Eileen held the reins firmly, hugged the horse's side tightly with her knees, her legs, her thigh muscles almost achingly taut. She permitted the horse to *go*, to simply *go* to the place where they both must now be, as fast as she could, which she did, travelling, Eileen could sense, at a seemingly impossible, ever-increasing speed.

To the few people—farmers and their wives and children, coming in from the spring-warmed fields—who saw them fly past, so fast was the mare racing that none would have believed she was returning to a place from which she had only recently departed, at a speed, if anything, now exceeding the swiftness with which she had so recently travelled.

Those who did not immediately recognise her would learn that it was Eileen O'Leary who had passed them, on her husband's horse, and what had happened, but until then they would remember only a beautiful chestnut, the rider a young woman, her hair flying as one with the horse's black mane and tail as they sped past. One man, one of the O'Learys' most trusted men, a friend much more than a tenant, knew immediately it was Eileen, and having heard the words on the wind, he instantly knew what must have happened, and that the horse was carrying her to Arthur. . . . The man, his face as gnarled as an oak, almost the colour of light saddle leather, his white hair thick and mussed, both his clothing and his hands rough, sat heavily on a granite outcrop and wept.

As she straddled Banrían, hurtling through and blessedly unaware of the disarmingly, placidly beautiful emerald countryside, the young mare's speed and endurance now beyond belief, her eyes straight ahead, Eileen did not weep.

She focused on what she was certain was now her reality. *This I know: Art O'Leary is dead; my Rider of the Bright Eyes is no more.* She repeated these thoughts and others, over and over, as if she were saying the saddest Rosary ever prayed. *So that when it is at his side I kneel, I shall then know this, know that he is gone and that I am not . . . that alone I am, that without him I shall remain . . . for the rest of my life . . . for so it is that I shall never love another as I love you, Arthur O'Leary . . . never!*

It was as if the mare knew precisely where she was, as approximately a half mile before they would reach the furze bush, Banrían began to slow, seemingly so that Eileen would know they were drawing near. The young widow understood, bent and gently stroked the horse, then sat regally erect, her hands resting on either side of the gentle mare's neck, barely holding the reins as, Banrían now walking slowly, timidly, almost reverently, and just ahead there appeared a tableau that remained seared in Eileen's memory until she herself died.

There sat a very old woman, hugging her knees. Bent slightly, she struggled to stand whilst beside her lay—Eileen was certain, had no doubt at all—Art O'Leary. She saw wisps of his hair above the shawl that covered him; she recognised his boots.

Banrían halted to one side and Eileen slowly dismounted, the old woman now standing. Eileen saw her gather the rough cloth of her skirts in her skeletal hands and form as best she could a curtsey. Instinctively, Eileen did exactly the same, and as she rose, the woman came forward, speaking softly in Irish as she moved. "My lady, you are the Lady Eileen. . . . Certain I was that you would come." She silently gestured her to where O'Leary lay and stepped back next to Banrían, stroking the glistening, trembling horse's neck.

Eileen nodded at her and wordlessly stepped forward; kneeling, she gently removed the woman's shawl and bent to her husband. Raising him, holding him in her arms, she kissed his lips powerfully, and embraced him equally so, then rocked them both for a long time. The massive volume of blood that had soaked his shirt and riding coat now, by the sheer force of her embrace, again flowed, coursing out of the linen, the tweed. Her palms gleamed, then, as she closed her fingers, pooled with O'Leary's blood; shamelessly, she drank it, her lips, chin and hands smeared with it, the bodice and much of the front of her dark grey wool dress stained a deep red.

Watching the younger woman continue to hold her husband, her eyes looking down on him in her arms, the old woman then heard Eileen's voice for the first time. Though not loud, it was husky, strong, powerful even, as she began, in Irish:

My love and my delight,
The day I saw you first
Beside the market house
I had eyes for nothing else
And love for none but you.

I left my father's house
And ran away with you,
And that was no bad choice;
You gave me everything.
There were parlours whitened for me
Bedrooms painted for me,
Ovens reddened for me,
Loaves baked for me,
Joints spitted for me,
Beds made for me
To take my ease on flock
Until the milking time
And later, if I pleased.

My mind remembers
That bright spring day,
How your hat with its band
Of gold became you,
Your silver-hilted sword,
Your manly right hand,
Your horse on her mettle
And foes around you

Cowed by your air;
For when you rode by
On your white-nosed mare
The English lowered their head before you
Not out of love for you
But hate and fear,
For, sweetheart of my soul,
The English killed you.

My Love and my mate
That I never thought dead
Till your horse came to me
With bridle trailing,
All blood from forehead
To polished saddle
Where you should be,
Either sitting or standing;

I gave one leap to the threshold,
A second to the gate,
A third upon its back.
I clapped my hands,
And off at a gallop;
I never lingered
Till I found you lying
By a little furze-bush
Without pope or bishop
Or priest or cleric
One prayer to whisper
But an old, old woman,
And her cloak about you,
And your blood in torrents ~
Art O'Leary ~

I did not wipe it off,
I drank it from my palms.

She then grew silent, reluctantly lowering her husband gently back onto the ground, again pillowing his head with the old woman's kerchief. Eileen rose slowly and stood for a time facing him, her head nodding occasionally at O'Leary. *Did you hear what I said, Arthur? Do you understand that Banrían came for me, and carried me here to you, my darling? Together, we shall be taking you home, my love.*

The old woman watched in silent awe as, tears silently streaming down her cheeks, her arms dramatically held open at her sides, Eileen then resumed:

My love and my delight
Stand up now beside me,
And let me lead you home
Until I make a feast,
And I will roast the meat
And send for company
And call the harpers in,
And I shall make your bed
Of soft and snowy sheets
And blankets dark and rough
To warm the beloved limbs
An autumn blast has chilled.

Stopping abruptly, she shook her head. Her passion, at least for the moment, stanched, she stepped back; Eileen had begun to think about how it was that she was to get Arthur home, for she believed it was up to her alone to do so. "As I know full well that you shall not stand up now . . . or ever again . . . beside me, my darling horseman," the old woman heard Eileen say softly, her lips trembling, silent tears only now finally falling, mingling with the blood smeared on her face.

The old woman still stood in silence, still holding the mare's bridle. She suddenly felt, at least to some small degree, fearful of this woman in whose commanding presence she found herself; never had she seen a woman who looked as Eileen did, and certainly never had she heard a woman speak thus. *Is she a banshee?* she wondered, trembling, finally concluding, *perhaps she is* bean caointe. She hoped she was correct as she tentatively stepped forward to Eileen.

"My lady, may I assist you? I am most aged, I agree, though not at all feeble, madame," she said softly.

Eileen nodded and very softly whispered, *"Go raith maith agat."*

"But first, my lady, if I may," she stepped closer, "your husband, he spoke of things to me, things he wished you to know . . . for me to tell you, were you to arrive after he . . ." Her lips began to quiver, tears again streaming down her face.

The words surprising her, Eileen now looked with gratitude on this ancient woman. "Please, yes, tell me these things, all that he spoke. . . . I should be most grateful   . . ."

As in a stronger, more certain voice, the woman related her observations about O'Leary's death and repeated his final thoughts and words, Eileen stood, regally straight, her bloody hands folded beneath her waist, silent tears falling, streaking the blood on her cheeks. She said not a word, made not a sound, though she smiled sadly at the mention of "our little archduchess" and nodded in approval at the old woman's precise recollection and correct pronunciation of the names of the Austrian palaces. When she mentioned Conor and Fiach, as had Art wept, speaking of them to the old women so, too, now Eileen's shoulders shuddered, her sobs becoming audible. She asked the old woman several questions, and, by listening and studying her weathered, creased face, became conscious of her concerns, perhaps her fears, even.

Eileen spoke gently to her, calming her, reassuring her. "Ah, I am as mortal a woman as one can be, 'tis my heart being broken . . . and my love for my darling . . . from whence have come the words, the passion."

Sometime later, as the lengthy spring dusk had slowly begun to fall, with more than a little difficulty, Eileen—refusing to even consider draping her husband's body over the horse's back—with the amazingly spry woman's help, finally had been able to seat O'Leary back on the horse, his boots again in the stirrups, Banrían standing virtually motionless, her huge eyes straight ahead, only occasionally flicking her tail. Eileen gently leaned him forward, placing his arms at Banrían's neck, and secured him as best she could with the reins, the old woman continuing to watch, to marvel, transfixed in wonder.

She stirred herself and offered to Eileen a significant length of rough rope: "From my basket, my lady, I know not why 'twas there, if not to be of use to you, madame."

Eileen reached for it with a trembling right hand and spoke again directly to the old woman. "Thank you, old woman. I shall use it to secure the captain to the stirrups." She bent and tied one end firmly on the left stirrup and tightly around the instep of O'Leary's left boot, draping the rope across his thighs. She then rounded the horse, pulling the rope as taut as she could over O'Leary's legs, and knelt next to the right stirrup. Eileen then repeated her motions as to the boot and the stirrup, checking the rope's tension. Finding it satisfactory, she stood with a glance at her husband, his head resting now against that of his beloved horse.

"We shall now depart, old woman," Eileen said softly, gently stroking the mare. "Be assured that never shall I forget your many kindnesses this horrid day . . . to Captain O'Leary and to myself." She paused. "I feel I am unable to either touch you or kiss you in gratitude," she added, quietly raising her bloodied hands, gesturing to her blood-streaked face and clothing, and the old woman nodded. As Eileen reached for the horse's bridle, she turned once again. "Be also assured that I shall seek you out and find you, old woman, to thank you in a fitting fashion, but, for now, we must return home." Nodding, she finished firmly, finally taking Banrían's left cheek strap and clicking to the horse.

Suddenly, into the silent dusk, the old woman called out hesitatingly but in a strong, firm voice, "My name, my lady! . . . *Maire Nic Amhlaoibh is anim dom!*"

Eileen tugged the horse to a gentle stop and turned, staring; she was shocked that it had not occurred to her to ask the old woman her name. At that, she shook her head and called softly, *"Dhia leat, Maire Nic Amhlaoibh, Dhia leat!"* "God bless you!" Turning, she resumed walking, only to stop this time abruptly, again turning. *". . . agus . . . agus, Eibhlin Ni Chonaill is anim dom!"* she said softly, her husky voice trembling.

Mary McAuliffe stood in the settling dusk for what seemed a long time. When last she saw them, Eileen was walking, as slowly, as precisely as she had begun, leading Banrían, her right hand in the mare's bridle, carefully watching that her husband's body was secure.

In silence, she would walk thus for the better part of two hours, the still night of this brutally sad, violent day now gently illuminated by a soft May moon.

Eileen knew neither how long she had been travelling nor where precisely she was when she heard the familiar and strangely welcome pounding of what sounded to her like a single set of horse's hoofs, heralding, she was nearly certain, the approach of a solitary rider. Almost as soon as she had halted, the silhouette of a flying horse and rider appeared in the placid moonlight at a bend in the road not far ahead, travelling so quickly that she could almost hear the horse's breaths in the still air.

As they came upon her, she gratefully recognised that the horseman was John Collins, who, reining in his panting, foaming Andalusian gelding, immediately jumped down, his arms open to her. She held her palms open, then, gesturing with her bloody hands to her clothing and face, shook her head. No words were exchanged; coatless, hatless, his shirt open at the neck, an ashen Collins stood still until Eileen finally mutely gestured, then softly managed, "'Tis Arthur, Squire John," as a single pair of silent tears streamed down her blood-streaked face, "'Twas Morris, I *know* it was, Morris he, he. . . he killed him . . . he *murdered him. . ."*

His own face set solid in grief and determination, Collins stepped closer to Banrían. "I have come for Arthur and for your good self, my dear," he said, his voice barely above a whisper, though still in his familiar, always formal tone. Eileen stepped aside as Collins closely examined the brown mare and her deathly rider, silent tears streaming down his smooth, ruddy cheeks. At one point he wordlessly retrieved a length of rope from his saddlebag and draped it over O'Leary's legs, quickly tying it tightly parallel to the extraordinarily placid young mare's leather girth.

He finally nodded at Eileen. "I believe Arthur to be now even a bit more secure." Eileen returned the nod in gratitude. Only later would she tell Collins and Anna how she had been able to place her husband aboard his horse.

"Would you please permit me to accompany you both to Rathleigh?" Collins then asked, his soft voice close to breaking.

Eileen smiled sadly. "In your gentle company, John . . . Banrían." She stroked the weary animal. "She and I and you, our dear friend, we shall now take Arthur home."

As she finished, despite Collins's gently firm insistence that she ride his horse, she shook her head softly and wearily took Banrían's gory bridle in her own bloodied hands. "I must do this," she whispered. Collins nodded and silently cast his eyes down at Eileen. She then nodded, and he gently clicked to the gelding. Collins permitted Eileen to set a gentle walking pace, such that he barely held his horse's reins, as in silence the tiny, poignant convoy finally wended the last miles to Rathleigh House, the bright moon now high, though delicately veiled in a lacy fog.

It was only during the ensuing days that Eileen would learn that, as the time following her dramatic departure from Rathleigh had lengthened into the cusp of early evening, Mary and Ann, by then fearing the worst, had, upon locating Seamus, dispatched him to Derryleigh. Knowing only the barest of details of Arthur's plan, Collins, also fearing the worst, raced towards Carriganima, whilst Seamus brought Anna and little Maria Theresa back to Rathleigh in the Collins's trap.

It was thus that as they made their way up the Rathleigh lane, the first person Eileen saw was Anna Collins, who, her arms folded, her eyes lowered and now walking alone towards her, had been awaiting Eileen's sad homecoming all evening long.

News of the tragedy having circulated quickly, a number of people had already gathered. Eileen and Collins reined in their horses near the front door, and at that moment a hush fell over Rathleigh. With Eileen still gripping the horse's bridle, the largely male gathering stepped aside as Collins, with Seamus's and Henry's help, gently lifted O'Leary from Banrían's back and slowly carried his body into the house.

Standing in the yard, with a now-riderless Banrían stubbornly refusing to leave her side, Eileen and, seemingly, her listeners, ignoring her blood-drenched appearance, spoke softly to several people and told the older Rathleigh men, "The captain's wake . . . my thought was that 'twould begin at dawn then; of that you will please tell all the people . . . all are welcome." She thought a moment, then continued, "Because he is now home, any and all of you are welcome to remain, and all of those who may come during the night, even before the dawn, they will all be most welcome . . . please." She gestured towards the house, where Ann, Mary and the other girls of the household had already begun to lay out food and drink as they continued to arrive, and at her urging would immediately begin being consumed.

Once inside, she declined, thinking silently, *Not just yet, I cannot, no . . . I shall, but . . . not now,* Anna's tearful offer to wash her face and hands. Rather, the women went together immediately to O'Leary's armoire in the couple's bedroom; there, her hands quickly, subtly, by Anna gloved, Eileen withdrew his finest dress uniform, a spotless white ruffled shirt and other items, whilst Anna set out his dress cavalry boots, which she would ask Seamus to have polished to a gleaming brilliance.

As they carried O'Leary's clothes back downstairs, Anna told her that word had gone out to Squire O'Leary and Catherine, and that she expected they would during the night be en route from Cork City, as would Conor O'Leary the Younger, he from Dublin.

Finally yielding to Anna's urging that she wash, though she had difficulty turning away from the water, now blood red, in the basin, pleading in a barely audible whisper that it be "gently poured in the near pasture, where Banrían usually is," and, shedding her bloodstained dress for a dressing gown, Eileen returned upstairs to see to her little boys.

In the meantime, John Collins, along with Seamus and Henry, both young men tearful, solemn, obviously heartbroken, had seen to the washing and dressing of O'Leary's body. Collins then stood alone for a long time at the foot of the white linen–draped trestle table upon which, in his magnificent uniform, Collins thought, *Captain Arthur O'Leary of Höeninger's Regiment, Her Imperial Majesty's Hungarian Hussars of the Armies of Austria and Hungary* now rested. He shook his head in numbed silence, *slain, murdered, by a vicious, worthless little man for no bloodygoddammed reason.* The master of Derryleigh's expression was sombre, his jaw set; it was only when Anna gently slipped her arm through his that silent tears began to stream down the distinguished man's features. Anna leaned her head wearily against her husband's right shoulder and, both weeping, together began to mourn their lost friend.

Eileen remained for some time upstairs with her little boys, who, when she had arrived, were racing about the house, calling for Mama . . . and Papa. Whilst Fiach could not grasp the situation, he was nevertheless weepy and frightened; Conor, however, understood what had happened and was inconsolable, sobbing uncontrollably as Eileen, finally giving vent to her own tears, did so as well, her arms wrapped protectively around both her sons, as they sobbed for "Papa . . . Papa. . . ." Fiach cried himself to sleep, and when Conor finally did calm, he wiped his eyes and asked plaintively of his mother, "Will Papa be a soldier in heaven, Mama? Will he be a captain of Hussars?" Eileen tearfully but firmly assured him he would indeed be one of God's most devoted soldiers and, after shedding yet more tears, mother and son finally fell asleep, together with Fiach, in Conor's bed.

At Eileen's invitation, a number of people had remained at Rathleigh, and many others had begun coming, so it was already a significant gathering that Squire O'Leary and Catherine O'Leary came upon in the predawn hours of 5 May.

At the sight of her dead brother, Catherine's steely reserve gave way to a flood of emotion, though as she emerged from the large formal parlour where Arthur and Eileen had been wed, her first mention was of Eileen's whereabouts, her absence ". . . as her husband lies shot and murdered, am I to believe that the woman is herself abed and sleeping?" she demanded of no one in particular.

"You shall not dare to do so!" Eileen's voice rang out angrily as she stepped off the staircase and into the suddenly hushed large parlour.

Eileen would later memorialise their exchange, having Catherine speak first:

My little love, my calf,
This is the image
That last night brought me
In Cork all lonely
On my bed sleeping,
What the white courtyard
And the tall mansion
That we two played in
As children had fallen,
Ballingeary withered
And your hounds were silent,
Your birds were songless
While people found you
On the open mountain
Without priest or cleric
But an old, old woman
And her cloak about you—
Art O'Leary—
And your life blood stiffened
The white shirt on you.

My love and treasure,
Where is the woman
From Cork of the white sails
To the bridge of Tomey
With her dowry gathered
And cows at pasture
Would sleep alone
The night they waked you?

Then having Eileen herself reply:

My darling, do not believe
One word she is saying,
It is a falsehood
That I slept while others
Sat up to wake you—
'Twas no sleep that took me
But the children crying;
They would not rest
Without me beside them.

O people, do not believe
Any lying story!
There is no woman in Ireland
Who had slept beside him
And borne him three children
But would cry out
After Art O'Leary
Who lies dead before me
Since yesterday.

For Eileen, the ensuing days were—and in her memory, would always remain—a complex, emotionally draining series of events and people, of words spoken, some connected, many others not.

With some effort, by morning she and Anna, assisted by Mary and one of the other serving girls, had located the elegant black mourning robe Eileen had worn after the death of Emperor Francis Stephen, and so attired, she moved regally through the remainder of the wake, the prayers and, finally, O'Leary's wrenching burial at what would prove to be only his temporary resting place at the graveyard at Dun na Radharc, the ruins of the ancient O'Flynn Castle in Kilnamartyr, of which she would say:

> *My love and my darling*
> *When I go home*
> *The little lad, Conor,*
> *And Fiach the baby*
> *Will surely ask for me*
> *Where I left their father,*
> *I'll say with anguish*
> *'Twas in Kilnamartyr;*
> *They will call the father*
> *Who will never answer.*

There, too, she would make her stunning first public utterances about the man she viewed as being responsible for Arthur's murder, as well as, for the second time, about her pregnancy:

> *Grief on you, Morris!*
> *Heart's blood and bowels' blood!*
> *May your eyes go blind*
> *And your knees be broken!*
> *You killed my darling*
> *And no man in Ireland*
> *Will fire the shot at you.*

Bittersweet Tapestry

Destruction pursue you,
Morris the traitor
Who brought death to my husband!
Father of three children—
Two on the hearth
And one in the womb
That I shall not bring forth.

It is my sorrow
That I was not by
When they fired the shots
To catch them in my dress
Or in my heart, who cares?
If you but reached the hills
Rider of the ready hands.

My love and my fortune
'Tis an evil portion
To lay for a giant—
A shroud and a coffin—
For a big-hearted hero
Who fished in the hill-streams
And drank in bright halls
With white-breasted women.

My comfort and my friend,
Master of the bright sword,
'Tis time you left your sleep;
Yonder hangs your whip,
Your horse is at the door,
Follow the lane to the east
Where every bush will bend

And every stream dry up,
And man and woman bow
If things have manners yet
That have them not I fear.

My love and my sweetness,
'Tis not the death of my people,
Donal Mór O'Connell,
Connell who died by drowning,
Or the girl of six and twenty
Who went across the water
To be a queen's companion—
'Tis not all these I speak of
And call in accents broken
But noble Art O'Leary,
Art of hair so golden,
Art of wit and courage,
Art the brown mare's master,
Swept last night to nothing. . . in Carriganima—
Perish it, name and people!

And then it was over. The final prayers were offered by the O'Flynns' priest, the gathered murmuring in response. Lowered into the grave, resting on and covered by layers of fresh, sweet-smelling hay, O'Leary's coffin was slowly covered with the soil of County Cork, Eileen kneeling and tossing the first handfuls onto it, placing a final rose on top of it.

Other than tersely acknowledging the final condolences of their friends, Eileen was unusually mute. As the crowd of mourners quietly dispersed, some insight into the complexity of her mental state was shortly apparent when, as she turned to walk to the waiting carriage, Anna delicately approached her, whispering, ". . . *three* children, my darling?"

As Eileen embraced her friend, she bent slightly, then spoke softly into her right ear. "Arthur did not yet know. I sensed it was so at the time of the races, thus my sidesaddle." Stepping back slightly, she shook her head. "My ride to Carriganima . . . the exertion of settling my darling back on his horse . . . my walking with them until your good husband came upon me . . . I do not see how that . . ." She rested her head on Anna's shoulder and wept briefly as her friend rocked her, stroking her hair.

In the hushed, darkest hours of the night that followed, Eileen was awakened by a sharp stab in her stomach. She sat up abruptly in the bed she and her husband had first shared in the Hofburg, where she had been sleeping on Arthur's side. As she somewhat unsteadily stood, a spasming series of cramps came in quick succession, followed by a pounding, near-paralyzing pain that gripped her midsection. Gasping aloud, she grabbed on to the high post at the right foot of the bed, clinging to it with both hands. After a few long moments more of the exquisite pain, she sensed a warm rush of what was water and blood, the fluids carrying a small bit of still, formless tissue away with them, out of her and onto the floor. Suddenly, the knifelike pain had ended. Breathless, lighting her large, high chimneyed bedside candle, she sat weakly back against the bed pillows; looking down, in the flickering light, Eileen saw a small, sad tarn on the gleaming dark wood of the floor. She knew. . . .

She sat up, gazing quietly at it for a few moments before she stood and reached for her dressing gown, which had lain across the bottom of the bed. Taking a linen cloth from the toilette cabinet, on the marble top of which rested a bowl of washwater and soap, she quickly cleansed herself, carefully folding the cloth and setting it back on the toilette. Looking about, she reached back for the cloth; kneeling, she slowly gathered what lay on the floor. Gently making sure the space was fully dry, she carefully wrapped the cloth yet again, this time twice about itself, and stood weakly, with some effort.

Drawing her long gown about her, holding the small bundle of fine linen to her breasts with her left hand, without a candle, Eileen, her bare feet slapping gently against the uncarpeted wood, padding on the carpets, made her way slowly, to a degree unsteadily, down the stairs and towards the back of the house. Stepping outside into the wispy moonlight, not closing the door, her feet quickly wet by the night's heavy dew covering the thick grass, she continued to walk slowly to the kitchen house and entered, the packed-dirt floor cold and slightly gritty beneath her feet. There she promptly located a small trowel, which the girls used to plant herbs, which, with their shallow roots, grew and were consumed quickly, thus requiring constant replenishment.

She exited and came about the far side of the compact building; again, ignoring the now-rough, wet grass beneath her bare feet, she walked as quickly as she was able towards the closest enclosure, the one where Banrían was most frequently pastured, the one where Anna had gently poured out the water she had used to wash her husband's blood from Eileen's hands and face.

This then, Eileen thought with certainty, *'tis the most suitable place, a place where Arthur's light, laughing spirit frequently will be . . . and the ground never disturbed, save by the hoofs of his beloved horse . . .* the place where, after slowly, painfully scaling the stacked-stone fence, she now knelt, setting down her tiny bundle on the thick wet grass. With some effort, she plunged the trowel several times into the thick grass, stabbing it; finally reaching the dirt beneath, with her long, fine fingers she pulled and tore at some clumps of grass and their roots. Digging silently, first in the shallow layer of heavy, pungent loam, and then into the sandy, stony soil that was County Cork, she quickly created a narrow, very deep horizontal hole.

Setting down the trowel, she reached for her bundle. Holding it in both hands, raising it to her lips, she kissed it softly. She then slowly, reverently laid it in the tiny fissure she had made. Tears now streaming down her cheeks, with the trowel and her hands she gathered the small mound of soil, fully covering the starkly white wrapping, then pressing the turf she had torn away back in some rough approximation of place. This done, she softly patted the tiny knoll, her wrenching sobs now audible in the hauntingly still night air. "Farewell, tiny wee angel," she whispered, bending low, her hair falling about her and her work. "Join now your papa in God's heaven . . . embrace him . . . I shall live now certain that ye and he are together and that Mary, the Blessed Mother of Jesus, will care for you, as she does for all the angels. . . ." Her shoulders and her breasts heaved as, resting her forehead on her hands, Eileen now wept bitterly beneath the mantle of her raven locks. When she finally stood slowly, unsteadily, her tears remained unwiped, and there was dirt on her soft, full lips.

She would tell only Anna what had occurred and what she had done; though Eileen had quietly experienced another early miscarriage during the course of her marriage, she somehow believed that this, along with so many other aspects of her life since the fourth of May was different, so she would hold the crushingly sad event and the spirit of her *little wee angel* forever in her heart.

Even before the small measure of catharsis provided by O'Leary's actual interment, Eileen sensed her emotions slowly changing, subtly reordering themselves. Her grief, which she accepted would always and forever be part of her life, and which would, at least in part, define her, in her psyche came to be separated, to be sublimated above all other emotions. Her grief began to take on the nature of a second living soul within her; it would daily be her companion as she lived and raised her sons. She would come to believe and then accept that her grief was not something from which she at some future time would emerge, but, as she would explain to a number of people, "Grief, I believe, 'tis an expression of how deeply we love . . . as my love for Arthur was boundless, so, too, shall be my lifelong grief for him." She felt that never more apt than now was her mother's original remark on the death of Donal Mór, that she had "buried a huge part of my heart, a huge part of my soul," as Eileen felt that she, too, had now done, that an integral part of her own life, her own being was absent—gone forever.

All this remaining true, Eileen soon discovered that as her primary controlling passion, rage would, for a time, overshadow grief. *I shall grieve and mourn my darling forever in the silent darkness of my heart. My rage against those who murdered my husband, it shall not, like my grief, be forever: It shall be finite; when the price has been paid by those men, when my very public vengeance is accomplished, my retribution realised, as it shall be by violence and in fury . . . only then shall my rage abate, but abate it ultimately shall.*

Eileen's rage was and would prove to be far more complex than simple anger. Rather, it was a concerted fury, an immeasurable wrath. She envisioned it as being a merciless gale that flattened, that destroyed all in its path, akin to the foaming, grey, mountainous waves of the winter Atlantic, as they crashed against the shore at Derrynane, reshaping the land, sometimes it appeared even the rocks, at their whim. It was a living wrath against which there would be, could be no defence.

She clearly envisioned the appearance of the type of devastation she contemplated befalling these men as she stood alone at Rathleigh one gentle evening some two weeks and several days following O'Leary's burial. With a sweep of her arm across the moonlit landscape, she pictured utter desolation: a grassless, treeless prospect, the gentle, verdantly emerald hills become a grey dust, beneath the blackest of skies, devoid of sun, moon and stars, a windless, airless, breathless void.

This—she extended both arms, now laying upon them her silent though terrifying curse—*this is what awaits Morris, his men, anyone howsoever remotely involved in the murder of Art O'Leary. 'Twill mean much more than mere death . . . no, death—at least the fleeting moments between its occurrence and their swift damnation into the flaming abyss that shall be their eternity—death shall prove to be a respite, a reprieve from what I envision for them, from what I this night invoke: They shall suffer as no men have ever suffered; they shall cry out for mercy, for relief from what I shall cause to befall them. I pray only that God Almighty shall make of me and mine His vengeful servants, empowering us to bring His righteous wrath crashing upon these most evil, these most vile, these most contemptible of men . . . and that He shall Himself turn a merciless, deaf ear to their pitiable moans.*

After some moments in silence, just as she had begun walking towards the house, to her little boys—to her own respite, as it were—she stopped suddenly and again faced the horizon, both of her arms raised to the heavens, her hands forming clenched fists. "May God's righteous wrath, vengeance and retribution for what they have done commence now . . . *this night!*" Eileen cried aloud in the near darkness.

She then walked quietly back to the house, her eyes lowered, her arms folded beneath her bosom. Her eyes were dry; she had no more tears left.

County Cork, Ireland—the remainder of May 1773

Ironically, it was one very close to Eileen upon whom her wrath would first fall.

As spring slowly began to display signs of becoming summer, even as several late-blooming spring wildflowers began to delicately appear, poking through the once-disturbed, now-settling earth covering Art O'Leary's grave, Dr. James Baldwin heard his name called aloud as he strode across the market square in Macroom. The voice was high, raspy. As the physician turned warily in the direction from whence it had come, he reluctantly confirmed that it was—unfortunately for him, he immediately felt—the voice of Abraham Morris.

"A moment of your time, Doctor, if you please, sir," Morris demanded rather than requested as he caught up to the man's long strides.

Dr. Baldwin stood, eying the much-shorter man warily, uncomfortable in his very presence. "If you must, please, speak then, sir," he invited Morris coldly.

"We have not had occasion to speak since—" Morris began.

"—for what for me has been a pleasantly long time," Baldwin completed.

"I meant, since the death of your wife's sister's *apparent* husband." Morris made the convoluted reference to O'Leary in an impatient tone.

"So what then *of* this, Morris?" Baldwin demanded. "Concerning what of this sorry affair could you suddenly now have *any* need to speak with me? The man is dead. I should think you would be quite satisfied. What then remains to be said?"

Morris stepped what for Baldwin was uncomfortably close, gesturing to a bench along the facing wall of the market house. "Sit, Doctor. As it involves you, sir, I should think you would wish to hear my *suggestion*."

The lanky physician sat, though not at all close to the magistrate, wary, uncomfortable, a sense of dread settling over him.

Morris cleared his throat. "Now, then . . . for a number of years, in fact since your marriage to Mistress Baldwin, little note has been made of, at approximately the same time, shall we say, your change in doctrinal status." His eyes fluttered, and he cackled, slapping his left knee with his palm.

Dr. Baldwin viewed him as a strange little man, behaving strangely. "And what of this event, a decade and almost one year more ago, is suddenly of current import?" he asked, his expression cold, harsh.

Morris's tone continued, even. "At the time, your rather *unusual* . . . to say the very least . . . embrace of Papist beliefs . . . you would agree, would you not, that the supposed *conversion* of a lifelong adherent of the Church of Ireland, of one whose family has been for generations the same, is, if nothing else, quite *odd*, yes?"

Baldwin sat silently, his face devoid of emotion.

"As I recall, many good Protestants saw it as being the means necessary for a significant dowry of an O'Connell of Derrynane to be settled on yourself, sir, as being a matter of finance, of business."

Baldwin remained impassive. No one had spoken to him for years of his embrace of Catholicism at the time of his marriage to Mary O'Connell. It was a fact, however, that Maurice O'Connell had made it clear in late 1761 that, whilst he approved of the proposed union and would sanction his sister's marriage to Baldwin, a Protestant, under such circumstances, a nominal, but still generous dowry would accompany Mary to Cork. He unsubtly suggested, however, that the O'Connells would be even more pleased were Mary to be marrying a fellow Catholic, ". . . and how better to express our feelings than by settling a significant sum" on him.

In time, the young physician had, somewhat to his own surprise, grown quite comfortable with Catholicism, coming to view the Church of Ireland as a wispy reflection of the deeply vibrant faith he had come to embrace, though now . . . Dr. Baldwin leaned slightly forward towards Morris. "And yet again I ask, what *of* this, sir? The circumstances were known, and little mention of it was made at the time, sir. My loyalty, perhaps indeed more correctly, my fealty, and that of my family, to the crown was not questioned and, I would suggest, was not at all compromised, by what you correctly refer to as 'a matter of finance, of business,'" he said coldly.

"Precisely!" Morris exclaimed. "The circumstances were indeed known . . . few questions were raised . . . no efforts to enforce the laws then . . . and now . . . in effect, specifically those requiring the forfeiture of your lands . . . were undertaken."

Baldwin's face flushed, his fingers drumming nervously on his knees as he sat rigidly.

"Ah, you *understand!*" Morris, who had noticed the physician's agitation, again laughed frigidly. "It is your recent close, I would say, *intimate* association and involvement with the executed outlaw O'Leary and his woman that has led many good Protestants here to perhaps now reconsider what was previously widely viewed as being an unfortunate and potentially self-defeating . . . in terms of your own salvation . . . conversion to Popery, to the extent that your recent actions have given most loyal men true cause for concern now of your own *loyalty* . . . such that many of us see now the need to reconsider the quiet decision to let rest the issue of your lands and your business and professional activities. In sum, many now see the need to perhaps more strictly enforce the law as it is presently in place. . . ." His voice trailed off.

Baldwin's eyes, his expression tightened. "What is it that you are *suggesting*, Magistrate?"

Morris sat back in self-satisfaction, saying nothing.

"What is it that *your people* would expect of me, sir?" Baldwin's voice evidenced a very slight tremor.

Morris now smiled peculiarly. "I would say, sir, a dramatic act . . . a *single dramatic act* . . . so significant a display that it would in their minds forever eradicate your apparent close and intimate association with the dead outlaw O'Leary and the woman . . . and thus dispel any notion that your loyalty should be in question. I should think that the thought now being given by many to a more strict enforcement of the laws of Ireland in your case . . . I believe that process would most likely be halted."

"And were I for some reason to be reluctant to . . ."

Morris's normally dull, listless eyes flashed, the muscles in his face trembling. "If a man who were to find himself in the position we are discussing were to be so foolish, so ignorant—or indeed so arrogant—as to the reality of life in Ireland as to display any reluctance to act in light of what has been said here today . . . I would suggest that such a man could well and quite soon find himself and his family stripped of lands and home, of inheritances, and that his continued plying of his trade or—" Morris laughed cruelly—"continued practise of his profession would be in question. I should think that such a foolish . . . or arrogant . . . or *stupid* man would be well served to consider life in America." He cackled, tossing his head back, such that he had to straighten his tatty, ill-cared-for wig.

Morris stood abruptly. "I have *so* enjoyed our conversation, Doctor. . . . I hope to be able to continue to address you as such . . . not to mention as 'Squire.'" He extended his hand, which Baldwin did not take, and Morris turned sharply away.

Baldwin remained seated on the bench, his expression blank, his face ashen. As he watched the compact little man stalk away, he said weakly, though half aloud, "They were wed . . . married they were, you little bastard!"

During quiet moments in the course of the following day, Dr. Baldwin could not but help hearing Morris's grating voice, speaking again and again of ". . . a dramatic act   . . . *a single dramatic act* . . ." and found himself reflecting constantly on what he now felt compelled to do to preserve the well-being of Mary, the children and of himself.

One morning, several days later and unannounced, Dr. Baldwin entered the barn at Rathleigh.

Seamus appeared as soon as he heard his never-used English name called, in his former employer's scraping tone. "Dr. Baldwin, sir—" the young man began.

"*James*, where is the chestnut mare, the one called Banrían?"

Without waiting for a response, the physician stomped about the barn, his eyes peering into the empty stalls. "Where is the animal, boy?" he demanded.

"Captain O'Leary's mount, she is afield, sir. Why do you ask?"

Baldwin said simply, "Bring the horse to me, boy . . . now . . . I have . . . I have seen Mistress O'Leary; I . . ."

Unaware that Eileen was not at Rathleigh, Seamus then unquestioningly retrieved the mare from the near field. At Baldwin's direction, he affixed a fine leather lunge line to her halter and, without a word, Dr. Baldwin led a whinnying, struggling, clearly resistant Banrían away, delivering her to the then-triumphant squire at Hanover Hall that very afternoon.

On her return from Derryleigh in the early evening, Eileen was greeted by an obviously uncomfortable—indeed she quickly, correctly concluded, a quite frightened young man. She had dismounted from Bull, who immediately wandered to the grass on the fringe of the broken-stone-covered yard, and nibbled whilst Seamus, crushing his hat between shaking hands, his voice trembling, his words spoken in gulps, unburdened himself to his mistress.

To the young man's patent relief, Eileen's reaction was calm. "You did not know he had not seen me nor had you any reason to be aware of my absence. I shall in the morning address the matter directly with Dr. Baldwin.

Worry not, lad," she said as she gently touched his shoulder, the young man's eyes tearing up as, after her hand rested there for a long moment, she finally squeezed it reassuringly, softly murmuring, "All will be well, Seamus," to which he stammered, "Thank you, mum."

It was barely first light when Eileen, again in her Viennese mourning robes, and Bull thundered through tiny Clohina and up to the front of the Baldwins' imposing residence, Eileen sliding off her horse almost before they'd fully halted, almost immediately pounding on the door with her still-gloved, fisted right hand.

As James Baldwin, just risen from his breakfast table, tentatively began to open the door, Eileen swept it forward and burst into the entryway, almost knocking him over. "In there!" she snarled, literally pushing her brother-in-law into the small parlour on the right side of the hall. When she slammed the front door closed, the house reverberated with the sound, the near-immediate slam of the lighter interior door seeming a weak echo.

Within moments—with no prodding from an eerily silent Eileen and after haltingly relating what he had done with the chestnut mare, failing in his admittedly weak effort to fully describe, much less attempt to justify his actions—James Baldwin found himself for the first time personally confronting the unbridled rage of his sister-in-law.

After dramatically stalking about the comfortable parlour, her husky voice loud, its tone powerful, Eileen had turned imperiously to him, her eyes wide, her right forefinger already pointed in accusation. "*How dare you* for *any* reason arrogate to yourself any capacity to relinquish something that is not yours to surrender, Doctor?" she thundered. "And how dare you lie to that young, innocent lad, you feckless bastard!"

As Baldwin stammeringly attempted to formulate a response, his wife gently began to open the door, peering in. "Leave, sister! Do not dare to enter this room!" Eileen raged. The door immediately clicked shut.

Eileen then again turned to her brother-in-law, who thought it best to remain silent. After briefly telling her of Morris's threats, seeing nothing but searing rage on Eileen's face, even as he spoke, he abandoned attempting any defence, finally whispering instead, "I do not have a satisfactory response, sister."

"You do not because there is none, Doctor . . . and you shall henceforth refrain from *ever* again addressing me in any form of familiarity," she snapped.

Eileen walked towards the blazing fire; though it was now approaching June, the morning and the parlour were both unusually chilly.

Facing the fire, she reached into the right-hand pocket, deep in the folds of her robe and, as she turned again towards Baldwin, withdrew her gleaming pistol, which she had begun carrying each day even before the armed attack on Rathleigh.

Wordlessly, she fully cocked the weapon and levelled it at a shocked James Baldwin. She smiled cruelly, silently sneering at the man's expression of disbelief.

Walking slowly towards him, her throaty voice level and frighteningly cold, "You shall take yourself even now, sir, at this very instant, to Morris," Eileen began. Her voice deeper, more threatening than Baldwin had ever heard any woman's, "and retrieve the singular horse which is Banrían."

Disregarding the fact that Baldwin had begun to speak, Eileen continued. "On his murder, by his will, certain of my husband's property became mine alone . . . most significantly, the mare; she is now mine . . . so you will now go and recover *my* property!" she shouted, the direction of the weapon never varying.

Baldwin appeared desperate to speak; Eileen ignored him.

"Know this well, sir, despite that you are husband to my sister and father to her children, should you appear before me at Rathleigh . . . to whence I shall now repair to await my horse . . . or should I be compelled to return here . . . in either instance with Banrían still remaining in the unlawful, immoral possession of the accursed Morris, I shall then and there . . . or *here*," she smiled viciously, "without a single thought . . . kill you, sir."

Baldwin's hands were clenched at his sides, in sweating, trembling fists, his eyes averted from her steely gaze.

Her expression one of deliberate, measured rage, Eileen moved even closer to Baldwin, ultimately holding the barrel of the gun a mere two or three inches from his heaving chest. Despite her having just provided him with perhaps some slender chance of salvation—by ordering him to retrieve the mare—the man now certain he was about to die, she seethed, "The 'tales' I am certain you have heard through the years involving my use of firearms . . . whilst first at Ballyhar, in the rough country of Kerry and Cork and, just recently, in defence of my home and family . . . I assure you, all of those are quite true."

She raised the beautiful weapon so that it was pointed at his forehead. Baldwin was visibly shaking, his ashen face dripping with sweat, his now-open hands trembling at his sides.

"Thus, have no doubt that the moment you stand before me in the yard of Rathleigh or in this place," for emphasis, she gestured with the pistol to the outside of Baldwin's home, "without Arthur's beloved mare, in the very next instant you shall lie before me dead . . . your wife widowed . . . your children orphans. . . ."

Eileen calmly uncocked her pistol and replaced it beneath her cloak. "'Tis thus your decision, Doctor, how to, the manner by which you will recover the horse, but recover her you shall . . . you must . . . as, I assure you yet again, sir, should you fail in this effort, I shall indeed kill you."

Wordlessly, Eileen turned and dramatically swept out of the room, out of the house, and it was at a gentle, steady canter that she and Bull returned to Rathleigh to await Banrían's return.

Mid-afternoons of the day following their confrontation, a still obviously shaken, again ashen-faced Baldwin appeared at Rathleigh, leading Banrían by her fine leather lunge line, its brass clasp on her bridle, the fittings of both gleaming in the sunshine. Ann had called out to Eileen of his coming, and the physician was yet again confronted by his sister-in-law, this time standing with a fully cocked rifle cradled across her bosom.

Seeing Banrían, she smiled—at the horse. Saying nothing to Baldwin, after first pointedly uncocking the gun, with her right hand, Eileen casually lifted the rifle over her right shoulder such that its barrel faced away from a visibly relieved Baldwin. After again smiling softly at her and leaning forward, Eileen kissed the mare on her nose and unclasped the line.

For the first time, she looked up at Baldwin; as he released the leather belt from his hand, Eileen flicked her wrist sharply, thus drawing it towards herself, as if retrieving a delicate fishing line. The soft leather strap was quickly gathered in her left hand. As she turned, the horse did as well, remaining close at her side, both now facing the physician.

Finally, she addressed the still-mounted Baldwin. "So ... you accomplished it," she began, her voice sarcastically icy. "You did as you were told." Baldwin nodded, saying nothing. Wordlessly, Eileen began to lead the horse to the barn.

Sitting, watching Eileen, seeing her by then resting her head against the horse as they walked, hearing her speaking to the mare softly in Irish, Baldwin finally called out in English—he had no Irish— "I was compelled to menace Morris, you know! . . . I threatened to shoot him, I did!"

Eileen stopped, turned her head, then slightly her body, and looked sardonically back at him, calling, "And at that threat from *you*, he relinquished the horse? As Arthur maintained, Morris is indeed a snivelling coward. Would that he were not in this instance but that he had stood up to you . . . and would that *you* would then have had the courage to kill him. . . ." She laughed cruelly. "Ah, no matter; our girl is home." She turned and continued walking the horse towards the barn.

As May progressed quietly and sadly at Rathleigh, virtually unnoticed— as none of the O'Leary family, nor any friends or neighbours had been informed, much less called for testimony, so none were even aware that it was being convened—was the publication of the terse findings of a coroner's inquest, held on 17 May in Macroom, advising that it had produced a verdict of the *"wilful and wanton murder, on 4 May this year, of Capt. Arthur O'Leary, late of Rathleigh House, near Macroom, against Hon. Abraham Morris . . . "* as well as against all the members of the military detachment at that time under his ostensible, highly questionable command.

Eileen learnt of the findings late one afternoon, not quite two weeks afterwards, as she scanned the Cork newspaper in which they were reported, nodding sadly into the low fire before her as she reread the notice. *So, it states the obvious . . . but no action shall be taken by the crown against Morris or any of them . . . as all they did was kill a Catholic outlaw. . . . Why should* that *be the crown's concern?*

Expressionless, she offhandedly folded the paper and set it on a side table; rising, she walked in the direction of the sounds of Conor and Fiach being returned from play with another pair of brothers close to their own ages who lived in one of the closer cottages.

A week or so following her learning of the coroner's findings, after a series of nearly sleepless nights, purposely having told no one of her intent, Eileen rose before dawn on what would become a grey, windless and unusually heavy, humid morning. Having assembled the cache as she'd quietly roamed about the house deep in the night, once she was dressed in one of Arthur's white linen shirts, her own black breeches and gleaming black boots, as well as, despite the prospect of the day's sultry heat, a heavy black wool, hip-length and rarely worn riding coat, she trundled towards the stables, carrying a pair of already-loaded rifles, as well as a pistol that belonged to "the house" and which was kept—loaded—on top of a high breakfront near the front door; the weapon was much larger and, it being double-barrelled, considerably more lethal than her own elegant one. In preparation, also during the night she had quietly padded out to the stables where she slung across and affixed a pair of handsome, hand-tooled leather rifle scabbards to Bull's saddle, at the same time slipping additional powder and shot into both of her saddlebags. Lastly, she laid a plain, unadorned black tricorn hat on the shelf in Bull's stall.

Now this morning, humming a random tune, softly murmuring in Irish to her still-drowsy stallion, Eileen effortlessly tacked Bull, eased the rifles into their sheaths and the pistol into her left saddlebag. Deeming all to be in readiness, leaning against the rough wood of Bull's now-wide-open stall gate, she gathered her long, thick locks together behind her head and drew it all to her left side; letting the mane fall over and well below her breast, she deftly braided it into a tight rope, which she then flipped back over her shoulder, the long plait coming to rest inches below approximately the small of her back, effectively melding with the colour of her coat. Finally, she firmly placed the black tricorn squarely on her head, resting it well down on her forehead, such that if she lowered her head even slightly, her face would be obscured by the hat's extended brim. *Attired thus, from any but the closest of distances I shall most likely be seen as a man.*

Once mounted, after tugging on a pair of soft black leather gloves, with a gentle touch of her bootheels to Bull's sides, she was quickly away, briskly heading north on the coach road in the direction of Doneraile, near which lay her destination: Hanover Hall.

Though her husband's beloved mare was younger, more agile and considerably faster than any horse in the Rathleigh barn, especially Bull, she was purposely riding her own horse for the simple—and, to Eileen, compelling—reason that she'd promised Banrían that "never anywhere near accursed Carriganima shall you go, darling girl . . . indeed never shall you ever again journey any distance at all north on the coach road; *never, ever!*" In addition, she felt Bull and she had been through so much of life together, *plus he is my horse, mine alone, and this is my revenge . . . mine alone.*

The hour being so early, she was more than halfway gone from Rathleigh before she'd passed anyone, and pass quickly she did, with barely an acknowledgement to the pair of fast-moving riders whom she encountered some distance north of Carriganima, as well as, considerably further along, a man and woman in a plodding pony cart not far from Doneraile; though her face was obscured on both occasions she could not be certain whether the bristling pair of rifles had gone unnoticed or not.

As she rode north, she was barely aware of her surroundings, conscious only of her direction and the approximate distance until she estimated she would arrive at Hanover Hall, a place she'd never before been. Her only thoughts were of Arthur and his murder, little else. Later, when queried about her early morning trek, she would, in all honesty, advise Anna that she recalled very little. Indeed she had no explicit memory of even taking note as she passed near the site of her husband's murder.

Having ridden for some time through what appeared to her to be a sad-looking, seemingly largely unpopulated countryside, as she finally rounded a gentle arc in the by-now poorly tended thoroughfare, the hulk of a large, dark, menacing-looking, even house came into still-distant view. "So, my darling love," she spoke softly to Bull—or was it to Arthur?—"So, this is the murderer's supposed sanctuary, though his place of execution it shall become . . . the time for which, it has now arrived." She slowed her horse to a walk; from Arthur's description of the place, she expected to see a lane, more likely a rough boreen, and some moments elapsed until she did: an ill-kept cut off the road to the right. Following it as best she could with her eyes, she concluded it would lead her to Abraham Morris, and him to his own death.

Without removing them from their scabbards, she reached forward and half-cocked both rifles; reaching into her left saddlebag, she similarly cocked the house's pistol; returning it, she left the bag's brass clasp open. Gently touching Bull's withers with her heels, she had him take her alongside the boreen, guiding him into and riding through, at some places briefly weaving in and out of the continuing long stand of scraggly saplings and wispy high weeds that bordered it.

As she drew closer to the dismal, unsightly dwelling perhaps some three hundred feet distant, she saw a trio of men ambling, it seemed almost casually, about what appeared to be the house's main entrance, another pair on the near side of a rough, unkempt hedgerow some distance in front of the house. Drawing closer still, for the first time she could also see clearly that each of the men was carrying a long gun—either a rifle or a musket, she could not be certain at this distance—whether casually slung over a shoulder or cradled across a chest, a finger on the trigger.

She slowed Bull to a gentle walk, first sighing deeply. "Bloody hell!" she suddenly exclaimed far too loudly into the heavy, still air; immediately lowering her voice, seething quietly, albeit still-aloud, she told herself, "The little bastard has guards; *of course he* does!" she hissed, shaking her head, appalled at her failure to accept, much less even consider this possibility beforehand.

Still progressing very slowly towards the house, now two hundred feet, perhaps even less, from its roughly defined close, after tugging Bull to a halt, deeming herself still at least partially concealed, protectively hidden by the vegetation, she sat silently, the only sounds in the still morning air being the random chirping of birds and the swish of the horse's majestic black tail as he reflexively flicked away bothersome insects. Her mind was clearing, seemingly beginning to again function normally: *Of course he bloody well does have guards, Eileen! Why in bloody hell would you think he would bloody not?*

Resting her still-gloved hands on the pommel, she shook her head. *Because you did not think this through,* then, as she gazed about the setting, as were she at least to some degree surprised that she was even there, *Bloody stupid woman! Foolish, thick, dense! Bloody brainless bitch!* she raged in her spinning thoughts.

She slowly recalled that her "plan"—she could not help but laugh ironically, softly now at the thought of her even believing she had conceived an actual one—such as it was, had been quite a simple one, one based on the sole premise that she would not attempt to kill Morris from cover, from any distance away. *The unseen, the concealed, the anonymous shooter; 'tis the way of a coward. 'Tis the manner in which he murdered my Horseman of the Bright Eyes.*

Rather, she would confront the man: *His last vision on earth will be my rifles aimed at him; the last sound he will hear, my laughter.*

She sat very still, her toes resting in Bull's stirrups. *My "plan"*—she shook her head and laughed again, quietly, though most bitterly—*my "plan" indeed!*

Her rifles, and the pistol as well, already fully cocked, she would ride, perhaps even gallop Bull straight up to the house, drawing him up sharply; perchance he would rear up spectacularly, his massive fore hoofs pawing the air. Remaining mounted, she would dramatically announce her arrival— *Hello, the house!*—immediately then calling out *Abraham Morris*—loudly, certainly more than once—*Abraham Morris!* Clearly identifying herself, leaving no doubt the purpose of her presence: *I am Eileen Ni Chonaill, the widow of Captain Arthur O'Leary, he whom you have slain, whose blood stains your hands, whose murder further darkens your already-blackened soul!* Morris would of course cower within his dwelling—*bloody dammed coward that he be!*— but he would finally emerge, white-faced and trembling, from behind the perceived safety of its heavy front door.

She would look scathingly at him, and he would, in his shock and cowardice, stand mute as she made a grandly theatrical speech, amply scattering through which words such as *cowardly, murder, justice, vengeance, retribution.* After a pause—she knew he would by then be sweating profusely, visibly quaking before her—she would describe, in excruciatingly vivid detail, *the deepest of the flaming pits of hell* to which she had come to dispatch him, to end the *miserable, useless, contemptible excuse for a life* he had thus far led. By doing so, she would, she was determined, make certain that he *shall smell the sulphuric flames, hear the searing of human flesh, indeed the crackling sound of his own flesh being forever scorched, though never consumed, by Satan's eternal, unquenchable fires.*

Perhaps he would by then fall to his knees, wringing his hands, beseeching her mercy, in response to which she would laugh: cruelly, dispassionately, coldly, finally, employing the characterisation she recalled Arthur had frequently used in referring to him, she would demand, *Have you finished begging, you worthless little sack of shit?*

Firmly squeezing Bull's sides with her muscular calves, steadying herself, she would withdraw both rifles simultaneously. Permitting herself sufficient time to absorb fully, so as to never forget, the look of unspeakable horror on Morris's pasty, sweat-streaked face, she would raise the brace of weapons and, still laughing, or at least smiling, looking directly into his terror-filled eyes, she would fire both rifles virtually as one into the little man's heaving chest, which would immediately explode in a bloody, gory, tissue-, sinew- and bone-filled spew, the detonation shattering the morning calm, the sultry air thick with bitter smoke, reeking of burnt black powder.

The force of her killing shots—so powerful such that they had nearly unhorsed Eileen—having caused him to fall backwards, the dead Morris would lie flat, his arms perhaps spread, his bandy legs askew as blood gushed from the massive, gaping cavity of what had been his chest, perhaps momentarily pooling on, surely soaking into the vividly green spring grass where he lay.

She would halt but for the moment in which it took her to slowly return the still-smoking rifles to their holsters, after which she would have Bull take a step, perhaps more, turning if necessary, until she gazed down upon what remained of Morris, at which point she would withdraw the house's pistol, lean over and, using both hands, fire its double barrels simultaneously. As a result, his skull would shatter, bursting brain, bone and blood. Perhaps by this point the pitifully plain, long-embittered Hannah Morris might have appeared, shocked, perhaps hysterical. Were that the case, Eileen would have coldly acknowledged her, *Mistress Morris*, and gestured cruelly to the slaughtered man, *your husband, madame. . . .*

In either case, unfazed by the horror she had caused, she would perhaps then sit quietly for another moment, possibly even smiling at the bloodbath. Only then would she gently turn Bull's head away from the house called Hanover Hall and the carnage that but moments before had been its master and, undisturbed, trot calmly away.

You reckless, foolish woman!

Eileen had been so absorbed in her sanguinary daydream, her blood-drenched reverie, that she hadn't realised she'd finally been noticed by Morris's coterie of armed men, but suddenly now she did. Although no one had yet fired at her, both of the men who'd been stationed before the hedgerow were quickly moving in her direction, apparently calling to their fellows, seen and unseen, until several of them finally fired their rifles at her.

The clouds of smoke and the echo of the rifles being discharged lingering heavily in the air, she instantly felt chilled, her heart beginning to pound. Resolving only that *I shall not be taken by the English!* she had turned Bull sharply out of the high weeds, immediately easing her grip on the reins, as she firmly booted him, such that he knew his head was his own, and they were sharply away, albeit still well within range, when she heard the next round of gunshots, as well as the whine of not-distant lead projectiles. *Shame! Shame on you, stupid girl! Dear God, Heavenly Father, help me! Please!*

So focused, as she would tell Anna, "on getting the bloody hell out of there," she failed to notice a well-separated pair of riders coming wide, both galloping directly towards her, just beyond her right periphery; only the sudden, much closer burst of rifle fire and the virtually simultaneous chilling whistle of a lead ball just narrowly missing her head caused her to reflexively pull up, turning Bull sharply, grabbing for her left-holstered rifle in the process. Eyes aflame, heart racing, she fully cocked the weapon; unable to do any more, she pointed it at the nearest of the two men and fired. Near-instantaneously, the short, redheaded man—she could see him clearly, he wore no hat—lifted in his stirrups, his right arm spasming, he appeared as if to be tossing his still-smoking rifle skyward, at the same time dropping a pistol from his left hand, fell sideways off his still-charging mount: unbeknownst to Eileen, dead.

Thrusting her spent weapon into its holster, Eileen again turned Bull, the massive stallion responding immediately.

Even as the horse did so, Eileen could see that, despite when she'd shot his fellow, the man had halted—perhaps he'd even instinctively turned away—her victim's companion was again in motion, now at most one hundred feet, mere seconds from having a clear pistol shot—she saw no evidence of a rifle—at her, as his lithe little horse continued to close in.

Innately accepting that Bull could not outrun the smaller, sleeker animal, unwilling to chance trying to defend herself whilst being pursued, in a rapidly fluid motion Eileen instead pulled him up sharply, withdrawing the rifle holstered at her right knee, fully cocking it as she did. Seeing the fast-approaching man levelling his pistol at her, Eileen—this time aiming carefully, she could clearly make out the man's face— unhesitatingly fired her own gun. Its effect was as lethal as had been her first shot. The man's body shuddered, his weapon falling from his hand as he toppled heavily backwards.

By the time his no-longer-spasming, lifeless body lay still, her rifles both again securely holstered and Bull having easily cleared the remnants of a tumble-down dry-stacked stone wall, Eileen and he thundered in what would be a long, wide arc across rough, ungrazed, unploughed open land on the far side of the thoroughfare, taking them away from disaster, until they finally rejoined the coach road, upon which Bull's hoofs pounded 'til she felt they'd travelled a sufficient distance so as to be relatively safe from being shot or captured. Heartened that there had been no more gunfire, or other sounds of an obvious pursuit, as she walked the sweat-sheened stallion for a few brief moments, after hugging his neck, she took note of where she was, and—this time much more gently—immediately touched her bootheels to his sides, sending horse and rider briskly, though no longer quite so urgently, down the still blessedly empty road for several more miles, thence across the rolling Cork countryside at a steady canter, riding in a roughly south-westerly direction, maintaining the pace until they finally entered upon what Eileen was near-certain were the lands of John Collins, the vast estate of Derryleigh.

She rode for perhaps a quarter-hour more, relieved beyond all measure as the sprawling, subtly elegant red-brick Georgian residence that was home to the Collins clan, its graceful Palladian windows reflecting the dull, late morning sunshine, finally came into view. Eileen slowed, and then gently walked Bull the distance to the house and smiled weakly when she saw Anna waving effusively as she drew near. She removed her hat, wanly raising it with her right hand in greeting.

She drew up to the house and, as Anna reached for Bull's bridle, lifting her right leg over his head, Eileen dismounted easily and wordlessly stepped into her friend's embrace, in the process dropping her tricorn onto the crushed stones. Anna was shocked by her haggard, wide-eyed, ghostlike appearance, more so when she began to cry, almost instantly dissolving into heaving, uncontrollable sobs, the taller woman's few words made unintelligible by her weeping. Anna continued to hold Eileen tightly, gently rocking her, a flick of the delicate fingers of her left hand sufficient to subtly halt the progress of the young groom who was loping up from the stables to take Bull.

Ultimately, even more red-eyed than before, ashen-faced and breathing heavily, Eileen quieted. Anna's right shoulder was damp with her friend's tears. As she gently released her, Eileen lifted her head and, as they looked into each other's eyes, began to speak, her husky voice shaking but finally coherent. "Oh, my darling, I have done the most foolhardy, perhaps the most terrifyingly stupid and dangerous thing I have *ever* done," Eileen admitted, as, having just grasped her hands, Anna gently released them. Appearing genuinely pained, after first gesturing for the lad from the barns who'd been waiting patiently some distance from them, the young Austrian then draped her arm around her friend's waist and led her into the house.

For the better part of the next hour, the tea service that had been set for the women remaining untouched, Eileen unburdened herself. Anna somehow managed to sit, her hands folded in her lap, quietly listening, despite that she was shaken, both by the nature as well as the frightening extent of Eileen's recklessness, a trait she'd rarely seen in her friend, certainly not to this degree. A shocked Anna finally gasped aloud as Eileen related her confrontation with the armed horsemen, though so stunned was she by the final revelation, she listened again mutely as Eileen calmly related,

"Shot them both I did . . . 'tis quite possible I killed them . . . 'tis virtually assured that I did the second man; he was closer, I saw . . ." Her words faded as she leaned back, her eyes fixed, staring, finally managing, surprisingly, in a stronger, more even voice, "In truth, my love, I would not be surprised if both of them were dead."

The morning waned, to the obvious shocked surprise of the new young serving girl of whom Anna had requested the switch, the women having traded their tea service for a large decanter of exceptionally fine Scotch whiskey well before the time John Collins came in from his rounds; even as he was greeting his wife and their guest, he was visibly stunned by the sight of them, each with a hefty cut-crystal glass of whiskey in hand, taking note that the large matching decanter was barely half-full. As soon as she appeared, he requested of the girl water for himself. Returning almost immediately, she quietly closed the door as she withdrew.

"I shall spare you the torrent of details I have just poured out upon your darling," Eileen began unhesitatingly, gesturing at Anna.

At this remark, his facial expression quizzical, Collins rested back in his slightly worn, high-backed, saddle-leather wing chair, slouching slightly, crossing his long legs, his boots dusty from the morning afield.

"Suffice it to say, dear friend John, I am just come from making an unsuccessful attempt on the life of the accursed murderer Abraham Morris . . ." Eileen began calmly, her husky voice even more so. Seeing the usually unflappable Collins's patent shock, hearing his audible gasp as he sat up straight, uncrossing his legs, Eileen paused. The silence hung heavily about the trio of friends.

Collins finally exhaled deeply; leaning back, he first gestured with his right hand, *continue* . . . "Please, I should like to know all, indeed I believe I must know all if I am to protect you," he said candidly, his demeanour gentle, the tone of his voice even.

Perhaps it was hearing that she might be in need of protection, but Eileen was atypically flustered. "I am almost unable to speak, sir, I am so terribly ashamed of myself, of my foolhardiness . . . I had formed no rational plan, just a wild scheme, born of my grief, fuelled by my rage and hatred for the detestable murdering Morris, and 'twas the rage and hatred that blinded me to the peril that lay in what I was attempting. Indeed so blinded was I that the menace did not become apparent until I was already at Hanover Hall." She shook her head, then looked down.

With Collins's gentle, though pointed verbal prompting, after first relating a shortened version of what she'd concocted in her imagination as to how, viciously and wholly unimpeded, she would successfully assassinate Arthur's murderer, she paused abruptly, shaking her head, her silently shed tears drying on her cheeks, first describing when and how she had finally been noticed and shot at by the guards on foot, she then managed to relate in almost painfully minute detail the pursuit by the armed horsemen. After which and following a long additional pause, her eyes again atypically fixed on the wall rather than on her listener, her voice again approaching a whisper, her visage ghostly, she finally concluded, ". . . and I believe at least one, and indeed quite possibly both of these men I have killed."

A deathly silence hung over the threesome, John and Anna Collins sitting in momentary voiceless horror, their eyes following her as Eileen abruptly rose, dominating the small parlour, her half-drained whiskey glass in her hand. She inexplicably took several steps towards the closed door, Anna wondering, *Is she now to make a dramatic exit?* just as she halted and turned to again face them.

Her husky voice becoming customarily strong, she declared, "Aye, I could indeed have been shot by Morris's make-believe 'soldiers' . . . or—and perhaps even worse—been taken by the English." She shook her head at the thought. "My poor wee little lads . . . their papa murdered, their mama in the Sassenach's prison or, aye, dead; just as well I realise fully that I could have been *killed*. . ." Her countenance steely now, she added, "So, you see, I could not—*I did not*—allow that to happen," she said firmly, and paused.

A distant expression yet again on her face, with her long, elegant fingers she formed a tight fist out of her free left hand, raising it as high as her waist, speaking very slowly now, vesting each word with importance. "*I did what I was compelled to do . . . if indeed I have killed one or both of my pursuers, to God Almighty I am prepared to answer for it!*' she proclaimed strongly, immediately then downing the remainder of the whiskey in her glass. Anna smiled almost imperceptively as she thought, *My dearest friend, she does indeed possess a powerful sense of the dramatic.*

Eileen had completed the few steps back to her chair; setting the empty glass gently next to the decanter, her voice again softened. "I know now and freely acknowledge that only the gracious mercy of a kind, benevolent God protected me, is all . . . of this I am wholly now certain! Had but one of those men been able to . . ." Apparently shocking herself by the unspoken but harrowing thought, her voice trailed off, her eyes lowered as, once again, although silently, tears dropped onto her tightly woven breeches as she resumed her seat.

Collins exchanged knowing looks with his wife, and then, resting his elbows on his legs, he leaned towards Eileen, his voice soft, his tone temperate, causing her to slowly look up at him. He spoke slowly, at one point gently taking her hand. "My dear, I shall think nothing, say nothing—now or ever—in judgment of what has happened, of what you may or may not have done, and indeed even of what our good and gracious Lord has prevented from happening." He paused and slowly releasing her hand, leaned back. "What I shall say, however, is that very few men have *ever* deserved killing more than Abraham Morris does. I, too, experienced a degree of rage I have never before felt . . . upon learning of the findings of the coroner's jury, certain, as were you, that the crown would not act upon them.

"Since that time, I, too, have likewise considered how, given the circumstances, what can only properly be called the man's"—he paused purposely—"*execution* shall be accomplished. I know not yet precisely how or where or even by whom the deed shall ultimately be done, but, without even a shred of doubt, it *shall* be done, and well before the chill of autumn . . . of *this* I assure you, as well. I must speak again with Conor O'Leary and, in his company, perhaps with the assistance of others, create a design for the killing of this fetid, foul excuse for a man.

"As soon as the preparations are in place, you will then know when it will be done, and indeed when I am certain of the means, *how* it will be accomplished . . ." Suddenly leaning forward, reaching for his large, empty water goblet, he poured himself a full-glass dram of whiskey, upending it and swallowing it in a single swig, he sat silent for a moment, his eyes closed, finding the warmth of the whiskey especially soothing, comforting even, his cheeks flushing.

"In the meantime, my lady. . ." he paused again for another long moment as he slowly lowered his glass, his tone gentle, "I shall undertake a discreet inquiry in an attempt to determine the outcome of your gun battle this day."

After momentarily pondering all that he'd taken in, as well as what he had said, the youthful squire shook his head and sighed, not quite smiling. "In truth, and for whatever my opinion may be worth at this point, my dear friend, I believe that the killing in self-defence of two armed henchmen of Abraham Morris by their intended victim—'tis of little or no consequence. . . ." Pausing for a long moment, he looked firmly at both women. "Indeed 'tis of *absolutely no bloody consequence* . . . at all!" His tone was now harsh, cruel even, accompanied by a dismissive sweep sideways of his right arm.

Anna, who was still acclimating herself to the more than occasional need for native Irish Catholics to take such matters as were customarily—*and quite capably*, she thought—dealt with by the Habsburgs' invariably efficient police, into their own well-armed hands, unhesitatingly nodded firmly in agreement with her husband and rested her hand on Eileen's right thigh, squeezing it gently, as he completed his thought. "They, these men . . . they need not, indeed *they should not* . . . have pursued you. 'Twas only doing the bidding of the murdering Morris himself that most likely has cost them their lives. 'Tis no great loss, no small one either; anyone doing the bidding of, not to say providing protection in any form to Abraham Morris, especially by use of violence, well and fully deserves to be shot to death." He nodded firmly, as did his wife.

The three friends then sat in a benevolent silence for a long moment, absorbing Collins's conclusions, his comforting pronouncement.

Her heart by then considerably lightened, Eileen sniffled and gently looked at Collins and Anna. "Thank you, my dear friends; there is little else I can say other than that. I believe I should shortly take my weapons of war as well as my good self and return home," she smiled weakly, "to leave you, my *dearest* friends, to your own peace." Both John and Anna Collins joined her in a shared and welcome sense of relief. They sat and chatted a bit more of pleasanter topics, and after first undoing her braid and gently shaking loose her hair, Eileen gratefully lifted a squirming little Maria Theresa Collins into her arms, as she'd bounced into the room, immediately bypassing both of her parents, chubby arms outstretched, attempting to wriggle herself up onto Auntie Eileen's lap.

When she was finally ready to depart, Collins and Anna, now carrying her still- fidgeting daughter, walked Eileen out of the handsome house; as the women stood to one side, the little girl out of her mother's arms and racing around them in pursuit of a butterfly. After first undoing the buckles of the straps that held them to Eileen's saddle, the young squire removed the holstered rifles from Bull's back. "I shall deliver these," he held up the pair, "to Rathleigh in the next day or so; though I suspect you will already have done so, I shall come prepared to make your fine brother-in-law aware of what has today transpired, I assure you now, and should you speak with him before I, you will quickly learn that he shall think no less of you, but rather that he shall fully appreciate and understand your motivations. Indeed given the alternatives—being shot yourself or, I agree, perhaps even worse, being taken by the English—whether your attackers be they dead or not, given the thankless choice you were compelled to make, he would see the merit, as I do, as *we* do," he nodded at Anna, "of your defending yourself. At the same time, I am also certain he will keep *our*—"he gestured from himself and Anna to her and back—"confidence. I feel we need not involve Squire O'Leary, and certainly not the Lady Catherine, *aye?* At least not for now." He nodded. Finally, he cautioned Eileen to quietly replace the house's pistol in its customary place, "and think no more of today."

Before remounting Bull, Eileen stuffed as much of her heavy, sweat-soaked coat as she could into her right saddlebag and, brushing it off, donned her tricorn, this time deliberately setting it at the rakishly jaunty angle at which she'd customarily worn one in and since departing Vienna. Smiling gratefully, she again hugged Anna and Maria Theresa before bussing Collins's cheeks with a pair of effusive Viennese kisses, which, as always, caused him to blush brightly. She looked back and waved to her friends at least twice as she headed up Derryleigh's smoothly gravelled lane towards the coach road—and home.

No one had noticed that the house's pistol had been missing.

As June approached, the tumult of O'Leary's murder, followed by Eileen's successful effort to secure Banrían's return, as well as her having given full vent to her rage by calling down the wrath of God on Morris and the others, once the young widow had put behind her the ill-conceived solitary attempt to slay the man herself, and had at least begun to absorb the shock of knowing for certain that she had indeed killed both men near Doneraile, the few remaining, still crushingly sad days of May were, at least to a degree, remarkably quiet.

Seeking spiritual comfort, as she had since she was a small girl, a calmer Eileen felt herself drawn to both the Blessed Mother and St. Brigid. Of the latter, Eileen could only recall there being a rough sketch at Derrynane, one depicting an almost-generic young Irish woman, distinguished by her long, thick hair, said to be golden, wildly windblown, the gusts not having disturbed the halo's aura about her head. When she spoke with and prayed to Brigid, Eileen closed her eyes and pictured the drawing.

At the times she prayed to Mary herself, whether outside, in her mind's eye or in her room, where it regularly hung, Eileen gazed upon an icon of the Blessed Virgin, its gold leaf almost garish, and Mary, who shared the wooden block, about the size of a midsized book with a small depiction of the Greek St. Spyridon, appearing less gentle, indeed almost stern to the young widow, who had originally found the depiction of the Virgin as a dark-haired, striking Semitic girl, rather than the more typical blonde, if not off-putting, different. That Donál Mór had gifted it to her upon his return from a lengthy trading voyage that had taken several of the O'Connell vessels to Venice and Corfu, where he'd acquired it, being the island of which Spyridon was patron, was almost as important to Eileen as that it provided her with an image of the mother of Jesus. It was only as she'd hung it next to her side of the bed that she and Arthur had shared at Rathleigh that it had occurred to her that the dark-haired, striking Semitic girl was indeed a much more accurate depiction of how Mary of Nazareth most likely appeared.

In either case, as she prayed to, and more frequently simply spoke with, both holy women, the horrendous events of May 1773 replayed themselves constantly in Eileen's vivid imagination, although, with time, the horror lessened, the pain was less sharp and her tears fewer.

Ultimately, inexorably, that horrid month drew to a bitter close.

"I have resolved things with Mary and Brigid," Eileen would tell Anna, whose own spiritual relationship with the Blessed Mother was considerably more formal than that of her friend, who spoke frequently of both the Irish saint and the Blessed Virgin Mary as "dear friends, and advocates for me before the throne of God Himself." Anna had still not grown comfortable with the phrase Eileen frequently added, "Jesus, though God, is still a Son, is he not? How hard is it for a Son—even one in His position—to ignore His mother's wishes?" she would laugh. "'Tis why I have long cultivated a good relationship with the Blessed Mother!"

By month's end, Eileen would write a number of letters—to her mother and siblings in Kerry, to Daniel, Hugh and the princess in Paris, to Abigail, the empress and to Morty O'Connell and his wife, the Countess von Graffenreit in Vienna, to Marie Antoinette at Versailles—finding the experience heartrending, draining, *exhausting*. "'Tis a fact," she had explained to Anna, who, early on in the process, along with little Maria Theresa, it seemed had all but moved in at Rathleigh. The sounds of the children at play served to lighten the otherwise funereal atmosphere of the household and often provided the background as Eileen sat at Squire O'Leary's desk to write, virtually all of her letters being substantially similar to the one she'd written to her mother:

Rathleigh House,
Co. Cork, Ireland
10 May 1773

My Darling Mama—
Though I have endeavoured to do so, I remain unable to find any words that could make the following any less difficult for me to write or for you to read:

Late in the afternoon of 4 May 1773, my beloved Arthur was ambushed by soldiers of the crown near Carriganima and then and there shot dead. Since that time, with John Collins's and Conor O'Leary's assistance, we have determined that the accursed Abraham Morris, of whom I have written you prior, had somehow, I know not by what means and, on whose authority, managed to procure a detachment of mounted soldiers from the garrison at Macroom, which provided the means by which he succeeded in having my darling murdered. I know very little more than that.

It was only when Banrían, the sweet, pretty mare gifted to Arthur by the empress on the occasion of what has now proven to be his final departure from Vienna, appeared here, fore hoofs pounding at the entrance, blood streaming on her saddle and flanks, the reins trailing, that I knew something horrid had happened. As if by magic, the beautiful animal carried me to the place near Carriganima where Arthur had been slain and awaited me, in death.

She'd started to include a detailed reference to Mary McAuliffe but began to sob bitterly at the thought of her husband's final moments and decided to spare Maire and herself that pain.

It was only with the help of an old indeed ancient woman, who had come to Arthur's aid, that I was able to remount and secure him on Banrían. We thus walked towards home for some hours until John Collins came upon us and shared the final miles of that sad journey.

Not satisfied with murdering my husband, the authorities have made even his interment difficult: Arthur is buried at the moment in the cemetery at Kilnamartyr; we hope to have him rest finally at Kilcrea Abbey.

To say that my heart is broken nowhere approaches the sense of loss, the desolation I feel. How I wish you were here for but a day!

Please pray for Arthur . . . for the lads, and me, and know I am and remain

Your loving daughter,

Eibhlin Ni Chonaill

Perhaps the most heart-rending of these communications was the one Eileen wrote to their—her and Arthur's—one-time little archduchess. Given the length and level of intimacy of their collective relationship, as well as the crosscurrents of emotion arising out of what Eileen understood to be Marie Antoinette's ongoing joylessness in her marriage, as well as with her life in general at the French court, she had begun writing only to stop in frustration on several occasions. Finally, using the text of her letter to her mother as a rough template, she would ultimately succeed in writing to Antoinette, now in her third year of residence at Versailles.

Within mere days of completing her letters to Paris and Vienna, a young officer of Dillon's Regiment, a Kerry lad named Fitzgerald home on leave, had appeared at Rathleigh and received a pair of thick envelopes, one of the two letters the first one contained would be delivered to the palace at Versailles. The second wrapper he was given was bound ultimately for Schönbrunn, outside of Vienna; the imperial family, including Abby and her own family, having been in residence at the lovely palace since the first week in April, Easter having fallen early, on the eleventh, this year.

Paris—late May 1773

It was approaching seven thirty on a cool, sunny Wednesday morning— Louise and Hugh were enjoying an unusually leisurely breakfast on the broad balcony, overlooking the suddenly lavishly blooming gardens, just off the dining room of Louise's apartments at Toulouse—when a young other-rank of Dillon's Regiment clattered through the high iron gates of the magnificent mansion's understated courtyard, his uniform almost as begrimed as his weary-looking horse's dull, dusty, brown coat. His French spoken in urgent tones and with a distinctive Kerry lilt, the young man was quickly escorted to the princess's quarters, where, following a brief, intense conversation with one of her ladies, he was immediately taken to the couple.

Bowing to "Your Royal Highness," sharply saluting "Left-tenant, sir!" the young man managed only, "'Tis an urgent message from Ireland," before Hugh gently plucked the hefty, somewhat-battered envelope out of his gloved right hand. Louise quickly at his side, Hugh thanked the courier, the princess requesting her servant to escort him to the kitchens, "for food and drink, with our thanks," she said softly.

By the time his fiancée had dismissed the soldier, Hugh had already broken the thick packet's green wax splodge, into which was impressed the O'Connell stag, and had withdrawn a pair of smaller envelopes similarly sealed, one addressed to the princess and himself . . . the other to Marie Antoinette, all written in Eileen's elegantly swirling hand. The prescience he shared with Eileen chilling him, he muttered softly, "This cannot be good . . . not good at all" as he broke the seal on their envelope. He handed Louise the wrapper addressed to the dauphine, which she'd slipped into a pocket as he tore at their envelope.

The rough, heavy paper held now between Hugh's right and Louise's left thumbs and forefingers, neither had read beyond . . . *Late in the afternoon of 4 May 1773, my beloved Arthur was ambushed by soldiers of the crown near Carriganima and then and there shot dead* . . . before they sank almost as one onto a small, cushioned, wrought-iron settee, overlooking the mansion's magnificent gardens, each seeing instead unspeakable images of blood, death and irredeemable loss. The young couple together read on in stunned silence, tears streaming down their faces, until they'd finished all Eileen had written, to which she'd added, *I must entrust you with the delivery of the envelope which accompanies your own . . . I leave how and when you share this horrid news with my wee archduchess to your wisdom . . . with love and gratitude to you both.*

The following afternoon the couple, both mounted—this not being a typical visit to Versailles, requiring their finest outfits—Hugh in his uniform, the princess in a fine, black wool riding habit, consisting of a short black jacket, worn over a simple silk shirt and a long, full skirt, thudded in near-silence along the familiar road, both lost in their thoughts, their sorrow, dreading their visit with the dauphine of France.

Clattering into the vast courtyard, they handed off their horses and quickly circled the expanse of the building, reaching a simple door—Louise unlocked it with a small brass key—and they made their way up an interior staircase, which led directly to Marie Antoinette's apartments.

The audience having been requested and scheduled, Antoinette was standing casually at the door to her quarters, barefoot and with a gaggle of puppies and several noisy small children whose mothers were attached to her household, chatting animatedly with one of the women.

Seeing the engaged couple, her animus surrounding how they met and came to be as one having by now passed, gesturing to the rollicking chaos about her, she laughed and greeted the pair warmly. With the help of her ladies, she succeeded in shooing puppies and children away, and admitted the princess and Hugh to her home.

Settling on a settee in a small, intimate parlour off her principal audience chamber, she effusively offered her guests "wine, coffee, tea . . . sugared water," she said, laughing, as that was her primary beverage. Both declined, their expressions seeming to Antoinette devoid of their usual animation. She finally chanced, "My dearests, you seem unlike your normally cheerful selves. I must ask, I feel compelled to, is something perhaps wrong, is someone unwell?"

Hugh and Louise eyed each other quickly, both beginning uneasily to speak: "My darling . . ." began the princess, and "my . . . my dear friend," stammered Hugh.

The dauphine stood abruptly, spreading her arms in front of herself. "What has happened? What is wrong?" she demanded firmly. "Is it that someone has . . . the empress, is it the *empress?*" Her voice was sharp, pained. Her eyes darted back and forth, until Louise rose slowly, gently assisting her mistress back on to the settee, she sat next to her, reaching into the deep pocket of her full skirt.

Louise withdrew the still-sealed envelope, Hugh joining his fiancée just as she passed the envelope to Antoinette. The younger woman's eyes immediately went to the front, instantly recognising her beloved "Mama's" near-singular script. Her hand shaking now, with her slender fingers, she tore the back flap away, shattering the green wax seal, its shards falling into her lap, onto the sofa and the rug.

Both Hugh and the princess watched her as her light-blue eyes travelled quickly across and down the rough Irish writing paper, Lamballe gripping her hand as, obviously having read . . . *Late in the afternoon of 4 May 1773, my beloved Arthur was ambushed by soldiers of the crown near Carriganima and then and there shot dead . . .* the young, future queen's left hand went to her mouth, though before she could silence herself, she had already shrieked, "*Non! Non!* Papa! *Mon* Papa . . . *Assassiné? Coup? Tué? . . . Non   . . . ça ne peut pas être!*" Lamballe's arm reached around Antoinette's trim shoulders, murmuring "*C'est vrai* . . . my darling . . . it is true, sadly it can be, it is . . . please read your mama's words . . .We"—she gestured to an ashen-faced Hugh and then to herself—" . . . we have received the same dreadful, horrid message. . . ."

The dauphine did so, reading Eileen's words slowly, her face a mask of horror and disbelief; at one point she'd buried her face in the soft black wool of Lamballe's riding coat, sobbing bitterly, screaming several times, "Oh, *mon Dieu . . . Non!*" as she read on, weeping gently as she read Eileen's final words:

Would that I were able to embrace you as I relate this sad, sad news to you, my darling, as I know how deeply you cared for him, and he for you. As do I at this very moment, he had come to think of you as our own child . . . and so you shall always and forever remain, and as Conor and Fiach's elder sister . . . and our beloved daughter. Now you have two loving papas to watch over and love you from God's heaven. . . . May that be a source of comfort for you in this sad time we share.

Antoinette smiled weakly as she noted that, casting caution to the wind, Eileen had signed the painful missive, as she had always preferred doing so, stopping only when she'd learnt that her letters would most likely be read by enemies of France and Austria, perhaps even friends as well, . . . *with my abiding love and affection, always—Mama.*

The dauphine wept even more, until she finally cried herself out, Louise shedding even more tears, Hugh's cheeks again wet, his eyes red.

The sad trio then sat for a time, holding hands . . . seemingly unable to speak, yet having no desire to end the visit. Hugh finally managed to speak softly, his voice seeming to Antoinette to be huskier, more like Eileen's than his own. "We know no more of this horrid crime than Eileen has written. . . . General Dillon has requested of his people in Ireland to find out what they can. When . . . should we learn more through this kindness, we shall certainly tell you what he has discovered. . . ." His voice trailing away, Louise, now again her servant, politely suggested that perhaps the dauphine would prefer to rest, to which Antoinette responded with a grateful expression, an extended hand and rose almost immediately. She nodded to Hugh, whispered in adieu "my dear friend," and hand in hand with the princess, she otherwise silently exited the room.

Schönbrunn—late May 1773

Late on a busy Tuesday morning, Abigail O'Sullivan was at her as-usual-paper-strewn desk, her recently, reluctantly acquired reading glasses resting pertly on her lightly freckled nose, at this moment in the midst of trying to make sense of an obviously quickly scrawled note from her uncle, General the Count Moritz O'Connell: *Your auntie and I and wee Caitríona are en route to Schönbrunn this day; urgent that we see you as well as HIM, if she is available. Sorrowful news—Morty*

Abby sighed, reflecting, *There is always some sorry news . . . Mama and Morgan write of deaths at home, lost babies, fights and quarrels, business losses, shipwrecks . . . Hugh bemoans life at court, though from what I understand, his bride-to-be should simply acquire the whole bloody place and toss all the troublemakers out*—she laughed—then, realising that Morty rarely shared unpleasant news, *'Tis simply not his way; the dear old boy prefers to have others be messengers of doom.* This time she did not laugh but was puzzled.

A half hour or so later, her door minder's triple knocks sounded, the door swinging wide almost immediately as the small, *so terribly officious*, she felt, the miniature bewigged man named Fritz began to announce, "His Grace, General the . . ." until Morty O'Connell's six feet and as many inches, three hundred-plus-pound frame stepped around the tiny fellow, followed by his wife, the Countess Maria von Graffenreit, their treasured two-year-and-several-months-old, late-in-life daughter, Caitríona, in tow, the general closing the door sharply behind them.

A now-standing Abby, her glasses perched on her head, was laughing at the typical Morty O'Connell entrance, though she caught herself as she absorbed her relatives' pinched, sombre expressions, simply gesturing to the leather chairs that faced her own across her writing table, reaching into a tall armoire set against the wall next to her work area and producing a smiling-faced stuffed doll with yellow yarn hair she'd had sewn for her little cousin, a beautiful toddler, in a miniature of her mother's elegant riding habit, a mane of unimaginably golden-blonde curls already almost tumbling over her shoulders.

General O'Connell leaned back and withdrew an envelope from his waistcoat, passing it across the desk to his niece. "If you would, darling Abby, it would perhaps be best were you to read the letter enclosed." Noting Eileen's distinct swirling hand, the envelope addressed to *Abigail O'Sullivan* and, as she turned it, the O'Connell stag frozen in the splodge of green wax, settling her spectacles back onto her nose, she immediately broke the seal, the pieces dropping onto her papers, and began to read her sister's message.

Maria von Graffenreit O'Connell, who for a number of years had occupied this room, this desk, as the principal lady-in-waiting to the Empress Maria Theresa, rested her eyes on the niece she had come to love dearly, following the younger woman's eyes until she read . . . *Late in the afternoon of 4 May 1773, my beloved Arthur was ambushed by soldiers of the crown near Carriganima and then and there shot dead . . .* and gasped a purposely-muted "Oh, good God, nooooooooooooooo, oh my dear God in bloody Heaven . . ." looking up plaintively, frozen momentarily until she burst into tears, muffling them by placing her arms before her, her head buried into them as she sobbed softly dampening some of her papers. . . . The countess rose reflexively and rested her delicate hands on the younger woman's heaving shoulders as Caitríona wriggled up onto her massive papa's lap, innocently showing him her new dolly.

Within moments, Abby rose, remarkably composed though red-eyed. "There is no reason to delay the inevitable," she stated almost matter-of-factly to the O'Connells, cocking her head in the direction of the door that connected her chambers with those of the most powerful woman in the world. Without waiting for assent or dissent from her family, with a *swishhhh* of the ample skirts of her pale-yellow afternoon dress, the slender young woman stepped to the door and knocked gently twice with the knuckles of her right hand, immediately receiving the customarily soft-spoken, *"Entrez, s'il vous plait."*

Looking up from her own paper-covered writing table, Maria Theresa smiled broadly as Abby led the small O'Connell contingent into her office, little Caitríona racing ahead, calling out, "Dolly, dolly!" and offering her new friend to the empress, who greeted them both with an all-embracing hug, settling the little girl on her lap as she gestured for the adults to, "Sit, sit, my dearest friends."

Maria Theresa had turned fifty-seven mere days before on 13 May and had reigned over Austria and Hungary for more than thirty of those years. Though no longer the lithe, striking young woman she had once been, the empress had lost none of her acute powers of observation, insight and the ability to act on what might seem to others to be minute amounts of information.

Even as the three adult O'Connells were settling themselves into their chairs, Maria Theresa addressed them. "You bring me news, information, I see . . . and it is not good tidings," she said softly, "Given that it is *you*—"she gestured broadly at the three of them in their matching, embroidered wing chairs, arched in front of her desk, the general seated between the two women, even as Caitríona had settled on the monarch's lap, her head resting against the her ample bosom. Hugging her dolly, peacefully sucking her left thumb.

"Given that it is you, the news is from Ireland, it is from France, please do not weary me, my dearest friends, just say what you must."

The women looked uneasily at each other and the general cleared his throat and leaned forward, his palms on his knees. "Our darling Eileen writes us from Ireland, Majesty. . . . She advises of the death of Captain O'Leary some weeks ago, on the fourth of this month, she . . ."

To Abby and the countess's relief, "How . . . where . . . how did, how could this happen, General?" she inquired coolly directly of O'Connell, as she had for a number of years of his military and political service.

And, as he had always been, as he remained, the dominating officer's response was direct and pointed: Without referencing the background in any great detail, he advised, "The Captain was ambushed from cover . . . a man of some standing in the county, a one-time sheriff, now a magistrate, a minor judicial officer, had long been at odds with Arthur, and apparently having somehow gotten the captain declared an 'outlaw,' this man, his name is Morris, also somehow succeeded in hectoring the officer commanding a small contingent of English troops there in Cork to detach some men to his command, perhaps to arrest the outlaw." He sighed and drew a breath.

The empress sat rigid, her hands around the general's daughter, who had fallen asleep, cuddling her doll.

"In any event, it was not an arrest this Morris had arranged, probably on the advice of informers—that curse of Ireland—he knew where Arthur was, that he was alone and in a remote spot, and lined up his wee, make-believe troop and commanded the men to fire, which they did. . . . Arthur O'Leary is died, Majesty. . . . Speaking as a military man in your service, and as an Irishman: *Arthur O'Leary was murdered.*"

By this point, the countess and Abigail were weeping softly. The empress's eyes and her cheeks were moist, but her expression was blank, almost chill. "Were I able, I should invade this miserable excuse for a kingdom and level it, destroy it and leave no evidence of it standing . . . slay these men who occupy it . . . you did not say it, but I am assuming this Morris is a Protestant . . . who use their power to . . . to do things like this. . . ." Her voice shook audibly.

Still seated, she crossed herself. "Let us pray for Captain O'Leary's soul . . . and for Eileen and for their sons, and . . ." She looked up, her face now a mask of pain, of loss ". . . and for their *daughter* . . ." she smiled sadly, "for their *wee archduchess*. . . ." Her voice trailed off as, resting her forehead in her left hand, she began to cry. The others then crossed themselves, and the four prayed briefly in silence.

The little girl stirring in her arms, the empress gestured to the countess, who stood and retrieved her daughter—and her doll.

As the two women were already standing, the general and Abby joined them.

"I am assuming this dreadful news is reaching the court at Versailles," the empress said softly.

Abby gently responded, "Hugh and the Princess de Lamballe, Eileen has written to them, enclosing a letter for Her Royal Highness, the Dauphine, with a request that they deliver it and tell her in person . . . as we have Your Majesty."

Satisfied, as best one could be, Maria Theresa kissed her friends, hugging Caitriona and gesturing that they withdraw informally. As they did, she resumed her seat and picked up a report of road conditions in lower Austria.

By the following morning, the empress had decreed that the court at Schönbrunn was in full, formal mourning for *Captain Arthur O'Leary, late of Höeninger's Regiment, Her Imperial Majesty's Hungarian Hussars of the Armies of*

Austria and Hungary, a brave, proud and faithful officer and servant and dear friend of Her Imperial Majesty, a loving faithful husband and father. In the young officer's honour, black was worn, mirrors were draped in crepe, flags fluttered at half-staff until 7 June. Eileen would learn of this exceptional honour, this graceful gesture, by means of a simple letter from the empress, and a more detailed, much more emotional one from Abby.

County Cork, Ireland—June 1773

Eileen was pleased both that Conor the Younger, Art's brother, had chosen to remain after Catherine O'Leary had reluctantly returned to Cork, and that Squire O'Leary had chosen to, as he put it, "stay at home." She was also relieved that, prior to her departure, Catherine and she had reconciled to some significant degree.

The men provided Eileen with good company and, more importantly, from them, almost casually, she learned that she now possessed a permanent home and security, neither of which many a widow of a younger son in eighteenth-century Ireland could hope for.

Conor was especially candid. "For a time, I have had a mind to depart Ireland. I had first considered France, but your brother, Daniel, appears to believe that France is itself in some measure of decline. I know not more than that of which he has to me written, but as I result, I have come to see my future in the New World, in America; for 'tis of America that I have received nothing but the most positive news, and 'tis *for* America that many Irish depart monthly, including a significant number of Ulster Dissenters, who are said to be populating America's seemingly immeasurable interior wilderness. They are fleeing Ulster, as the Protestants there seem to treat them in much the same way as they do us—rather poorly!" He laughed ironically.

Growing serious, and leaning forward on his arms, Conor related that several younger legal colleagues, Catholic and Church of Ireland communicants alike, had settled in Philadelphia, and several more in

Baltimore, ". . . and are even now there in both locations already prospering."

He had agreed with his father to formally relinquish his interest in Rathleigh in favour of Eileen's eldest son, in return for which the squire would provide him, for an extended time, with an income. In response to Eileen's unspoken question, he said simply, "'Twill be relatively soon . . ."

"So, you see now, my dear, should you so desire, *this* shall remain your home." Squire O'Leary gestured expansively that evening at dinner, and Eileen had jumped up spontaneously, wrapping her arms around her father-in-law and holding him silently for a moment. When Conor stood and joined them, she then embraced both O'Learys and they her; "my benefactors," she added.

"Your *family*," the squire said and, after first tipping his raised glass towards Eileen, took a deep swallow of claret.

Beyond the O'Learys providing a secure life for Eileen and her wee lads, the young widow felt herself fortunate to be sensitively embraced by them, including Catherine, following and despite her strange behaviour at Art's wake, as the O'Connells of Derrynane had proven themselves to be largely emotionally distant.

She had sent word to Derrynane, and to Morgan at Carhen, some six miles west, of Art's murder within days of its occurrence, mentioning his temporary interment and the plan to move him to Kilcrea Abbey as soon as possible; other than a gentle though brief letter the messenger brought with him from Morgan, both Maurice and Maire had taken some days to author what Eileen felt were purely cursory letters of condolence. Despite his many kindnesses to her, Eileen had long believed her second-eldest brother to be detached, almost cold in relation to the feelings of others. She knew he bore his wife's childlessness stoically; she never questioned how, if at all, solicitous he was of Mary Cantillon's own feelings.

As she read and reread her mother's letter, which she would tell Anna she saw as being "gracious, kind but little more," Eileen finally permitted herself to feel a deep, profound degree of disappointment in Maire Ni Dhuibh. Pondering her mother's words—*Whilst most deeply I of course regret your loss, and the sorrow that I know must accompany it for you, that Captain O'Leary would have lost his life as he sadly did seems to me regrettably predictable in light of the reputation he had earned even prior to your marriage, does it not, my darling?*—Eileen could only shake her head, in disillusionment, in disenchantment, and such was the degree of both that she found the words themselves frequently coming to mind thereafter. When they did, she was yet again saddened and, eventually and for some not insignificant time, embittered.

Eileen had accepted that Maire had distanced herself after her marriage to O'Leary, and that her mother was aging; she also concluded—in doing, she wondered whether she was attempting to reconcile her feelings about her mother?—that Maire had suffered numerous losses: of a dozen children—in the womb or soon after birth—as well as two brothers whom Eileen had known, John in 1751, when Eileen was but seven, in addition to Conaill's perishing at sea and of course of her beloved Donal Mór. For Maire O'Connell, death was perhaps as much a part of life as birth. Her faith was deep and constant. She believed, never doubting, she would see her husband and her children in God's heaven; as to the fact that they had preceded her thence, once the initial wrenching that accompanied their actual deaths had passed, she simply went on living.

One steamy, windlessly still early June afternoon, an odd-looking group of horsemen entered Macroom, proceeding through the Market Square and directly towards the nondescript building that housed various government offices, including that of Major James MacAteer, commander of the small detachment of British troops resident in the Muskerry Barony.

Other than that they were obviously and unusually heavily armed, rifles bristling, sidearms in various types of holsters, what was especially strange about the horsemen was how they were riding: A man in front was immediately followed by a second rider, who, in turn, was flanked by two men, one on each side, and followed by two more at the rear. People stopped and stared, as the men appeared to be strangers to the vicinage, as they plodded towards their destination.

Just as they neared it, a rotund little man, virtually the shape of a child's ball, was walking with a surprisingly light step in the opposite direction. A massive Irish wolfhound trotted alongside, his tail swaying, at least until one of the horses noticed him and shied, the dog lurched forward. "Git away, whore-hound! Git!" roared the closest outrider, pointing his rifle outward at the dog.

"Rufus! Rufus!" cried the fat man, and the dog instantly calmed, his tail again wagging.

Taking him by the scruff, the man began to scurry away until he looked up and saw the middle rider, the one who was apparently, for some reason, being protected, whose face was ashen, his hands trembling.

"Why, Morris, *Morris*, where have ye been, man?" queried the round fellow in a dry, Lowland Scots burr. "I've no seen ye for weeks, man! Is there some cause for ye to secrete yerself at the Hall?" Though the small man's mouth had fallen open, no words had come. "Hah, ye coward . . . ye coward and ye murderer. . ." Turning towards the small group that had instantly gathered around the riders, he continued, " . . . lookee all, the *Great Abraham Morris* deigns to descend to our wee village. . . . Oh, will ye have a drink perhaps, *your honour*?" At that word, the man spat on the ground and turned coldly away . . . muttering, "Never! N'er would I drink with a murderer!" The little group muttered in seeming agreement.

Within minutes, a shaken Abraham Morris sat trembling before Major MacAteer, who, having listened to what he immediately had determined were the first few sentences of a plea he had heard several times already, slammed his right palm on his tidy wooden desktop and snapped, " No! Not again, sir . . . you *will* understand, as I have advised you repeatedly, but I shall say it yet again and for the final time, I am *not in any way* responsible for your safety or security, nor are any of my men. Not one man! The crown is not in any way beholden to you!"

Leaning forward, looking harshly at the sweating little man, he continued coldly, "I now know that this O'Leary was a popular figure, said to be viewed as being a solid man even amongst many of our kind. And as for the bloody Papists, as I have learnt, his foolish 'outlawing' by your make-believe 'court,' why, it simply made him a fucking hero, an even more bloody 'romantic' character! Stupid men, you and your bloody ignorant friends. Hah, *stupid man—you*!" his right forefinger pointed accusingly.

"On the other hand, you blithering fool, in case you are somehow unawares, you are generally despised in this vicinage by men of all beliefs!" The officer stood abruptly, his creaky chair scraping the rough wooden floor. "Now, be gone! Be fucking gone, you bloody bastard! How I wish I had never . . . Get the bloody hell out of here, and do not bloody ever come back! *Mister Magistrate*!" He shook his head.

Morris and his guards quickly gathered their rifles and clambered out of the little room and onto the sun-bright, bustling street, only to be met by a group of rowdy young men, appearing to be farmers' sons and their hands, taking an afternoon off from the fields.

"Why, 'tis the *former* high sheriff of Cork himself, lads!" a tall, hulking man of perhaps twenty years named Kenney observed, gesturing to Morris.

"Ah, aye indeed, the coward . . . it is indeed he, sir . . . took O'Leary's life as sure as if he'd fired the killing shots, though he had a lad do his dirty, his filthy work he did!" scoffed one of his companions loudly.

The two youngest, mere boys began shouting, "Murderer! Murderer! Killer! Killer! Coward! Coward!" As they continued their accusatory litany, all the young men began jostling Morris and, despite their weaponry, his obviously terrified protectors, some of whom pushed back, two of them quickly landing on the ground, one struggling to raise his rifle.

"I wouldna do that, stranger," snapped Kenney. "Would no be wise."

"Lads!" Another of the group suddenly began waving his arms, gesturing at an open door where stood Major MacAteer, his own arms folded. "Let us be gone, lads!" and they hastened away.

As did a terrified Abraham Morris, his armed guards notwithstanding.

One morning, towards the middle of June, Eileen reflected that too much time had passed since she had promised Mary McAuliffe, the old woman who had come on a devastatingly wounded O'Leary and remained with him, even as and after he died, until Eileen had arrived, to "seek you out and find you, old woman, then to thank you in a fitting fashion."

"How does one properly express adequate gratitude to a person such as this ancient woman for what she did? How does one compensate a person of some ninety or more years for such an act?" Eileen wondered aloud as she and Anna sat in a grove of trees at Derryleigh, the children frolicking under the watchful gaze of John Collins whilst he and John Daly were repairing a shattered fence board. Anna had no ready response but agreed that it was likely not something to be easily accomplished.

As had her husband, Eileen had come to regard John Collins for his thoughtful wisdom and wise counsel, so the women posed the same question to him when he had strolled towards them, the children circling him like puppies as he walked.

"McAuliffe, you say?" Collins asked quickly. "There are several large McAuliffe families, a number unrelated, so there a McAuliffe not infrequently and separated by any significant number of degrees, weds another McAuliffe amongst the tenantry on the Lipton estates; above and about Carriganima . . . she is most likely of those people. Though generally well thought of himself, Lord Lipton is rarely in Ireland, as a result so many overseers have been engaged, only to be sacked or depart, that I know not who might be on the property at present. I *do* know, however, that, by and large, the people there do not live as they do here—" he gestured about Derryleigh—"or at Rathleigh."

Eileen sat quietly for a few moments. "What think ye were I to perhaps permit . . . or, more correctly, to *invite* . . . the old woman and her family to come onto Rathleigh . . . to a new cottage and, given what you say about the conditions at Lord Lipton's, a new and perhaps even better life?"

Collins smiled broadly. "'Tis a grand idea, such that I wish 'twas I who first conceived of it!" he cried out, adding, "Daly and myself, we could assist your man Walsh and the Rathleigh lads in putting up a cottage, eh?"

Eileen literally jumped up and embraced a shocked Collins, soundly kissing him on both cheeks and causing Anna to laugh. "Ah, see—you are still Austrian!"

That afternoon, as painful as it was to do so, Eileen rode once again alone, though this time on Bull, to Carriganima. Once there, after speaking, mostly in Irish, with several men in the village, she located one who was one of the Lipton tenants, in whose company and that of his wide-eyed daughter, who behaved as if everything about Eileen, beginning with her singular black mourning robes, and everything she said was fascinating, she rode to the massive estates of Lord Lipton.

Less than a half hour later, Eileen was seated on a rude bench in front of an aging cottage that was home to Mary McAuliffe, who had greeted her warmly, refusing to accept apologies for any tardiness on Eileen's part, "My darling girl, a widow ye have only just become," along with one of her numerous great-grandsons, himself appearing to be approaching forty, his wife, one of their daughters, her husband and, Eileen counted, though she did not ask, at least six younger children of varying ages. Though the distressed-looking cabin was spotlessly clean inside, the people appeared to Eileen to be somewhat cheerless, perhaps even ill-fed. She pointedly inquired if anyone, especially any of the children, could read or write, and all shook their heads sadly in the negative.

As she sat with the adults, conversing in Irish, asking and answering numerous questions, the old woman had joined her on the rough bench and would occasionally whisper a comment in Eileen's ear or pat her maternally on her knee. As the conversation continued, the children quietly, one by one, came to sit on the ground by the women's bench, several of the girls' wondering eyes focused solely on their visitor.

Finally, leaning back against the, rough stone of the house, made comfortingly warm by the sunshine, Eileen spoke softly, admitting "of money I have no great amount, most of my possessions being of value to me alone . . . What I do possess, however, with my husband's family, is land, a good place on which live good people, like your good selves. . . . At Rathleigh, everyone labours to their abilities, no one is hungry or ill-clad . . . and the children—even the grown people, should they desire—learn to read." She smiled.

At that, their eyes wide with wonder, several of the children mouthed Eileen's phrase, *ag léamh*, softly amongst themselves, *to read*, and nodded and smiled.

She then made her proposal, including John Collins's offer of construction assistance, additionally providing that "so long as the O'Learys have a home at Rathleigh, so, too, shall the McAuliffes."

The decision was quickly made, qualified only by Patrick McAuliffe, a thick, solid, handsomely tousled blond man with rough hands, who declared, "We, the McAuliffe men, we shall work with your men, my lady, in building our home, mistress."

Eileen smiled broadly. "Come tomorrow morning, then, and we shall find you a site."

They did, and by mid-July, the multigenerational McAuliffes had moved into what had, given the size of the immediate extended clan, become a pair of snug, large-roomed, high-lofted cottages, each with a tightly thatched roof and a chimney, as all of the Rathleigh tenants' homes now had. An ample, shared garden plot was being turned, and work arrangements had been arrived at, as had a commitment by the O'Learys to see that the family would be assured of having adequate food until their own crops were in.

One evening several days after the family had moved their few belongings in, Eileen rode Banrían out to the pleasant site, a gentle knoll the McAuliffes had chosen, a wisp of smoke lazily drifting away from the cooking fire, several of her great-great-grandchildren playing under Mary McAuliffe's watchful eyes. Eileen had approached quietly; she was not at first noticed and enjoyed the sight, smiling broadly as Mary leaned back against the still-sun-warmed wall of her new home, delicately puffing on a clay pipe, an expression of contentment on her deeply tanned, heavily creased face. Finally noticing Eileen, she smiled as she rose and ambled slowly to greet her caller, causing Eileen to chuckle as Mary observed "what a nice young man" she had found Squire O'Leary to be.

This was the first of a number of visits Eileen would make there; she and Conor and Fiach and Squire O'Leary, Catherine even, would grow close to the exuberant McAuliffe clan and they to the O'Learys, to the extent that when, several years later, Mary, having marked her hundredth birthday, and by the clan's estimate perhaps at least two beyond that, died peacefully in her sleep, the McAuliffes and the O'Learys would mourn her passing and celebrate her remarkable life as one family.

Both Eileen and Anna observed an increasingly close bond quickly developing between Conor O'Leary and John Collins; the young men frequently rode, fished and hunted together, drank together and, as June progressed, took long walks before or after dinner on those evenings when the Collins family was at Rathleigh or Eileen, her brother-in-law and her sons were at Derryleigh.

It was a breezy though hot evening in mid-June when, following a light meal at Rathleigh, the two men had gently asked of Anna a few minutes of Mistress O'Leary's time and company alone. As she watched Eileen going to join the men in Squire O'Leary's study, with twinkling eyes Anna muttered softly under her breath in German. John Collins had learnt just enough of the difficult tongue to understand and told the O'Learys that it was by "yet one more strange Irish custom" that his pert wife was bemused.

Once settled, Conor O'Leary was both serious and quite direct. "Squire Collins and I have been in discussions these weeks over what steps to take as to killing Morris." Eileen leaned back, her interest piqued, as she and the men had previously agreed that, whilst they were not yet through with Morris, given her own potentially disastrous attempt, she permit them to formulate what Conor had at the time gently referred to as "shall we say, *a more realistic . . . though none less lethal strategy.*"

Conor cleared his throat and began earnestly. "We—Collins and I, I should say Collins more than I, he seemingly being the more devious one—we have together devised a general plan, at least some of the salient details of which we wish to advise you."

For the ensuing hour, both men outlined for Eileen a precise, carefully calculated attack on Morris, who, following her bloody foray to Hanover Hall, was known to have been hiding in several locations in Macroom but had recently, seemingly inexplicably, returned to his estate. In this regard, Collins voiced an opinion he'd heard being generally repeated in Macroom: "This English officer, MacAteer—the spineless bastard Morris hectored into giving him the contingent that cost Arthur his life— 'tis said he has told Morris that he cannot, indeed he will not provide him with any security in Macroom, will not assume any responsibility for his safety.

"We believe 'tis best to await his return yet again to an urban setting . . . as it will be safer for the assassins," Collins said.

"Though not for *him!*" Conor added.

"How can we be certain he shall yet again depart Hanover Hall?" Eileen wondered aloud. "Does it not make sense that he deems himself most secure there, in his own place, on his own lands? Especially given that the English have seemingly cut him loose?"

The men exchanged knowing glances. "Ah, but even now we have begun to sow the winds of County Cork with *words*, with *rumours*," Conor said, employing a conspiratorial tone, lowering his voice for emphasis. "Indeed, with *terrifying tales*." He laughed icily.

"If he has not yet, very soon the contemptable Morris will learn of there being a band of assassins engaged by . . . engaged by *someone*," he laughed again, "perhaps by the king of France . . . or perhaps even the Empress Maria Theresa herself. . . . Indeed your own solitary effort," Eileen, gasped, blushed and momentarily lowered her eyes—"It has itself proven most positive, as it affords a tangible basis for all these wild tales we are sowing." He smiled and, to a degree puzzled, Eileen winced at the still-sore memory of her poorly planned, potentially catastrophic attempt on Morris's life, not to mention her killing two men sent in pursuit of her as she fled the place.

"In the event," Conor continued, Eileen now looking fully up, drawn to his effusive tone and gestures, "the talk . . . indeed, it has truly begun . . . a great deal of it amongst the people of the countryside—and it is and will continue to be of men . . . *men who are skilled assassins* . . . attacking him in the remote fastness of Hanover Hall—men for whom it is even now being spoken aloud that *the lone, tall, black-clad rider was a scout! Indeed 'tis said that this man's killing of Morris's henchmen is to have been meant as but a foreshadowing of the fate to befall their master."* As both men laughed cruelly at the spectre of a terrified Morris, Eileen finally smiled weakly.

Collins added, "Indeed the deaths of these two guards, it has apparently made obtaining and retaining a force of any size virtually impossible for Morris." O'Leary quickly qualifying, "Indeed he has no more than two or three men, is what I continue to hear!

"So then, that the authorities would provide him with some form of military protection, which we are certain now is not going to occur, so vast and so secluded are his estates he shall be forced to conclude that he cannot there adequately ensure his own safety and survival. We shall make certain that of this vulnerability he shall become fully convinced . . . indeed in this effort Johnny O'Callaghan has already arranged for several of the taller young lads in his neighbourhood to don black clothing and, thus clad, they are already being seen on the roads and especially in the precincts of Hanover Hall itself.   As Morris apparently did following the event of *the lone, tall, black-clad rider* when he attempted to hide himself in Macroom, he shall thus feel himself virtually compelled to repair this time to the perceived sanctuary that only Cork City offers."

"Though 'twill be in Cork City that he shall meet his just and deserved fate!" Conor exclaimed.

Their faces gleaming with sweat, both men smiled, and Eileen nodded quietly, her expression now growing grimly firm. "So then . . . thus it commences in earnest . . . and with a sound plan . . . revenge   . . . retribution . . . In this instance, I firmly believe that your chosen assassins, whoever they may be, they *shall* be doing God's holy work, administering

God's holy justice, as the crown does nothing." She nodded again, firmly, as did the men in response.

As Conor and Collins began to rise, a distant expression in her eyes, Eileen said, "A moment, please, gentlemen," and they both resumed their seats, though she now stood. "As you have been making me aware of your plan of attack, a thought has just come to mind. I should be grateful were I to be able to make a suggestion, which it is that arises out of this thought; perhaps you might take it as a widow's request: If 'tis at all possible, rather than killing him outright, I should think it would be most fitting for whomever you may charge with the act to somehow deliver wounds that will condemn Morris to a lengthy, painful and horrid death," she said in a calm, even voice. "Might this possibly be done?"

The men exchanged nods, and both nodded at Eileen. "Yes," said John Collins in his elegant tone, "'tis a fine idea it is . . . indeed, an excellent one! 'Tis one that shall assure that the wretched, murdering bastard Morris will suffer the most miserable of prolonged deaths possible."

We shall speak with some men," Conor O'Leary volunteered, nodding at his co-conspirator, who nodded back, their thoughts apparently the same.

"All that remains now is for us to be certain that our quarry has bought the lie and sought what he will see as safe refuge in Cork City," added Collins.

In the depths of a deathly still, abnormally hot night in late June, Anna heard the pounding first; though both women would now deny the fact, her years of being at Eileen's beck-and-call in Austria had rendered her an extremely light sleeper. After rocking, practically pummelling, her soundly sleeping husband semi awake, she hastily drew a long, blue satin dressing gown about her trim, naked body. Having withdrawn one of a pair of pistols kept ready on the top shelf in her husband's armoire, and leaving the doors ajar, should Collins wish the other one, she raced barefoot down the stairs;

once in the broad entryway, she was satisfied with the adequacy of the light provided by the short, thick candle flickering safely in a two-foot-high hurricane glass on a table at the foot of the stairs.

Cocking her weapon, Anna finally then peered through the right one of the narrow, glazed glass windows that flanked both sides of the door; recognising John Daly, one of the Collinses' most trusted men, she unbolted and pulled the door open, her invariably proper, now almost comically dishevelled, husband, stuffing a rumpled shirt into his breeches, lumbering barefoot down the stairs, the second upstairs pistol at the ready.

As the couple laid down their weapons, without hesitation, even before taking a proffered seat on a bench in the hall, having declined Anna's offer to sit in the drawing room, Daly began slowly, in precise Irish, then repeating his words in English, "Squire, Mistress Anna . . . 'tis time: The murderer Morris, he has again removed himself to Cork City, as, sir, you and Master O'Leary said he would, sir. Three days before yesterday he did . . . and he was alone, sir, madame."

Collins began to speak, but Anna caught his sleeve as, primarily for her benefit, Daly continued now wholly in English.

"He is secreted at the house of a man called Boyce . . . 'tis on a street called by the name Hammonds Lane in Cork City, though I know not where that place is, sir, m'lady."

Collins draped a heavy hand on the slightly smaller man's shoulder. "How certain of this are you, John?" he asked firmly. "From whom have we learnt of this?"

The older man nodded, equally firmly, continuing still in English. "My younger brother, Liam . . . the handsome lad, sir." Lifting his right forefinger in pause, rising from the bench, he managed a smile, taking a few steps, he reopened the door and gestured a wide-eyed Liam Daly into the house, a place he had never before been, there to find himself standing before the dressing gown–clad, barefoot Mistress Collins, who understood and smilingly indicated he should step forward into the broad entryway, which he did tentatively, even as his brother resumed speaking.

"The lad, he had gone with Curran, my Lady Anna, sir, to Cork City, to deliver the very large load of tanned hides and, as you'll recall we'd told anyone heading to Cork to keep a sharp eye out for the man, he saw Morris there, alone on a street. He's only just arrived home this evening. . . . Now, tell the squire, tell the mistress, lad; go ahead, now."

Young Liam's mouth opened, but no words came. He appeared on the verge of tears and shook his head at his brother, who immediately continued as both Collinses listened in silence.

"The lad"—Daly affectionately cocked his tousled head at his still awestruck brother—"the lad, he tells me he followed Morris on foot and saw him enter the back of a house." Liam was nodding vigorously at each fact his brother delivered, confirming the accuracy of what was being said.

"Other than this moment," Daly rolled his eyes and, unable to help himself not to, laughed aloud, "the boy, he is such a glorious talker he is, sir . . . and nice-looking as well he is, you would have to say so, would you not, Mistress Anna?" Anna smiled softly, nodding, her hands folded as if in prayer at her bosom. "So, now . . . so he manages to catch the eye of a serving girl in the yard . . . and, with very little prodding on his part," he proudly placed his arm around his brother's shoulder, as the boy smiled shyly now, "before he knows it, she has told him who the man is, from where he has come and, if you can believe it, mistress," he nodded respectfully at Anna, "even where in the house he is lodging!"

"Liam, is this indeed what happened then in Cork, is this what you have discovered, lad?" Collins asked sharply in Irish.

The boy nodded and pushed some of his thick, blond, thatchlike hair out of his eyes and finally began to relax, managing in careful English, "Aye . . . yessir, yes, Squire, sir, it is, it was . . . indeed, sir!" He smiled, still shyly.

"You have done well, lad!" Collins firmly clapped a hand on the boy's other shoulder. "Very proud of you I am, Liam, very proud indeed!"

This having made him even more at ease, Liam began now to relate in his halting, Irish-laced English, much of what his brother had already reported, adding qualifiers such as "the girl, she was lovely, she was, sir . . . madame . . . and she asked me to tea, though I of course said no, though I must admit I would very much have liked to have taken tea with her, pretty as she was and all. . . ."

Though the couple continued to listen with warm, proudly parental expressions on their faces, he quieted as his brother finally gently nudged him, quickly finishing his tale, ". . . and that's how it went, sir . . . mistress."

The brothers shortly took their leave of the squire and the mistress, young Liam indicating, as they strolled towards the grouping of the Daly cottages, that he was bemused by the fact that, "She talks in a funny way, does she not, brother, the mistress; does she not now?"

John Daly smiled, and again wrapped a lanky arm around Liam's shoulder as they walked. "You will know that she comes from a place called Austria, lad, where they speak the German tongue, but I have no doubt that she is now as Irish as are any of us!"

Cork City, Ireland—7 July 1773

A trim, gleaming black coach, its curtains drawn, carrying most likely—judging by the level ride of the carriage—two unseen passengers, lurched through the streets of Cork on what, having dawned foggy and chill, had proven to be a delightfully breezy midsummer Wednesday afternoon. Turning the corner from busy Whitefriarschurch Road, the coach made its way slowly up Hammonds Lane, halting finally in front of a plain, though quite large brick house in the middle of the short, narrow street.

Exchanging no words with the coachman, whose gaze remained fixed between the shoulders of the two sleek horses in their traces, the passenger seated on the carriage's right-hand side reached through the window space, opened the door and alighted; smacking the side of the coach once, it immediately lurched and then rolled away. He hoisted the strap of what was a relatively large, well-worn leather satchel over his right shoulder and turned to the brick footpath leading to the house's front steps.

The passenger, who walked slowly, heavily, was an odd-looking man, with loose-hanging, frizzy, dull black hair covered by a worn, broad-brimmed hat, its distinctive shape strikingly similar to ones usually affected by male members of the Society of Friends. At first, he appeared to be thick, hulking, almost ungainly, of difficult-to-determine age, his shoulders round, his middle thick in a baggy, nondescript grey suit; yet his calves were incongruously spindly in comparison with his rotund upper body, encased in white hose, wearing dusty black shoes, his posture slouched. Reaching the top of the steps, the man lifted a heavy brass knocker and let it drop. The door was almost immediately answered by a pretty—*a very pretty indeed,* reflected the visitor—girl, her long, loose hair the intriguing colour of a fox's coat.

After determining from her that he for certain was at the house of Mr. Boyce, he announced that he was calling on "The Honourable Magistrate Morris, if you please. I am Squire Dodson Goodfellow, just arrived from Dublin, indeed from the Castle itself, Dublin Castle, I have come . . . with vital news for his honour, most crucial as to his safety and security. . . ."

Her mouth somewhat agape at the apparently distinguished, unexpected visitor, the girl wondered aloud, "Would you be seeing the gentleman in his rooms, your honour, or in the parlour, sir, your pleasure, sir"—she pointed into the parlour with her left hand—"or, perhaps in the garden, sir, 'tis quite a lovely day, is it not, sir?" She smiled, gesturing him to a window from which the visitor could see a simple, green-grassed, lightly planted garden, enclosed by a hedge, rather than a wall, with a gap in the hedge at the far back, appearing to open onto the adjacent street.

His immediate unspoken reaction, *yes, the garden . . .bloody perfect!* notwithstanding, the awkward man permitted himself to appear to reflect a moment, finally saying, almost diffidently, "The garden, girl, yes, the garden would be quite satisfactory. I shall await the magistrate there, if I may," he added as she held the door at the far end of the front-to-back corridor, open for him, before immediately hustling to Morris's rooms.

Clearing several steps into the garden, Squire Goodfellow seated himself on a black wrought-iron bench that faced the house and awaited Abraham Morris. He set his satchel next to him and opened the pair of gleaming brass clasps that held it shut; he hugged it to his right hip as he sat.

Approximately a quarter of an hour later, Magistrate Abraham Morris stalked through the same door and proceeded across part of the yard on a brick footpath. Adjusting his wig, as he was often wont to do, the compact man was sombrely dressed in a simple black suit, white hose, black shoes; as was his caller at the moment, he was hatless.

The visitor stood as Morris struttingly approached the grouping of black-painted, wrought-iron furniture and bowed slightly, as did Morris. Extending his hand to the Corkman, Goodfellow proceeded to introduce himself. Waving off both the proffered hand and the introduction, Morris immediately took the sole chair of the furniture grouping and set it catty-corner to the bench on which the other man would sit. "You certainly know who I am, and I have been told who you are; Goodfellow, the girl says you are just arrived from Dublin Castle? Assuming this is correct . . . and true . . . what is it precisely which brings you here? Something concerning my safety, you said to the girl, about my security?" Morris appeared uneasy, uncertain.

"What the pretty girl has said is quite correct and most certainly true, of this I assure you, sir!"

Morris immediately appeared to relax at what he now felt was his visitor's credible demeanour and calm, strong voice.

"Now then . . . word has reached *the Castle*," Goodfellow began in what seemed to Morris to be an officious tone. "Sir, we believe your life may be in danger."

Instantly reflecting that he had had the same terrifying belief for some weeks now, Morris asked cautiously, "Of what concern of the Castle is my present safety, sir?"

Unruffled, the apparent emissary, his palms now resting on his knees, leaned towards Morris and continued. "A loyal servant of the king, are you not, Magistrate? The word we have received is that it is in connection with your ridding this county of an individual said to be a dangerous, seditious outlaw that this peril has arisen. We understand it may be that a foreign power has sent one or more assassins; you know how those French and Spanish Papists can be, eh?"

Morris nodded. "If it is as you say, which would surprise me not . . . as the *vermin* whose life I took is . . ." he sniggered coldly, ". . . or should I say *was* . . . a sworn, commissioned officer in the Austrian armies." He shook his head dismissively. "Thus, I could believe that the Austrians, Papists, too, you must know, might behave as you suggest, especially as it is said that the outlaw of whom we speak was one well-known to the accursed Habsburgs, to the fucking popish bitch Maria Theresa herself."

Goodfellow had been listening closely. "Was this man, in truth, *vermin* as you say, sir?" he inquired somewhat incredulously, a look of slight puzzlement on his face. "Our information was that . . . despite that he was traitorous, disloyal and said to be arrogant in demeanour and behaviour . . . or perhaps the reason he was all of these! . . . in any case, we understand O'Leary was extremely well-educated, of good repute, being of the better class of Papists and rather quite well wed."

Morris flicked his hand dismissively, scoffing. "I most certainly meant what I said, sir. This O'Leary was nothing but a violent, treacherous, seditious Papist bastard, his 'well-wed' wife being much the same. I am certain the O'Connells of Derrynane are well-known to the Castle, sir; smugglers, thieves, murderers . . . the lot of them, that's who *she* is. We are well rid of this, yes, this *vermin* indeed, yessir!"

The visitor nodded, seemingly, to Morris, in agreement, and then continued. "So I understand, your honour, it was *you* who both commandeered and then bravely led a detachment of the king's soldiers, and it was one or more of those gallant men who succeeded—under your firm direction, of this I am most certain, sir—in killing this man, this O'Leary."

Morris was warming to the subject. "Quite so, though it took much effort on my part to convince the local military here to support this undertaking, but I finally succeeded in doing so, and it was in Macroom that I assumed command of a detachment of mounted men of the king. As often is the case in such circumstances, we were fortunate that more than one dirty, greedy, ill-bred Irish informer approached me and practically led us to a place from which this most successful execution was accomplished."

The visitor nodded yet again, several times slowly repeating the word *execution.* "Ah, well done, your honour, well done indeed!" Dodson Goodfellow called out. "Now that I know that 'twas *you,* the one virtually solely responsible for this *execution,* I shall do all in my power to see that you are both protected and suitably rewarded, eh?"

Morris smiled now and sat back smugly. *Perhaps I shall finally now be recognised as I deserve. . . . Perhaps someone at the Castle has at long last begun paying attention to affairs here.*

Dodson Goodfellow raised his right hand. "For now, sir, we must first see to your security." He slid to the far-right side of the small bench, placing his satchel on the ground beneath his right arm. Gesturing with his right forefinger, Goodfellow said softly, "Come, come, sit closer to me, if you would. I do not wish to speak at all loudly." His eyes cast cautiously about the house and yard, looking anxiously from side to side, Morris quickly stood, moved, then quickly sat, his dull eyes still darting about.

Goodfellow leaned slightly to his left, his long arm seemingly casually draped over the right armrest. "We must make certain, sir, that you—" His eyes suddenly flashed, as from beneath his coat, with his left hand, he just barely withdrew a small pistol. "That you are—" he hissed—"*never* again able to harm, much less murder, anyone. . . .

"You shall not move nor cry out; be still!

"You have murdered Arthur O'Leary . . . and for this you will pay with your miserable life."

All blood drained from his face and Morris now sat frozen, seeming to have no thought of even attempting escape.

Not taking his eyes off Morris, with his right hand, Goodfellow now retrieved from his satchel and deftly hoisted a frighteningly large—some thirteen inches in length—double-barrelled pistol, loaded, fully cocked and as lethal as it appeared.

Save for visibly trembling, the little man had been sitting perfectly still. Suddenly, he attempted to pull away. With a muffled roar, a surprisingly agile Goodfellow grappled the smaller man back to the bench. His left hand wrapped around Morris's throat, the veins in his own neck pulsating,

Goodfellow roughly shoved him forward. Coldly, dispassionately, as Morris squirmed and wriggled impotently, he aimed the pistol's double barrels at the base of his spine and immediately pulled the trigger. The massive blast muffled only somewhat by the close quarters, the sound of the simultaneous explosions of both barrels immediately filled the afternoon air, though the rising breeze from the harbour immediately lifted it, and the smoke with it, speedily dispelling both.

Propelled by the blast, Morris tumbled forward, half-kneeling onto the ground and turning his head. "You bastard! Who the . . . what the fuck . . ." he said weakly, but a smaller pistol then exploded, almost immediately followed by yet again another explosion, and again . . . and again . . . and . . . again . . . as, using, in all, five small pistols in rapid succession, roughly turning Morris onto his back as he lay on the ground, the attacker swiftly fired lead balls deep into the fleshy parts of Morris's thighs, as well as into the region of his lower abdomen and chest. Morris's eyes fluttered wildly at Goodfellow as he struggled to speak.

"You . . . have . . . killed . . . me!" he finally barely managed to whisper.

"I trust I have, you bastard, as that was the purpose of this visit," Goodfellow hissed caustically. "I also trust you shall not die for months, many months. You do not yet know it, but you are most likely now no longer able to walk, to even stand upright. You also may no longer be able to control your piss or your bowels. You shall die a helpless, repulsive cripple . . . disgusting to all and, quite possibly, mad!"

Morris appeared about to cry out. The attacker smacked the stock of his last-fired weapon across his victim's face, rendering him, at least briefly, unconscious.

His own face still scarlet with rage, Goodfellow stood quickly; gathering and immediately tossing the spent weapons, the barrels of several of them still gently smoking, into his satchel, he swiftly fled the yard through the ungated opening. In the adjoining street, onto which the gap in the garden hedge opened, waited the shiny black coach in which he had arrived, its right door already open. Dodson Goodfellow flung himself into the coach and, with a clatter of hoofs, it sped away.

At the Boyce house, a heavily bleeding, shocked and barely conscious Morris lay on the grass, crumpled against a leg of the bench. Even as Goodfellow was escaping through the hedge, the pretty girl and three men from the house were racing out into the yard. "I am shot!" Morris whined, though so faintly no one heard him.

As two of the men attempted to stand him upright, his now useless legs immediately buckled beneath him. Finding himself unable to tell the men, the words seared in his mind: *my feet, my legs . . . I cannot feel. . . .* Morris collapsed back onto the bench, the front of his breeches wet, an unmistakable stench akin to that of an untended, overused privy swirling disgustingly in the suddenly still air as his bowels emptied. Unable to speak, Morris could only think: *Not walk . . . he said I would not . . . he, he . . .* His eyes fluttered open momentarily and fixed on the gap in the hedge. Bleeding even more heavily now from, it would be discovered by a surgeon, seven gunshot wounds, Abraham Morris fell unconscious.

Meanwhile, in the bustle of Cork City perhaps, it was later thought by the local authorities, amidst the constant activity at its inner harbour, Dodson Goodfellow had seemingly made good his escape. In the ensuing days, after a very seriously wounded—his legs, indeed, paralyzed, control of his bodily functions no longer his own—Morris and the pretty housemaid had been able to provide a deputy under high sheriff with Goodfellow's description, a wide search yielded nothing and no one. "He was a very peculiar-looking gentleman," the girl maintained. "I do not see how he could simply disappear!"

But Dodson Goodfellow had indeed vanished, never to be seen or heard from again.

His disappearance had commenced even as the glistening black carriage sped away from the rear of the Boyce house. With the assistance of his companion, a woman, Goodfellow first doffed what was a long, scraggly black wig and, after first removing his coat and waistcoat and then struggling, grunting and tugging at the mounds of cotton batting that had been stuffed under the waistcoat and into his breeches, speedily shed an apparent twenty-five or even thirty pounds of bulk, Goodfellow had departed, to be replaced by a trim, albeit sweating and red-faced Conor O'Leary.

As he did so, herself elegantly clad in a brilliantly white summer linen dress, Catherine O'Leary's deep sigh was one of genuine relief, though she immediately after that exclaimed, "I shall not feel fully comfortable until you are rid of that horrid suit! What sort of a man would wear such a pack of rags?"

"I myself believe an ill-bred, self-important, toadying Dublin Castle sycophant most certainly would!" Conor exclaimed, himself relieved, though not yet able to laugh. Catherine was and did heartily, which broke the tension.

The coach made its way as quickly as possible to the hummingly alive docks at Merchants Quay. As it clattered and jangled to a halt at the edge of one of the farthest—and quietest—slips on the quay, seven men, heavily armed with gleaming rifles, several with pistols as well, stepped up on both sides, quickly enveloping the O'Learys as they alighted, one on each side. Walking as one, appearing an ungainly, multifooted creature, four of the men and Conor O'Leary approached a shed, the door of which one of the men promptly opened.

As Catherine remained with the others—who, along with O'Leary's protectors, were employed by one of the several large Cork trading companies with which she had been affiliated for a number of years— Conor quickly rid himself of the heinous garb and emerged in a fresh black suit, clean white shirt and neckcloth as well as fresh hose; the once-dusty, black, silver-buckled shoes, now wiped clean, were his own.

The men, continuing to provide an armed, protective barrier between the O'Learys and any prying eyes, Catherine and Conor stood quietly for a few moments, savouring, being enveloped by the sweet moistness of the salt-laced air, a sense of security settling with a cool breeze and a warm July sun. As Conor watched a flock of seagulls swooping and circling above them, Catherine finally spoke. "So, a sound plot it was, brother. I am . . . more than pleased the little bastard received precisely what he deserved. I shall quickly journey to West Cork and tell Father and Eileen . . . and I shall thank Squire Collins and his sweet little wife."

". . . and I thank *you*, sister," Conor said, taking Catherine's velvet-soft hand in his own. "This would not have been possible without your assistance."

"Our brother deserved this deed to be done and done well, as you have!" Catherine said sharply. "'Tis the least I could do to aid you and John Collins . . . and Mistress O'Leary." She smiled, not at all harshly indeed almost playfully.

Conor's surprise was evident.

"Ah, most certainly I see the subtle hand of Arthur's beloved *Eileen of the Raven Locks* in the design of this scheme." Catherine nodded. "Only a brilliantly conniving *woman* would conceive of condemning the man who murdered her husband to a lingering, horrific death. I applaud her. Indeed I shall so tell her!" She looked a moment at her brother, her voice much softer. "Please know that I have never disliked the woman. . . . In truth, I have been deeply, intrinsically jealous of her, is all . . . and now the reason for my jealousy, it . . . he . . ." She quickly brushed away her tears before they fell.

The master of the vessel set to take Conor to France gestured to Catherine.

"The tide, brother, 'tis time," she said firmly, embracing Conor and he her; they stood in each other's arms for several minutes.

"I shall write you from France. I shall not write Rathleigh or Derryleigh for a time, I do not think," Conor murmured.

"That is wise, brother. I shall journey to Rathleigh by week's end and tell them all that the deed is done, and write to them nothing save, perhaps, a warning—"she laughed—"of my imminent arrival."

After first stepping back, Conor now looked at his complex, complicatedly frustrating but fascinating sister. Reading his mind, the woman patted his upper arms maternally. "I shall behave at Rathleigh . . . and behave quite well towards our sister-in-law, of that I promise you from now on."

As the ship slipped away from the quay, the siblings waved, though long before the vessel was out of sight, Catherine O'Leary had turned and busied herself in conversation with several well-dressed older gentlemen. Conor could only smile and shake his head, sensing they might well never see each other again. Though when she looked up and raised her arm, he was glad to have seen her do so, and returned the gesture.

The sturdy vessel gingerly—the cut was narrow, the current contrary— made its way about the west side of Great Island, finally easing out of the greater harbour and into Ringabella Bay and thence into the Atlantic.

Leaning against the warm wood of the ship's starboard rail, Conor stood for a long time in the welcomingly warm, dazzling July sunshine, watching Cork and then, ultimately, Ireland herself slip away. One of the ship's officers quietly indicated the direction of "Kinsale, sir," but Conor was primarily left to himself and to his thoughts:

The seventh of July 1773 . . . this day, one I shall n'er forget: On this day I killed a man . . . at least I trust and pray I did . . . for the first time. On this same day as well, I am leaving my country as an emigrant, fairly certain I n'er shall see Ireland or any of mine again, and yet . . . yet, I am to no small degree elated.

I have destroyed he who murdered my brother, have proudly caused Dark Eileen's vengeance to fall violently on the monster that was Morris . . . 'tis my gift to her . . . to her and Arthur's lads.

And now I commence my own—what has Eileen called their, her and Abigail, going to Vienna? Ah, yes, my own "great adventure"! Perhaps I shall be lawyering in Philadelphia as the Dublin lads are, perhaps somewhere else. Baltimore? . . . Perhaps even doing something else.

He again found himself studying the swooping gulls, though he sensed fewer as the ship drew closer to the open ocean, farther away from the Cork coast. His eyes traced their loops and dips and upward movements, reflecting, *I am as free as any of you are!* Then, surprising the deckhands and the ship's officers alike, he called aloud, "I said, 'I am as free as you are!'" and he raised both arms to the blue Irish sky.

County Cork, Ireland—August 1773

As a sultry August descended on West Cork, some semblance of normalcy appeared to have settled over Rathleigh. The little O'Leary lads were more like themselves, playing and roughhousing, their laughter and other happy—and frequently not as well—noises become again more frequent. Save in public, Eileen had largely forgone her mourning robes; as she was still spending most of her time at home, she favoured breeches, boots and one of O'Leary's white linen shirts over dresses of any type. Though the Collins family, especially Anna and Maria Theresa, were frequent visitors, mother and daughter had ceased their semi residency at Rathleigh.

Eileen was less moody, laughed more frequently. Conscious that she and the beautiful mare would forever be linked in a sadly singular way, she spent time with Banrían each day, riding her several times a week; she nevertheless quietly returned to riding Bull as her regular mount.

Catherine O'Leary's mid-July visit had lasted into August and was exceptionally pleasant. On her arrival, she advised that Cork City was rife with rumours of the mysterious, stealthy attack on Morris, Eileen responding that John Collins had independently confirmed the fact.

Later, when Catherine sat with Eileen and Squire O'Leary one oppressively muggy evening and related the events of the afternoon of 7 July, thanking Catherine for the news and for her help, Eileen said softly, "'Tis now real. . . . It actually has begun, has it not?" and she smiled ever so slightly.

Afterwards, when the women were alone, Catherine was effusive in her praise of her sister-in-law. "Following the deed being done," she began, "even as we were departing the Boyce property, I told Conor that indeed I saw the subtle hand of Arthur's beloved *Eileen of the Raven Locks*—she smiled and nodded at Eileen—"in this scheme. . . . Only a brilliantly conniving woman would conceive of condemning the man who murdered her husband to a lingering, horrific death and, as I promised Conor that I would, I applaud you! Indeed I do, sister!"

Both Catherine and Collins had heard from reliable sources in Cork City that Conor had indeed succeeded in rendering Abraham Morris paralyzed, and that, whilst the surgeons had calculated that the man had been shot a total of seven times, including the pair of wounds from both barrels of O'Leary's largest pistol, they removed only those lead balls that had irreparably damaged his spinal column. As to the others, they concluded, and so advised Mistress Morris, that "their locations in the body medically render excisions extremely difficult and, with regard to one or two of them, quite dangerous, as those, they lie quite proximate to, though not immediately threatening, vital organs."

What the surgeons did not tell Morris, his wife or anyone else was their unanimous conclusion that whoever it was who shot Morris, injuring him thus, knew precisely what he was doing. He had shot not to kill the man immediately but rather to fatally wound him in such a manner that he could conceivably live or more correctly die over a matter of many months, perhaps even a year or two. . . . "He shall experience a lingering, miserable death. . . . Already a cripple, with no control of his bodily functions, he shall most likely be poisoned by the lead balls. . . . He shall suffer horrendous pain and, depending on how long he manages to survive . . . and *survive* is the correct term, for he shall be but existing by this time . . . may well become mad. Death, when it does come, will be a relief for the poor bastard," as one Scottish-born, University of Edinburgh–trained surgeon named Jones advised his fellows.

It would be several years until Eileen would learn, from John Collins, that the means by which "Dodson Goodfellow" was able to accomplish rendering Morris as he was to become was a series of detailed conversations about human anatomy and physiology Collins and Conor O'Leary had held with Dr. James Baldwin, who had carefully scripted out the types of pistols and the trajectories necessary to achieve the desired result. Even then, Eileen was still dismissive of her brother-in-law as a weak and cowardly man, though she ultimately would approach him, convey her thanks for his role in Morris's assassination and become, at least to some degree, reconciled with both Baldwin and her twin sister.

Amongst the many subtle and not-so-subtle changes that had resulted from the murder of Art O'Leary in the lives of those people closest to him was that aside from, as he confessed to Anna, being "lonesome; I miss the man," Squire John Collins had grown quieter and even more reflective than before. Though with his wife and little daughter he remained largely the lighthearted man that marrying Anna had caused him to become, in public he appeared sombre, often annoyed, if not outright angry and sad.

It was his brooding anger that was apparent in Macroom early one humid August afternoon when he learned that one of the soldiers who had ridden with Morris on 4 May, a corporal named Greene, had been publicly commended for "gallantry" for his central role, it being officially acknowledged for the first time that it was this Greene who had actually fired the shot that had killed Arthur O'Leary, in what the authorities were now seemingly proclaiming was a successful execution.

Andrew Baggot, the strikingly handsome, elegant young Protestant squire, who was also a magistrate, with whom both Collins and O'Leary had become friends, was the one who had advised Collins of the commendation as they strolled towards Macroom Castle and Collins's pub. Himself seething with rage, Baggot briefly feared that, in the fury the news provoked, Collins might perhaps attack *him*.

Though that fear was unfounded, as Collins's anger exploded, the Catholic aristocrat clearly appeared as if he would welcome the immediate opportunity to physically attack any other member of the local officialdom. "How dare they!" John Collins bellowed as the two men stopped in the road, "'Twas murder, pure and simple! The bloody coroner's jury issued a verdict of wilful and wanton murder against that snivelling coward bastard

Morris, as well as all of the members of the military detachment with him, specifically Greene as the one who fired the killing shot, did it not?"

Baggot nodded in the affirmative but said nothing.

"'Tis ghastly enough that the inquest's findings are ignored, but to then bestow on this assassin a medal, or whatever in holy hell these bastards have done . . . I cannot imagine the evil that poisons these men's minds, their very souls, Andrew, *their very souls.*"

As his friend calmed and they resumed walking, Baggot draped an arm over Collins's shoulder. "I believe, friend John, 'tis over the porter that I would suggest we now repair to your good establishment, there to consume, that we should *speak quietly . . .*"

Baggot was a brilliant, thoughtful graduate of Magdalen College, Oxford, who had several times mentioned to Collins and O'Leary briefly considering continuing his education at Grey's Inn, London, through which both a cousin to whom he was close, and his uncle had passed, the two men now distinguished barristers in London. "I am a countryman, as are your goodselves," he had gestured on one occasion to his relatively new friends, "and my place is here, not in filthy London . . . or even in Dublin."

He was active and visible in the community, and when he spoke in meetings, formal or otherwise, of the Muskerry Constitutional Society, most of his colleagues listened carefully to what he had to say, and many regularly agreed with him.

Baggot, now thirty, lived a comfortable life; the eldest child and the only son—he had four sisters—of a now-deceased father, he had inherited significant land holdings, in Cork and elsewhere and, financially, had become an extremely wealthy young man. A devout though far from pious member of the Church of Ireland, he had come to seriously, though only within himself, question the viability of a church set down in what to it and to many, if not most of its adherents, was a foreign land, a land in which it could count but approximately 10 percent of the population as communicants, though in which it was, incredibly, the established church.

Though he had known Catholics, both in England and locally, and despite that he knew John Collins relatively well, it had not been until he met Arthur O'Leary and, through him, Eileen, that he began to understand the depth, the profound strength that was to many of its adherents, Irish Catholicism. That men and women such as these continued to feel compelled to leave Ireland, for which they expressed an abiding devotion, so as to achieve what they had abroad, when such advancement was, solely on account of their Catholicism, denied them at home. "Never shall the most vigorous proselytizing yield any but the most negligible number of converts in this kingdom," he had said to the Reverend Arthur McGee, whose Church of Ireland parish encompassed the area around Dunisky, and the clergyman had not disagreed. Baggot had also come to feel that, unlike many of his coreligionists, the O'Learys and the Collinses wore their religion comfortably, as were it no burden but rather a welcome part of their very being. *Their God, He laughs . . . ours all too often scowls.* Eileen, he noted on more than one occasion, spoke of St. Brigid as were she a friend, a companion, of the Blessed Virgin as a cherished, wholly approachable older woman.

It was through this acceptance that Baggot had come to at least begin to understand the alienation of his Catholic contemporaries such as O'Leary and Collins, not to mention that of those he simply called *the people*—the tenants and landless peasants—the extent of whose isolation from the world in which he and, at least to some degree, the far fewer Catholic gentry dwelt, was unimaginable.

In addition to having come to know the O'Learys as a result of Arthur's history with Abraham Morris and his related legal difficulties, as a magistrate Baggot was intimately familiar with the wholly arbitrary, ofttimes capricious workings of the dysfunctional criminal justice system in Ireland as a whole and in Cork in particular, the worst aspects of which had cost O'Leary his life.

During the weeks and into July following O'Leary's death, Baggot had reached out both to the O'Leary family and to Eileen particularly, and to John Collins. It was with Collins that he spoke in early June of what he deemed the shocking injustice that no official action would follow the verdict of the coroner's inquest. "I believe that justice may have to be served in other ways," he told Collins. It was only after the successful attack on Morris had become common knowledge in the community that John Collins suggested that he and Baggot might speak quietly. Even as he did, Collins kept Eileen's confidence as to her own ill-advised solo attempt to kill Morris.

Before they had had an opportunity to meet, the commendation of the shooter Greene had been publicized, which had led to Collins's outburst and their subsequent evening at his pub.

As Collins had calmed, and they had discussed in a general way Morris's shooting, Baggot surprised his friend by observing, "As it appears that *someone* has properly dealt with Morris, I now suggest that *others* endeavour to devise a suitable reward or act of approbation for the soldier Greene . . . reflecting the feelings of men other than the low-bred, ill-educated bigots who populate what masquerades for local government in Macroom."

The following evening, the men paid a call on Mistress O'Leary at Rathleigh. Just as they were departing, after an hour and a bit more of animated conversation and brandy, Eileen smilingly advised them that "I am pleased to learn that men as well are capable of proving themselves to be brilliantly conniving," though she did not elaborate.

John Greene was nineteen years old that August of 1773; he had taken the king's shilling three years before in his tiny village, located in the area of Tunbridge Wells in green, bucolic Kent, on the coast in southeast England. His father had been a groom on the estates of a lesser noble there, and John was familiar with and enjoyed being around horses. He was also a good rider, so it made sense that he ultimately found his way into the frequently mounted component of a small regiment stationed for the past twelve months in Macroom. Though it was green, like Kent, he found Ireland rough and raw compared to the gentle English countryside and would say frequently that he "could not understand the people, why they hate us so. . . ."

He had met very few Irish people directly; he found a number of the girls to be pretty, "especially the ones with red hair, but they do not like us any more than anyone else does." Once, in Macroom, when a red-haired girl had smiled at him, he immediately saw her father grab her arm roughly and berate her through gritted teeth in Irish, a language that caused John Greene to simply shake his head. *Like cats they sound, squawking and . . . hacking.*

When he learned that Squire Andrew Baggot was at barracks, seeking a word with him, Greene was thus extremely surprised. He found the youthful landowner, whom one of the officers had quickly reminded Greene was also a magistrate, to be effusively pleasant. By that he had advised that he had come to invite him to a small gathering of men, for "a bit of a celebration of your recent commendation." Greene was nonplussed.

"This is a personal gesture of my own, mind you, nothing official," Baggot had said. "This entire O'Leary affair has these last many years grown more wearisome, and the fact that it was you, displaying what I understand was *gallantry* in a most perilous situation, who have brought it to a close, I, along with several of my friends, should simply like to extend our thanks in this small way."

Greene had been most surprised by what Baggot had proposed, that they celebrate this evening . . . *and why should we not, eh?*

"Your commander advises you are tonight at liberty. You are a mounted soldier, so you shall simply accompany me to my home . . . and from thence return to barracks."

The well-dressed young aristocrat on a striking black stallion and the uniformed soldier, accompanying him on his nondescript grey-brown gelding, would have perhaps seemed an odd pair riding out of Macroom, if anyone had taken note, though none seemingly had.

They rode northeast out of the town, ostensibly in the direction of Ballymagree; as Greene had no idea where Baggot lived or to where they were headed, he could not have thought it unusual that they would be going to a location with which Baggot had no prior relationship. They had cantered pleasantly for just short of an hour, as the late summer dusk had finally begun to settle over the green land, when they came upon a group of mounted men, gathered at the top of what appeared to be a boreen.

Baggot raised an arm, and calls of welcome echoed in the still, humid evening air.

"Come, join us now," Baggot said to Greene as he gently touched his heels to the stallion's sides. They were quickly surrounded by men whom Greene believed were Baggot's friends, to whom he announced, "Here we have the *gallant* Greene, gentlemen, the man who with a single shot from his rifle *heroically* took the life of Arthur O'Leary!"

"Welcome!" called out John Collins jovially, and with an arm gestured the group to follow him down the boreen, to a clearing in a thick, boggy wood where, Greene noticed, a fire gaily flamed, and saw evidence of food and drink.

The men all dismounted, leaving their horses to nibble at the green shoots of weeds and wild herbs, and walked towards the fire.

"So, Greene, 'tis indeed true that you were the one who actually killed O'Leary the outlaw?" wondered John Collins as the others stood close.

"I did, sir, yes . . . on the command of the Magistrate Morris, I immediately took my shot. Dropped the outlaw from his horse right there, I did. . . ." Greene nodded affirmatively, his tone firm, no small degree of pride evident in his voice.

"If I may," began John Daly of Derryleigh, "of what were you made aware concerning this outlaw O'Leary? What did you know of the man?"

Greene paused at the odd, unexpected question, now suddenly eying the group carefully. "I . . . why . . . he was an outlaw of course . . . decreed by the judges some months before, he was . . . and a traitor . . . yes, a violent, disloyal man who on several occasions had attempted to murder . . . to kill . . . loyal people . . . he . . ."

John Collins stepped now so he was standing in front of the soldier. "Were you aware that he was a decorated captain of Hussars in the imperial armies of Austria and Hungary?"

Green shook his head tightly.

"Were you aware that he had passed through university at Louvain . . . a student of literature, of poetry, of history and of languages?"

Greene had never heard of, did not know what or where Louvain was, so a now nervous gesture in the negative followed.

Johnny O'Callaghan, a lifelong friend of O'Leary's, then stepped to Collins's side. "I do not suppose you knew he had two wee lads . . . not to mention a fine, handsome woman for a wife, all of whom he loved dearly, and they him."

Eyes widening, Greene found he could not have spoken the word *no* if he had wanted to.

Michael MacCarthy, a powerfully built older man, in rough clothes, his hands massive and gnarled, then asked, "You are of course *proud* of what you did, *proud* that a commendation you received, aye?"

Greene cleared his throat. "Yes . . . yes, I am." His voice quivered and he felt a chill despite the close, almost steamy atmosphere in the clearing.

John Collins's eyes were wide, his face now red with rage; he had clearly heard and witnessed enough. Before Greene knew what had happened, the normally quiet, almost gentle man had smashed him powerfully with an uppercut to his jaw, sending him sprawling in the mucky dirt where they stood.

"Get up!" John Daly roared.

As with great effort he managed to stand, Greene's jaw dropped as Andrew Baggot twisted the gleaming blade of a short rapier in front of his eyes, the magistrate then turning and suddenly turning back, with the tip delicately slicing both of Greene's lightly downed cheeks. "You murderer!" Baggot hissed, the blood streaking down the soldier's cheeks in two fine rivulets. As soon as he heard the word *murderer*, Greene had no doubt as to the purpose of this evening, and immediately understood that he was going to die.

John Collins stepped back in front of Greene, and this time his powerful right fist smashed into the left side of the soldier's face, his jaw seeming to have been broken by the force of the blow, and the man crumpled to the ground. Dragging him to his feet, holding him up with his left hand, Collins, again using his right fist, delivered a crushing blow to the man's midsection, which sent him to his knees, doubled over and vomiting. With his boot, Johnny O'Callaghan forced his face into the puddle of it.

Daly and MacCarthy then roughly drew him back upright, supporting a barely conscious Greene under his arms as he swayed. Andrew Baggot tossed a full tankard of cold spring water in his face, rendering Greene gaspingly alert, which was his cruel intended purpose.

Collins stood now in front of him, holding a fully cocked pistol. "Unlike Captain Arthur O'Leary, you shall know the face of the man who killed you," he sneered, leaning towards the terrified young soldier, pointing to himself with his left forefinger. "Look well, you bastard murderer," he commanded. "*Look at me!* So you will always remember it as the face of one of the men who killed you. Take this sight to hell, to burn with you forever!" he roared, firing the weapon point-blank into Greene's chest.

His palms open, his arms spread slightly at his sides, the soldier sank heavily to his knees, his mouth agape, a look of disbelief on his face. Before Greene touched the ground, Andrew Baggot reached down and, with his powerful left hand and by his uniform coat, dragged the fatally wounded man to his feet, continuing to hold him up with a vicelike grip. Seeing Greene's eyes open, he ordered, "You shall remember me, as well!" and plunged his rapier into the man's heart. "May you burn in hell; may the fires never consume you and never be quenched . . . for all eternity!" He released his grip on Greene's coat and, a look of contempt, of triumph on his tired face, pushed the dead man away, as he would a tree being felled. Greene landed sprawled on his back, arms spread, his eyes still open in horror.

Letting him lay where and as he was, Baggot and Collins both stepped back, Collins diffidently repocketing his pistol, Baggot almost casually wiping his blade on a kerchief, which he then stuffed in his coat pocket as he resheathed the knife. They looked down at the corpse they had made and then at each other and nodded and shook hands firmly.

Baggot simply muttered, "Bastard," whilst the normally thoughtful Collins did not appear at all reflective.

"He earned this, Andrew; he deserved this. I have no regret . . . I am proud that *we* . . ." he spread his arms wide and raised his voice, "that we all had the courage to do what needed to be done."

The men gathered around and all nodded and spoke softly in agreement, before Collins gestured all to the fire. "Drink and eat we shall now!"

As he started to walk, Collins turned around and with the toe of his right boot almost gently rolled Greene's body, so it was facedown, eyes open in a mere of blood, vomit and mud.

Some thirty minutes later, John Daly stepped forward. "Gentlemen," he addressed Collins and Baggot, "you both did Ireland—Gaelic Ireland, the *real* Ireland—and yourselves proud this evening. . . . The captain, he would have done it for either of ye, indeed for any of us. You will please tell the Lady Eileen what we *all* did. . . . Please say to her that we did it for the captain . . . for her and the wee lads." His jaw was set, his eyes clear and his expression hard. "And that we all did it proudly."

Addressing Baggot and Collins, "You gentlemen, you should head on, sirs . . . you have done your part of the deed," Johnny O'Callaghan then said firmly. "We shall take care of the remainder . . . Corporal Greene, he will simply *be gone* . . . never to be seen, ever again." He gestured the two squires to their horses, and all of the men stood and watched as they mounted and thudded up the boreen.

The following morning, bright, breezy and much cooler than the days before, by agreement with Andrew Baggot, John Collins brought Anna and Maria Theresa with him to Rathleigh.

Whilst Anna ran ahead with the children to play, Collins stood quietly with Eileen on the broad veranda at the rear of the house. As they watched Bull and his best friend, the gelding, romp and chase in one fenced pasture, and Banrían frolicking with the mares, some distance away in another, Collins provided details of the previous night. Eileen asked several pointed questions, and he answered them graphically, as she had asked that he do. As he spoke, she nodded, occasionally, saying, "Good . . . very good . . . I am most pleased. You have done well; thank you, my dear friend."

Finally, Collins turned away from the horses at play and looked quietly, directly at Eileen. "So our vengeance thus continues, additional retribution has been extracted, paid it has been."

Eileen nodded and looked calmly at Collins. "As so it should . . . as so it shall continue until the full price is paid by all of them. Thank you, John. . . . Arthur, I am sure, thanks you as well . . . and Squire Baggot, and all of the others." She nodded again and smiled softly.

Turning their attention then to Anna and the wee ones, they laughed as, screeching like a banshee, Maria Theresa chased Conor, and laughed again as Conor stopped short and turned, screeching himself and chasing Maria Theresa back towards her mama. Laughing louder still as, waving her arms and screeching, Anna playfully chased them both, an apparently undaunted little Fiach then toddling along as the three of them chased Anna, who purposely dropped onto the thick grass, laughing, and, as she rolled on her back, the children piled on top of her.

Then Eileen and Collins walked to where Anna and the children were rolling about in the grass, and both dropped to the ground and joined them.

The merry sounds of children and adults' voices filled the morning air, as did their laughter: Eileen's distinctive hearty one, Anna's equally so, though higher-pitched, and Collins's distinguishing rumble. In the kitchen, Mary and Ann heard the sounds and peered out, and they, too, smiled and laughed.

"Improving, it is, is it not?" Ann observed.

Stirring a steaming pot, Mary smiled. "Aye, 'tis very much so."

When John Greene failed to return to barracks that night, his mates laughed about him getting drunk with the gentry. When he did not appear by mid-afternoon of the following day, his sergeant put him on report. By week's end, he had been classified as a wilful deserter, subject to the lash, imprisonment or even the firing squad. No one in the local military or government gave a thought to seeking out Andrew Baggot or anyone else in search of any information about the deserter. Other than his family and friends in the little village in Kent, no one ever again thought about John Greene.

During the course of that week, Eileen, in her now customary breeches—today, buff-coloured—and boots, again wearing one of Arthur's blousy white linen shirts, had ridden Banrían to the graveyard at Dun na Radharc, where, kneeling, and after first advising God that she believed He had immediately taken Art into His heaven, she nevertheless prayed for her husband's immortal soul. Then, for a much longer time, whilst sitting on her heels on the lush summertime grass, fully relishing the sensual comforts of the sun and the breeze, she simply visited with Arthur, silently advising him: *So twice you have now been avenged, my darling: As I have told you, by Conor's gallant hand, the monster Morris lies crippled and stinking, already dying though his passing lies, God willing, many miserable months ahead . . . and, thanks now to John and Andrew, and to Daly and MacCarthy and Johnny O'Callaghan as well . . . the soldier who fired the rifle that killed you, he now lies deep, already rotting, in some nameless bog after first having been educated about who you were. He was then duly thrashed, until finally, by Squire John's pistol and Andrew's blade, he was dispatched to God's Holy and Final Judgment, and from thence by His hand most assuredly cast immediately into the fires of hell, there to burn and suffer agony and torment for all eternity.*

I promised you, my darling Horseman of the Bright Eyes, that I would pursue and attain very public vengeance and retribution, both accomplished by violence and in fury . . . as it has begun, so it shall continue . . . until all who were in any way responsible for your murder shall pay . . . by forfeiture of their own wretched lives, and by an eternity spent in the flames of the deepest nether reaches of Satan's hell. . . . She nodded at the grave for emphasis.

She then sat quietly, in thought, for a while longer; finally, after bending and kissing the ground above her husband's lips and whispering, "I love you, my darling," she rose and strode back to where Banrían had been grazing.

She was experiencing a sense of lightness, of peace and calm, such that as she was riding home, Eileen even stopped for a chat with an old woman and her granddaughter as they sat on a large, rough stone watching the clouds. As Eileen leaned back against the rock, stretching her long legs out on the ground in front of her, the little girl caused her to laugh when she respectfully inquired, "Have you lost your dress, my lady?"

Ireland—September 1773

When word of Arthur O'Leary's death reached North Kerry in late-May, both Lord and Lady Moyvane were deeply saddened. In the years since departing Firies as a very young widow, Eileen had periodically corresponded with the couple to the extent that they had at a distance followed her life from Ireland to Vienna, her marriage to O'Leary, the births of her sons and her return to Ireland as her time in Vienna came to a close. Receiving Eileen's letter, they both regretted not pressing their former neighbour and her husband to accept their offer of hospitality. "Now we shall never have known this seemingly extraordinary young man," the countess told her husband.

"Though Maurice O'Connell had apparently opposed her match with O'Leary, looking on the man as dangerous and arrogant, 'tis a far cry from these attributes being applied by a conservative eldest brother to a man he views as an unacceptable suitor for his sister to the same man being declared by the crown's representatives an outlaw," the short, still-rotund nobleman had informed his wife as they discussed Eileen's bitter loss. Curious as to the overall situation surrounding Arthur O'Leary, he had made inquiries amongst his vast network of friends and acquaintances and, as a result, a significantly different, much more favourable picture of the unfortunate O'Leary had emerged. "High-spirited, perhaps arrogant, handsome in a way that renders men less so envious, apparently not given to paying consistent obeisance to the British crown and proud of his Continental status," he would report to his wife, concluding firmly, "but, all of this being true, I do not believe the young man deserved to die as he did."

When he had completed reading Eileen's lengthy letter, seeking his assistance in obtaining an audience with the Earl Harcourt, who had succeeded Lord Townshend as lord lieutenant of Ireland, in which she wrote candidly and quite extensively of the running feud with Morris and in great detail of the events leading up to her husband's death, Moyvane stalked through the castle in search of Lady Elizabeth. Finding her in a cosy room—unlike much of the starkly stone-walled and-floored castle, it was thickly carpeted and hung with several strikingly intricate tapestries from Bruges—visiting with the couple's somewhat late-in-life three children, he requested the younger girls' nurse to take them elsewhere, whilst having his son, heir and namesake remain. "You must hear this, lad . . . this is of the young solider of whom I have spoken to you."

Once a suitably solemn young George was seated beside his mother on a flowered sofa, standing before the large hearth, Moyvane related, "This man O'Leary . . . Captain O'Leary . . . he was murdered, slain, assassinated, pure and simple!" he sputtered, the pages of Eileen's letter gripped in the chubby fingers of his left hand, his right forefinger thumping against them, both of his hands shaking, his cherubic face red with rage, as he once again told the tale of Art O'Leary's killing—*murder* he now called it—by Morris and the soldiers, *who had no bloody business at all being involved in this!* he spat. *There should be bloody hell to pay!*

It was in this frame of mind that he wrote the lord lieutenant a rambling, anger-, indeed even rage-driven missive of a kind rarely addressed by an Irish noble to the crown's representative at Dublin Castle, purposely having his twelve-year-old son read it once he was satisfied with what he had written.

In it, Moyvane had quickly moved through the niceties required by and in such correspondence, promptly reaching the sole topic of interest to him:

. . . If I might, my lord, please permit me to speak of a matter of some grave note in County Cork and indeed to an extent here in Kerry as well and then to introduce with a request of you, sir, a rather extraordinary young woman both the Lady Elizabeth and I have considered it a privilege to know for a number of years:

I am quite certain that Your Lordship is at least in passing familiar with the matter of one Arthur O'Leary of Cork, killed there in May this year. I shall not elaborate on the event, save to say that, based on a great deal of competent information I have succeeded in assembling from a variety of trustworthy sources, it is my considered opinion that the so-

called "official version" of what was, I am now fully convinced, in truth, an illegal execution carried out by perhaps unwitting, perhaps not, servants of the king, is far from the full truth. I say this, sir, on my oath!

It is in this regard that I trust you will permit me to introduce to Your Lordship, and to, most respectfully, sir, commend to your attention, the Lady Eileen O'Leary, the widow of the referenced deceased. I came to know the woman when, as a young girl some thirteen years ago, she was brought from her family's home at Derrynane—yes, it is of the O'Connells of Derrynane she is!—to become the bride of my then (and until his untimely death in that very same year of 1760) dearest friend, John O'Connor, Esq., late of Ballyhar, this county. Reflecting on this time, I am reminded that I initially employed the term "extraordinary" with regard to the Lady Eileen the very first time, it being, indeed, on the day of her wedding that I came to know her. How she has conducted herself and, to the extent I can be aware, lived her life since that time has only increased my estimation of the woman.

Wed at age sixteen, in the all-too-brief seven months she lived as the wife of my dear friend and, in doing so, became a dear friend as well, she displayed attributes of maturity, loyalty, foresight and, yes, bravery that few women of any age do. I recall advising her husband at the time that. though she was still a mere girl, a child, in truth—and only then just beginning to grasp the reality of who and what she was—even at that juncture she was as poised as a woman twice her age, and more regal than most I have encountered in London. Making the most of these qualities, she assumed with ease and grace the role of mistress of the O'Connor home and estate; respected by tenantry and nobility alike, she proved a perfect consort for a gentleman such as John O'Connor. I believe it is quite accurate to say that O'Connor's death and the Lady Eileen's subsequent departure permanently diminished the quality of life in this neighbourhood.

Brilliant, strong, determined—there are not sufficient adjectives that would permit me to adequately state the high regard in which I hold the woman. Neither her years of service at the imperial court in Vienna nor the fact that her deceased husband was a commissioned officer in the Austrian armies in any way cause me to think any less of either of these young people. My grave misgivings as to the religion they embrace notwithstanding, I have said in public and I am certain you are quite aware that I have long been of the firm belief that the brightest and most capable of much of the old Gaelic order has departed this kingdom, and will continue to do so, to Ireland's detriment, until the horrors of that which Cromwell wrought are, to the extent that this is possible, significantly reversed.

Thus qualifying his appeal, Lord Moyvane simply requested, as he wrote, that an audience be extended to the Lady Eileen, and that the lord lieutenant

Listen carefully and give serious, very serious consideration to acceding to her requests——lest this situation surrounding and continuing in the wake of Captain O'Leary's killing be permitted to fester . . . without speaking for her, I am merely advising Your Lordship that it is my strong belief that the woman offers the crown a wise solution that will provide her with the justice she seeks and a means to defuse a potentially most contentious matter, rectifying it by having those military men directly involved in the tragedy disciplined. Given the circumstances, it is neither an unreasonable nor unusual request nor resolution. Thus, I say, sir, most respectfully: Hear her out!

In mid-September, Eileen received a brief letter of invitation, respectfully requesting that she make arrangements to call upon the Honourable Lord Lieutenant of Ireland at Dublin Castle as soon as possible, advising her that "accommodations at the Castle will have been arranged in anticipation of your arrival in Dublin in the coming weeks," and requesting only that she arrive fully prepared for an immediate audience with His Lordship. So confident had she been in Lord Moyvane, immediately upon learning from him that he had written to the Earl Harcourt on her behalf, she had indeed begun making arrangements in preparation for her journey to Dublin.

These near-immediate preparations were such so that a mere two days following receipt of the message from Dublin Castle, Eileen, having already sent word from Rathleigh by a messenger advising Dublin of her itinerary, was in Cork City. Catherine O'Leary had arranged water transport for Eileen on one of, as she phrased it, "my ships," and had invited her sister-in-law to spend the night prior to her departure with her, an evening that had proven to be most pleasant, including a sumptuous dinner, "of banquet quality!" Eileen had exclaimed, served to just the two women in Catherine O'Leary's large, comfortable dining room. They chatted generally of Conor's recent progress from France to America, of Eileen's little boys and their coping with their father's death, as well as of horses, the weather and light gossip of the Rathleigh neighbourhood.

As they lingered over brandies by a gentle fire in what appeared to Eileen to be Catherine's study or personal sitting room, after sitting quietly, her eyes studying the fire, Catherine wondered softly, "If I may, sister, your precise purpose in seeking audience with the lord lieutenant is . . .?"

Eileen could only smile at this still more than a bit strange but increasingly, to her, fascinating woman. She reached over, taking Catherine's hand lightly in her own. "My precise purpose is to begin the final act, the completion of the full revenge, the total retribution I have sought against and from those men responsible for your dear brother's, my beloved husband's, murder."

The normally steely Catherine's eyes grew wide.

"I have certain requests to make of the lord lieutenant as to the soldiers who were involved in Arthur's ambush and murder. . . . I wish them to be made to pay, much as Morris and the actual rifleman Greene already have."

Though the phrase *firing squad* immediately came to mind, Catherine had come to understand Eileen, and so she asked no further questions.

In the morning, Catherine accompanied her sister-in-law to Merchants Quay in the same gleaming black coach that had carried "Dodson Goodfellow" on his travels within Cork several months prior.

As soon as Eileen alighted from the coach, a covey of men immediately swooped down to gather her luggage; Catherine took her sister-in-law's arm and led her to the quick, compact, gleaming black clipper, of recent American design and manufacture, that would carry her to Dublin overnight. The women embraced just as Eileen, again regal in her elegantly Viennese version of widow's weeds, turned and, with a quick wave to Catherine, strode up the gangway, which was raised almost as Eileen's feet touched the ship's deck; as soon as she was aboard and the ship's master was standing with her, the ship loosed her moorings and was quickly away, the ends of Eileen's black mantle billowing, her hair contained within it, as, the master returning to the helm, she stood alone on the deck, watching Cork slowly disappear.

Though women of a certain station, particularly young widows, did not typically travel unaccompanied, it was apparent that Catherine O'Leary had frequently journeyed alone on this particular ship, and in her own mind, Eileen O'Leary was perfectly comfortable doing so. She dined that evening with the master and his first officer and took coffee and bread with them in the morning, read in her cabin or strolled about the deck, occasionally asking questions about the ship's precise location or the condition of the sea of anyone, seaman or officer, she cared to, the journey bringing back pleasant memories of jaunts both brief and of longer duration with her father.

When, having fortunately arrived in the arc of Dublin Bay on an incoming high tide and thus being able to readily navigate into and up the River Liffey, the trim vessel arrived the next afternoon in Dublin at Wood Quay, near Christ Church Cathedral, a carriage arranged for by Catherine awaited Eileen.

She was whisked towards Dame Street, quickly passing Trinity College, set on its aptly named green, and the majestic, semi-circular Georgian building that housed the Irish Parliament, to the looming assembly of buildings that comprised Dublin Castle, the seat of English power in Ireland. There, Eileen knew, amongst other things, the lord lieutenant was headquartered, and the Privy Council met.

The coach finally clattered to a halt in the ornately cobblestoned Upper Courtyard; alighting, Eileen, looking to her right, faced a striking, broad Georgian red-brick building, to the left of which the State Apartments fronted. As soon as the coachmen had exchanged words with one of the sentries, a young officer quickly appeared to greet Eileen, the orderly accompanying him promptly gathering up her baggage. "Accommodations have been arranged for as long as my lady wishes to remain in Dublin," the officer crisply informed her, gesturing towards the formal, six-pillared granite entrance to the State Apartments. Eileen smiled a soft thank-you, feeling a gentle prick in her heart: The handsome young man in his brilliant red uniform coat reminded her of Arthur, and the emotion reminded her why she had come, strengthening even more her resolve to achieve her goals.

Eileen was provided with warm water and an opportunity to refresh herself in her rooms prior to being escorted, again by the young officer in the bright red coat, to the lord lieutenant's chambers. Her substantial black skirts rustling as she moved easily along the serpentine, uneven passageways of what she found, other than some truly striking rooms, to be in many ways a disappointingly drab and largely unimposing structure or, more correctly, a hodgepodge of a number of buildings that was Dublin Castle. She felt it paled—*most of the floors creak!*—before any of *my palaces*—she smiled to herself—in Austria.

Awaiting Eileen in the elegantly ornate chambers of the lord lieutenant was Simon Harcourt, the first Earl Harcourt, a not unattractive, somewhat sad-faced gentleman of fifty-nine, with distinctive, heavily lidded grey eyes and a prominent nose. Born in Oxfordshire, he had been created Earl Harcourt of Stanton Harcourt in 1749, becoming governor to the then Prince of Wales, the now King George III, in 1751. Under George III, he had held a number of appointments at court and in the diplomatic service, most notably as British ambassador to Paris from 1768 to 1772, in October of the latter of which he had succeeded to the lord lieutenancy. He had been a widower since 1764.

Despite being intrigued by Lord Moyvane's glowing introduction of his visitor, in truth Harcourt was not altogether pleased with the prospect of meeting yet another member of the native Irish Catholic gentry. In the months since taking up his post in Dublin, he had, for the most part, found those of the once-proud Gaelic order to whom he had been introduced to be either pretentiously arrogant or snivellingly obsequious. Eileen would prove to be an altogether striking exception.

As she and her escort reached the door, the young man knocked and was greeted by a similarly attired officer. *The Lady Eileen O'Leary of Rathleigh House, Co. Cork,* read the elegant cursive script on the stiff card the officers exchanged with their white-gloved hands.

The door clicked closed and was almost immediately reopened.

"Mistress O'Leary," the Earl Harcourt, attired in an elegant suit of fine black wool, with a dazzlingly white ruffled shirt and hose, his black, silver-buckled shoes gleaming, spoke in a voice that was crisp and precise without being cold. He stood in the middle of the room.

"My Lord Lieutenant," responded Eileen as, to his surprise, she executed a deep, full curtsey, her eyes lowered, rising only when the lord lieutenant took her right hand and raised her himself, smiling softly.

"My Lady Eileen, we welcome you to Dublin . . . please." He gestured for Eileen to enter the massive room and conducted her to a pair of comfortably worn, high-backed, dark saddle leather–covered winged chairs, facing each other over a gleaming mahogany field desk, upon which was set a full tea.

Harcourt stood at Eileen's side until she took her seat, only then crossing to his own, absorbing what he immediately thought of as being the young woman's striking appearance, taking special note, as did many on first meeting Eileen, of her height and the captivating quality of her blue eyes. The sombre elegance of her mourning robes immediately reminded him of those worn by the preeminent women of the English court upon the death of King George II.

The atmosphere in the room was more cordial than it was not; host and guest—or, Eileen had wondered, was she perhaps more correctly the supplicant?—were to some extent generally aware of the other's history, and each well understood his or her role this day.

The initial pleasantries were just that: Yes, Eileen's journey from Cork had been agreeable. No, she did not experience seasickness. Yes, her accommodations were quite lovely, thank you. It was when Harcourt observed, "Ah, quite . . . I recall now that you have travelled a good deal by sea . . . as a child, yes, and of course your several journeys to and from Vienna," that he smiled pleasantly.

"My lord, you are quite well-informed." Eileen smiled in response.

Harcourt, taking note of her husky, almost-sensual voice, nodded.

It was Eileen's turn. "During the second half of your posting in Paris, Your Lordship undoubtedly made the acquaintance of my one-time charge, the former archduchess of Austria and Lorraine, Maria Antonia?" she inquired softly, her eyes, he thought, twinkling almost playfully. "I trust that you found Madame la Dauphine to be a pleasing hostess, sir, as well as a charming and delightful young woman?"

Harcourt now smiled warmly, silently reflecting, *no simply resentful Gaelic Irish countrywoman this.* Whilst he had been told that Eileen had served for some years at the Viennese court, because of Abigail's presence at court, as well, he had received conflicting reports as to what her precise duties had been.

"I found Madame la Dauphine to be both beautiful and charming, witty and most enjoyable company. I should think that her governess of some years," he chanced, "might claim a measure of credit for the young woman's poise."

Lowering her eyes in acknowledgement and appreciation, Eileen purred softly, "Aye, sir, 'twas approximately nine years, my lord. . . . She was but a wee *cailín* when I arrived in Vienna in 1761. We departed there together, indeed in the very same coach."

They chatted a bit about Paris, Eileen telling him of her and Abigail's whirlwind visit en route to Vienna the first time, and she pointedly mentioned that Arthur had stopped at Versailles to see the dauphine en route home to Ireland.

His significant reservations notwithstanding, as he discovered that everything Lord Moyvane had said and more was proving to be correct, Harcourt found himself quickly becoming most comfortable. He now committed himself to listen seriously to what Eileen had to say. To set her at ease, he offered and poured tea.

"Lord Moyvane has spoken most highly of you, madame," he began. "He has also shared details of your husband and his views surrounding Mr. O'Leary's death that . . ."

"If I may, my lord," Eileen interrupted, her tone delicately sharp, her expression one of both annoyance and sadness as she lowered her cup, "I should be most grateful were my husband to be referred to as *Captain O'Leary*, as that was his rank in the Hungarian Hussars of the Imperial

Armies of Austria and Hungary, at the time of his murder, this rank being by commission and decree of Her Imperial Majesty, the Empress," she finished firmly.

Having immediately realised his wholly unintentional slip, his cheeks instantly bright red, Harcourt studied Eileen and nodded. "My true apologies, my Lady Eileen; of this fact I was quite fully aware. I misspoke. Please forgive me."

Looking up, Eileen flashed one of the dazzling smiles that had not been in evidence for some months, the tension instantly dispelled.

Harcourt cleared his throat. ". . . Lord Moyvane advises quite candidly that he believes Captain O'Leary's death was as the result of what he termed an 'illegal execution,' this being contrary to the position of the local authorities. If it would not be too painful for you to do so, might I ask that you elaborate, so that I may be better, more fully informed?"

Setting down her teacup, Eileen sat regally, her broad shoulders just barely touching the high back of her chair, her long, elegant fingers resting delicately on the arms, her knuckles elevated slightly. The position was not lost on the Earl Harcourt; it was identical to that of the seated dauphine of France.

Eileen believed, accurately, that she now had his full attention as she spoke, at first generally, of the painful history between Morris and Arthur, proceeding to cover in some significant detail O'Leary's failed attempt to reconcile with the man, including its violent culmination; the confrontations at the Christmas ball in Macroom several years before, as well as those at the Muskerry fox hunt and the horse races at Dunisky, noting that "despite my husband's reputation for hotheadedness, he was the provocateur in none of these instances." Also in connection with the latter two events, she did not neglect to mention Banrían and the horse's history, even to the extent of explaining her name, nor was she defensive of Arthur's cocky, ofttimes arrogant public persona, as, in addition to providing several other examples, she briefly described their first meeting in the square at Macroom, which elicited genuinely warm laughter from the lord lieutenant.

As Eileen spoke, Harcourt's expression advanced from attentive to serious, then quickly to sombre and finally to one of barely concealed contempt as, along with the overall circumstances, he now more fully understood the manner of man Abraham Morris was, and how he conducted himself. Thoughts and images cascaded: *Low-bred Cromwellian spawn, as so many of his ilk in Ireland are,* his mind raced, *stupidly, unthinkingly, for no rational reason, they loathe what little remains of the old Gaelic order, knowing full well that only their Protestant religion and the positions they occupy as a direct result render them superior to people like* . . . His eyes fell on a now-animated Eileen as she was speaking in detail of O'Leary's thrashing of Morris at the racecourse. As she finished relating that episode, she paused and then added, "My husband, many believed him, not entirely incorrectly, arrogant. I felt him to be nevertheless justifiably rightly proud of who he was, of what he had made of himself. . . . You must understand, my lord, 'tis hard for men such as Arthur, fortunate in being well-educated and well-travelled, their military training superior to many, when they return to Ireland, which so many eventually do, for 'tis here that lie their hearts, when they find themselves confronted with or by small, ill-bred, uneducated and seemingly always-angry men, such as this Morris, and others. . . ."

At this Harcourt nodded and sighed, as, with considerably less reluctance than he had ever thought he would have, he silently conceded, *of these men we are of the same mind.*

Harcourt then queried as to Arthur being outlawed. As she began to speak, Eileen shook her head, and an errant lock of hair fell over her right eye. With her right fingertips she pushed it back in place, Harcourt viewing it as an elegant gesture, as she answered. "In Ireland, in all candour, my lord, an *outlaw* is all too often a Catholic gentleman who stands tall and moves freely about a land that he strongly believes is his country, a man who sees the *Sassenach*"—her tone was sharp, direct; she did not hesitate, did not divert her gaze but looked directly at her listener—"as do most of us, sir, as being *invaders* and *occupiers.*"

Harcourt, who had heard and come to understand the words' meaning, said nothing. He nevertheless felt his cheeks unexpectedly flush and his eyes narrow as she elaborated on what he quickly determined to be the wholly arbitrary process of outlawing, at least as practiced in County Cork, and he reflexively clenched his fists as she related that, though Arthur had appealed the ruling and requested both a formal stay of enforcement and a full assizes court trial, neither entreaty had been acted on by the time of the armed assault on Rathleigh, – nor indeed by the time of O'Leary's murder.

Eileen completed her narrative with a pair of additional meticulously detailed descriptions—of the armed attack on their home and, finally, of the day of O'Leary's death. As her listener did not interrupt and indeed appeared deeply interested, she made a point of telling the full, dramatic tale, beginning with Arthur's blood-drenched horse returning home and taking her to where O'Leary lay dead, and through the old woman's vivid description of O'Leary's final moments and words, as well as of, with the woman's assistance, remounting and securing her husband's body . . . and the long, wrenching, moonlit trek towards home.

As she finished, the lord lieutenant rested his head back for a long, quiet moment, closing his eyes and finally taking a deep breath. "This is a troubling narrative, madame, an extremely troubling one . . . and a most moving tale."

Eileen sat quietly, saying nothing.

Harcourt permitted the silence to settle over the room for a time before he resumed the conversation. "Lord Moyvane indicates that you perhaps might provide something of a *solution* . . ." He broke off and rose, striding to his large desk and returning with what proved to be Lord Moyvane's letter. "I wished to state it as his lordship did to me . . . He indicated you might perhaps have '*a wise solution which will provide* you *with the justice* you seek *and a means to defuse a potentially most contentious matter, rectifying it by having those military men directly involved in the tragedy disciplined.*'

"Does his lordship accurately represent your desires, my lady?"

Eileen nodded firmly. "He does indeed, my lord."

Harcourt sat and gestured gently for her to continue.

"My requests of Your Lordship are relatively simple: As a result of the roles they played in what undoubtedly was indeed the *murder* of Captain

O'Leary, I would ask that Major MacAteer, the officer whom, as I have said, provided Morris with his little army, one of whose number killed my husband, be reassigned to Jamaica . . . and that the remaining members of the contingent—all other-ranks, I believe—who are still in Ireland be similarly redeployed, but to Barbados."

Harcourt nodded at Eileen. "Some would liken both reassignments to being virtual sentences of death, would they not?"

To his surprise, Eileen immediately smiled, *rather cruelly,* as Harcourt would later recall. "Would they now? . . . As indeed so might they prove to be." She continued in all seriousness, "Though in the case of Major MacAteer, I have suggested Jamaica, given his relatively limited role, and considering that my eldest brother has been resident in Jamaica now some ten years and more and remains quite alive."

Harcourt coughed. "My lady, would you agree that unusual happenings have already occurred relative to the two individuals said to have been most proximately involved in your husband's death?

"This man Morris, the ex-high sheriff, the former magistrate, he is said to have been gravely wounded by an unknown assailant, being even now in danger of death, we are told.

"Whilst the other-rank, Greene, now known to have been the rifleman who made the killing shot—" he lowered both his eyes and his voice—"he is said to have disappeared. Originally thought to have deserted, we are informed that he is believed, at least by some, to have been killed."

Eileen's expression was now deliberately one of almost girlish guilelessness. "How fascinatingly coincidental, would you not agree, my lord?"

Harcourt had difficulty not smiling, particularly when she suggested that "If perhaps the difficulties these two gentlemen you mentioned have experienced may have indeed been in some way related to their roles in my husband's murder . . . it might be said . . . might it not, sir? . . . that were you to authorise the transfers to the West Indies, as I have suggested, you would perhaps in one way possibly be seen as *saving* these men's lives." She smiled innocently.

". . . and should I not to do as you request? What then, madame?" he could not resist, though his tone was gentle, not at all challenging.

Eileen sighed softly. "With great respect, my lord, should you not, sir, then 'tis the king whom I shall find myself compelled to approach. I have done so prior, as you may be aware, sir."

Harcourt took a moment, now studying even more carefully the woman, whom he had difficulty thinking of as being *not yet thirty years of age, much less as being an Irish Papist from the depths of distant County Kerry, of a family of, as is ofttimes said, "smugglers, thieves, murderers and cattle-rustlers . . . who nevertheless speak Latin and Greek . . . some of whom serve at the courts of Europe and who now sits here before me, calmly discussing murder, revenge, transportation and the manner in which she previously has and shall perhaps yet again directly approach His Britannic Majesty.* He shook his head.

He was very much aware of the outcome of her prior written plea to George III, which had led to a full investigation, uncovering serious abuses committed against members of the community that, he knew now, had included Eileen, resulting in the very public sacking of Abraham Morris as high sheriff and the further curtailment of the power of the Ascendency officialdom in Cork, reflecting as she spoke, *neither endeared the O'Learys to Morris, of this I am certain, but . . .*

"Though I believe I should, in this instance, seek to have audience with His Majesty in person," Eileen added firmly.

The lord lieutenant could only very gently again nod his head. The topic was dropped.

"If I may, Mistress O'Leary, am I correct in understanding that, in addition to Captain O'Leary and yourself, a number of your family, have, shall we say, *served abroad?*"

She smiled. "Indeed, sir, your understanding is quite correct. If I may, sir, in Vienna this would include my dear uncle, General the Count Moritz O'Connell of the Imperial Austrian Armies and personal counsellor to Her Imperial Majesty, as well my brother-in-law, Major Denis O'Sullivan, of the Hungarian Hussars, the same military force . . . he being the husband of my dearest sister, Abigail, who herself now serves as primary lady-in-waiting to

Her Imperial Majesty, having succeeded the now-wife of General O'Connell, the Countess Maria von Graffenreit-O'Connell." She could not help but laugh softly. "Whilst in France, my lord, there are—"

Harcourt shared her mirth, laughing heartily, both genuinely and warmly. "You would thus be referring to your two brothers, both commissioned officers of the Irish Brigade in the armies of Louis XV, yes?" he asked, still chuckling warmly.

Eileen lowered her eyes. "If I may yet again say it, Your Lordship is indeed quite well-informed."

"Your family is quite well-known to us, madame."

They then unexpectedly grew quiet, each seeming to be pondering a thought. It was Harcourt who resumed the conversation, expressing something he had reflected on more than once, prior to but especially this day. "If I may now say, and with the greatest respect, as well, madame, were you people of but a, shall we say, different religious persuasion, many of these valuable individuals, including perhaps even yourself, might have been or might even yet now be in the service of good King George."

Though appropriately deferential in her tone, Eileen was imperturbable as she answered without hesitation, "If only that *good King George* and His Majesty's wise and trusted counsellors would come to realise and recognise the value of having loyal, royalist and devoutly Catholic Irish officers, gentry and nobles in His Majesty's service ... that which you suggest might well become the case, my lord ... but not until such time, sir."

Harcourt could only nod slowly in respectful, noncommittal response.

At that, Eileen nodded and winked at him, eliciting from Harcourt an expression of utter surprise and a barely audible gasp and, finally, a shy laugh.

Though he had clearly enjoyed intellectually sparing with this most attractive young woman, Harcourt realised his time was limited, as were his options in, as Lord Moyvane had characterised it, *defusing* the *O'Leary matter.*

Standing, he extended his hand to his visitor, who surprised him yet again by gripping it and shaking it firmly.

As Eileen immediately then curtseyed as deeply and flawlessly as she had on her arrival, and the lord lieutenant took the momentary opportunity to gather his composure and his thoughts, as he raised her, saying, "Though I am certain you are able to appreciate the fact that I am unable to even informally commit to what actions, if any, I might take in response to your requests, I do want you to know that when final determinations are indeed arrived at and communicated to you, my lady, they shall be the result of lengthy and deliberate thought."

He nodded firmly, and Eileen smiled broadly, whispering softly, "Thank you, my lord; for that alone, sir, I am most grateful."

At that, she quietly took her leave, the nobleman's eyes following her closely as she was escorted out of his office, watching her as she walked down the long corridor with the seemingly omnipresent young officer in the bright red coat until she turned a corner.

Eileen spent a pleasant, inconsequential day after in Dublin, during which she visited Trinity College—*'tis truly a pity such a fine school is wasted, virtually solely educating Protestants . . . and only men, at that!*—and St. Patrick's Cathedral, where Jonathan Swift had for many years been dean, stopping briefly at the Church of Ireland cleric and celebrated author's crypt. Sending word to Catherine's man in Dublin that she was prepared to return home, she was advised that a ship would depart for Cork the afternoon following, and that a carriage would be sent for her.

Within several weeks of Eileen's return home, she would receive a brief letter from the lord lieutenant's aide-de-camp, advising that

. . . Major James MacAteer shall be forthwith reassigned to the king's resident forces on the island of Jamaica, whilst the eight men who remain in Ireland and who, whilst under the questionable command of one Abraham Morris, participated in the armed assault on the late Captain O'Leary, they themselves shall be reassigned to the king's resident forces on the island of Barbados; of the four remaining men, one, Greene, is missing, presumed to have deserted, two have indeed deserted and are believed to have fled Great Britain, whilst one man has legitimately left the service, his period of enlistment having ended.

Sometime later, a short personal note from the handsome young officer in the bright red coat confirmed that the nine men—the officer as well as the other-ranks—would together depart Southampton aboard the same West Indies–destined troopship, "sometime prior to Christmas."

Eileen read the young officer's letter several times, smiling harshly as she whispered softly, "Christmas at sea," finally stepping outside and strolling to the area overlooking the fenced pastures, the place where she had stood, invoking the wrath of God on the men responsible for Arthur's murder; the place where Banrían was now romping with her barn mates, the place where she felt Arthur's joyful spirit often hovered over Rathleigh and all of them, especially their *wee little angel.* At the moment, she could manage no more than a whispered, "Thank you, God . . . all of it, 'tis now nearly over . . . it is. Thank you, Sir." She found she was too emotionally exhausted even to shed a tear.

That night, for the first time in many months, she gathered her little boys up on her bed and, as Maire and Donal Mór had done with her and as she had with Hugh, her little sisters and, even more recently, with the archduchesses and indeed with the boys themselves—though, sadly, she reflected, not once since Arthur's death had she done so—she again told them her favourite Kerry stories, including the ones about the *Fianna of Ireland,* "Way up over the mountains from Derrynane," she gestured, the little boys' eyes following her thin right forefinger as, in her mind, she pointed towards Killarney, "in the village of Cill ár Ne, and 'twas *there* that the Fianna came to hunt," her throaty voice, calm, measured now, she told stories until her sons were both asleep.

In midmorning, Eileen rode first to O'Leary's grave and then in a wide, lengthy arc on to Derryleigh. She was now both emotionally and physically exhausted; even her conversation with Arthur was brief. *The soldiers, they shall soon be en route to the Caribbean, to the West Indies . . . where in God's good time, I have no doubt of that, they all shall die . . . so 'tis now finished, completed, my darling, all of those who murdered you . . . they have or will pay a price beyond what anyone could have believed possible. With our friends and family—I surely could not have done this alone!—I have accomplished what I promised you. . . . Whilst to restore you to life I am unable, I believe that you and I shall both now rest better. . . .*

As had become her practice, she bent and, resting on her palms, gently kissed the ground, now soft and green with thick, late-summer grass.

Arriving at Derryleigh, she shared the young officer's letter with Anna, and together the women wept and embraced. Though it had been patently obvious to Anna for some time, to her dearest friend Eileen now finally admitted her exhaustion. Anna provided tea and biscuits and gentle conversation; after a while, she gently sent her own dearest friend back to Rathleigh. "You have completed all that you promised Arthur and yourself you would. . . . As soon as word is received that he can be brought to Kilcrea Abbey, so shall we all do that, my darling, but even now . . . now you must resume your life. The wee ones need you, Rathleigh needs you, I need you . . . so rest and begin again."

That night Eileen slept soundly for the first time in what had been several unimaginably long months.

Summer, its peaceful days, weeks even, had inevitably progressed, punctuated primarily by the dramatic, the bloody events that Eileen had unleashed not long after O'Leary's death, beginning with the shooting of Abraham Morris in July by a mysterious outlaw and culminating in her own visit to Dublin Castle in September.

So focused had Eileen been on her own vengeance that it was with a shock that, shortly after returning from Dublin, she learnt from Andrew Baggot that Morris was to be tried for Arthur's murder later on in September. He would, she was told, be transported to Cork City and brought into court in a rolling chair.

"'Tis to be a mere formality, I fear," Baggot said bitterly, cautioning her; he then advised, "Clearly desiring to have nothing to do with this case, the assizes judges have . . . as they possess full authority to do . . . empowered the magistrates themselves . . . *ourselves*," he shook his head in irony at his position, "to try the bastard, Cameron and I have only yesterday been informed. They—Noble and some of the others—even delayed advising Davidson; they seem to see him as becoming 'weak.'" He shook his head again.

His original assessment notwithstanding, Baggot succeeded in shedding his sense of the inevitable. "I do not believe that, in good conscience, we can stand by and do nothing," he told Alexander Cameron, who immediately agreed, adding, "The little bastard is said to be dying; no one is going to hang him, but I believe we should at least try to have him convicted, should we not?"

Thus agreed, and during the ensuing days, unbeknownst to the general public, including the young widow, an eclectic group composed of individuals generally regarded as being stalwarts of the Protestant Ascendancy would be delicately assembled, initially by Baggot and Cameron, joined almost immediately by the Reverend McGee.

It was only when a third magistrate, George Davidson, unexpectedly indicated to Cameron that—despite his virulently outspoken anti-Papist views—"Given the present set of circumstances," he, too, wished "only to see justice truly done in this case" that Andrew Baggot was surprised and grew at least minimally optimistic. In the meantime, the Reverend McGee had successfully approached several other well-regarded Church of Ireland clerics, whose reaction was similarly and, in the case of most, surprisingly favourable.

The men would within two days' time be joined by the eminent Earl of Cork and Orrery, whose favourable impression of O'Leary—and Eileen— had seemingly carried over from the spring races, sufficient in this instance to prevail over his own, unrentingly lethal anti-Catholicism. The only Catholic involved in the effort would be Lord Clancarty, and his quiet efforts remained purposely unseen, unknown.

By the time of the trial, a number of Protestant squires, whom Baggot smilingly referred to as the "lads from the hunt, from the races," had informally pledged to appear in Cork, ostensibly in support of a fair and impartial trial, which, virtually all agreed now, was the same as favouring a finding of guilt against Morris. "We shall be present, and we shall be heard!" declared James Walker, the husky, distinguished-looking, prematurely grey-haired squire of perhaps forty who, aboard his sleek black stallion, had provided O'Leary and Banrían with their most serious challenge at Dunisky.

On the chill, heavy Saturday morning of 26 September, fewer than half of the magistrates were in attendance in a medium-size, drably undistinguished room, customarily used as the officers' mess at the headquarters of the British army detachment billeted in Cork, the long dining board having been turned so that it stretched across the chamber's narrow breadth, the magistrates seated in array at it, whilst the more junior members were seated behind them to hear the cherubic deputy under high sheriff, Harry McCain, the man who had first confronted Morris with his cheating at the Dunisky races in April, bring the matter formally before the Muskerry Constitutional Society in an almost perfunctory manner. As soon as McCain wheeled Morris into the room, almost before Madame Morris was seated, he began.

His voice a not unpleasant singsong, he outlined the facts, the allegations, and read the formal charge, its wording taken from and being based on the damning findings of the coroner's inquest, that

on the fourth of May this year, at or near that place known and commonly referred to as Carriganima, this County, the Hon. Abraham Morris did there commit and cause to be committed, the wilful and wanton murder of Capt. Arthur O'Leary, late of Rathleigh House.

Barely had McCain completed reading when a nasty exchange between Wilfred Noble and Alexander Cameron ensued, prompted by Noble's shrill complaint that it was inappropriate to include O'Leary's military rank in the charge, arguing that "Even were indeed it legitimate, which I have always questioned . . . it was one bestowed on him by a foreign power—a foreign *Catholic* power—and an enemy of Great Britain!"

"Be still, you brainless lout!" Cameron exploded, slamming his right palm on the table in front of him. "Is there no aspect of life that the hatred begot by your bigotry does not control?"

Before Noble could respond, James Aiken, at ninety the oldest magistrate and a former high sheriff of Cork, impatiently snapped, "Indeed! Will you shut your bloody mouth, Noble? This man O'Leary is dead, and who but you and . . ." he gestured derisively at Morris, who slumped awkwardly in his rolling chair, "on this earth gives a bloody damn what he is called . . . a rotting corpse is a rotting corpse . . . even a Papist . . . bloody hell, even a Musselman, even a bloody Jew! The only thing that matters here is whether a murder was committed in the creation of this particular corpse." He sniffed derisively.

Noble sniffed as well but said nothing further.

At Davidson's direction, Sheriff McCain first produced Major MacAteer, seemingly already shaken by his recent receipt of unexplained orders transferring him to Jamaica. Clearly uncomfortable, he described in detail Morris's hectoring of him, shaking his head as he acknowledged, "I sorely regret that I provided *him*," he dramatically gestured to Morris, slumped in his rolling chair, "with the means by which Captain O'Leary's life was taken."

Under McCain's softly spoken questioning, MacAteer said he "had no doubt" that if he had known that Morris's true intent was to slay rather than to capture O'Leary, he would have "most definitely not" acceded to the little man's demands, adding with a deep, almost-theatrical sigh, "I am sad for the man's death."

Watson and Noble rolled their eyes at the remark, the most junior magistrates snickering audibly, until Cameron turned and stared them into an abrupt and, in the case of the younger men, embarrassed silence.

For a moment it appeared McCain was finished with his questioning until, almost casually, with, people would later say, the *ease of a well-practised* barrister, he turned back. "Major, just one additional question if I may: What specific authority did you possess so as to be able to detach these soldiers from your command?"

MacAteer sat dumbly, his face glistening with sweat. McCain stood quietly, saying nothing, the men staring uneasily at each other, until MacAteer began, "I was, I am in command of . . ."

"Aye, that, but in truth you possessed no independent authority to release these soldiers, did you, *sir?* To place them under the control of a civilian magistrate, *did you, sir?*"

Again, MacAteer said nothing, hardly moving until he finally, wordlessly, shook his head back and forth. *"The commonly accepted gesture for an unspoken but negative response!"* a gesturing Harry McCain informed the magistrates. "He admits having no authority, gentlemen. None at all!"

The second and final witness was a young other-rank, Simon McCall, not much older than the still-absent John Greene, though longer in the king's service. In a rolling Yorkshire burr, he related in surprising detail the activities of Morris and the soldiers on 4 May, emphasising that it was Morris who was "in command, yessir, he was indeed that, sir, yes, wholly and fully in charge," testifying that, as O'Leary and Banrían appeared on the low ridge just above the coach road, roughly across from their position, Morris had given the order to fire, emphasising that he had been compelled to growl out more than a single order, adding quietly, "It was only after he threatened to charge us with cowardice—or to shoot us—that we fired, sir. . . or some of us did, sir," he added in a much quieter voice.

Baggot and Cameron shook their heads, whilst, looking at Morris, old James Aiken muttered audibly to no one in particular, *"He* should bloody well know about being a coward!" He then smacked the table and cried out loudly, "The little shit should hang for his cowardice alone . . . and twice for misusing the king's men in this manner!"

When McCain pressed the soldier as to why there was a reluctance to obey Morris's order to fire on O'Leary, there was a long pause, a sigh and an admission: "All along, sir, we believed we were there to capture the man, this O'Leary, sir, that it was that purpose why we were sent out with the magistrate, sir, to bring in an outlaw . . . not to kill him," he said softly, his eyes, piercing black now, drilling into Morris's own as he stared at him.

The youthful deputy sheriff queried the witness as to Morris's demeanour, as to what he might have said before the shooting.

Taking a deep breath, the soldier continued softly, "The magistrate, sir, he said something like, 'Men, it has been a long time that I've been trying to kill this outlaw, this disloyal Papist bastard. Today justice shall be finally accomplished . . . a great service to king and country you are performing.'"

McCain calmly inquired, "To assure that the magistrates fully and clearly understand . . . are you saying *that* was the first time anything was said to you men about shooting or killing O'Leary?"

The young soldier nodded firmly, softly adding, "Aye, yessir, yes it was, sir. Yes, the very first time, sir."

"And after the shooting . . . what did Squire Morris say afterwards?"

After a moment's hesitation, the sheriff's deputy nodding at him to do so, McCall responded. "Then, he—" he pointed a steady right hand at Morris—"he looks down alongside the post road where the man, O'Leary it was, sir, is lying on the ground there, where he fell from his horse, sir, and smiling like, sir, he says, sir, 'The . . . fucking—'" he blushed, his pale cheeks instantly a bright red, lowering his eyes, waiting for McCain to indicate for him to proceed—"'the fucking traitor,' that's what he called the man, '*the fucking traitor*,' he says"—the soldier's voice now strong, its tone condemnatory, " . . . and he pointed at O'Leary . . . and he says something like 'that's precisely how I have been waiting a long time to see him, dead in the dirt. . . . '*the fucking traitor*!'" Then he says for us to get along, to get out where we were, sir."

A profound silence hung heavily over the room for several long moments, not a word being said, not even a whisper heard.

Finally, a low, indistinct murmur rose from the windowed side of the room, though it was Squire James Walker's voice that was heard clearly above it, as he intended it to be, chilling in both its tone and content, as he stood and began moving forward, "After hearing this, what this young man says under oath, I am strongly inclined to simply shoot the fucking little bastard right now . . . and be done with this, and him!"

Before anyone could react, barely pausing after speaking, whilst still walking across and towards the front of the room, he withdrew a massive, gleaming double-barrelled pistol from the deep pockets of his fine, black wool broad-skirted coat. Hesitating not at all, in a near-fluid movement, he cocked one barrel and levelled the lethal-looking weapon directly at Morris, perhaps six or seven feet from where Walker finally stood, saying almost offhandedly to an aghast Reverend McGee, "Well, why the bloody hell should I bloody not?" and calmly squeezed the trigger.

In the closed room, the roar of the pistol's explosion was deafening, the spew of thick, bitter smoke instantly blinding, choking. As the pall slowly began to clear, so too was it that Reverend McGee had managed to just barely grab at the hem of Walker's coat, and it was that alone that had caused the squire's shot to go high and wide of Morris, smashing instead into the rough, whitewashed wall above and behind where Andrew Baggott sat. Baggott calmly turned around, surveyed the damage as well as the proximity of the ball to him, shook his head and laughed ironically.

Shouts, curses and Hannah Morris's screams easing as the smoke lazily continued to dissipate, the room grew deathly silent until Alexander Cameron, once again quietly elegant in the gleaming, brass-buttoned, dazzling red uniform coat he had worn most recently as a major in the 4th King's Own Regiment of Foot, calmly, placidly— as if nothing had happened—rose in his place. It seemed as if the stunning brilliance of his striking scarlet coat had compelled virtually all eyes to focus on him, so that simply by rising, thus attired, he restored some measure of order. Resting his knuckles on the highly polished table at which most of the magistrates were seated, he leaned towards Morris, demanding slowly, "Have you *anything* to add to what has been said? Have you *anything* to say in contradiction to what has been testified to?" The former officer's voice was harsh, his expression chilling.

His jaw slack, his eyes glazed, a sweat-drenched, clearly terrified Morris gasped for breath, struggling to speak. He finally succeeded in righting himself in the awkward chair, which rolled slightly forward and then back each time he moved. "I cannot, I am unable to . . . I have nothing to say save that I was acting solely to rid Cork of a disloyal, violent man, a man who had been declared, I would remind you, *by this Society* . . ." he screeched, "to be an outlaw . . . who was and always had been nothing more than an arrogant, a wilful Papist traitor, a . . ."

"Enough! Silence!" James Aiken, whose apparently extreme loathing of Morris had never before been publicly evident, snapped as he waved his birdlike claw of a hand dismissively. "I have heard this same, whining, tiresome litany about this now-dead man from you far too many times before. I believed you could only contradict the testimony by lying," he laughed harshly, "yet, for once in your miserable life, you have actually spoken the truth, admitting that you have no defence at law . . . and for doing so, you should bloody well hang, you fraud, you worthless coward!"

Wordlessly, Morris slumped slowly back down in his seat, the chair squeaking mournfully.

In the abrupt silence that ensued, the tension, which had only been heightened by James Walker's gunfire, – was thick, powerful and unexpected, as, in the normal course of things, having prejudged the matter before them, thinking as they did largely in unison, the magistrates would customarily merely exchange glances and nods and render, with rare exceptions, a near or totally unanimous and predictable verdict.

Not so this day, as George Davidson loudly announced the Society would "duly consider the matter, here and now, this day, in public!" surprising all by adding, "The deputy under high sheriff will remove . . ." He gestured at Morris, not speaking his name, as well as the two witnesses. Even as Harry McCain began to do so, along with Madame Morris, who was loudly protesting their removal, a hurried discussion amongst the magistrates ensued. In what was virtually the day's sole instance of equanimity, they agreed that Morris and the others could remain for their deliberations.

Try as he might to avoid it, his apprehension obvious, Wilfred Noble, Morris's long-time ally, viewed by many people as his sole friend, looked over at Davidson. "What is it that we have to consider, sir?" he demanded. "O'Leary was a declared outlaw, a threat to the peace and well-being of the vicinage, was he not?"

"*No!* Quite possibly he was not!" a stentorian, patrician voice rang out. "Even so, whether he was or was not, *that* is not the issue here," began His

Lordship, Hamilton Boyle, 6th Earl of Cork and Orrery, rising in a shadowy corner in the rear of the now-stuffy room.

Slowly walking forward, purposely achieving the full effect of his surprise attendance, his black suit of the finest wool, his gleaming black boots of the softest leather, his hair impeccably powdered and perfectly tied with a black satin ribbon, the tall, spare nobleman stopped as a shocked Josiah Watson began, "My lord, you do not—"

"I do not *what?*" the noble shot back at the still-seated commoner, gesturing with a sweep of his right arm. "You are not suggesting that I am not permitted to speak . . . are you?"

As if only then conscious of his failure to stand in the earl's presence, Watson stood, visibly shaken. "No, no, my lord, not at all, my lord . . . It is just that . . ."

"What is it *just* then, whoever you are?

"Could it be that you do not know—as you seemingly did not know to stand whilst in my presence, most certainly whilst daring to address me— how to go about considering this case? I have only recently learnt that virtually all the matters that have come before you men in the relatively brief time your little assembly has existed are neatly, quite tidily disposed of with virtually no debate amongst yourselves, that a fact or circumstance of a matter is relevant only to the extent that it may permit effortless prejudgment by yourselves and, lastly, and what in my mind, sir, is the most dastardly practise of all, is that you routinely ignore and selectively enforce the laws of this kingdom."

"Is *that* what it is, sir?"

Wilfred Noble came to stand next to Watson, bowing slightly to Boyle. "If I may, my lord, I—"

"You may *not,* sir," snapped the earl. "*Whoever* you *may be* . . . and I assure you that I care not a whit who you are . . . it is well-known, and I say again that I am not now, have never been and I *shall never* be a friend to the native Irish Catholics in this kingdom, nor to Papists anywhere, for that matter. Again, I say I find their idolatrous, superstition-ridden religion reprehensible . . . the hocus-pocus, about which they obsess laughable and their patent disloyalty to the crown appalling. All of this notwithstanding, in this instance, O'Leary, despite being one of these people, albeit an officer . . . sadly of a foreign power . . . and a gentleman . . . well-educated, though wholly contra to the laws of this kingdom . . . " he shook his head, "should have nevertheless been properly adjudged as to the crimes he was *said* to have committed, as I understand he had repeatedly requested be done . . . and if I may add, gentlemen, not even an Irish Catholic, such as O'Leary, should have been summarily executed under the guise of an official act.

"This being said, no matter the outcome, Magistrate Morris should also be fairly judged, judged by you on the facts and the laws of this kingdom applied to them . . . as O'Leary was most assuredly not," he paused, and the shocked silence in the room was profound.

"You do not disagree with me, sir, do you, gentlemen . . .?" Lord Boyle's inquiry remained heavily in the air, which was rank, in addition to the lingering bitter smell of burnt black powder, with musty leather, damp wool and worn-too-many-days linen, until Harry McCain instinctively eventually opened a window.

No one spoke.

Finally, George Davidson resumed his occasional priority amongst the members. Rising, bowing to the earl, he cleared his throat. "The matter before the Society is whether the Honourable Abraham Morris is guilty as charged of the murder of the deceased, Arthur O'Leary. This is the only question before us."

He looked around the room, warily eying Lord Boyle and the several clergymen of the established Church of Ireland, who were now in the front of the room gathered with him. His expression was one of shock as Lord Clancarty admitted himself and, walking forward, seated himself next to his fellow peer, immediately followed by a second group of tardy Protestant squires, who joined their fellows, some seated along, most standing, leaning against the wall.

Wilfred Noble finally whined, "The deceased had been declared an outlaw by this Society months prior to his being brought to justice, he—"

"Immaterial! He was murdered, pure and simple!" raged Alexander Cameron, rising again from his chair, its legs scraping the worn floor. "This was nothing less than a self-sanctioned—by the defendant alone—judicial murder, the forces of the crown being used by the accused to settle a wholly private, wholly personal score with the deceased."

"How dare you?" Josiah Watson demanded, a weak, perfunctory chorus of "hear, hear" echoing from the seats of those magistrates who had not spoken.

"How dare he? How dare *you*, sir?" a visibly enraged, trembling Andrew Baggot roared, half-standing, jabbing a finger at Watson, challenging him. "You demonstrate to me, to this Society, to this assembly, one indication, *a single one*, based on the evidence produced, all of which remains unrefuted, that the accused is not guilty of murder as charged!"

There ensued a raucous, bitter debate:

Judicial murder . . . legal murder . . . not at all—'Twas of course murder—the bloody 'unlawful killing by one person of another'. . . in this instance by an illegally assembled posse . . . pure and simple, it was . . . disloyal native Irish Catholic, he was . . . guilty as charged! . . . An innocent man is Magistrate Morris . . . only doing his duty as a loyal subject of good King George! . . . Innocent? What then was O'Leary? . . . A loyal subject? . . . Bah! Rather as a rank, snivelling coward, using the soldiers of the king to do his dirty work! . . . .

As the nasty deliberations raged, fuelling the already roaring intellectual fires were the usually reserved Church of Ireland clergymen, who had unexpectedly and quite spontaneously decided amongst themselves to speak. Gathering near the front centre of the room, they freely interrupted the magistrates at will, their contributions being a mix of theological reasoning, biblical quotations and personal reflections on the uneasy relationship between native Irish Catholics and those who Reverend McGee repeatedly characterised as being "we *strangers*, as many if not most of the Gaelic Irish view us."

At one point, having noted puzzled expressions, especially on the faces of the younger, newer magistrates, at the first and then the second time he employed the term, he paused, "You have assuredly heard the Gaelic word

'Sassenach,' have you not?" he asked the assembled, especially these young men, rhetorically. "In Irish, in the Gaelic it simply means 'stranger'. . . and as such it is used interchangeably with the designations 'British' or 'English' . . . you see then, it is all the same, we are viewed by those whom many of *us* caustically refer to as 'the mere Irish,' as being 'strangers' in this, *their own* land."

Not unexpectedly, Baggot and Cameron led the charge for conviction and execution. When pressed, Baggot refused to concede that, given the state of Morris's health, he should, in the event of his conviction, receive a sentence of death by hanging, with the stipulation that it would be suspended. "If found guilty of the foul deed for which he is accused, he should surely hang," Baggot pressed. "Were it up to me alone, I should have him drawn and quartered as well!"

Wordlessly, Aiken stiffly rose from his chair and, his left hand leaning heavily on the chair backs as he did so, walked delicately over to Davidson and bent to his ear, whispering. He sniffed and slowly made his way back to his own place.

As he was resuming his seat, an aristocratic voice again rang out from the far side of the room. "I say, why should he not be hanged, gentlemen?" cried an unabashed Squire Walker, who, having remained standing, leaned diffidently against a windowsill as he again withdrew his large pistol, this time from his belt, his long coat folded back, permitting him ready access to the weapon.

His query unanswered, wordlessly again striding forward, he stopped mere feet—perhaps as close as a yard—from where Morris's chair sat insecurely parked. Looking disdainfully down at the clearly terrified man, his voice and expression murderous, Walker informed him that "I still have a good mind to simply shoot you . . . you worthless, piss-soaked, puny little sack of shit, as I am well able, as I only emptied one barrel!" He laughed cruelly, waving the weapon's barrels before Morris's ghostly white face. Given his prior action, his remark shocked the room into momentary silence, as Davidson abruptly, wordlessly, with a cock of his head, indicated to the youthful sheriff to step towards where Morris, sat and Walker stood.

Having done so, McCain said softly, almost pleadingly, "Squire, if your honour would *pleas*e, sir . . . please." Nodding, his general disgust expressed by a growled "*aaahhhh* . . . aye, very well, then," Walker reluctantly stepped back, very slowly moving away, this time returning his pistol into the recesses of the deep pocket of his coat.

As the debate continued, Aiken made his detestation of Morris yet even more evident. A litany of pejoratives reflective of what had apparently been years of anger towards, frustration with and disdain for the accused man spewed venomously from his mouth, in his dusty, raspy voice: *ill-bred, unlettered, ignorant, dishonest, deceitful, thieving, corrupting* and *corrupt* were but a few.

Most damning of all of his remarks were those he made directly to Morris, repeatedly stabbing his bony right forefinger through the air at him.

"You are more guilty of the murder of O'Leary than was Pontius Pilate responsible for the death of Christ. To my knowledge, to the knowledge of all here, *you* had tried and failed repeatedly to kill O'Leary, on at least two occasions that we are aware of, most recently at your home, where he came with your consent and unarmed, only to be attacked by you not once but twice, and seriously wounded, this we now know. At the race meet at Dunisky, where you attempted with whip and gun to attack O'Leary, only to be easily disarmed of both by him and, when challenged to a duel by the man in front of a large crowd, you snivellingly squirmed out of it, you *miserable . . . gutless . . . worthless . . . coward*!" his hissed.

Though he paused, Aiken was not finished; he was only taking deep gulps of air into his thin, arid lungs.

Purposely avoiding specific mention of the armed attack on Rathleigh, which Aiken and a number of the other magistrates had nominally sanctioned, he completed his tirade. "Failing in these attempts, you succeeded, as the major has testified, in somehow hectoring him into providing you with a detachment of His Majesty's troops, in ostensible command of which," he rolled his eyes, "you gave the order to fire—an order which, as we have just heard, resulted in the death of O'Leary, an order which you had *absolutely no authority* to give. You are guilty, sir, guilty of the wanton murder of, although a disloyal Papist, an arrogant soldier in the thrall of an enemy power he was . . . a man over whom you had no legal authority, much less the authority to *execute* him. If I have my way, Morris, you shall this very day hang!"

The gasps in the room were audible. In their shared numbed amazement, Cameron and Baggot spontaneously laughed aloud; even they were stunned into silence when the ancient man added, ". . . and I, too, would see you drawn and quartered and, for good measure, have your pieces burnt!" he cackled, before he finally leaned back in his chair.

Masking his own shock, Lord Boyle again rose, his voice strong. "Very powerfully phrased, sir, very powerfully indeed. I shall say nothing further."

Half-rising, Aiken bowed stiffly in respect.

"Nor, then, shall we!" called out the Reverend McGee, gesturing to himself and his fellow clergymen.

In the momentary silence, again in the company of the squires who had joined him, early and latecomers alike, all wealthy, none known for anything other than their general disdain of Irish Catholics, along with a stalwart fealty to the crown, Squire Walker smacked the windowsill. "Guilty, I say then, guilty . . . hang him!"

The others, several of whom had been passing Walker's large, burnished silver flask of fine Scotch whiskey amongst themselves, picked up his words, chanting loudly, "Guilty . . . hang him! . . . Guilty . . . hang him!" until Aiken held up his trembling hands almost plaintively.

Wilfred Noble was seeking Davidson's attention. Leering at him, Davidson only waved his right hand dismissively. "You may speak, sir, with your vote alone. I rule . . . and aye, it is a *totally* arbitrary ruling . . ." he laughed caustically, "that you have nothing intelligent to add to this discourse, to these deliberations."

"Hear, hear!" thundered Baggot, Cameron and Aiken, rapping their palms on the table.

Squire Walker, his threatening pistol suddenly yet again in his hand, concurred. "Indeed! Hell, yes! Shut up, Noble!" The other squires cheered loudly, stamping their boots on the floor as Walker, only half in jest, aimed the weapon at Noble.

When the vote was then taken, those of Baggot, Cameron, Aiken and Davidson were in favour of a finding of guilt and a sentence of death by hanging, to be carried out immediately.

In voting for a finding of not guilty, Noble and Watson were supported by the four most recently seated magistrates: young, outspokenly anti-Catholic men, men James Aiken had already grouped with Morris as being ill-lettered and ignorant, but men who had been selected—ironically, in a vote in favour of which both Aiken and Davidson had joined with Morris, Noble and Watson—because of their unyielding support of the Ascendency, coupled with a vehement and vocal form of anti-Catholicism.

Morris's expression was blank, his eyes seemingly fixed as it was announced by Davidson that he had escaped guilt—and execution—by a mere two votes.

The published version of the proceedings, appearing in the Monday edition of the *Corke Evening Post* would duly and tersely report only that, *Last Saturday, 26th September, at Cork City, Abraham Morris was tried for the killing of Arthur O'Leary, where he was honourably acquitted.*

Though no formal acknowledgement, much less any official mention, of the narrow margin of acquittal was ever to be made, the *words on the wind*—as they always had, as they always would—quickly carried the full account of the trial throughout County Cork and beyond, eventually throughout Ireland and on to London itself, along with the details of the tumultuous nature of the proceedings, the heated words exchanged and by whom and, perhaps even more damming, of the fact that those openly urging an impartial trial for Morris, one conducted solely on the facts and the law, were also those who would have had him convicted and, it was said, despite his condition,   hanged forthwith, seemingly included the region's preeminent Protestant peer, at least a dozen prominent Church of Ireland clergymen, more than that number of stalwartly Protestant squires, as well as a vocal minority of the all-Protestant members of the Muskerry Constitutional Society, who had judged the case.

So, it was said that in death, Arthur O'Leary had brought about the first significant public fissure in the Protestant Ascendancy of County Cork. Never again would there be the absolute certainty, as there had been for generations, of the hegemonous unity of the Ascendancy, that when its leaders spoke, they spoke for all, that when Protestants acted, they did so in full accord, that the Ascendancy was single-mindedly strong, its permanence in power certain and assured.

It would never be the same again. This would never be the case ever again.

Kilcrea Abbey, Ovens, County Cork, Ireland—mid-November 1773

For Eileen—and for Squire O'Leary, as he had slowly, sadly settled back into life at Rathleigh House, as well as for Catherine, now returned to spending most of her time in Cork City—a continuing frustration was their inability to have Art's final interment on the grounds of the ruined Kilcrea Abbey, located in Ovens, some eleven miles west of Cork City.

Even as she numbly watched as her beloved Arthur was interred at the graveyard at Dun na Radharc, the ruins of the ancient castle of the O'Flynns in Kilnamartyr, Eileen knew that it was at Kilcrea that she ultimately would see him rest.

O'Leary had first introduced the site to her on a blissful spring day not long after his return from Vienna. The little boys happy with their doting grandfather, the couple had headed off very early and ridden largely aimlessly for miles over the verdant green countryside, first in one direction, then the other, until early in the afternoon they reached the banks of the gentle River Bride, at which point O'Leary observed, "'Tis for sure in the very heart of the Barony of Muskerry that we now are, the ancient domain of the MacCarthys, it is."

He sat quietly for a moment and then smiled at Eileen. "You must see a place ... 'tis not far, my love." Without awaiting a response, he gently booted Banrían and she shot ahead, Eileen and Bull promptly joining them.

They had ridden up from the riverbank onto higher ground, which looked back down at the sprightly waterway. As they came up over a rise, O'Leary slowed, gesturing with his gauntleted right hand. "Kilcrea," he'd said softly, "Kilcrea Abbey ... or 'Friary,' some say," and Eileen's eyes fell upon a sprawling ruin of what she immediately concluded must have been a truly magnificent monastic house.

As they approached it slowly, her mind gently wandering to Gaelic Ireland, Eileen silently thought of Ballycarbery Castle, where, during those times, her O'Connell forebears had served the Lords of Desmond as hereditary warders, it, too, having fallen victim to English hordes. She heard O'Leary's resonant voice just as he was saying, "... the Observant Franciscans," and she realised he had been speaking. Smiling, she apologised for being distracted.

Undaunted, O'Leary continued, "... so 'twas in the mid-fifteenth century—1465 or so, I believe—that Cormac MacCarthy, the lord of Muskerry himself, established Kilcrea for the Franciscans. He lies buried here ... I shall show you, as I have always felt it a special place." Dismounting, permitting the horses to graze in the thickening grasses, they ambled, hand in hand, into the roofless ruin. Eileen could readily see that a fine church it had been; gazing about, she could tell that they were approaching the choir. Its bell tower, looming from its place at the far wall, appeared much like an ancient Gaelic tower house, constructed to protect noble families from invading enemies. As she gazed up at it in silence, O'Leary recalled, "Up there—"he gestured along her line of sight—"'tis said a magnificent rood cross enhanced by gold and silver once hung."

"One must wonder if the poor holy monks awaited the English invaders *up there*," she gestured, an edge to her voice. O'Leary nodded, and they walked a moment in silence before Art recalled, "'Tis also said that the rood cross—indeed the place—"he gestured wide—"the entire friary, the church, the monastery, all of it itself was destroyed in the 1580s." He shook his head. Indeed history records that in 1584 the great friary and its, in many ways, breathtaking interior was plundered by English soldiers, who were said to have hacked at statues and paintings of Christ, His Blessed Mother and various biblical scenes, slashing at ancient tapestries, regardless of what scenes or subjects they depicted.

They walked perhaps another twenty-five feet.

"There," he pointed, "there 'tis Cormac's tomb." They took a few more steps and halted.

Eileen leaned forward, reading the Latin inscription. "'Here lies Cormac, son of Teig, son of Dermot MacCarthy, lord of Muskerry, and founder of this convent, 1494.'"

She straightened. "So . . . worshipped here presumably he did for almost three decades," she observed, "and after a long life was well-spared witnessing the Tudor hordes and Cromwell's blood-drenched armies desecrate and ultimately destroy what he had built." She shook her head. O'Leary could hear the hostility in her voice. They rarely spoke of the dispossession of the native Irish Catholic nobility and aristocracy; they both knew who they were and from whom and what they had come.

Shaking off her bitter reverie, she took her husband's hand. "'Tis a striking and a moving place, indeed my darling love. I agree 'tis a most special place, and lovely . . . yes, in a sad way, 'tis quite lovely indeed."

The thought of it as a fitting resting place for her husband had come to her the night of his murder, though she knew that arrangements could not be made in time and, in her numbness, she was thus grateful for the proximity of the burial site offered by the O'Flynns.

It was only after Arthur had been dead several weeks that Eileen would learn that, yet again, the Penal Laws could impact even the most private, most profound of decisions, of actions: burying one's dead.

Beginning in mid-June, Eileen, with the help of Andrew Baggot, had laboured to dislodge the enforcement of what they all viewed as being a mindlessly vindictive and obscure provision of *An Act for explaining . . . an Act to Prevent the further Growth of Popery*, which provided, amongst a number of other things, that in order for Catholics to bury their dead in a ruined abbey or monastery, they would incur a penalty of ten pounds. When she first learnt of the fee, Eileen expressed her willingness to pay virtually any amount to have Arthur finally interred at Kilcrea. It was then that she came to understand that the real issue was that the strict construction of the provision, as practised in Cork, held that burial in Catholic monastic grounds remained forbidden; despite that, as with so many other aspects of the now unevenly enforced, solely punitive legal regime, as the eighteenth century moved towards its final quarter, the local authorities in many Irish counties more frequently looked away from its strict enforcement.

This was not so in County Cork, as they had discovered that, from his sickbed, Morris had threatened an elderly Franciscan friar, who lived in Cork City and had no connection with Kilcrea, that "punishment under the full weight of the laws of the United Kingdom" would befall him were O'Leary to be buried at the ruined abbey.

In the weeks following Morris's trial, Cameron and Baggot succeeded in convincing Davidson and Aiken to join together with them to overturn the prior ruling of the magistrates. Several unsubtle visits by Squire James Walker and a number of his like-minded friends to the four young, silent magistrates, as well as others who rarely participated in any proceedings, convinced them they should support it. At the request of the Muskerry Constitutional Society, in early November, the assizes court for County Cork issued a formal decree permitting *the earthly remains of Capt. Arthur O'Leary, dec'd* to, at long last, be interred at Kilcrea.

Well before dawn on what would be the appropriately gloomy, grey morning of Wednesday, 18 November, under John Collins's and Johnny O'Callaghan's sombrely watchful gaze, the two friends standing shoulder to shoulder in near-silence, by the efficient efforts of a pair of diggers flanked by several blazing torches stuck in the ground, O'Leary's coffin had been disinterred at Dun na Radharc and brought in Collins's simple farm wagon, lying atop a bed of fresh, clean hay, to Rathleigh.

There, a small cortege of carriages and traps had formed and awaited them.

Led by a today extremely weary-looking young widow, once again regal in her magnificent Viennese mourning robe, holding her sons' hands, a small group composed of Squire O'Leary, John and Anna Collins, Andrew Baggot and Johnny O'Callaghan, together with the close-to-the-family coterie of servants, Ann, Mary, Seamus and Henry, as well as perhaps a dozen representatives of the O'Leary tenants, along with several neighbours, all journeyed from Rathleigh to Kilcrea Abbey, a distance of some sixteen miles, necessitating the dawn departure. Catherine O'Leary would await them at the ruined friary, having been driven out of Cork City in her own coach, planning to return to Rathleigh, with her father joining her in her conveyance for that journey.

In addition to being both emotionally and physically weary this melancholy morning, Eileen was also extremely bitter. Though she'd said nothing to anyone but Anna, once it was clear that Arthur could be reinterred at Kilcrea, she had written to her mother as well as her brothers, Maurice and Morgan, advising them of the fact and of the approximate date of the burial, noting that, unlike his temporary interment on the O'Flynns' property, this arrangement would now afford them adequate time to journey over from Kerry. In doing so, she wrote hopefully, they would *bring the spirit of great Derrynane and some of the legendary strength of the O'Connells* to the occasion, and to her and her sons.

Only two days before the date set, she'd received a pair of notes. "They are not at all worthy of being characterised as letters," she'd scoffed bitterly to her dearest friend. There was no response at all from Maurice, whilst her mother, Maire Ni Dhuibh, pled *advancing age, ever-increasing infirmity* and opined that *It is* your *legendary strength that shall sustain you, daughter—not something one might "bring" from this place from which you have been long absent.*

Her brother, Morgan, was at least candid, *the circumstances surrounding O'Leary's death have caused much talk, much rancour in the neighbourhood all spring and summer, indeed a pair of British officers stopped here some weeks back to specifically inquire of me the closeness of our, the O'Connells', connection to your slain husband. To deflect their interest and avoid further discussion, I felt compelled to indicate the relationship was a "distant one," for which I apologise to you, dear sister . . . nevertheless, believing that attendance at the rites at Kilcrea would exacerbate an already-tense relationship with the current men of the king in Iveragh, I shall not be present.*

"So much for the dashing, powerful clan spirit of the bloody O'Connells, aye?" she observed to Anna as she tossed both messages into the fire before which they'd been seated.

"We shall go and return in a single day," Eileen had requested of Collins unsubtly, with which he took no issue. He agreed with her when she added, "I have no desire to prolong my stay away from my home . . . 'tis at Rathleigh that I believe Arthur's spirit dwells and comforts me, 'tis his bones alone shall lie in this sadly majestic place where I feel he would wish them to be."

Despite O'Leary's attachment to the location, and Eileen's commitment to have her husband interred there, as her carriage, in the lead, directly behind Collins's wagon, turned from the Cork City road into the oak-lined entranceway leading up to the friary itself, Eileen could not help but note that the rough, poorly kept road was, in addition to the impressive stand of oak trees, flanked by what a historian would, in a book to be published within a year, describe as being "high banks formed entirely of human bones and skulls cemented together with moss . . ." She gazed upon the gruesome site and shuddered, grateful that her sons, snuggled up against her, distracted by an ample basket containing some picture books, several issues of the *Lilliputian Magazine,* as well as some small toys, did not notice. Reflecting on the grisly image later on, she realised that when Arthur had brought her to Kilcrea, the only other time she'd been there until today, they'd come cross-country and had not approached the ruins via the oak-lined road.

As the small, sad cortege lurched to a halt near the ruined friary, the collective mood was not quite anticlimactic, but, as Anna Collins reflected, *We have done our grieving, shed our public tears; 'tis as much a memorial to Arthur as anything else. We have simply brought him to where he is meant to rest.*

The wagon carried O'Leary's simple wooden coffin to what had been a side entrance to the now-roofless abbey church, grass and weeds growing where once the monks and the Catholic faithful had stood and knelt to pray. Collins, O'Callaghan and Baggot, joined by Seamus and Henry, hoisted the casket one last time and lumbered it through the entryway and, turning right, walking gently towards the choir, shortly reached a spot along the wall between a pair of gaps in the thick stone that had, before Cromwell, held magnificent stained-glass windows. There, a grave had been dug, its dirt piled to one side, some half-dozen or more rough-handled shovels left by the diggers resting against the wall.

As, similar to the lane outside, the ruined interior of the once-majestic monastery church now, as the local historian would describe in his book, contained "several [thousand more skulls], piled up in the arches . . . and windows," someone, most likely 'twas whoever had dug the grave, had thoughtfully scoured a significant space some fifty feet in both directions about the area where O'Leary was to be buried of this impossibly sad detritus of the charnel house.

Eileen and the others came together in a semicircle, the little O'Leary boys between their mother and Aunt Catherine, the four of them holding hands, the group growing quiet, almost sombre.

The O'Learys' not having had a regular priest in residence for some time, and Father Tomás Ó Sé, the heroic Jesuit so long in service to the Collins clan at Derryleigh having died in the past year, Eileen made it clear that she did not desire a strange priest to be present, ". . . the ground in which Arthur shall rest surely being consecrated by the blood spilt here in centuries past by the English marauders," she told an understanding John Collins.

Eileen had also advised Collins that she would not approach the coffin, and so it was that, under his direction, the now grim-faced bearers took several heavy ropes, with which they cradled the simple casket and gently lowered it into the grave.

An awkward silence lay heavily on the gathered whilst Collins and the others as respectfully as possible, swiftly covered the unpretentious coffin with the grave's sandy dirt until, gently letting go of her sons' hands, Eileen finally stepped forward, her eyes fixed on the head of the casket, looking directly upon the wood beneath which her husband's stilled, upraised face lay, and began slowly, her husky voice firm, certain:

My love and my treasure,
Though I bring with me
No throng of mourners,
'Tis no shame for me,
For my kinsmen are wrapped in
A sleep beyond waking,
In narrow coffins
Walled up in stone.
Though but for the smallpox,
And the black death,
And the spotted fever,
That host of riders
With bridles shaking
Would wake the echoes,
Coming to your waking,
Art of the white breast.
Could my calls but wake my kindred
In Derrynane beyond the mountains,
Or Capling of the yellow apples,

Many a proud and stately rider,
Many a girl with spotless kerchief,
Would be here before tomorrow,
Shedding tears about your body,
Art O'Leary, once so merry.

Her voice grew suddenly gentle as she seemingly spoke to her husband:

My love and my secret,
Your corn is stacked,
Your cows are milking;

Then grew louder, harsher, evoking her raw pain:

On me is the grief
There's no cure for in Munster.
Till Art O'Leary rise
This grief will never yield
That's bruising all my heart
Yet shut up fast in it,
As 'twere in a locked trunk
With the key gone astray,
And rust grown on the wards.
My love and my calf,
Noble Art O'Leary,
Son of Conor, son of Cady,
Son of Lewis O'Leary,
West of the Valley
And east of Greenane
Where berries grow thickly
And nuts crowd on branches
And apples in heaps fall
In their own season;

What wonder to any
If Iveleary lighted
And Ballingeary
And Gougane of the saints
For the smooth-palmed rider,
The unwearying huntsman
That I would see spurring
From Grenagh without halting
When quick hounds had faltered?
My rider of the bright eyes,
What happened to you "yesterday"?
I thought you in my heart,
When I brought you your fine clothes,
A man the world could not slay.

The last line spoken in a strong voice, she paused before continuing,

Rider of the white palms,
Go in to [she raised her voice] Baldwin, [turning her head, she spat on the ground]
And face the schemer,
The bandy-legged monster—
God rot him and his children!
(Wishing no harm to Maire
Yet of no love for her,
But that my mother's body
Was a bed to her for three seasons
And to me beside her.)
Her husky voice now again softened:
Take my heart's love,
Dark women of the Mill,
For the sharp rhymes ye shed
On the rider of the brown mare.

> *But cease your weeping now,*
> *Women of the soft, wet eyes*
> *Till Art O'Leary drink*
> *Ere he go to the dark school—*
> *Not to learn music or song*
> *But to prop the earth and the stone.*

Scanning the setting, lifting her eyes to the roofless reaches of the ruin, Eileen softly but firmly repeated, "*. . . to prop the earth and the stone*," finishing with a deep, audible sigh.

Without hesitation, shaking her head gently, she abruptly turned and began to walk away, her expression trancelike, her sons quickly scurrying to catch up, immediately grasping her reflexively outstretched hands. She did not stop; she did not look back. Nor did the little boys.

Derryleigh, County Cork—late November 1773

It was shortly after breakfast on a tumultuously windy, brilliantly sunny day in late November. Both of "my wee lads," as she had come to collectively refer to Conor and Fiach, had been sick with heavy colds, and Eileen felt she had been house-bound for long enough. Announcing to Ann and Mary merely that she was "headed out," without changing from her full-skirted, heavy, grey wool dress, she wrapped herself in her arasaid; clasping its heavy pewter brooch, gathering the thick leather belt about herself, Eileen strode to the stables, saddled Bull and thundered away cross-country.

For the next several hours, horse and rider were as one: Sharing the exuberance of effortlessly flying over walls and outcroppings, unexpected ditches and through surprisingly fast-flowing streams, even then barely slowing, taking no notice of her billowing skirts, and boots becoming wet and mud-spattered, Eileen experienced an emotional, nearly a physical release as, more than once, she merely gave the stallion his head and let him carry her wherever he wanted to go.

As she had thought she ultimately would when she'd departed Rathleigh, shortly before noon, her skirts still damp and, along with much of the rest of her, muddied, a weary Eileen and Bull thudded slowly up the serpentine track leading to Derryleigh. The impressively large though simply constructed red-brick Georgian dwelling appeared stark against the dramatic late-autumn sky. The backdrop was first sunny then not, darkly clouded then lightly so then blue sky and sun. As she drew up in front of the Collinses' home, one of the younger stable boys, whose name she did not know, called out, "Mistress O'Leary!" as he raced to take Bull.

Leaning back and throwing her right leg over the horse's head, Eileen slid easily off Bull, drew off her gloves and, lifting the gleaming brass knocker, rapped sharply at the brilliantly bright red door. The colour made her smile; *so like Anna, so unlike John Collins.*

Having spied her unexpected caller from an upper window, Anna Collins herself responded to Eileen's knock with, as she sometimes did, a playful, "Mistress! How may I serve you today?" and the women would laugh and embrace, effusively cheek kissing, as they invariably did.

Just outside the door, Eileen removed her boots and shook the mostly dry clumps of mud from her skirts. She then followed her friend into her home, and up to Maria Theresa's nursery, where Anna had been reading to the bright little not-quite-eighteen-month-old, flaxen-haired girl, who greeted "Auntie Eileen!" as Anna called out to her, announcing Eileen's arrival with gurgles and an exuberant hug with her chubby arms and hands.

The little girl having fallen asleep in Eileen's arms, Anna easing the child into her tiny bed, the women ultimately settled by a fire in a cosy, back-of-the-first-floor nook of the house, an alcove with its own hearth—the fire was roaring at the moment—and two luxurious, high-backed, padded chairs. They chatted briefly about the weather and the children. Anna no longer inquired specifically as to Eileen's well-being; her friend had been a widow for just six months, and she was doing as well as any woman whose husband had been slain could be expected.

The conversation had momentarily ebbed, and both women were gazing into the dancing flames, each lost for a moment in her own thoughts.

Anna reached for her friend's left hand with her right; the chairs were that close, and Eileen looked at her, as the shorter woman began to speak quietly, Eileen noticing her German accent more today than usual.

Having wanted to for some weeks, Anna began, "I have been for a time wondering, my darling," she said, and Eileen cocked her head slightly. "There is perhaps no correct, no gentle way to pose the question, but . . . you have never expressed your feelings, and indeed I have never inquired, but if I may, have you feelings in terms of the vengeance you and others have extracted for your darling Arthur's murder?"

Anna paused, but then continued, her voice gentle, though she felt her words were challenging. "Does it not matter, for example, that at least some of these men could be said to have been doing nothing more than their duty, that their actions were controlled by other men?"

She instantly regretted posing the questions, especially the second one.

Eileen's expression was at first almost quizzical as she actually smiled slightly; sensing Anna's feelings and hoping to dispel her regret, she shook her head gently. "I have posed this very pair of questions to myself, my love; considered the topic from time to time I have . . . and my conclusion each time remains the same:

"Whilst Morris is the most craven, the most evil of them all . . . and Greene, the soldier, the one who actually fired the shot that killed Arthur . . . all of them, each of them bears responsibility for his murder: MacAteer for his weakness in permitting the dastardly loathsome Morris to browbeat him into providing him with the soldiers; each of the soldiers for nothing more than being armed and firing on command . . . were it not Greene, 'twould have been one of the nameless others, Morris being too much of a coward to take the shot himself." Her voice was even, almost detached.

Anna studied Eileen's calm demeanour, her peaceful expression, then chancing to inquire further, "Do you not for an instant regret their deaths, my love?"

Her friend's passion evident only by the fact that Anna saw her eyes flash, her cheeks instantly flame and her hands momentarily become fists in her lap, Eileen shook her head firmly and leaned slightly forward, her palms resting on her knees. Thinking *the shortest response is simple and true*, so she answered, her voice coldly unwavering. "No . . . I do not, not at all, not for an instant, *no*." She finished firmly and shook her head for emphasis.

"Lest you think me callous or cavalier concerning such a grave subject, I would say to you further that 'twas I who begged for the wrath of God. I implored God in his Holy Trinity to make of me and mine His instruments of punishment for what these men did to Arthur. . . . Even after these months, I believe that my actions, my instigation . . . and indeed the deeds of dear, brave Conor O'Leary, not to mention those of your own darling heart, and Baggot and the others with them . . . With all my heart and to the very depths of my soul, I believe we were doing the work of the Almighty and indeed only His work, and that solely as His temporal authorities in this realm had failed utterly in doing their duties."

Anna nodded, saying nothing, her eyes moist.

Eileen in turn nodded firmly again, continuing, "No, my love, 'twas God's Holy Will that we succeeded . . . how else but by the hand of God Himself could the complex plan, devised by your brave husband and Conor the Younger, equally brave, to lure Morris out of his lair, so as to make his execution possible, have unfolded so perfectly?   . . . No matter this, should God come to feel differently, I have more than once told Him that 'tis I and I alone whom He must hold responsible for these deeds. . . . If someone is to be cast into the flaming pits of Hell, it shall be myself and no other. My only prayer is that I am able to see my beloved before being dispatched into Hades." She paused, continuing now in a softly but deeply passionate tone, "This having been said, I know God, God most certainly knows me . . . I have been a loyal if not always meek and pious nor an always obedient daughter to Him; I have the greatest, the most certain faith that I shall not be punished for seeking vengeance on those who murdered the love of my life, the father of our sons."

She looked at her friend, whose eyes were brimming, her lips quivering and then turned to the fire.

After a few moments, Eileen stood, opening her arms to Anna. "Now, my love, might we have tea?" Anna smiled in relief and, standing, stepped into her friend's embrace. Arm in arm, then, they walked towards the kitchen house.

Rathleigh House—December 1773–Spring 1774

A dreary, chill mid-December day—the latest in a series of them, it seemed— had dragged itself towards a nearly imperceptible dusk when pounding on Rathleigh's gleaming black front door summoned the inevitable dogs, along with, as was often the case these days, little Conor O'Leary racing in their midst.

As Eileen had cautioned him to never admit any visitor, ". . . not until a big person is with you, my love," after peering through one of the delicately frosted parlour windows, the little boy impatiently awaited his mother, who had only herself just arrived from a visit to the McAuliffes' cottage. Learning that Mary was suffering a heavy cold, she had brought her a fresh box of tea and some biscuits and, as was frequently the case, wound up staying longer than she'd planned.

Still in her heavy black, wool riding cloak, covering a short, tweed coat, buff-coloured breeches and, but for some streaks of mud, otherwise gleaming black boots, Eileen strode to the window, ruffling her son's blond hair as the unexpected visitor helpfully held up a battered envelope, addressed in what she recognised as being the precise hand of an imperial court scrivener, to the window. She gestured for an impatiently ready Conor to open the door, admitting its bearer, a short, red-haired, red-faced little fellow, almost buried in a too-big greatcoat, who smiled an endearing, slightly gap-toothed grin as he handed her the envelope, advising in Irish that, "Squire Collins, he sent me, mistress." His eyes grew slightly wide as he added, almost solemnly, "The message, the squire says, 'tis come from *Vienna*, mistress. . . . I know not where that place is, but the squire, he says 'tis very, *very* far away, mum!"

As she plucked the thick, water-stained and rather battered envelope from his gloved fingers, Eileen flashed one of her gleaming smiles, replying in her lyrical Kerry Irish, "Ah, m'lad, aye, Vienna, 'tis indeed very, very, *very* far!"

Ann had by then bustled into the hall, immediately gesturing to the obviously grateful young courier. "Freezing it is you must be, lad; come for tea . . . and . . ." Hearing the word ". . . biscuits" spoken as an afterthought, Conor immediately hurried to join them.

Smiling at her little boy and calling out her thanks again to the chilled little courier, after draping her cloak over a chair and tearing open the envelope, Eileen dropped casually into a large, leather wing chair, half-facing the generously warm fire, tearing open the scruffy envelope as she did. She smiled again as she began to read the letter within, headed, *Vienna, 3 October 1773*, the elegant hand, the idiosyncratically swirling script belonging, she knew, to Colonel Wolfgang von Klaus.

Beginning with what Eileen felt were, despite their brevity, additional thoughtful and sincere condolences on Arthur's death, he having sent a lengthy letter from Vienna in May, speaking of the younger junior officer as *a true gentleman, a rising star in the firmament of the armies of Her Imperial Majesty,* von Klaus spoke feelingly of her widowhood and what he called her *innate bravery, I am certain evidencing strength beyond that of most people.* She stopped reading and rested her head back, the gentle hiss and popping of the turf fire, the barely audible swinging of the heavy brass pendulum of the tall clock in the corner being the only sounds, as she shook her head gently, visualising, for the first time in ages, what seemed like a lifetime ago when she and the letter's author had periodically shared her bed. She sighed and smiled weakly, ironically.

It was the next paragraph that caused her eyes to widen, as it was therein that von Klaus quite casually announced that

as I am told by those—being your beloved and honoured sister and General the Count O'Connell himself—familiar with such a journey, I shall arrive in your country before Christmas, and I shall thus very much enjoy spending Christmas with you and your family.

She laughed aloud. "Ah, Wolfgang, you are nothing if not your dearly presumptuous self!" Then she read on:

Thus, I write now as I am also informed that a letter carried from Vienna requires not more than six weeks to reach Ireland—indeed frequently less, your dearest Abigail advises—so you shall know well in advance of the time when to anticipate my arrival.

Eileen laughed again, thinking, *So much for mail from Vienna in six weeks . . . Christmas is in but a week and a few days!* Standing abruptly, she stalked through the house in search of Squire O'Leary, to whom, upon locating him in the library, she would announce, "My darling Father, it appears we shall be having an unexpected guest for Christmas. . . ."

And so they did.

Catherine O'Leary made a gift-laden arrival, her gleaming new black coach bursting with wine and food baskets as well as books and toys, on 18 December, followed on the 20th by that of a magnificently uniformed Wolfgang von Klaus, mounted on a handsome hired horse, leading a wagon filled with what Eileen could not imagine, driven by a slightly awed-looking young lad.

But it was the day separating the two joyous comings that, for Eileen, would prove to be amongst the most profound she would ever experience, for it was but six years prior, on 19 December 1767, that she and Arthur O'Leary had been wed, in this house that she now considered to be her home.

Awakening before dawn, on what was to be a brilliantly sunny though bitterly cold day, the young widow remained abed, a pair of puffy, densely filled goose-down Vienna quilts and simple white Egyptian sheeting between her naked body and the chill of the bedroom. She slowly rolled towards Arthur's side, her hair loose about her, tousled on the mound of pillows, closed her eyes and let her silent tears come and pass, remaining there as morning's light slowly, almost grudgingly appeared. Lying still, she heard Rathleigh creak softly once or twice in the frigid air, heard the distant sound of at least one pair of falcons circling, she thought, low above where she lay, and a husky though solitary bark of one of the family's lumbering Irish wolfhounds, whom she pictured still asleep and perhaps dreaming, sprawled before a barely flickering fire, somewhere downstairs.

As a ribbon of sunlight appeared to slice the space between the gleaming dark wood of the floor and the delicately worn splendour of the Chinese carpet upon which stood her bed, Eileen wriggled from beneath the covers, immediately donning a heavy dressing gown, into the right-hand pocket of which she had the night before slid a thick envelope. Retrieving that envelope, she removed a small newspaper cutting from the weekly Corke *Journal* ,published shortly after their marriage. Sitting on the edge of her bed, she held it in her long, elegant fingers, and for how long or how many times she could never be certain, she read softly aloud its few words:

MARRIED,
MR. ARTHUR O'LEARY, MACROOM,
TO
THE WIDOW O'CONNOR OF IVERAGH,
19 DECEMBER 1767

As she did, a myriad of images appeared, vivid and immediate: the bustling market square at Macroom in the autumn of 1767; her early morning gallop the following day from the Baldwins' to Rathleigh and the first time she and Arthur had spoken words of love, of marriage, only to be followed by the disaster of their mission to Derrynane and the dangers of their flight from thence. She smiled at reflections of their wedding—*just downstairs*—and of O'Leary's presentation at court in Vienna, when the empress had been so wonderfully coquettish! . . . and of Conor's arrival at Laxenburg and the awe of the handsome young father.

Permitting her mind's eye to wander freely, it ultimately presented her with visions so horrible, so powerful such that they caused her to gasp aloud, to involuntarily drop the cutting on the carpet and to hold herself as she sobbed bitterly and aloud, hugging herself, rocking gently as her body heaved, some of her tears falling on the newsprint as she gazed down on it.

She wept until she ultimately stopped, feeling as if she had yet again shed every tear she ever had for Arthur and herself. Taking a deep breath, she finally stood and, bending, retrieved the tear-splotched newspaper cutting, laying it on her dresser, smoothing it. Running her fingers through her thick hair, she let her robe slide off and within moments was dressed. Stepping before the long looking glass on the door of the armoire that still contained O'Leary's uniforms, swords and pistols, a pair of boots and his elegant, fur-trimmed pelisse, she studied herself, something she rarely did anymore.

That her eyes were puffy and red she did not care; her long hair hung loosely and barely brushed over her broad shoulders, down her back and over the front of her thick, rough, brown tweed redingote, beneath which she wore one of her husband's white linen shirts, its blousiness made less so by her full breasts. Gleaming black boots peeked out from below the hem of a flowing, heavy, grey Scottish wool skirt. She nodded at herself—the *Widow O'Leary*, she shook her head gently as she yet again heard the words in her mind—and headed downstairs; donning her coarsely thick, dull plaid arasaid, which she had lifted from a rack by the door to the kitchen house, gathering the wool's folds at her bosom, clasped with a heavy pewter brooch, the one with the O'Connell stag at the centre, then belting herself about her hips with the heavy strap meant for that purpose, she stepped immediately outside.

She strode silently past the structure and towards the barns. Having spoken to Seamus the evening before, he emerged from the stable with a fully tacked Banrían, the horse nodding and whinnying at the sight of she whom she now saw as her mistress.

The young man nodded as well, then, with a cock of his head at Banrían murmuring, "Herself, she has breakfasted, mistress."

Eileen whispered, "Thank you" and mounted. First feeling for the rough envelope, the words on its cutting repeating themselves for her, she drew on her gloves and clicked to the gentle mare.

Stopping first at the dry-stacked wall of the horse's pasture, horse and rider sat quietly as Eileen felt O'Leary slowly enveloping her mind, her heart, her body even. *Good morning, my darling love. Share with me today the joyous memories that it brings.*

Her gaze then fell upon a patch of ground, the existence and precise location of which only she knew, only she would ever know. *Good morning, my wee little angel . . . I am certain you are the most beautiful of God's tiny angels. . . .* She shook her head as she began again to weep—and stopped as abruptly as she had begun. . . . *Enough, no more,* she heard her mother's long-ago admonition.

She turned Banrían's head away from the pasture and they trotted silently away. Eileen almost immediately giving the gentle young mare her head, they were soon racing across the countryside, Banrían taking rocks and streams, the occasional random fence with ease. They would slow and pause, Eileen stroking her husband's beloved mount, speaking softly to the horse, whose head turned, and ears flicked as she did, only to shortly resume their at-times-frantic pace.

As the late December sun set almost abruptly and the gloam came upon them, Eileen instinctively slowed the horse, took measure of where and how approximately distant from home they were. Turning Banrían's head in that direction, they cantered and even walked some for well over an hour thence.

They arrived at Rathleigh well after nightfall.

Seamus having taken the still-sprightly mare, Eileen nuzzled her and kissed her nose before she strode towards the house, where Catherine O'Leary silently greeted Eileen at the door, her arms open. Stepping into her sister-in-law's embrace, it was only when the shorter woman began to speak what she clearly intended to be words of comfort, of affection and herself began to weep that Eileen leaned back and gently placed the tip of her right forefinger on Catherine's slightly chapped lips, gently shaking her head, silently conveying, *Enough. No more.* With her thumb, she wiped the tears from her sister-in-law's ruddy cheeks, then, leaning forward, she kissed the older woman's forehead. *Enough. No more.*

Arm in arm for the first time ever the women walked towards the empty dining room, Squire O'Leary and the lads being at Derryleigh for the night, where Catherine would see to her sister's evening meal. She would also assist her in preparing for bed. Between the two events, having mutually committed to and succeeding in not weeping, over brandies by the fire they shared soft memories and more than a few funny stories of the young man they had both loved.

Eileen would long remember the day as an altogether profoundly sad, albeit remarkable one.

The following morning—closer to noontime actually—one of yet another series of brilliantly sunny though bitterly cold days, Colonel Wolfgang von Klaus arrived.

In the course of the noisy canine and little boy–led welcome by the household, Eileen again noticed the colonel's still striking appearance: Though she found it hard to believe, she knew he was nearing, if he had not already reached, fifty, von Klaus stood an imposing six feet and at least three inches; he had grown bulkier in the chest and around the middle, yet he remained solid, his thick blond hair longer, tied in a dramatic plait, his face fuller, his eyes no less blue. Unlike many Austrian and Hungarian officers, he was, as were virtually all the Irish officers in the Austrian military, clean-shaven.

As he stepped into the broad hall, looking up at him, Conor observed softly, "My papa, he has a red coat, too, sir," and the distinguished officer's eyes misted over.

Dropping his gauntlets to the floor, von Klaus instantly knelt before the now- sombre lad, placing his large hands on his shoulders. His eyes looking deeply into Conor's, he said softly, speaking his English slowly, precisely, "Your papa was a brave and beloved young officer. I am much older than he, yes . . . and I was not fortunate to have been with him a Hungarian Hussar, but, as you and your mama and brother, and—" he looked around the gathered adults, quickly verbalising his correct assumptions— "your grandpapa and your auntie," he smiled at Catherine, "I am certain all miss Captain O'Leary, so, too, you will know do all of his brothers-in-arms in Vienna . . . very much so, as does the empress herself."

Tears streaming down his cheeks, still ruddy from the cold, the usually reserved officer stood slowly, bending again to embrace both little boys as Mary came to lead them away. Only then did he retrieve his gloves.

Noting that, given the colonel's accurate surmises, they might not be necessary, Eileen moved quickly through the brief introductions of family and staff, smiling gratefully as von Klaus softly kissed her hand.

As Seamus and Henry assisted the still-agog young lad driving von Klaus's heavily-ladened wagon in unloading its contents, the adults then gathered in the smaller parlour, some coal added to the turf having made the room quite warm. It was only as she casually took her seat that Eileen noticed that Catherine, already having completed a deep formal curtsey, was now standing mutely agog, her hand resting in the elegant officer's, her mouth ever so slightly agape, a delicately pinched expression on her face as she appeared to be experiencing difficulty understanding the colonel's thickly German-flavoured English. Eileen found it too amusing to interrupt, as her own ears adjusted more easily to the manner of speech.

The family's first Christmas without Arthur was more festive than Eileen had ever imagined it could be. Unexpectedly buoyed by Colonel von Klaus's effusive presence and the ongoing comic relief unintentionally being provided by her obviously smitten sister-in-law, Eileen had conducted a successful search for the heavy, broad-skirted, fully trained, deep red velvet robe she had worn on several happy Christmases in Vienna. For the little boys, the focus was primarily on gifts, though presents, largely a variety of fine books, were exchanged amongst the adults. In addition to the gift books he'd brought, von Klaus also presented the O'Learys, to Eileen's special delight, with cases of fine German wines and several substantial packages of the hardy Austrian Christmas bread, Christstollen, which had somehow managed to survive the journey from Vienna fully intact and delicious.

The colonel had brought a number of sets of small, exquisitely hand-painted metal soldiers for the little boys, including a perfectly rendered detachment of Hungarian Hussars, which he was both pleased and relieved to see delighted rather than saddened Conor, for whom, being the older one, they were specifically intended. Though he had never before done so with any child, von Klaus joined Conor on the floor as, for the first time on Christmas night the little boy set out all the miniature soldiers in his idea of battle array on the ornately detailed, thick wool Chinese parlour rug. Von Klaus patiently explained to him the position each man held and his responsibilities. As Eileen watched warmly, the two created and fought a mock skirmish, which ended as von Klaus assisted Conor in placing his Hungarian Hussars such that they encircled their opponents, compelling an immediate surrender. She almost burst into tears as the little boy jumped up and embraced his still-kneeling new friend, who looked up at Eileen in wonder, his own eyes full.

It was also von Klaus who provided Eileen with what she effusively exclaimed was the "best, the most wonderfully thoughtful Christmas gift!" in the form of Arthur's uniforms, personal effects—including a striking miniature oil of Eileen, painted at Laxenburg—his second formal dress sword and—she wept in the colonel's embrace as, the family looking on, she accepted the bundles from von Klaus—virtually all her letters to him, neatly tied up in a colourful array of ribbons.

Even as Christmas was approaching and throughout the festive days, Squire O'Leary almost immediately began using his Louvain-acquired albeit now-rusty German, as did Anna Collins, who announced softly—in English, Irish and German—at the Collins's traditional St. Stephen's Day festivities that she was again with child. The gathering erupted in cheers and applause as John Collins's beet-red face provided an additional cause for mirth.

Despite that Arthur's absence was profoundly felt, the atmosphere at Rathleigh was, if not wholly joyous, both pleasant and relaxed. In addition to taking delight in her sons' Christmas awe, Eileen's amusement was unexpectedly provided by her ofttimes starchy sister-in-law, whose continuing behaviour with "the colonel" had become, Eileen told Anna, "girlishly giddy." Eileen was, of course, aware that von Klaus enjoyed bright and attractive women and saw he was clearly amused by Catherine O'Leary, whom she noted, was liberally using "*Ja!*" at every possible opportunity and giggling coquettishly.

Catherine remained until after Twelfth Night and left a small birthday present for Eileen before she departed. Observing that her leave-taking from the colonel appeared to be a most reluctant one, Eileen smiled saucily but said nothing. Though he bid her an effusive farewell, complete with a formal kiss of her hand, which resulted in one final giggle, von Klaus appeared, to some significant degree, relieved as they together watched her carriage clatter through the open gate, observing to Eileen only that "your *dear sister*, she is a most, shall we say unusual woman, *ja?*"

Eileen took her friend's arm and led him back into the house, nodding. "*Ja*, she is indeed that!"

As the household began to settle into its post-Christmastide, midwinter routine, Eileen was pleased that von Klaus had remained. They rode almost daily across the frosty countryside, including paying a solemn visit to Arthur's grave at Kilcrea Abbey. Though attired in a heavy, rough Scottish tweed coat and well-worn breeches, von Klaus stood silently at attention, deep in his thoughts for a time, finally smartly saluting before he turned back to Eileen. "Is this not a very sad place—"he gestured with open arms—"a ruined monastery, a place of God and of learning, destroyed by those who would likewise seek to destroy our Holy Faith?" he wondered and observed.

It was only as they quietly took leave of the place, as they walked to where the horses were grazing on the thin winter grass, that Eileen had told her friend an abbreviated version of the day Arthur had first brought her here, "despite, or perhaps on account of, the abbey's history, even its sad, bloody aspects, I came to believe that Arthur would lie peacefully here, in a way more profound even than were he to be laid to rest at or proximate to Rathleigh." To this von Klaus nodded, though he would never again look upon Englishmen or their king in the same light as he had before coming to Kilcrea.

When they returned to Rathleigh, after handing the horses over to Seamus, Eileen took her friend's arm and led him to Banrían's pasture. "'Tis *here* I believe Arthur's joyful spirit dwells," she explained, "whilst his earthly remains lie at Ovens . . . which is, in a number of ways, yes, a very sad place indeed, it is here he is with us." Her left arm swept the prospect. As she looked at her friend, she saw that his eyes were yet again filled with tears.

One evening, after the little boys had been put to bed and Squire O'Leary had excused himself earlier than was his custom, von Klaus joined Eileen for brandy in the small, cosy family parlour. The pair was as comfortable as the setting, Eileen wearing a winter-heavy Scottish woollen dress with a simple blue-and-grey-plaid pattern, her bare feet tucked under its ample skirts. Von Klaus was relaxed in a well-worn linen shirt and black breeches, though he still had his boots on. Feeling chilled, he playfully wrapped a thick, voluminous Aran-made shawl about his ample shoulders as they settled by the fire.

Taking a deep draught, after gazing silently into the flames, he rested his intricately cut crystal snifter on his knee and looked gently at Eileen. "If you would permit me an observation, my dear . . . as an old friend, *ja?*"

Eileen nodded and sipped her brandy.

"As lovely as this place is—indeed more beautiful even than you and your beloved horseman and the other fine Irish in Vienna have described— I believe that, in time, you will waste away here. You are a vital, a wise and thoughtful . . . indeed, and of this you are well aware, a very handsome woman, *ja?*"

Eileen forced herself to remain silent, her eyes warm on her old friend.

After a long pause, he continued, almost abruptly announcing, "At some point, my dear Eileen, I believe you *must* return to Vienna!"

Eileen stifled a laugh when she saw how deadly serious he was.

Gently setting his glass on the small table their winged chairs flanked, von Klaus rested his elbows on his thighs, his large hands folded as if in prayer, leaning slightly forward towards Eileen. "The fact is, my dear friend, my beloved papa lies near death at Salzburg; he suffered a massive apoplexy in the autumn and remains unconscious, though still alive."

Eileen conveyed her thoughts with her eyes, with her expressive face.

"I am thus, you will know, then, soon to become Count von Klaus." He paused. "I thus shall be able to—and I would do so most joyfully, I assure you—offer you a title, a position, abundant, *ja*, virtually limitless resources." He smiled warmly. "I am very much aware indeed from the empress herself, that you declined much of this, in fact *all* of this—wealth, titles, lands—to depart Vienna when the Archduchess Maria Antonia did, and I so respected you for doing thus at that time, but . . . but, now . . . *now* is it not all wholly, entirely different?" He paused, looking deeply into Eileen's eyes. "I know that nothing—no honours, no title or vast wealth, certainly no man, could ever ease the hurt your heart daily bears for the captain, but, perhaps . . ." His voice drifted into momentary silence.

The wood in the fire crackled, whilst the turf hissed softly, the atmosphere in the room equally warm, gentle, even intimate, von Klaus let the Aran wrap slip off his shoulders. Not having seen him in shirtsleeves for some years, Eileen once again noticed how massive his shoulders were.

Her immediate thought was that she should be shocked, perhaps even appalled by von Klaus's suggestion. Discovering to her surprise that she was neither, she instead inquired softly, "So . . . you, you are . . . you are making a proposal of sorts, is that what you are doing, my dear Colonel?"

Von Klaus nodded, lowering his eyes and smiling sheepishly, almost boyishly. "*Ja* . . . one could say that, yes.

"I so desire not merely your happiness . . . your good company, *ja?* . . . but also your safety. My dear friend, I genuinely fear for you in this place. These men, the English king's men, they appear barbarians, no? What they have done here for years, for centuries, the abbey you showed me, and killed your beloved. I wish you and your lads to be safe."

Her eyes cast ever so slightly up at his, Eileen reached over and took his rough right hand in her smoother one, patting it with her left and smiling affectionately. "Ah, Wolfgang . . . never could I have imagined you here, much less here at *this* Christmastime, much less bringing me the treasure of Arthur's belongings and being so gracious and charming to my family—*especially* my dear sister!" She twinkled as he rolled his eyes. Quickly growing serious again, she continued, "But to suggest that I . . . that you . . . we . . . that we might wed; by this gesture, kind sir, you have truly stunned me."

Her mind whirring, a swift vision of a tall, dark, elegantly robed Countess von Klaus unexpectedly appearing, she paused momentarily, summarily dismissing it. "Though it is mere months since Arthur's murder, given, as you correctly suggest, the significantly changed circumstances of my life, I believe I must, and thus I shall indeed reflect on this, Wolfgang. . . . I am of course unable to make this decision whilst you are here, and . . ."

Von Klaus patted her arm. "I had no such expectation. . . . Take a year, *take more.*" He laughed, taking and kissing the back of her hand. "As I must indeed *ultimately* marry, I desire to wed only you, my Lady Eileen. We are friends these many years, yes—and I understand how deeply you loved Captain O'Leary, and he you. Never to replace him in your heart; I could not, I would not even attempt to . . . but, *friends.* It is not a bad thing for friends to wed, no?"

Eileen shook her head. "No, 'tis not a bad thing at all, my dear, dear friend."

Von Klaus was quiet for a moment. "An heir, *ja?* An heir I must have. Were we to, were you to . . . this would be, for us to . . ."

Eileen could only shake her head gently, smiling softly again. "Were we to wed, the activities involved in procuring for you an heir . . . I should find them most enjoyable, of this I am certain, my friend." They both blushed, each knowing the other was recalling their frequent and passionate nights in bed, though—to both—those years in Vienna now seemed much longer ago than they were.

"Should you reject me," he smiled affectionately, almost playfully, hanging his head, "you will know I shall be compelled to take a flighty, fluffy-headed little blonde German noble girl, but I would do so *solely* out of the requirement to produce a male heir. . . . You, however, *you* I should wed with only the greatest of joy, though I would hope an heir we would produce, *ja?* . . . Whatever you decide in your own good time, we shall forever be dear friends." He lifted her hand to his lips, kissing it gently.

He departed the following day.

As to von Klaus's proposal, Eileen would, in the ensuing months, through what proved to be a strange, dreary winter, one of frequent intense rain and thick fogs, of suffocatingly dank, oddly warm, windless days and often deathly still, heavy black nights, reflect more deeply and with a greater degree of intensity than she originally thought she would.

Conversing only with God—or, perhaps more frequently, with the Blessed Mother and St. Brigid, as well as with her own her heart and soul— Eileen grew increasingly certain that her immediate future lay in West Cork, coming to feel that months, perhaps even years might pass before she would, if ever, arrive at any life-changing decision, though fleeting images of Countess von Klaus and the life she and her sons could live in Vienna, unexpectedly but frequently intruded, repeatedly distracting her from what she sometimes believed was her firm conclusion. With her usual prescience, she nevertheless anticipated that, as more time passed, she would frequently permit herself the reverie of being Countess von Klaus, entertaining thoughts of what it would be like to be back in Austria, this time permanently, and as a titled woman.

As for now, however, as the powerful winds of spring 1774 ejected the singularly bizarre, snowless winter from West Cork, and as Eileen returned to her near-daily, much more lengthy rides on Bull, her thoughts turned more to whom she had become, who she now was, as opposed to whom she had been, or even to whom she might become. Sensing the powerful intimacy of her relationship with this place, with West Cork, she felt her once- and perhaps yet-again beloved Kerry and Derrynane, Ballyhar—Vienna even—all receding into the swirling Irish mists of the few still, grey days of spring, all ultimately being swept away by the arrival of the steady, south westerly winds from the Atlantic's warm ribbon of blue.

It was on a flawless, sun-dappled afternoon in mid-May 1774—two weeks more than a year since O'Leary's murder—that a boots and breeches clad Eileen, wearing as she still occasionally did one of her husband's linen shirts, found herself standing alone by the fence-topped, dry-stacked stone wall at Banrían's pasture, watching the mare frolic with her girlfriends, their background being the emerald-green hills of Cork as they gently fell away towards the horizon. She felt Arthur's spirit especially profoundly this day. "I am *home,* Arthur, my darling love," she spontaneously announced softly into the steady, fragrant breeze, her words on the wind reaching him, she was certain. "Home with you, my darling, I am," she said.

Hearing her sons at play in the distance, she added, ". . . and with our wee lads." She glanced at Banrían, who appeared to be looking directly at her, at the same moment thinking she might also have heard Bull's unmistakable whinnying two short fields away. "And home with the four-legged children, as well I am." She laughed.

She leaned her arms against the top rail, feeling the afternoon sun warm on her back, inhaling the spring-perfumed scents. She watched in amusement as a flock of what she still thought of as being "black-faced Kerry sheep" ambled about in a circle, bleating loudly, doing their very best to ignore a young border collie as, under the watchful maternal eye of his mother, Millie, for some years now as much a pet to the family as a valued working dog, he instinctively circled the flock, barking in joyful surprise at his apparent power as the sheep—albeit reluctantly—ultimately moved to their pens. Casting her eyes upward in response to their familiar piercing shrieks, Eileen followed a pair of falcons in the effortless elegance of their aerial dance.

As the birds arched high, then streaked away, her gaze again fell on the panorama spread before her.

"Yes, my dearest love, I am home," she said with certainty. "Indeed, I am."

And so she was.

And so it was that a sense of calm, perhaps one might even say one of peace, would come to settle upon Eileen, as well as upon Rathleigh and West Cork—at least for a time.

An Deireadh

As were were *Beyond Derrynane* and *Two Journeys Home,* so too, is *Bittersweet Tapestry* a work of fiction, and, once again, it has been the tantalisingly few facts that are actually known of Eileen's and the other O'Connells' lives that have provided the basic threads around which the tale itself is woven, into which strategic additions of numerous fictional and historical personalities and events have, I hope, seamlessly intertwined.

I have been a relatively serious student of the history of Eighteenth Century Europe, especially that of Ireland and France, for much of my life; one significant aspect of this being a continuing scholarly as well as personal interest in my extended family, many distant, and long-ago members of which, especially the characters of whom I write, I feel I have come to know intimately. Some of the tales which I grew up hearing, and later reading about, were the genesis for parts of both *Beyond Derrynane* and *Two Journeys Home.* This is even more so the case with regard to much of the Irish history fictionalised in *Bittersweet Tapestry.*

All of this notwithstanding, none of these books could have been written absent almost six decades of reading and studying the works of a number of extraordinary historians and other authors, to all of whom – living and dead – an immeasurable debt is owed, especially to those noted below.

Though many of these works are cited in this same section of both *Beyond Derrynane* and *Two Journeys Home,* given my continued reliance on virtually all of them, in one way or another, in the writing of *Bittersweet Tapestry,* at the risk of appearing repetitive, I feel it is only right to, once again, acknowledge the books and their authors.

My formal research has included standard works such as the still-brilliant *Course of Irish History,* by T.W. Moody and F.X. Martin; *Contested Island (Ireland 1460-1630)* by S.J. Connolly and *Gaelic Ireland (1250 – 1650:*

Land, Lordship & Settlement), edited by Patrick J. Duffy, David Edwards and Elizabeth Fitzpatrick.

Raymond Gillespie's *Seventeenth Century Ireland* as well as Ian McBride's *Eighteenth Century Ireland*, both volumes in the Gill New History of Ireland series, and Patrick Moran's *The Catholics of Ireland under the Penal Laws of the Eighteenth Century* proved invaluable in that they permitted me to more fully immerse myself in the period and, hopefully, to write at least to some degree with a sense of immediacy – as had the events unfolded almost contemporaneously, rather than centuries before. I would also add, with gratitude to both gentlemen, that Messrs. McBride's and Moran's works provided valuable insights into the political and social setting and some of the events which, whether they actually occurred or not, have come down to us as part of the lore surrounding the murder of Art O'Leary.

Daniel Corkery's *Hidden Ireland*; volume one of Mrs. Morgan John O'Connell's classic work, *The Last Colonel of the Irish Brigade, Count O'Connell and Old Irish Life at Home and abroad, 1745-1833*, Richard Hayward's *In the Kingdom of Kerry*; Patrick M. Geoghan's splendid two-volume biography of Daniel O'Connell, *The Rise of Daniel O'Connell, 1775-1829* and *The Life and Death of Daniel O'Connell, 1830-1846*; Sean O'Faolain's still largely-definitive *King of the Beggars: The Life of Daniel O'Connell* and *Daniel O'Connell's Childhood* by Brian Igoe, which appears on *The Irish Story* website, have all played the same role for me concerning the O'Connells, the O'Sullivans, Derrynane and County Kerry in the period covered.

These works have been augmented by John Crowley and John Sheehan's breathtaking book, *The Iveragh Peninsula: A Cultural Atlas of the Ring of Kerry* and *Derrynane House National Historical Park: A Guide to the Country Home of Daniel O'Connell* by Jim Larner (vice Alain Craig's prior version)

Priceless background for the history of the various Irish brigades not to mention the lives and careers of some of the (both fictional and historical) Irish officers who appear in the book was provided by John Cornelius O'Callaghan's massive classic, *History of the Irish Brigades in the Service of France* – as well as by Stephen McGarry's *Irish Brigades Abroad, From the Wild Geese to the Napoleonic Wars*, George B. Clark's *Irish Soldiers in Europe 17th-19th Century*, and the *Wild Geese – The Irish Brigades in the Service of France and Spain,* written by Mary McLaughlin and beautifully illustrated by Chris Warner.

Beginning with the events which unfolded and the new character (Princess Marie Thérèse Louise of Savoy) who was introduced in the closing pages of *Two Journeys Home,* and the resultant increasing prominence in this volume of both the Princess and Hugh O'Connell in Paris and at Versailles, I have continued to rely on the extraordinary biographies of Marie Antoinette by Evelyne Lever (*Marie Antoinette: The Last Queen of France)* and Antonia Fraser (*Marie Antoinette: The Journey),* as well as Munro Price's *The Road from Versailles;* Carolly Erickson's *To the Scaffold,* Caroline Morehead's *Dancing to the Precipice: The Life of Lucie De La Tour Du Pin* (the daughter of General Arthur Dillon – who deserves an insightful biography of his own) and *Marie Thérèse, Child of Terror The Fate of Marie Antoinette's Daughter,* by Susan Nagel. In addition to these works, specifically regarding Hugh and Louise's visit to Louis XV at Versailles, the section, *The King's Apartments/Palace at Versailles* which the Chateau Versailles makes available on its site, http://en.chateauversailles, was extraordinarily helpful.

Since I have mentioned Hugh O'Connell's "Louise," I should say that creating a significantly-different temperament, indeed, personality and, in most ways an entirely dissimilar life for a relatively well-known historical character has been daunting.

I must admit that, as with many of the twists and turns throughout the writing of the *Saga* to date none of this was planned, but rather developed as the story progressed and began to take shape. As Marie Thérèse Louise of Savoy and Hugh were, in effect, circling each other in my imagination, and in researching the princess, in effect getting to know her better, reading, studying literally dozens of portraits, visiting her homes in Paris, including the Hôtel de Toulouse (now the headquarters of the Bank of France), I developed a sense that she was perhaps a more complex, indeed certainly a more interesting person than history has shown her to be. Several of her portraits depict (at least to me) a very pretty young woman with a gentle, perhaps even playful sense of humour, one who laughs and makes others do so as well. She is, at least at this stage of her life, to a degree both shy and guileless, most likely a result of her sheltered life in Savoy and despite her singular position in the French monarchy. As she appears in *Bittersweet Tapestry* her life is undergoing rapid, totally-unforeseen changes – it and she are clearly both works-in-progress.

All of this said, the genre of historical fiction permits its practitioners to depict not only actual historical events in a fictional manner but also events – and people – which could have happened . . . and who could have lived. Taking dramatic advantage of this latitude, I believe and hope that I have stayed within these bounds.

Though Daniel Charles and Hugh O'Connell's separate periods of study and training there pre-date Napoleon's by some fifteen to twenty years, early chapters of the extraordinary biographical work, *Napoleon Bonaparte* by Alan Schom, provided valuable insights into the history of and the academic and military training provided by Ecole Militaire to cadets in the Eighteenth Century.

Writing a fictionalised account of the murder of Art O'Leary has been both an emotional experience as well as a significant challenge. There are any number of different versions of all or part of the grim tale, conflicting, inconsistent and – as long-ago events frequently still are in Ireland – discussed, debated and argued about as if they had only recently occurred. I realise some may take issue with my fictionalised version of what could possibly have happened, and to them I would apologise for any unintended offense I may have given, whilst at the same time respectfully reminding them that I am telling a story and am in no way attempting to provide a definitive chronicle of the happenings leading up to – and following – those of the first week of May 1773. In addition to creating a number of wholly-fictional goings-on (and ignoring things that may have occurred – or not) , I have selected a series of events which by most accounts appear to have happened – I have then fictionalised them in considerable detail, adding characters, dialogue and the like.

This being said, beyond the works of Irish history already mentioned, I would additionally credit John T. Collins's extraordinary, quite exhaustive piece, *Arthur O'Leary, The Outlaw,* which appeared in the January–June 1949 edition of the *Journal of the Cork Historical and Archaeological Society* as well as Mary Leland's truly wonderful book, *Lie of the Land: Journeys Through Literary Cork.*

In terms of what Oxford's Peter Levi has referred to as being the "greatest poem written in these islands in the whole eighteenth century," I am privileged to have been granted the rights to use Frank O'Connor's brilliant version of *The Lament for Art O'Leary* to provide the words for, and literally give voice to Eileen's bitterly powerful, heart-rending poetic response to her husband's murder, I have, over the years, become quite familiar as well with the extraordinary translations of Thomas Kinsella, Ellis Dillon Malachi McCormick and Seán Ó Tuma.

In this regard, so, too, have I relied significantly on the commentaries in a pair of what have become now-cherished books: Seán Ó Tuma and Thomas Kinsella's *An Duanaire 1600-1900 Poems of the Dispossessed* and Mr. Ó Tuma's *Repossessions: Selected Essays on the Irish Literary Heritage,* as well as Malachi McCormick's highly detailed, beautifully written notes accompanying his translation of the *Lament* I gratefully acknowledge that Mr. McCormick's notes proved especially valuable in connection with the "duel of words" engaged in by O'Leary and his nemesis Abraham Morris in the Cork newspaper. (As an aside, I must also mention that McCormick's work appears as and in a singularly magnificent hand-made book – a work of art in itself – published by his Stone Street Press.)

Invaluable details about Kilcrea Friary – the ultimate resting place of Art O'Leary, located near Ovens in County Cork – where Eileen speaks the final, bitterly-poignant words of the *Lament,* have been taken from a pair of brilliant essays written by Mary Leland: *Tomb of a lamented hero,* published in the 20 January 2001 edition of the *Irish Times,* and in her column *An Irishwoman's Diary,* which appears in the 4 October 2011 edition of the *Irish Times.* Especially in *Tomb of a lamented hero,* she has written dramatically and movingly of the ruined monastic setting – a place which, she says, "seems to sigh with emanations of a vast, cruel history."

Lastly, I must mention Professor Declan Kiberd's all-too-brief but marvellously provocative essay, *In Praise of Eibhlín Dhubh Ní Chonaill,* appearing in the 2 March 2015 edition of the *Irish Times,* for the simple reason that it made me think about and reflect on Eileen (with whom I have had for as long as I can recall something of a numinous relationship – and to whom I have been especially close these last seven-odd years) as a woman, a poet, and as the inventor of what he characterises as being a "new tense, neither past nor present." He is quite correct in saying that "We know little enough about Eibhlín" and that "(i)t seems somehow appropriate that we have no picture of her." That we do know so little has enabled me to "create" a version of the type of person whom I believe she may have been, and perhaps the life she could have led – that there is no portrait amongst those of some of the other O'Connells of Derrynane is indeed, in a way, fitting, and contributes to her "mystique" – this is one reason why no pictorial version of her has graced the covers of these volumes

ABOUT THE AUTHOR

KEVIN O'CONNELL IS A NATIVE of New York City, descended from a young officer of what had – from 1690 to 1792 – been the Irish Brigade of the French army, believed to have arrived in French Canada sometime following the execution of Queen Marie Antoinette in October 1793. At least one grandson subsequently returned to Ireland; Mr. O'Connell's own grandparents arrived in New York in the early Twentieth Century. He holds both Irish and American citizenship.

He has been a relatively serious student of the history of Eighteenth Century Europe, especially that of Ireland and France – for much of his life; one significant aspect of this has been a continuing scholarly as well as personal interest in the extended O'Connell family.

Mr. O'Connell began the *Derrynane Saga* in 2014. His first book, *Beyond Derrynane: A Novel of Eighteenth Century Europe,* was published in July 2016, whilst the second, *Two Journeys Home: A Novel of Eighteenth Century Europe* was released in November 2017. Both are in global circulation and have received a range of positive critical reviews, in the United States, the United Kingdom and Europe. *Bittersweet Tapestry* is the third of four projected volumes.

The *Saga* has been described as being "a sweeping, multi-layered story, populated by an array of colourfully-complex characters, whose lives and stories play out in a series of striking settings. Set against the drama of Europe in the early stages of significant change, the book dramatizes the roles – which have never before been treated in fiction – played by a small number of expatriate Irish of the fallen 'Gaelic Aristocracy' at the courts of Catholic Europe." It is with *Bittersweet Tapestry* that O'Connell again focuses in greater detail on their lives in English-occupied Ireland.

An alumnus of Don Bosco Preparatory School, Mr. O'Connell is a graduate of Providence College and Georgetown University Law Centre. For much of his forty-plus year long legal career, he practised international business transactional law, primarily involving direct-investment matters, throughout Asia, Europe and the Middle East.

O'Connell is married, has five children and ten grandchildren. He resides with his wife, Laurette, and their golden retriever, Katie, near Annapolis, Maryland, USA.

www.ingramcontent.com/pod-product-compliance
Lightning Source LLC
Chambersburg PA
CBHW021538110726
47902CB00004B/933